Question #2: How
with this woman?

Nicola knew Reese's answer by heart—9,999 times 10, on a scale of 10. The score of her next highest subject had been 8.

This had to be something more than her own meager powers of attraction. Could there have been a chemical interaction, somehow, between *Irresistible* and *her* formula to give him a supercharged sensation of bonding?

She would have to find out. "But how?" she said aloud, and her eyes fell on his message. Addressed to "D."

To me. She paused, feeling ridiculously guilty. It was addressed to "D."

Me.

Except that "D" had acted like someone else. Done things, allowed things... Felt things that Nicola had never felt.

It's for me. She opened his folded message.

Just two lines, penned as boldly as the words themselves.

> "D, If you felt what I felt yesterday, then come to me. Tonight.
>
> "The Twenty-Third Man."

Dear Reader,

How did I come to write romances? Good question. You could
maybe blame it on my childhood in Texas, home of the most gallant
myths and the tallest tales. Or blame my grandmother with her
wonderful, scary yarns of panthers, sleepwalkers and talking cats.
Or all those years I spent bored in school—I was the shy, quiet one
with an open book hidden under my desk. Or maybe
it's my fey, crazy mother's fault—with a role model who goes
paragliding at sixty, how could I turn out normal? And what about
my wildcatter father, who decided only last summer to search for
gold in backwoods Alaska? (I went along as camp cook and
chief worrywart. We came back with one-eighth teaspoon of gold,
ten thousand bug bites and five bear sightings. Oh, and I met a
prospector who spends his winters reading Harlequin romances.
Hi, Pete!) And then there's all those years spent restoring antique
yachts, the ultimate dream machines. And a certain sailing man,
who seems to resemble all the heroes I ever invented. So maybe a
better question, given the above influences, is…how could I not
write romances?

Sincerely,

Peggy Nicholson

Books by Peggy Nicholson

HARLEQUIN SUPERROMANCE
698—YOU AGAIN

THE TWENTY-THIRD MAN
Peggy Nicholson

Harlequin Books

TORONTO • NEW YORK • LONDON
AMSTERDAM • PARIS • SYDNEY • HAMBURG
STOCKHOLM • ATHENS • TOKYO • MILAN
MADRID • WARSAW • BUDAPEST • AUCKLAND

ISBN 0-373-70740-1

THE TWENTY-THIRD MAN

To John and Bonnie Row—
Every memory is a smiler

CHAPTER ONE

"WHAT D'YOU FIGURE it is, a pill?" The young man standing two places ahead of Reese bounced on his heels.

"Nose spray," suggested the kid next to the bouncer. Which would make him twenty-second in line, since Reese stood twenty-third. "If it's a pheromone they're testing, it's gotta be a nose spray."

"Who cares, if it drives women wild?" squeaked Twenty, looking up from the physics textbook he'd been reading all morning. With a face like an intelligent frog and a voice like a chipmunk, he could use a little help in the driving department, Reese suspected.

"But do they give the dose to the women...or to us?" Twenty-two wondered aloud. He slumped low against the corridor wall, his long legs braced at a gravity-defying angle.

"Whatever. Lead me to her. To a coupl'a dozen hers." Twenty-one spread his hands against the concrete blocks, backed his feet away and started a set of standing push-offs. "Use my poor body for science. I'm ready!"

"Yeah, they're going to lead you into this cubicle," predicted Frog-face. "A blonde in a tight white nurse's uniform, with a front like the Grand Tetons and a rear like a prize peach, will come *wigglin'* into the room..."

"*Yeah!*" breathed Twenty-one, pausing midpush, elbows locked.

"She'll bat her great big blue peepers and say—" Froggy's voice rose half an octave "—Drop *trou*, please, sir, if it's not too much trouble."

"Oh, no...no trouble at *all*," crooned Twenty-two.

"Then, with you standing at attention, ready to give your all for science, she'll whip out this *horse* needle and say, "Now if you'll just turn around and bend—"

A chorus of groans drowned out the fantasy, and even Reese winced, then casually swung around to prop his other shoulder against the wall. The line of bored college boys straggled on along the science-lab corridor, then around a corner and out of sight. Forty in all, Reese had been told, for this behavioral experiment. Forty males ready and eager to serve as guinea pigs, cheerfully willing to sniff or swallow any unknown substance at all if it would make them irresistible to the opposite sex.

Make that thirty-nine, plus me, Reese amended. He was here for something more important than sex, which had never proved much of a problem. Not since he'd turned fourteen and Janie-Jean Morton took him in hand.

No, he was here to save his company. His fast-dwindling fortune. Everything he'd worked for since the day he'd turned thirteen.

His thirteenth birthday... There'd been no cake that day, so soon after his father's killing, and thoughts of a present would have been laughable. Instead, he'd gifted himself. With a promise. That whatever it took to leave the breakheart streets of the East Nashville slums behind, he'd do it. Whatever price he'd have to pay, he'd pay it. He'd get out and he'd never go back. Not ever.

That vow was more than twenty years old, the determination that lay behind it as raw as yesterday. He was here today to keep that promise.

"Who's the geezer?" whispered somebody behind him.

Reese smiled wryly and didn't turn. *Thirty-five isn't quite over the hill, puppy.* Though the worry of the past five months often felt like the weight of years, a backpack of lead pigs strapped to his shoulders.

Well, with any luck he'd find the way to shed that load at the end of this corridor. Beyond that dark green door through which the test subjects were disappearing in batches of four. At molasses-slow intervals.

"A professor?" someone else guessed.

Not even close, kid. Reese hadn't bothered finishing high school. He'd been too busy finding his way out of Nashville.

Academics wouldn't do it for somebody like him. He had the brains but not the patience. And life lived at a desk was no life at all.

Gangs wouldn't do it. Fighting your way to the top of a gang made you king rat of a few squalid blocks of slum turf, but gangs hadn't offered a way out of town. Even if they had, he hadn't the stomach for hurting people. At least, not those who couldn't hit you back.

Besides, rule one in Durand's Rules to Live By was that you traveled alone. Which ruled out hanging with the home boys. It also ruled out team sports such as football or baseball, which might have paid off big. He'd checked out boxing—he had the speed and the punch—but he meant to leave town with his brains intact.

Then he'd found tennis. A rich boy's sport. A game for country-club sissies he'd thought at first, but then he'd learned otherwise. Played with do-or-die drive, tennis was the path to unbelievable riches.

Once his feet were set on that path, he'd been too busy earning his first million, backhand by smashing backhand, to finish school. Too busy following the pro circuit from Stockholm to Paris to Barcelona to Miami. Too busy learning how to talk, how to dress, how to pleasure the silken high-class beauties who wanted to boast to their friends that they'd bedded a young Wimbledon champion. Earning his first million had been the hardest, and yet the most fun.

Almost paradise, and like paradise, it hadn't lasted long. With that thought, Reese swung around—too fast. A razor-edged pain sliced up his leg, his daily reminder of that day he'd reached too far at the net.

No, tennis hadn't lasted, but it had given him his first

real grasp on the greasy pole of life. He was damned if he'd slip down that pole now.

"*Hup*—here we go!" announced someone up ahead. The line jostled forward as another batch of test subjects was admitted through the green door. The last of the chosen turned, gave those left behind a lecherous grin and a thumbs-up, then slammed the door in their faces.

"Ten dollars to stand here half a day or more coolin' our heels. Plus that interview yesterday... I figure we're making 'bout a dollar an hour," growled Twenty-two.

"Heck, if it's really an aphrodisiac they want us to test-drive, I'll pay *them*," declared Twenty-one, returning to his push-offs.

"If," Frog-face repeated on an ominous note. "I asked the interviewer yesterday, that redheaded ice cube in the lab coat? She dropped down to subzero and asked me where I got *that* idea. Wouldn't say yes or say no, just glared icicles. I'm still frostbit."

"Yeah, I tried asking, too," agreed Twenty-two. "But even if Ms. Tightbuns won't talk, the word's out. You see in the *Journal Bulletin* day before yesterday that some RIIT student in biochem was 'bout to test an aphrodisiac? And then later the same day this notice is posted in the library that someone needs paid volunteers for a test—to report to the biochem department? What else could it be?"

"I heard last winter that some kinky chick over here was studying the love life of voles and hamsters," added Twenty-one. "Gotta be the same thesis."

Reese had learned that much, too, quizzing the kid who'd written up the rumors for the *RIITWORD*. From that campus rag the gossip had been picked up by Rhode Island's statewide newspaper, the *Providence Journal*. Since Reese employed a nationwide clipping service to send him every whisper of pheromones, aphrodisiacs or love potions that appeared in print, the rumor had flown home to him, ninety miles up the road in Boston. Someone at the Rhode Island Institute of Technology was said to be experimenting with pheromones, the biochemical messengers that were now believed to underlie all sexual attraction for every species. This unidentified student was about to test a pheromone on human males, here in his own backyard.

So here he stood, determined to track that rumor to its source. Because after a year of hard work and some seven million of his hard-earned dollars poured down the drain, his own pheromonic cologne for men didn't work worth a damn. In spite of all the promise of the cologne's initial tests, in spite of all the efforts of the brilliant team Reese had put together—fragrance consultants, ad wunderkinds, superstar salesmen and celebrity pitchmen—in spite of all this, Irresistible was not proving irresistible to the women who sniffed the men who wore it.

At best, Irresistible apparently left women…cold. In fact, Reese was beginning to wonder if Irresistible might not actually *repel* women. For a man who'd paid one hundred dollars for an ounce of liquid passion, that would be unforgivable. Death of a young fragrance company. Bankruptcy for Reese Durand, entrepreneur. Overreaching poor boy.

So if somebody else, even some wet-behind-the-ears grad student, had found the biochemical answer to male-female sexual attraction, some pheromonic solution that Reese could use to make his own cologne work, he meant to *have* that answer. It was worth millions. Billions. *Survival.*

DON'T PANIC. There's no reason to panic yet. Nicola Kent took a deep breath, let it out, then said in a voice sharp with tension and lack of sleep, "She can't quit. We've got twenty or more left to test."

"She did. She's gone already. Flew down the back stairs yelling something about how she was sick of oversexed, underbrained, sophomoric octopuses—"

"Octopi." Nicola tugged at her braid, which was some nameless shade between chestnut and copper.

"Yeah, so she'd had it up to here with undergrad octopi groaning in her ear and snorting down her cleavage."

"She *didn't* say that, Joe. She couldn't have. The guards wouldn't let the subjects touch her." Nicola had stationed four husky guards, all members of the RIIT rugby team, at observation posts outside each of the four rooms in which her experiment was being conducted. "The guards are under strictest orders to stop any groping before it starts."

Her test monitor shrugged. "Don't think any of the guys grabbed her, really. It's just that they're all charged up, their imaginations working overtime, what with the blindfolds. They take one sniff in the dark and they imagine they're sniffing Miss Universe. I'm sure there's been lots of heavy breathing and groaning. And they can say whatever they want. Care to bet a few of 'em *aren't* making some pretty rude suggestions?"

"There was no way I could control that, short of gagging the lot," Nicola muttered, pressing her fingertips to her aching temples.

"A bit much to ask when they're already blindfolded," Joe agreed. "And you did warn your test women to expect some of this. You just needed steady types, women with rhinoceros hides and senses of humor. The quitter was your drama student. Theatrical temperament. Don't say I didn't warn you about that one."

"I know, I know. It's just that I couldn't find..." Nicola shook her head. Sagging back against the wall of the borrowed office, which she'd designated as experiment headquarters, she closed her eyes for a moment. "Funny how I have more male volunteers than I could use in a year of testing. But I had to bribe, beg and beat the bushes for just *four* women..." *And now one of them has quit on me. This ruins everything.*

"You think that's funny? After studying male sexuality for the past three years?"

"Male hamsters and voles, mostly."

"Four legs or two, a guy's a guy, Nic. Women are picky, guys are—"

"I know, I know, I know, and I think it's pathetic. Present company excluded, of course."

"Of course. Ha. So what are you going to do, Nic? The next four are getting restless. Do we call the whole thing off?"

"Can't." She'd been stampeded into conducting this experiment a year before she ever should have attempted it. Damn Hadley for his grabbing hands and grubby mind. But if she quit now, she'd lose *all* credibility, all chance of using the data she hoped to gain today to woo a new adviser. *So grit your teeth and press on regardless, girl.*

She sighed, straightened against the wall and squared her slim shoulders. "We have a few sweatshirts left, don't we?" She had dressed all her test women in freshly laundered cotton sweatshirts with the hoods pulled up to cover their hair.

"You're not..." Joe shook his head, then kept on shaking it.

"Yes, I am, since you won't do."

"Thanks, I think." The big New Mexican shrugged, then turned to a counter where a pile of sweatshirts lay. He sorted through them, then tossed her a medium. "Nobody will ever accept your data, kid, if you become one of your own test subjects. Scientific objectivity flies out the old window."

"I've got a choice here?" Nicola slipped her hands into the garment's fuzzy sleeves. "What should I do, Joe, run out on the green and yell, 'I need a woman, and I need her right now'?"

"That's been tried, and believe me, it doesn't work. Least, it never worked for me and my friends."

"Then that leaves me, doesn't it? And my test data won't be called into question—*if* nobody knows I was one of the subjects." Turning to face him, she lifted her eyebrows, a gesture as close as she could ever come to pleading, even with friends.

Joe sighed and drifted toward the door. "Okay, Nics. I'll keep an eye out for Hadley. Try to head him off if he shows."

"No worries there." She couldn't keep the bitterness from her voice. "Hadley won't show. He's only my doctoral adviser." *But not for long.* Not if this test gave her the results she hoped for.

"TYLER! WHERE THE HECK did *you*—"

Reese looked up to see a red-haired young man emerge from a side door in the corridor. The kid aimed a finger at Twenty-one and advanced till his fingertip nearly touched the other's nose. "Shut your mouth before you catch a fly, Bascomb," he said cheerfully. He nudged into line ahead of the other boy.

"What d'you think you're doing?" Twenty-two demanded.

Excellent question, agreed Reese. This floor of the science building was sealed off today, with a burly student guard stationed at the elevator and another sitting by the stairwell door. As well it should be. When Reese had arrived this morning, there'd been fifty or more frustrated RIIT men milling around the front steps of the building like tomcats below the window of a she-cat in heat—students who had heard about the experiment too late, or who had not passed the unspoken requirements of yesterday's interview.

On admittance to the fourth floor, the test subjects had been strictly admonished to stay in line until they reached the green door. Their order corresponded to the order of the five-page questionnaires, which each of them had filled out yesterday after acceptance for a place in this study.

That blasted questionnaire—the researcher had extracted a life and medical history that covered everything from the volunteer's early encounters with chicken pox and measles to his latest encounter with a woman. If Reese hadn't been determined to participate in this experiment, he'd have walked out the door at any one of those questions.

Because rule two of Durand's Rules to Live By was that knowledge is power. To make someone privy to the intimate details of your life was to give that person power over you. He kept himself to himself. But to gain the knowledge he needed about this substance they were testing, Reese would have to play their game. So he'd gritted his teeth and answered the interviewer—in his case not a redheaded, tight-bunned Ivy League ice cube, but a big, slow-talking, fast-thinking grad student named Joe Dominguez. No sex for the past two months, Reese had admitted grudgingly. He'd had more important things on his mind. *Like keeping my nose above water.*

"They sent me back in line," Tyler was explaining. "I was number three, but some bozo lost my interview papers, so now they're hunting 'em down. They said just be sure to give 'em my number when I come round the second time." He glanced at Reese, lowered his voice and turned away.

That was okay, then. If the kid had a lower number than Reese, then it didn't matter if he was reshuffled somewhere up ahead. That wouldn't affect Reese's place in line. Twenty-three. One of his lucky numbers. Not that he'd ever been lucky in the sense of lottery tickets, something for nothing. His kind of luck, he made himself. But you couldn't make it out of thin air. He needed an edge. A start. *Let it be behind that green door.* Because if it wasn't there, then it might not be anywhere....

AFTER SEVENTEEN, Nicola knew why the drama student had quit. She wanted to run down the back stairs herself. Blind, fevered males snuffling at your face, muttering comments and suggestions in your ear. Their desire beating against your own icy reserve like waves of some hot, sticky liquid. Their arrogant, utterly masculine conviction that if only they could make you see how much they wanted you—whoever you were—why then, you must surely melt.

But male passion had never impressed Nicola much. Never melted her. Perhaps it failed to move her because she'd studied it too long, knew too well the intricate ebb and flow of the brain chemicals that produced what most people thought of as simple, spontaneous emotion.

The emotion that all this groaning and whispering was inspiring in *her* was one of frozen distaste.

"Rhinoceros hide, sense of humor," Joe reminded her, handing her the premeasured dose labeled 18D.

She bared her teeth at him in a silent snarl, only half joking, and shoved through the door to which Eighteen's questionnaire was taped.

"Nobel prize, biochem," Joe murmured in soothing tones, handing her the bottle marked 19D.

"A hot shower," she snapped back, and marched off to Nineteen.

"Cure for *aut*ism," Joe practically sang as he passed her the bottle with Twenty's D dose, then aimed her toward the lab around the corner, the one that always held the last man of each foursome.

"Make that a bubble bath."

"You don't have a bath anymore, Nic. You live on a boat."

She had actually forgotten. She'd let go her apartment last week, moved aboard *Madame Curie*, her antiquated powerboat. The rent saved this summer should almost cover her experiment's expenses.

"But you can use *my* tub."

"Susie would scratch my eyes out. I'll bet Twenty will lend me his." As would Twenty-one through Forty. With their eyes blindfolded and their imaginations running wild, they were *all* obliging today.

C SMELLED MUCH like woman A and woman B. Reese took a last dutiful sniff of her cheek, the tip of his nose grazing baby-soft skin. He smelled warm woman, a whiff of mint toothpaste, a faint aura of laundry detergent. "You smell like a load of clean clothes." As had the other two.

She giggled, which was a violation of the experiment's protocol, at least as Joe Dominguez, the test monitor, had explained them to Reese, Tyler, Twenty-one and Twenty-two, once they'd been admitted beyond the green door. The four women who would come to each of them in turn would make no sound at all, though the men could speak if they chose.

"Very nice," Reese added with a final sniff, which was true enough. The verdict won him another giggle. For some reason he needed that small victory of making C break the rules, turning her from the unknown experimenter's creature into his own ally. Probably it was the blindfold that had roused his spark of rebellion. He didn't like being told to sit here on a stool in the darkness, waiting blindly for whatever and whoever came. Powerless.

No, not powerless, he reminded himself. He could rip off the gauze and tape that covered his eyes any time he chose. He was no passively compliant test subject to be picked apart and analyzed, whatever they might think. He was here with his own agenda.

How many minutes to go? he wondered. Each unseen woman was to spend precisely twenty minutes in his close company, the monitor had explained. During this period he must smell her face and throat at least ten times, more if he pleased.

Reese didn't please. He'd sniffed the obligatory ten times, and that was enough, thank you, sweetheart, as it had been with A and B. *I'm feeling nothing! Well, no more than I'd feel touching my nose to any warm female.* "This stuff doesn't work," Reese said aloud, not bothering to hide his disappointment.

She giggled again, uneasily, from very nearby.

I don't care if you sit on my lap, sweetheart. Whatever I inhaled from the jar you gave me when you entered this room twenty minutes ago, whatever the stuff was that A and B gave me, it doesn't work.

If it *was* supposed to be an aphrodisiac or a pheromone they were testing, it didn't work, he amended sourly.

Twenty-one had made one last attempt to pry the purpose of the experiment out of the test monitor as soon as their foursome had passed through the green door. "We are testing a pheromone, right?" he'd demanded. "Some sort of love potion?"

Dominguez's shrug dismissed mere rumor and those fool enough to believe it. "You're part of a study testing male emotional response," he said with weary patience, repeating word for word the nonexplanation they'd been given in the previous day's interview. "You'll inhale four substances, some or all of which might be placebos—just air in a bottle. Some of you *might* be given a gaseous version of a synthetic human hormone.

"Any substance that you might or might not inhale today has been approved for medical practice for years. In other words, we're simply testing out new applications for the same old-same old. There's no danger, but if anybody would like to bail out, I'll show you the back stairs."

Not one of them had budged, and the faces of the other three had reflected Reese's hope. That despite Dominguez's circumlocutions, they were indeed about to encounter some form of human sexual attractant.

But maybe the male emotional response they were helping to test here was the response to boredom. *I'm damn sure bored enough smelling squeaky-clean, bland little co-eds. I've wasted two blasted days.*

His irritation at this waste masked a deeper frustration. No way out. At least not from here. He'd been a fool to hope.

A knock on the door cut off his grim reflections. The guard, signaling the end of their twenty minutes. "Well…" he said, holding out the plastic bottle that C had given him on her arrival, the container that held whatever scentless substance he'd inhaled. *Probably nothing but air. A placebo.*

Which meant that he'd inhaled nothing but an empty bottle of air before sniffing A and B, as well?

Which then might mean that, come D, he'd be given the real substance to be tested at last?

Or it meant that he'd already sniffed whatever it was they were testing—and it simply didn't work. Not as an aphrodisiac, not as an attractant to the opposite sex. Reese felt the bottle being lifted from his fingers. "Well...it's been fun...sniffing you."

"Um...yeah." C's voice was as breathy as a ten-year-old's, a baby-doll voice surely not old enough to go away to college. "D'you think, maybe later, we could maybe—"

The guard rapped briskly on the door again and she gasped.

I don't think, Reese thought, careful not to smile. *At least, not till you grow up, girl. And believe me, I wish I felt otherwise.* "Bye," he said gently to the sound of her retreating footsteps.

The door opened, then closed, leaving him to darkness and silence. With hope fading fast.

CHAPTER TWO

BANDAGED FACES BLURRED; time stretched like melting taffy. She went through the motions, her body quivering with tension, her mind held precisely in neutral. Nicola Kent had fled to her lab, her data, her cages where her voles and hamsters spun exercise wheels in shining circles—the quiet, orderly, satisfying world where no one and nothing could touch her, where her mind ruled supreme. This woman being sniffed and snuffled was simply…D.

Joe handed her another bottle. "Last of this four."

"Yeah." But they had four more sets of four to go. Nicola trudged around the corner, stepped through the lab door, closed it behind her—and stopped short.

Her first response was surprise, which sliced through her protective veil of numbness. This was a man here, not a college kid. The others suddenly seemed children in comparison—unfinished, uncertain, not yet come into their power. *What's a man doing*— Then she remembered. Three of the volunteers they'd accepted were in their thirties—some sort of coach, an economics professor, a campus security guard. Joe had interviewed the prof and the coach.

If she hadn't interviewed the guard herself, an ex-cop, she would have said this was surely he. He stood relaxed, stone still, yet somehow she knew he was poised for action. *Almost as if he expects danger.* She brushed that notion aside. He simply stood with the grace of an athlete. This was the coach, then. An aging jock.

"It seems I've misplaced my seat." His voice was low,

with a touch of gravel and a hint of the South. Maybe a note of mockery.

So I see. None of the other volunteers she'd encountered so far had dared stray from their stools.

"I'm not in the mood for blindman's buff, D. Come here."

She felt a flick of temper at the command, then understanding. She would have felt the same, unwilling to make a clown of herself, groping blindly around while some stranger watched, maybe smiled at her antics.

He held out his hand. "Are you shy, D? Or just slow? Or maybe you're the kind of girl who likes to pull the wings..." He tipped his head when she started moving.

He's angry, she thought, her steps slowing with the realization. Was it just the blindfold? Or was he simply one of those angry types—old hurts, old injustices and the smoldering indignation the wounds left behind? She had a streak of that herself. A little anger put some steel in the backbone, iron in the will. More turned a person into a snapping dog, unable to know his friends, to be avoided at all cost. *And he's going to be sniffing me in a moment.* She shivered—from nerves, not fear. Avoiding his proffered hand, she touched his forearm.

His face turned to her oblique approach. He smiled for the first time, a slow half curve of beautifully carved lips, the lower one full, the upper austere. "Shy, then, we'll say for the moment."

Was she? She shied away from men, that was true. But that was from lack of interest—from an abundance of other, more compelling interests—hardly from fear. She made it a point of pride not to fear anything.

On that thought, she gripped his forearm—gripped rock-hard muscle beneath his shirtsleeve—then paused as all her senses focused on this discovery. It was oddly...pleasing. He was built so much bigger than she, so much more rugged, but why should that please? It never had before. Refocusing—their twenty minutes were passing rapidly—she guided him sideways toward his seat.

He came with easy grace, careful not to tread on her, looming alongside, almost a head taller than she. Slightly over six feet, she guessed.

His other hand reached out, found the stool. "Thank you," he said as she let him go.

Not too exasperated to be polite. She gave him a point for that, waited for him to settle, then nudged his hand with the bottle that held his D dose.

"Do I get lucky this time, D? Does this one hold the prize?" He twisted the top off with long powerful fingers. "I suppose since you're a guinea pig like me, you don't know, either."

Right, haven't a clue. Because this was a double-blind study. The contents of the numbered bottles would be matched to the men who had received them only *after* all responses had been tallied.

Half the volunteers would smell nothing but a placebo oday, just a sponge soaked in a saline solution, then lropped into an empty plastic bottle. Scentless and without ffect.

The other half would sniff from a bottle containing a sponge soaked in her formula.

But no man who got a dose of the real thing received a second one. If he'd really felt no effect with A, B or C, *then the chances are now fifty-fifty....* She shivered again, watching as he lifted the bottle to his nose and inhaled. Then held it. He exhaled at last, inhaled again, then again, till he'd reached his instructed total of five inhalations. He recapped the bottle and tossed it on the floor. She jumped at the racket it made, opened her mouth to protest, then closed it. *Okay, be that way.*

"Come here," he said huskily, holding out his hand.

He was not to touch her from the neck down, though *she* could touch *him* to steady herself. The guard was to interfere immediately if he tried.

But there was no guard outside this door. She'd sent him to take a break, telling him she'd stand this watch in his place. It was the simplest way to keep her role as subject a secret. *So there's no one here but you and me.*

"Shy," he mocked, hand still extended. "Don't be afraid, D. I never lose control. You're safe with me."

Am not. Shy? Or did she mean safe? Stepping to his side, her hip brushing the hard length of his outer thigh, she put her hands on his shoulders. He twisted to face her.

With the white blindfold over his eyes, and his dark, tousled hair, he looked like an illustration from one of the old novels she'd loved as a child, *Kidnapped*, perhaps, or *Treasure Island.* He had hollows in his lean cheeks and, already, the shadow of a beard. He looked like a pirate's prisoner—hers—no, the pirate himself, captured at last, dipping his head for the noose at the gallows. She was suddenly stunned by too many sensations—the warmth and sculptured elegance of his wide shoulders, the heat of his body, his head bending so deliberately toward her face. She let out her breath in a feathering gasp, sucked it in again— and breathed in his essence, a faint, intensely masculine fragrance, some sort of cologne. *I'm* not *afraid!*

She was. She had a sudden mad urge to twist away and bolt—*it's now or never!*—a sudden wild quickening of the heart, the fight-or-flight reflex kicking in for no reason she could name. But there was no way she was running. *This is* my *experiment!*

The alternative to flight was a sudden stiffening, a rush of all-over warmth that felt like anger, all the more angering for its utter senselessness. She was a woman who cherished her rationality.

Anger swirled, needing a target, and found one handy. *And you—you're such a…a guy, so sure you're in control! Why, I could knock that control for a loop simply by tightening my hold and tipping you backward off your—*

"*Hey!*" His hands snapped up to grab her waist, hard.

"You little..." Laughing, he brought his face to hers. "I take it back. You're not..."

His laughter faded and he drew a sharp breath, his forehead resting against her temple. "You're..." His voice was suddenly huskier, distant, as if he were waking from sleep, still reaching inward for a broken dream. "You're..." He inhaled again and pressed closer, his nose grazing her temple, nuzzling the edge of her sweatshirt hood aside, seeking her hair. His hands tightened when she shuddered.

You're...the One. The nonsensical words formed in his mind like a crystal distilling itself from a tear. Diamond bright. Shaped in sheer, immutable planes of utmost clarity.

She smelled...familiar. Reese sniffed again and something caught in his throat. Her hair smelled like...*home.* No, that couldn't be right. His home had held nothing to draw him like this. Somebody else's home, then, the kind he'd dreamed of as a child. He breathed into her hair and she trembled. *Are you feeling this, too?*

Inhaling again, he saw flowers, tiny and white. He'd buried his face in them one day long ago, lying somewhere in a park. They'd smelled of honey and hay and sunlight. Alyssum, he'd learned years later. She smelled of that. Sweet alyssum.

Greedy for more, he pulled her closer. Her body bent like a sapling—as if she yearned toward him from the waist down, her girl-sharp hipbones imprinting themselves against his thigh, her weight half resting on him. From her slender middle upward, she resisted, held herself upright, aloof, even though she'd granted him her face. As if she stood apart from him, frozen in thought. Or alarm?

Whatever its cause, her stillness didn't matter—yet. All the better to explore. His nose quested on. Finding the outer tip of her eyebrow, he traced it inward, a low tickling arch. He smiled against her when she shivered. Frozen, yet hardly unfeeling. *Good.*

So good. Even more than her hair, her skin smelled...familiar, evoking some teasing memory. The scent was different and more intense than her hair, honey without the hay, but not precisely that.

What, then? "You smell like—" he paused, the tip of his nose resting between her brows "—burnt honey." *And home*. He searched his memory and still couldn't find the event that triggered this response. Honey spilled on a hot stove? But when? In whose kitchen? His mother hadn't cooked to speak of, at least not after his father—

He plunged away from that thought. Refocused. His senses spiraling around her, he traced the delicate line of her nose down to her lips.

Then to taste her was only natural. Not an option, but a necessity if he was to know her. And he was.

But no hurry, he reminded himself. She was shy. He brushed his closed lips along contoured softness, out to the corner of her mouth, then paused, inhaling her essence. Sweetness, and something wilder. Wild honey. *Open to me, darlin'*, he demanded silently, his lips poised on hers.

Her lips moved, but it was neither smile nor surrender. *Yet*. He brushed her mouth the other way then, with a flick of impatience, caught her wonderfully full bottom lip between his own and waited. *You're mine. Don't you know that yet?* His hands tightened in spite of himself, his thumbs pressing into the softness below her rib cage, stroking her upward in lazy arcs.

Her head tipped back slowly…as slow as a dream, her mouth rising as she did so. His mouth rode hers, starting to smile. *That's right*. She parted her lips with a tiny gasp, and he was in. *Home*. Honey and darkness and home. He'd known her all along. Forever.

She made a wordless sound of despair or welcome, he wasn't sure which. It didn't matter. Dark or light, it still meant yes. The word was ringing in his ears. *Yes*. Of course. How could it be anything else? They were as inevitable as sunrise.

Senses swimming, he stepped down from his stool to gather her in. His hands slid around her waist, then up her supple back to cradle her against him from thighs to breast. *She fits me perfectly.* It came as no surprise.

But something had alarmed her, maybe his rising, looming above her. She tore her mouth from his and stood frozen, her head thrown back, panting soundlessly.

"It's all right." He waited for her to deny it, waited while she breathed against him, each shuddering breath pressing her breasts to his chest. When she didn't back away, he kissed the side of her throat below her ear, then dragged his lips down, down, to the velvety corner where neck curved to shoulder.

"*Huh!*" It was a rush of breath, a raw exclamation, not a word. She still hadn't spoken aloud. He smiled. *No hurry.* His hands smoothed down her back, molding her to him. She was the perfect size.

He filled his hands with boyishly firm hips, lifting her up on tiptoe, and returned to plunder her mouth. *Mine.* He slid one hand under her sweatshirt, if that's what the fluffy thing was, then under a T-shirt below that. Her skin was red-hot, silk spread to the sun at high noon. His thumb and fingers spanned the side of her narrow body and skimmed upward. *You're mine, all of you.* Every hill and valley was home. His thumb came to rest against the lower curve of her breast and he waited, not sure if she knew it, too. *Yet.*

She shuddered convulsively. Twisted away from his hand, but not his mouth, then slowly, hesitantly, as they kissed, she twisted back around.

Yes. His thumb stroked upward, found the prize, and she sang in his mouth, a tiny wordless song of yearning and worry. *It's all right, darlin'. Meant to be and you know it.* His fingertips cherished the top curve of her breast, small, perfectly round, then met to oppose his thumb across her nipple. He fingered her, rubbing lace against her hardness in a slow, sweet friction, promise of what was to—

With a hiss like a little steam engine, she bucked against him, her pelvis shuddering up against his erection in an unmistakable, importunate rhythm.

"Why, you…" He laughed aloud with delight. Wrapping his arms around her, he held her till it ended. *Hot. His.* And he didn't even know what she— "I've got to see you." One arm hooked around her, he reached for his bandage, edged one thumb under the tape. "Ouch!"

"No!" she whispered, and flattened a palm over the blindfold. "Don't!"

He felt the first lick of fear. She existed in the dark. But in the light? "I've got to." He ran his thumb along the underside of the tape.

"No!" She spun out of his hold, leaving a gap where she'd been, a cold wind blowing through the space between them.

"D, dammit, come back here!"

No answer, just a flurry of footsteps. "D?" He blundered after her, hit the stool, sent it flying. "Damn!" He stopped, rammed his thumb all the way under the bandage and ripped upward. *"Ouch!"*

A door slammed.

Light filtered under the lifting bandage, showing him a room that was brighter than the one he'd imagined, the rude shock of daylight after a theater's dark magic. Blinking, he tore the blindfold the rest of the way off and threw it aside. She was gone.

He yanked open the door to look out on a corridor, starkly empty. "D!" He swore and stepped out of his room, glancing both ways. "D?"

Footsteps clattered in the distance, around a corner. Reese swung around it, too, and ran head-on into Dominguez. "A woman," he said, catching the kid by his arms to hold him off. "D. Where'd she go?"

Dominguez scowled. "She's busy. And your part in this study is over, mister, except for your evaluation form. Let's go."

She's busy. It smacked him between the eyes. There were seventeen more punks, ready and eager to smell her. *No way.* No way at all. *"D!"* he yelled, glaring past the monitor at the closed doors that lined the corridor.

Three very large young men, lounging before three of those doors, turned to give him narrow-eyed stares. Two of them started his way with the zestful look of born brawlers, their boredom problem finally solved.

"Trouble?" one of them inquired hopefully.

Reese took a deep breath and held it. He could go over them—their eagerness showed their greenness—but he'd have to inflict major damage to do so. He didn't even want to start, with his mind still wandering through fields of sweet alyssum. And if he had to negotiate with these people tomorrow, then bloodshed today wouldn't—

But men sniffing her... He clenched his teeth till they ached, his eyes locked on Dominguez, who returned his gaze with wary interest.

When he could hold it no longer, Reese let his breath go in a ragged hiss. She wouldn't let them touch her, not as she'd let him...

Or would she? The question echoed in his brain.

No, he couldn't imagine it. Would not, if he hoped to sleep tonight. *Later, then,* he promised her silently. *Soon.* And turned to the waiting Dominguez. "Where's your friggin' form?"

with his team, and the fear of sleep while the experiment's full run concluded. Though Goss suffered much with their olfactory experiments, the analgon would have eased any tendency to a wide-awake response, and, despite Nicola's bomb, I bet Goss had a far, far better sleep with his one-hour—

"Hello?"

Hoof! She jumped to her feet, nearly dropping her

"UH, MASON? HE'S HERE someplace. Still sleeping, I bet." The sound of a jaw-cracking yawn came clearly down the phone line. Nine o'clock was near dawn to male undergraduates, Nicola was learning.

"He knew he'd be contacted," she explained with more patience than she felt. "As a follow-up to the experiment he took part in yesterday?"

"Oh, yeah—the love potion."

Nicola rubbed her aching head. "It wasn't precisely that. It—"

"Well, you sure fooled ol' Mase. He's in *love.* With every last woman he got his nose on."

Good. "Could I speak to Mason himself, please?" With a weary sigh, she tipped back in her office chair. Behind her, a soft-squeaking exercise wheel spun like her thoughts.

Every time she stopped pushing them in a purposeful line, they circled right back again. She should be worrying about where her experiment had gone wrong but, instead... A warm tide of blood started at her toes and swept upward. *Sex with an alpha male.* So that was what it was like....

Something between anger and restlessness crisped her nerves. Standing, Nicola stalked as close to the window as her phone cord would allow. It was humiliating. Even though she understood the precise mechanisms of sexual submission, to have it happen to *her*...

One-time aberration, she told herself, pacing at the end of her tether. Just a fluke response brought on by a freak occasion. Her defenses had been at an all-time low, what with the tension and the loss of sleep while she prepared for this experiment. Then all those sniffing males with their overheated expectations. The situation would have raised any female to a state of sexual readiness. She'd been a ticking bomb. It had only been luck that she blew when Twenty-three—

"H'llo?"

"Oop!" She jumped a foot and nearly dropped the phone. "Hello? Mason, er, Albright?" A look at the snapshot stapled to his papers brought him to mind, his wide lipless mouth like a frog. Anything *but* an alpha, poor kid. "This is Nicola Kent."

"The redhead?"

She stiffened. "The *biochemist*. You took part in my experiment yesterday. And as you agreed…" Quickly she reviewed the promise that had been extracted from all participants. To make themselves available for the follow-up evaluations she'd be conducting a day after the experiment, then again in a week, then after two weeks, then four.

"Now…my first question is the same one you answered yesterday on the form you filled out at the end of your test. If you had your choice *today*, Mason, of spending more time with any one of the women you sniffed yesterday— A, B, C or D—which one would you choose?" She waited, pen poised, his sheet from yesterday set side by side with the blank form she was filling out today.

"Uh…I thought they were all super. Foxes, every last one."

She nodded, smiling in spite of herself as she looked down at his previous response. For that same question he should have circled one letter, to show his preferred woman, A, B, C or D. Or he could have circled N for "no preference."

Instead, he'd enclosed A, B, C *and* D in a heavy-handed, joyfully lopsided valentine. "If you could have a date with just one, today, which would you choose?" she prodded just to be sure.

"Any of 'em," he said simply. "All of 'em. And if you've got any more like 'em tucked away somewhere, you can send them over, too. I'll be waiting with bells on."

"No preference," Nicola translated dryly, marking today's form. No particular woman had claimed his allegiance or attention. *The subject has not bonded.* Which was exactly as it should be. Because Twenty, alias Mason Albright, was a control. He'd been given nothing to sniff yesterday but air and saline solution. His bottles, marked 20-A, 20-B, 20-C and 20-D had each contained the placebo.

"Another question. Have you dated any other woman, or women, since yesterday?"

He sighed heavily. "Nope." Then his squeaky voice brightened. "But if I'd had your stuff... You know, you ought to bottle and sell it. If that was an aphrodisiac, it wasn't half-bad."

It wasn't, Mason. It was all in your head. The largest sexual organ of all, as the joke went.

"What *did* you give me, if you don't mind my asking?"

Revealing that he'd sniffed nothing but salt water and air would be bound to skew his future responses. "I'll send you a paper detailing what your doses consisted of after I receive your final evaluation form."

Winding up the interview, she promised to mail Albright a response form the next week, since by then he'd have left campus for his summer vacation. She stapled today's form to the back of his sheaf of papers and sat, frowning down at his photo.

Mason was one of the test subjects who had responded according to her predictions. As such, he didn't worry her. In fact, he was delightfully predictable.

It was the *other* half, the nineteen men who had *not* responded according to her thesis expectations. Those who had expressed a bonding with the wrong woman, or no bonding at all when they *should* have bonded, or intense bonding when they, like Mason, had received nothing to make them bond. "What the hell *happened?*" she muttered.

She'd been so sure of success. Was sure of it still, given her previous results with mountain voles. And yet her experiment had proved precisely *nothing.*

She'd have loved to ask Joe what he thought, but he didn't know about the catastrophe yet. Long after they'd called the test a wrap and Joe had staggered off home, Nicola had completed her paperwork, stapling each subject's numbered response form to his original interview packet. She'd thanked her lucky stars that only one of the men—Forty, she deduced by process of elimination—had forgotten to write in his identifying number at the top of his sheet.

But that was where her luck had ended. Once she opened the envelope containing the key to who had received which dose, placebo or real thing, and collated her results, she'd discovered the disaster—too late to call Joe. And at dawn this morning Joe had headed off with Susie for a summer research job in California. He'd only stayed this long to see Nicola through her experiment.

She wished he'd stayed one day longer to help her face Hadley. Her adviser was probably reading the copy of her test results that she'd left on his desk this very minute. *And hugging himself with glee!* He'd be along anytime now to sneer in person.

Press on regardless. It was all she could do. She flipped Mason's papers aside, flipped on past Twenty-one's interview, then Twenty-two's. They were among the nineteen who'd somehow gone awry. Nicola flipped again, to stare down at the photo of the last man in her experiment whose response had correctly matched the dose he'd received. *And what a response.* Twenty-three. This wasn't the first time, nor the tenth, she'd studied his picture since yesterday. And staring, Nicola felt something in the neighborhood of her womb throb in slow reply. *Yes...*

Stop it! She thrust herself out of her chair to stand, leaning over the desk, arms braced, hands flattened on either side of his packet—as if even that increment of separation might help.

"Reese Goforth," she read aloud. "Junior varsity tennis coach... Yes, she could see him playing tennis. That she never had came as no surprise. There were several thousand people on campus, and she hadn't time for sports, not the organized sort, anyway. *A jock, just an aging jock.*

With the jock's usual healthy ego. Accustomed to winning. She felt a flick of anger. *Well, you won yesterday.* And worse yet, he'd known it. *Point and game to you, buddy.*

But not the whole match. Not the whole match, by any means.

And the thing to keep squarely in mind, once she'd nerved herself to pick up that phone and call him, was that *he didn't know who he'd been playing.* She wasn't D today. In fact, D was gone forever.

The woman with whom he'd be speaking was someone Goforth had never met before. Nicola Kent, biochemist and animal behaviorist. Doctoral candidate with a dissertation that someday, once she'd worked the kinks out of it, was going to make everyone in her field sit up and swallow the ice in their drinks. Maybe would win her a Nobel prize. Maybe would even help Moo?

All you need is your Ph.D., hotshot, she reminded herself, and picked up the phone. *So just do it.*

Five minutes later, she banged the phone down and spun in her swivel chair. "I will be *damned!*"

On the counter behind her desk, in the nearest cage, Matthew paused, his paws resting on Matilda's furry head. Black, beady eyes studied Nicola's pink face for a whisker-quivering moment, then dismissed her. *Not our problem.* The prairie vole turned back to grooming his mate.

Not only did D not exist, no such person as Reese Goforth existed. Not in the Athletic Department at RIIT and not anywhere on campus, according to Personnel. "He lied!"

He'd come, he'd conquered, and he hadn't even bothered to tell the truth. There was a...black hole where the man should have been. She shivered. *No way to put my hands on you, damn you. Whoever you are.*

And he'd had the strongest response of any man in her experiment. If there was any *one* man she needed to study— She jumped violently as her door opened.

Peter Hadley, acting head of RIIT's Department of Biochemistry and Nicola's own doctoral adviser, breezed into her office with an expansive grin. "Well, I hate to be the one to say 'I told you so,' Nikki-luv..." He propped one ample hip on the edge of her desk and smirked down at her.

Then why say it?

But she knew why. Ever since that day last November when he'd cornered her in a supply closet, told her she had wineglass breasts, then tried to grope them. Ever since she'd responded to that compliment...by dumping a gallon of rodent feed over his head, Hadley had been seeking ways to pay her back. Or to make her give in. Or—ugly thought—probably both.

After that episode, Hadley's nasty put-downs, made behind her back to the overwhelmingly male grad students and faculty of their department, had escalated month by month. At first Nicola had simply put her head down and worked on, hoping her adviser's pique would pass if she simply ignored him. But ignoring Hadley apparently added insult to his imagined injury. By the spring, he'd graduated to savage public criticism of her work and her thesis.

And that Nicola would not tolerate. Her work was everything she lived for, her reputation for scientific excellence what she banked her future on. No man would take that from her.

Three weeks ago she'd retaliated with the threat of a

sexual-harassment suit—only to have Hadley smugly point out that she had no proof.

He was right. His worst transgressions had been committed with the practiced discretion of the habitual lech. She hadn't a single witness.

And his verbal attacks, heard by all and sundry around the labs?

Why, in a court of law, his remarks could be interpreted simply as a brilliant professor's disgust at a dull student, Hadley had assured her.

Provable or not, she would bring the charges, Nicola had insisted, if he didn't lay off. Because everyone knew that Hadley would have given his secretary's right hand to be appointed permanent head of Biochem. At this crux of his career, the last thing he needed was a sexual-harassment suit, proven or otherwise.

But the last thing Nicola Kent needed was a thesis adviser who hated her. Who, even if he didn't actually wreck her chances of earning a doctorate, would most certainly damn her with faint praise when she needed letters of recommendation to win a post-doc research fellowship.

This was a game of chicken nobody could win. The only rational solution was to walk away from it, find a new adviser and get on with her research. She'd proposed this armed truce to Hadley, and he'd magnanimously accepted it, provided she could find a new mentor.

And there was the rub. Every professor in biology or biochem had his full complement of grad students for the coming year, his research funds earmarked. She'd found no one willing to accept an additional burden.

Hence yesterday's experiment, her attempt to dramatically demonstrate the validity of her data. The applicability of her research to humankind, as well as to rodents. The sheer *glamour* of her groundbreaking thesis, which someday was bound to reap accolades for its adviser, as well as its deviser.

Admittedly she'd rushed it. But she needed to find an adviser before everyone wandered off for the summer.

Without a doubt she'd gambled, trying to apply to human subjects something that had worked so well with voles. But it was a gamble she'd fully expected to win. And now?

Hadley shook his head pityingly. "Egg all over your face, sugar."

She willed her hands to stay flat on the desk. "Twenty-one of the subjects behaved *precisely* as I predicted. Those who received my formula bonded to the woman who was present when they sniffed it. The controls bonded to no woman at all."

"And nineteen of your subjects bonded to a woman who was *not* associated with your hormone. Or they failed to bond. Or, for all you can prove, they bonded to the bottle they were sniffing, or maybe the hand that *held* that bottle. That's a failure rate of roughly fifty percent, Nikki. I'm sure that will impress everybody."

"There's an anomaly somewhere in my data, I don't dispute that. But still—"

"Aside from your pathetic results, the *proceedings* of your experiment were fatally flawed. Everyone on campus knew what you were trying to prove going into the study. Why, I dined at the Faculty Club night before last, and you should have *heard* the sniggering. Everyone and his grandmother knew, luv. Which means your subjects' expectations going *into* the experiment would color their responses coming out. Garbage in, garbage out, as they say."

"There was some sort of leak, I know that." Engrossed as she'd been in organizing her experiment, she'd been the last to know, and by then it had been too late to turn back. "But I still felt my results would show that—"

"You *felt?* That's women in science in a nutshell, Nikki-sweet, feeling when they ought to be thinking. It's perfectly charming in the bedroom, but in the lab? Fatal."

Do not lose it. That's just what he wants you to do, so don't do it! Hands trembling, she flipped Twenty-three's interview to the last page. "Look at this response." *It's as plain as that piggy little nose on your face.* "The subject received my formula in his D dose. You see he circled D as the woman he'd have chosen to spend more time with?" *He chose me, nothing-special-to-look-at Nicola.*

But then, he hadn't been looking.

"Twenty-three had a twenty-five percent chance of guessing that question correctly, luv. If that were my odds of winning the lottery, I'd bet the farm."

He didn't guess. He chose. Me. She jabbed the second question. "And does *that* look like a random response? He was asked, on a scale of one to ten, how much he'd like to meet with D again, ten being the greatest intensity of desire and one the least. You see how he answered that?"

Her phantom admirer had printed the multiplication sign, X, to the right of the number ten. Beyond that, he'd printed the number 9999, then he'd circled his equation—10 x 9999. His desire to meet her again was 99,999 on a scale of ten? "You call that a random response? My formula affected him *precisely* as predicted. And once I follow up his response—" She stopped as it hit her. There would be no follow-up. She had no way of finding her man.

"Do you know what *I* think, Nikkikins?" Bracing his hands on either side of hers, Hadley leaned across the desk till their noses almost touched. "I think you'd better give up and start over. Find a new dissertation. I'd be only too happy to help."

So *that* was what he wanted! Getting rid of her wasn't good enough—wasn't the point at all. He wanted her humiliation, her face rubbed in the dirt. He knew what this thesis meant to her...so he'd make her abandon it? She felt her eyes tearing with rage. *Don't go for his throat,* she told herself desperately. *If you do that, then—*

A large hand descended on Hadley's shoulder. The professor's smirk contracted to a pink *O* of surprise. "Who—" As he spun around to face his accoster, he slipped on Nicola's glass-topped desk. He would have toppled backward into her lap if she hadn't jammed a hand between his shoulder blades.

Snatching her hand from his softness, she wiped it on her jeans.

Twenty-three hadn't missed that gesture. His too-familiar mouth quirked up on one side as he met her rounding eyes. "Sorry if I'm interrupting something," he said, not sorry at all. "But I believe Ms. Kent and I have a prior engagement."

CHAPTER FOUR

GOD, SO HE KNEW! Nicola shoved her chair backward on its wheels till it bumped the counter behind her.

He didn't miss that reaction, either. Seen for the first time, his eyes weren't the dark brown she'd imagined, but a cobalt blue that was almost black, deep-set beneath level black brows.

Hadley brushed the sleeves of his jacket off and shook himself like a flustered hen shaking its feathers down. "And who the devil are *you?*"

"Reese Durand. And you're Peter Hadley, Ms. Kent's thesis adviser." He grasped Hadley's arm, apparently to steady him as he stepped away from her desk, then didn't let go.

How had he learned their names? And why? She watched Durand—if that really was his name—conduct Hadley toward her door. It was done too smoothly to be considered a bum's rush, but the effect was the same. And nearly as satisfying.

"Perhaps we'll have a chance to chat later." He eased Hadley out into the hall, then reached for the doorknob, his forearm barring reentry.

Hadley caught his breath as the door started to close on him. "Y-you're Reese Durand, the *tennis* player? That one—the champion?"

"That one, yes." He drew the door inward.

"The entrepreneur? Why *Forbes* interviewed you only last month—*that's* where I've seen you. I have the article down in my office. A pheromonic cologne for men, wasn't it?''

"It was." Durand shut the door—it cleared Hadley's nose by less than an inch. He swung on his heel, his eyes hitting Nicola like a slap. "When a bully sticks his chin out, you nail it, Nic. Or he'll keep on sticking it in your face."

"I'll remember that," she said absently. Pheromonic colognes? She felt as if her mind were sucking air, refusing to flow. She'd assumed he'd come for her, but *pheromones?* "So you do play tennis," she managed at last.

"Did."

"But you lied about your name." She caught her breath as he launched into motion, straight at her.

"Yes." He stopped at the far side of her desk, after all, to pick up a beach stone that she used for a paperweight.

Her stomach muscles eased a bit. "Why?"

"Your call for volunteers was limited to members of the RIIT community." He turned the rock over, inspecting its underside. "I wanted to take part, so I appointed myself RIIT's tennis coach for a day, with a name no one would recognize."

"Why?"

He tipped his head an inch or so, considering. "Nostalgia?" He shrugged. "It was what I did once upon a time. Back when you were playing with dolls."

Champion, Hadley had said. And she had never played with dolls. She'd been the tomboy—Nic, never Nikki—in her futile attempt to please a man who had wanted sons. "I meant, why did you want to take part in my experiment?"

"Business." Durand tossed the stone from left hand to right, then headed for her window. "I make it my business to learn everything I can about sexual attractants. You've heard of Irresistible?"

She recalled vaguely that she had, and had dismissed it. Pheromonic colognes had nothing to do with her aims.

There had been two or three brought to market in the past few years, but none very successfully as far as she knew. "Let me get this straight," she said evenly to his back. "You conned your way into an experiment arranged by me, financed by me, designed by me to gain data that I needed for *my* dissertation." Her outrage grew with each word. "And you did that to further *your* knowledge? You used *my* efforts—used *me*—for your own agenda?"

She found herself blushing, the image of his mouth coming down on hers, his hand on her breast. Her responding like a wind-up toy when its key is twisted. Oh, he'd used her all right! "Isn't that hijacking?"

His lips twitched, driving her temperature farther up the scale. "I suppose you could look at it that way. I'd prefer to see it as—" His voice dropped and softened, velvet spread over gravel "—the beginning of a most...*rewarding* relationship."

So he did know she was D! Her hands clenched on her chair's armrests, as if he could raise her to her feet with one look if she wasn't hanging on. *No way.*

"That's why I've come today, Nic." He prowled to the desk, stood looking down at her. "I have a proposition to make."

"No. Absolutely not." *That's not who I am. That's not what I do.*

"Just hear me out." His brows drew together when she shook her head violently, but he didn't stop. "I want you to work for me."

"What?" It came out as a strangled squawk.

"I want to buy your data, everything you've learned so far. I want all your research and I want you." He set the stone on her desk as if he was placing his offer there.

He doesn't know! The wave of relief was so strong she almost laughed aloud as it swept through her.

Its backwash carried an aftertaste of disappointment, bitter as quinine. He didn't know her. Somehow she'd thought he would, after yesterday. "W-w-why would you want to do that?"

"I told you, I'm in the business of selling pheromonic colognes. I want your brains on my team. I want to see if we can use your research as the basis for a fragrance."

She shook her head again. "That's not what I'm doing here or why I'm doing it. I'm not researching sexual attractants. I'm investigating bonding behavior and the hormones that cause it."

He shrugged. "I'm not a chemist, Nic. I'm the money man, the guy with the skills to bring a good idea to market. But I know what I felt yesterday. Your potion packs a kick like a mule. I'm still…"

"Yes?" she said softly into his sudden silence. *You bonded yesterday. Are you still feeling it?*

He changed direction as smoothly as a Porsche swinging into a turn. "Your formula has enormous commercial applications, is what I'm saying, Nic. The worldwide perfume market is ten billion per year."

"So go get it, tiger." She crossed her arms and leaned back in her chair, faking nonchalance, since the real thing eluded her. "You've got your cologne. If it really makes men irresistible to women, you won't be able to make it fast enough. You'll take a *big* bite out of that ten billion."

"Come take a bite with me." He sat on the edge of her desk, braced one arm and leaned closer. "Irresistible is just one fragrance. I want a whole line of scents, Nic. I want the whole market." *I want it all,* said the blue eyes drilling into her.

Alpha male, she reminded herself. *Challenge is his meat and drink, be it sexual, territorial or—in the modern male— financial.* "Good for you." And now he was *too* close, she realized, her pulse stampeding as she looked up into his face. Depending on how good a nose he had, at some proximity he'd smell her skin. D's personal aura, unique as a fingerprint. A starburst of panic lit up her brain. *No way.*

Ducking, she grabbed the spray bottle of cleaner she kept

under the counter for cage-cleaning time, and a roll of paper towels, then bobbed up again. "A *smudge!*" she cried on a note of outrage, attacking her desktop beside his flattened hand.

A stinging ammoniac cloud rose between them. "Hey!" He snatched his hand back as she sprayed his fingers.

"Oops. Sorry." She tore off a couple of paper towels and handed them to him, then bent over the desktop, wiping furiously. "Might as well do the whole thing while I'm at it." She picked up the bottle again. Squirting with abandon, she bit back her smile as he retreated to the window. "You can't *imagine* how dusty it gets around here, with all the cedar chips…" She tipped her head toward her cages with their bark bedding.

His eyes followed, and she used the moment to spray her own fingers. "There. Much better." Stooping to put the cleaning materials away, she touched the hollow below each of her earlobes, her throat, smoothed her hand over her hair…and wrinkled her nose. *Gak!* Her own mother wouldn't know her scent now. She settled back in her chair and gave him a magnanimous smile. "Now…where were we?"

Eyes narrowed, he studied her. "I was saying I need you," he said as if he was having second thoughts. "And I'm willing to pay—very well. We're talking a yearly salary, plus royalties, if your potion is translatable into a perfume. And since your formula would become my company's proprietary secret, I'd be willing to pay you a one-time flat fee for—"

"Proprietary secret?"

"Your formula becomes my secret, Nic, the way Coca-Cola guards their recipe for Coke. So no competitors can copy the product."

"No."

"What d'you mean, no? Secrecy's essential in this business."

"I mean, no deal, Mr. Durand. I mean, forget it, because

I'm not interested." She tapped the edge of a stack of interviews on the desk to line them up, turned them and tapped again, then looked up.

Into a gaze like a blue laser. She could imagine him aiming that beam over a racket as he waited to smash the last ball of a game down an opponent's throat. "Why?"

"Why? Because I'm in the midst of earning my Ph.D., that's why. Because I'll have to publish my dissertation to win that degree, and in that paper I'll spell out *precisely* what's in my formula—no secrets allowed."

"Nic, think about it. We may be talking millions here for you."

"Emphasis on the 'may be,'" she said dryly. "And that's not the point. I want to be a professor of biochem someday. I can't do that without my degree."

"So buy a college, instead. Buy this one. Let RIIT give you an honorary degree."

"No, thanks. I want the real thing." Honor, worldwide renown in her field, something few women had achieved. *I want to show them all. One man in particular. I can play with the big boys. Beat them at their own game.* Money meant nothing, compared with that lifelong goal. "So that's that," she ended brightly.

"Is it?"

Again that disturbing softness. Ignoring it, she reached for a blank form. "I'm sorry I can't help you. But on the other hand, Mr. Durand, you can help me. As you know, I have to reevaluate your response after twenty-four hours. So now that I have you here..." She lifted her pen. "First question..." *If you had to choose one woman to be with today, would it still be me? Uh, D?*

"No." He leaned against her windowsill, arms crossed. "No deal, Nic. If you won't play ball with me, why should I play with you?"

"Because you volunteered for my experiment, that's why!" He shrugged, and she tapped the end of her pen against the desk in frustration. "That was part of the agreement, that you'd submit to follow-up evaluations."

"Guess I changed my mind...about submitting." He looked as submissive as a half-ton chunk of granite, propping up her wall.

"I even *paid* you to participate," she cried, and realized it was absurd even as she said it. Her face reddened.

"You did, ten dollars." Reaching into his coat, he pulled out a wallet. "Here's your refund." He laid a twenty on her desk. "Don't worry about the change."

She lifted the bill by one corner and threw it back at him. It didn't throw very well. "I don't want my money back. I just want to know the answers to a few simple questions! If the intensity of your response has changed. If you've dated anyone since yesterday." The intensity of her own need to know *that* was as startling as it was sudden, a tiny jab of electricity, jolting her stomach muscles.

His eyebrows tipped. "I'm down from Boston, Nic. Don't know a soul in town."

"That wouldn't necessarily stop—" She stopped.

He didn't smile, but his eyes were amused. "No, that wouldn't stop me if I needed a woman."

"Well, did you?" *Pick up some lucky woman in a bar? Call a hooker?* If he had, then his response was already degrading.

He laughed under his breath, swept the rejected bill off the floor and placed it back on her desk. "I ask questions, Nic. I don't answer them."

Ooh, you arrogant— She ripped the twenty into halves, and his smile vanished. *Ha—that got to you!* Chin tipped defiantly, eyes locked with his, she held each half of the bill like a tiny banner. *You didn't like that at all, did you?* Funny reaction from a man who must have millions.

It lasted only a moment. "Tape works nicely." He headed for her door.

Wait! Come back here! She wasn't finished with him. She needed...she needed...*data,* she told herself fiercely.

That was what—*all*—she needed from him. She rifled her mind, seeking some way to compel him to turn. Come back. But "please" wasn't an option. She didn't beg.

As if he'd read her thoughts, he wheeled in the doorway. "Oh…there's one thing. Two, actually. Here's my card. If you change your mind about my offer, call me."

"I won't." Her fingers curled tight around the cream-colored rectangle. "And the other?"

He put his hands in his pockets, jingled some change he found there, the picture of casual, carefree masculinity. "I spoke with one of the women, during your test."

"You weren't supposed to do that!" She was outraged all over again, which was silly, considering he'd blithely broken every other rule to suit himself.

His half smile seconded her self-assessment. "We talked cars. She had an old Corvette I might like to buy. She gave me her phone number, but I've mislaid it. If you could let me have it…" As he spoke, he swung toward the window, wandered a step or two that way, peered out casually. "I didn't catch her name, but she was…D. The last one who came to me."

Got you! A wide grin of triumph lit her face. As he turned back, Nicola swept the whole stack of interviews off her desk, then dived after them. "Oops—darn." *Got him!* she told herself gleefully as she messed with the papers out of sight. He *was* still bonded. The impulse to be with D hadn't decayed yet. Was still strong enough that he was willing to fabricate that ridiculous car story as his excuse.

"Need some help?" He started around her desk.

"No!" She shuffled the papers. "I can manage, thanks." So she still had him, but now what? She was barely holding her own with him as it was. Admit she was D, the woman he'd reduced to a puddle of Jell-O? No way. Not in a million years.

"About that phone number…" Durand leaned over her desk.

There must be some way to use this, turn it to her advantage, but she couldn't think how. Not with him looming overhead. She straightened and gave him a prim frown. "I don't believe I could do that."

"*What?*" The word was very soft. Downright scary.

She gulped and shook her head. "I promised my test women perfect anonymity. I gave my word on that."

He planted his hands on her desk and leaned closer. "Read my lips, Nic. She *wants* me to contact her."

Oh, yeah? Nicola stared back, answering his scowl with haughty defiance. "I believe you said I should nail any bully who sticks his chin in my face?"

He swore and backed off. Turned a tight circle of frustration around the room and came back again. "Look, I *have* to reach her. I want that car."

"Sorry." His want would fade away soon enough. In mountain voles the one-hundred-percent decay rate was two weeks. In humans, she couldn't say yet, though some of the bonded men she'd reached this morning were showing diminishment of interest already. Of course, Durand's had been stronger from the start. Was probably stronger still. *I need to study you, dammit. You're the exception to every rule. Why?*

He looked as if he could cheerfully throttle her. She was suddenly jealous, ludicrous as it was, of D, who could inspire such allegiance, if only for a little while. It was more than *she'd* ever accomplished—except perhaps with Hadley in his own twisted way.

The silence stretched between them, long enough for him to count to ten. Three times over. "All right," he said bitterly. "If you won't give me her number, would you consider taking a note to her?"

She cocked her head, enjoying the power. Yesterday it had been all his. "I'd...consider it." He took a step forward and she added hastily, "In exchange for..."

"What?"

Silently she rose, rotated a blank evaluation form on her

desk to face him—and smiled. Hardly sporting, but victory was too sweet to be denied.

"Forget it."

As he spun toward the door, she stopped smiling. "Wait!" *Damn rock-stubborn male!*

He didn't stumble as he turned—nothing so clumsy. But there was a sudden check in his stride, accompanied by a tiny implosion of breath. He'd stopped moving, faced away from her.

"Are you...are you all right?"

"Yes." His hand slashed the air in a "stop" gesture as she thrust her chair back and stood.

"But—"

"I'm *fine!*" he snarled, then turned with his usual grace. "Just...fine."

He was gripped by some pain, the lines in his angular face etched deeper than they'd been only a moment before.

"Look, I'll pass your note on. No conditions," she said impulsively, and earned herself a savage look. Alpha males detested pity, apparently.

"Here." She yanked open a drawer, found envelopes, a pad of paper, a pen and slid them across the desk. Then she turned to inspect the feed cups of the four cages on the counter that held her old favorites. While Durand scribbled something on the pad, she added pellets to each tiny feeding trough.

Cuddled in blissfully sleeping pairs, the voles ignored her. Her one hamster, three-legged General Hannibal, reared squinting out of a drift of cedar chips, then gimped over to inspect the bounty.

She turned back to find Durand sealing the envelope. He slashed the letter D on its front, then shoved it across the glass. Neither smiling, they eyed each other. "I'll see she gets this."

He gave one curt nod, then glanced at the blank form on her desk.

Yes? He wouldn't take a favor without paying for it, she

realized, watching his brows knit. Wouldn't want to be beholden. He looked up, his gaze like an overhead smash, saw that she was waiting. That she understood. "One question, then."

She needed his response to *all* her questions, all but number one—his sealed message answered that. He still wanted D. But any answer was a start. "Number two, then. On a scale of one to ten, how much would you like to meet with—"

"Not that one."

She opened her mouth to cry, "No fair!" then closed it with a snap. "All right…" Which one, then? Which question would maximize her information? *Think.* If he was still bonded, then he hadn't seen another woman last night; he couldn't have. So she didn't need number three. Ask him about his dreams last night?

He stirred impatiently, and she sucked in a breath, trying to think. She could smell nothing but her own ammoniac camouflage, but that very act of sniffing—

The leap came, the kind of vaulting surmise that Hadley sneered at and she had come to cherish—her intuitive connecting of apparently unrelated facts, which one day might carry her all the way to the top of the scientific heap. "It's a two-part question," she said, forming it as she spoke.

"Then you can have half." He took a step backward toward the door.

We'll see about that. "Did you happen to wear a cologne yesterday during my experiment?" She knew he had. The hairs on the back of her neck quivered as she remembered. *The scent of his warm skin, interwoven with something that promised danger, whispered, "Come closer!"* And she'd come.

"Yes." Just the one fact, nothing more, like a hand of cards held tight to the chest. She bet he played poker, and won. He backed another step out of her life. Put a hand on the doorknob.

"What was that cologne?" She willed him to answer—

he *would* give her an answer if she had to chase him down the hallway to have it. Though she knew already. She was sure she knew.

His eyebrows drew together; he was framing his refusal. She put a hand to his envelope—not a threat, but a reminder. *I'm doing you a favor. And you don't take favors without paying, do you? No more than I do.*

"My own," he growled, and walked out her door.

She sat, dizzy with triumph. *His own!* Meaning simply a cologne that he'd purchased—or meaning the one his company had brought to market? Irresistible, a pheromonic cologne, designed to draw women to men? She was sure she knew which, though she'd no proof as yet.

But she'd obtain that proof somehow. She had to.

Nicola reached for his interview, flipped to the last page and sat, eyes only half-focused on it. She knew it already by heart. *Question two: How much do you want to be with this woman? With D?*

Nine thousand, nine hundred and ninety-nine times ten, on a scale of one to ten.

The score of her next-highest subject had been an eight out of ten. The average male, of those who had bonded, had answered six to this question. *Your level of wanting was off the chart. Through the roof. Why? Because I let you touch me? Kiss me?*

But she'd never roused that kind of passion in a man before. Saw no reason she should start now.

No, this had to be something more than her own meager powers of attraction. Much more.

Had there been a chemical interaction somehow? *Your pheromone interacted with my formula to give you a supercharged sensation of bonding?*

She would have to find out if she wanted to turn her experiment from a crashing defeat into resounding victory. And did she ever want to. "But how?" she said aloud, and her eyes fell on his message. Addressed to D.

To me. She dragged the envelope across the glass, lifted

it and paused, feeling ridiculously guilty. It was addressed to somebody else.

Me.

Except that that woman had acted like someone else. Done things, allowed things to be done to her, that Nicola Kent never would have permitted in her wildest dreams. Felt things that Nicola had never felt.

It's for me. She slipped a finger under a corner of the flap and opened it in one single slashing rip. Pulled out the folded message.

Just two lines, penned as boldly as the words themselves:

D, if you felt what I felt yesterday, then come to me. I'll wait on the front steps of the science lab from eight till nine tonight. 23.

CHAPTER FIVE

THERE WERE TWO possibilities here. Reese measured them off in long strides, from one end of the terrace that fronted the science building to the other.

First explanation: What he had felt yesterday during the test was unrelated to whatever substance he'd inhaled. D was simply the sexiest creature he'd ever encountered in his life. No more than that.

And no less! His stomach muscles tensed with a jolt. If that was all this was, he knew what to do about it. When and if she came.

She'll come. And when she did... Leaping ahead into the night, his imagination painted an image that sucked his breath away. Her, his hotel room with its king-size bed and its wall of glass overlooking the lights of Providence. He jerked his thoughts back to the present as he reached the end of the terrace.

Second explanation: D was nothing special. It was Nicola Kent's secret potion that had made the magic.

In which case that magic, bottled as a cologne or perfume, was worth millions. Billions. Nothing-special people would buy it by the bathtubful, splash it on themselves and go forth to conquer the world.

A wise investor would make dead sure he knew *which* explanation was the true one before he dropped half a million or more, securing that potion and its contrary young inventor.

Nicola Kent. He grimaced at the image that came to mind. Reddish-brown hair escaping in wisps from a thick, short braid. Sharp eyes, sharper tongue, a face like that of a too-pretty choirboy, the innocent-looking one who put the goldfish in the holy water. Or Billy the Kid at thirteen, practicing quick draws with an earnest scowl, the tip of his tongue caught between his teeth.

He stiffened at the sound of light footsteps—*Yes!*—then relaxed again when he heard girlish giggles. Each clutching an armload of books, two campus cuties hurried past on the sidewalk below his lookout post. Absorbed in hushed conversation, they didn't glance up the flight of stairs, didn't see him waiting there, motionless till they passed.

He glanced at his watch, an analog type, with hands but no numbers. Well past half-past. *She'll come.*

If the kid had kept her word and delivered his message as promised. Reese's jaw clenched at the thought. If there was anything he hated, it was not being on top of a situation. In control. He'd lived his whole life making sure that it was he who pulled his own strings.

But not knowing D's name, D's phone number, he was automatically one down in this game. A redheaded little Joan of Arc, without the street smarts to recognize a windfall and grab it when it was offered her, held the high card tonight. If she'd forgotten, or changed her mind about delivering, there was nothing he could do.

Till tomorrow, when I hang her by her heels out her third-floor office window. Shake her a few times and she'd cough up D's name and number quick enough. Striding past the doors to the building, he stopped and gave their handles a jerk.

Still locked. Not that he thought D was behind those doors, but since this was the last place he'd met her, touched her... He swore under his breath and paced on. If he had to wait till tomorrow to hold her again, he might explode.

Something smashed onto the concrete behind him. He was already whirling as the thing bounced, knowing that this was a mistake even as he reacted. *Damn!* He clapped a hand to his kneecap and stared through watering eyes.

A dark lump rested on a step a few down from the terrace. Where the devil had it...? Eyes narrowed, heart thumping, he turned his head, but not his body, to scan the twilight.

Across the green, students hurried along the lamplit walks, late for supper or a cram session at the library, downhill beyond this quadrangle of massive ivy-laced buildings. No one was close enough to have thrown the box-shaped missile.

He limped down the steps to glare at it—then, as the thought hit him, looked up.

One window on the fifth floor looked darker than its neighbors, no glass reflecting the distant lights. An open window. Almost straight up from his gift. Starting to smile, Reese bent to collect the object.

It was a cardboard box, palm-size, then made much bulkier. Someone had wrapped his or her offering in a good half roll of duct tape. *Not the secure type, are you, darlin'?* He pulled an oblong shape from his pocket, glanced both ways to make sure no one was watching, then thumbed the switch. A razor-edged blade jumped into view, and Reese commenced slicing.

FOURTH FLOOR, Nicola noted, swinging around the fourth-floor landing, then pelting on down the back stairs. Durand would be picking up her package about now. She calculated five minutes for him to fight his way through her wrappings to its contents. *And swearing all the while, I bet.* She laughed breathlessly.

Third floor. She'd beat him with minutes to spare. Once he'd opened the box and found the key to the building, he'd still need to study the map she'd drawn, then orient himself and set out. Assuming he took her implicit dare.

He will. Her breath was coming in puffs now, her body heating as she held the headlong pace. Which was good.

She'd showered this afternoon, scourging herself with a loofah to wash away every trace of ammonia. And now this exertion would give her back her own scent. The smell of D's skin.

You're crazy, she told herself, not for the first time. *Clear out of your mind, doing this.* She rattled down the first flight of floor two, grabbed the railing and swung out around it like a giddy child.

Granted, but how else am I s'posed to study him if he won't answer my questions? He'll talk to D, even if he won't talk to me.

As long as she posed those questions with exquisite care. Any hint of scientific inquiry and he'd guess. He was hardly slow, blast him. Alpha males were alpha from head to toe, not just from the neck down, she was learning, their brains as potent as their— Image replaced verbal thought. She was rushing downward to meet a mouth, a pair of hands, a body that overarched her own—

I'm not.

Well, she was, but she knew better than to let him lay those hands on her this time. Which was why she'd chosen this rendezvous, where she knew the ground and he didn't. Where darkness was her high card. *The ace of spades.*

First floor, she chanted mechanically as she passed it and clattered down the final flight. To the steam tunnels, the network of damp, dimly lit stone corridors that connected the buildings of the main campus like a gigantic subterranean maze.

But tonight the tunnels below the science lab would not be dimly lit. She'd found the fuse box an hour ago and flipped the breakers. You couldn't find a more perfect darkness anywhere. And she was queen of this night. She'd scoped out her path this afternoon. *Keep your right hand on the wall going, your left coming back, and it's easy. You can't go wrong.*

Halting before the steel door at the base of the stairwell, she stooped for the block of wood she'd left beside it. This door locked automatically when it closed. It could be opened from the stairwell but not from the tunnel side.

Her heart was pounding from her descent. Its *thud-thud* accelerated as she hit the light switch in the stairwell. The staircase to which her map would lead Durand lay at the other end of the building, around a corner and nearly two hundred yards away. There wasn't a chance that he'd be waiting on the other side of this door, but still, she wanted no light leaking into her underworld.

This is crazy. Why am I doing this? She stepped through the door into darkness, then turned back to wedge her block between door and jamb.

For science, she told herself, rising and turning. *And for Moo.* These were answers that had served her well for years. Had taken her far and would take her much farther before her life was done.

In the blackness they felt like lies.

But then, in the dark all perceptions felt...false. Wide-open eyes probed ungiving blackness and were first confounded, then outraged. Ten steps into the dark, and already they were inventing colors. Strange misty clouds of purple and deepest ruby drifted across her mind's eye.

Her ears seemed to crane out from her head, then swivel like a small animal's, scanning for danger. They reported a dull thumping—a prisoner locked in one of the many storerooms whose doorways breached the opposite wall? Hammering, hammering at his dungeon walls?

She stopped, held her breath, listened. *It's my own pulse,* she realized, the blood pounding in her ears. With a grimace, she pushed on.

Fingers dragging lightly along the right-hand wall. This side was solid for some thirty yards, up to a corner. A right turn, then the wall continued without a break for a hundred yards or so till it reached the entrance Durand would be using.

Why the hell am I doing this?

In the dark the mind supplied answers, true or false, to fill the nothingness. *To show them all. To show him.*

The mind supplied memories where perhaps no experience had ever existed—perhaps made them up, perhaps shoveled them up from some long-buried hiding place. *A sensation of being carried...warm, enveloping arms...her own arms wrapped around a wide, warm neck. Powerful shoulders. Utter safety.* Where? When? Ever?

Her fingers dragged on, her senses spiraling inward around the sense of touch. *Right hand to wall and I can't get lost.* But who could trust her own right hand? A hand that couldn't even catch a baseball.

Someone carrying her...a voice rumbling against her chest. "You're my girl. My big girl. Now stop. Big girls don't cry."

"I don't wanna be a stupid girl."

He'd laughed. "Don't be silly, Nic. Sure you do."

"I tried to catch it, Daddy. I tried."

"I know, darlin', I know you did. It's not your fault. The glove's too big. My fault for even thinking... You're just a little girl."

"I don't wanna be—"

"Hush! Now hush. There's my girl..."

Her hand dragged out into empty space as she reached the corner—a nasty sensation of falling. It wrenched her back to the present. A present of blackness...silence...no arms around her. A man coming any moment now whose arms could not be trusted any more than her father's—

Get a grip, Kent! Three minutes of sensory deprivation and she was hallucinating. Hand on the corner's edge, she turned right around it. The steps lay ahead. He'd be coming down them any minute.

She padded onward, eyes wide, ears straining, right hand kissing stone, heart pounding. *What am I doing here?*

Running a maze like a lady vole in search of her true love. *Been studying rodents too damn long. Dominguez would laugh to see me now.*

How far had she come since the corner? Wouldn't do to bumble right up to his entrance. *Stop here and wait.*

How long?

Maybe he's not coming.

She drew a shaky breath—and knew. *He's...here.* Hair standing straight up at the nape of her neck, nostrils flaring, she flattened herself against the wall, muscles taut for flight. Sniffing.

She could smell nothing but mustiness and damp stone, but he was near. *Close.* So close he'd hear her heart, which was going wild.

He couldn't be here. He hadn't had time to—

He's here. Mouth open, she gulped a silent breath of air. She couldn't smell him or hear him, but Durand was here. She could feel him through her skin as if their bodies touched. Some subliminal noise she'd heard?

Or I'm picking up his pheromones?

So now what? She'd meant to seize the advantage from the start, with him newly disoriented and her already at ease in this dark territory. But now her thoughts were scattering to the four winds, and with them, her plans. Blind instinct wrestled with intellect to take over and save her, whether she willed it or not. Something big and wild lurked in the dark nearby. Wanting her. *Flee, you fool, flee!*

"D?"

Her pent-up breath exploded at the sound of his voice, pitched low and cautious. The softest scrape—leather against stone. She scuttered backward, one hand clutching at the wall, eyes straining to see him. *Bad idea. Oh, this was a bad—*

"D. That's you, isn't it?" His voice held impatience, and command. *Answer me, woman.*

Quiet. Oh, move quietly! Backpedaling on tiptoe, she suddenly had to laugh, could hardly suppress it. Hysteria, sheer and simple.

"D? Are you shy?" A hint of reckless laughter underlay his question, that and coaxing. *Come out, woman.*

Her own laughter answered, a wild, crazy gaiety. *"Perhaaaps..."* She took three silent steps backward, her right hand brushing stone. He was across the corridor, following the opposite wall, wasn't he?

"Don't be afraid." His voice loomed nearer, though she'd caught no sound this time. An athlete, light on his feet. "Not of me."

"I'm n-n-never afraid." The blatant lie turned to stuttering laughter in her throat. Oh, this was crazy. And what had she meant to ask him?

And suddenly he was *here,* upon her—he was moving each time she spoke! She sucked in her breath and sensed him, no fragrance she could name, simply *him,* an impact out of the dark like a hammer blow. Overwhelming. *Terrifying.* All her instincts suddenly shrieked, *Run, girl, run! Run for the life you know!*

Or step forward into a new one.

She ducked instinctively, felt the whisper of sound—the swish of air as an arm swept over her head? Arms hugging her knees, she hunched close to the floor, a small animal making itself smaller while the predator walked.

Tiniest scuffing sound—he'd prowled on past her. Relief bubbled in her throat, then wicked triumph. *Ha! Fooled you, big guy.* And what had she meant to ask? "Did you miss me?" she whispered after him. *How much on a scale of one to ten?*

She heard his startled hiss, then his voice growing louder as he swung around. "I did. I missed you like sunshine in a month of rain."

Scientist meets poet, she thought wryly. How was she to quantify that on his response sheet? With a start, she realized he'd again closed the gap between them. And retreating before him, she realized she had no idea how the tunnels ran beyond the door by which he'd entered. Retreat past that, and she'd be as lost as he. *I've got to slip by him!*

"Did you miss *me?*" Reese countered, his left hand riding the wall, his right scything the blackness. Then he cursed himself for the question. It left him wide open to anything. To a mocking no. Well, he'd only asked it to make her speak. *Speak, oh, lady...witch....*

"Like rain in a dry year."

He laughed under his breath. Shy, maybe, but nobody's fool. Good. He liked his women quick. *And the quicker I get my hands on you, my lady, the better.* Stopping, he stood stone still, only his head swinging to pinpoint any sound. *Speak, temptress. Give me your real voice. Are you a smoky alto? A high, sweet soprano?* You couldn't tell from a whisper.

Or maybe you're a bass. The thought sent an ice cube sliding down his spine. For all he knew, what he chased was man, not woman. Without conscious thought, his fingers found the pocket that held his knife, touched the shape of it through the fabric.

Can't be, he told himself, his pulse hammering in his fingertips. Yesterday he'd made no mistake. She'd been richly, wonderfully woman, as soft and feminine as they came. *But who's to say she didn't send her big brother or some other bruiser to take her place?* He was walking blind and brainless into God knew what situation, leading with his—

At the sound, he took one lightning step sideways, then froze. That tiny clatter had come from...his left?

From inside that doorway up ahead, which gave onto a small storeroom, he realized after a heartbeat. He'd explored the space only minutes before she—he?—had arrived. It contained a collection of scrap lumber and pipes, stacked upright against the corner to the right of the door.

Got you, my sneaky friend! Left hand grazing the wall, he rushed the doorway. His fingers brushed the doorjamb, and he paused, arms braced to bar her way. "D?" *Speak, devil woman.*

Only silence, jangling his nerves. He sniffed the cold air, seeking a hint of honey and hay. Smelling only must, decay. Those pipes to the right of the door. Could someone have lifted one of those without his hearing?

Not possible. Still, his mind projected an image on the dark—a faceless enemy with lethal bludgeon upraised. While his memory promised an armful of warm curves...wild honey...

Ducking low, he swung to the right, hands sweeping at waist level. His fingers grazed vertical coldness. Something slithered against stone. He dodged backward as the whole stack of pipes came clanging down—hell's bell tower toppling. His back pressed to a wall, he stood, panting and swearing.

And heard her. Out in the hallway. A warm, bubbling laugh, just three notes or so, but unmistakably feminine. He laughed silently between his teeth and was suddenly rock hard. *Devil woman!* She'd thrown something from out there, a coin or some such, to draw him.

This point to you, my darlin'. He waited, holding his breath. Knowing she'd come to him.

"Twenty-three?" Her whisper came from the doorway.

Smiling more broadly, he waited, tensing for a spring.

"Are you all ri—" She gasped, must have heard his first movement.

He made the doorway in two bounds. His fingertips grazed sliding, silky softness—hair?—as his foot landed squarely on a pipe.

Which rolled. *"Shi—"* He stumbled headlong, one shoulder whacking the doorjamb as he plunged through. Flailing like a cartoon character, he smashed into the opposite wall with a grunt. And a growl.

From down the corridor, back the way she'd first come, she laughed.

Rubbing his shoulder, he had to laugh, too. "That one you'll pay for!" When she finally used it, she'd have a low voice, he was sure. The kind of voice a man would want sharing his pillow.

"You think?" The whispered taunt fading as she withdrew.

"Babe, I know." *Soon, darlin'. Meant to be.* He quickened his pace, half-crouched with arms outspread so that he'd touch her even if she ducked. He could almost span the corridor. *Coming to get you!*

The clatter came from the same side of the hall as before, muffled again. His fingers found the raised frame of another doorway. He paused, ran his hand along the far side of it. A small doorway. Another room, then, rather than an intersection. "D?"

Not a whisper. Which might mean she stood very near. Didn't dare answer.

Or was she just being contrary? He cocked his head. Heard only his own heartbeat, fast and hard. *Well, girl?*

Last time she'd thrown something from the corridor to fool him. But she was too smart to try the same trick twice. So this time she was really hiding within? Had accidentally bumped something?

Or she's smarter yet, and knowing I'd think that, she did the same as before? A double bluff.

A man could waste half a lifetime guessing and second-guessing himself. Action was the only sure answer. "Fool me twice, shame on me," he called into the room, and took three audible steps past the doorway—then silently doubled back and crouched on the floor. He waited, one arm spanning the entrance at thigh level. His head swung from the room to the corridor, then back again. Inside or out, he meant to have her. *Come to me, D. Darlin'. Devil woman. Whichever you are, come. Whatever your game, come meet the one who'll win it.*

Silence. A minute passed. She wasn't coming. Maybe had gone?

No. He wouldn't have that. This night wouldn't end that way.

The touch came from within, just a nudge against his forearm as she tried to edge out the door. She yelped and dodged backward as his hand curled around the back of her thigh. *"Gotcha!"*

Her momentum carried her onward. She would have gone down, but he was lunging to his feet. His other arm hooked her waist and he caught her in a perfect tango dip— her hair must be brushing the floor. *Gotcha!*

For a moment he held her there suspended, savoring his own strength and speed, letting her feel it, too. *A very good catch indeed.* Then, laughing under his breath, he reeled her back in. Swung her upright against his chest. "I've got you." It was reassurance, promise, a declaration of victory. He dropped his face to her hair, breathed in the scent of alyssum and knew it all over again. *You're mine,* the feeling so strong it stole his breath away.

And she was trembling.

Automatically, he cradled her closer. "I'm here." *Don't be frightened. With my arms around you, nothing can...* Then he realized, as she shuddered violently, a tip-to-toe convulsion that arched her back and shivered her breasts against his chest, nearly driving him right over the edge, *she's frightened of me.*

This wasn't a lab room, with a guard outside the door, him safely blindfolded. And she was shy, in the way wild things are. *But she called me here. Came to me.*

And now it was up to him to make sure she didn't regret that. Yet if he let her go, she'd be gone. She was shivering because every muscle was pulled wire-tight, ready to explode, preparing to fight him or to fly.

Clenching his teeth with the effort it took, Reese smoothed his palms slowly down her back, then around to grip her narrow waist. His hands nearly spanned her—he squinched his eyes shut with that sensation, so violently *pleasing.* Took a ragged breath.

Then, with every instinct howling for him to pull her close, he backed her gently away from his chest. Held her at arm's length. And more than that he could not do. To let her go was unthinkable. She was his.

Time passed—a heartbeat or a year. Small hands materialized out of the night to settle over his. Fingers curled delicately around his wrists to touch the undersides where his pulse hammered and the nerves ran shallow. Two lightning bolts scorched up his arms. Reese bit back a groan. She was assessing her chances of throwing his hands off, he knew. Still... *Do that again, witch! Touch me there, then touch me—*

She sucked in a sharp breath and her hands tensed.

No, babe, please don't try it. I don't know what I'll—

Her breath feathered out again. Finger by finger, her hands unclenched. He could almost hear her thought, that she could not break his grip. He felt a beat of pure triumph at that; he needed her to know his strength. That it overpowered her own. Always would. *But it's yours tonight, babe. Take it. Take it all.*

With a shuddering sigh he could feel through his fingertips—was it surrender?—she abandoned his wrists. Smoothed her fingers slowly, slowly up his arms toward his elbows. If she couldn't escape him, she would explore?

Yes...that's right...know me. Turning inward to her touch, he closed his eyes. Her fingertips brushed slowly upward. The hairs on his arms turned electric, a current of fiery gold running through them, heat flowing up his arms. *Yes, keep touching me.*

When she reached the hollows at his elbows, Reese clamped his teeth on his lip. She fingered the tendons there, and at this sensation, incredulous, exultant, he gave up and laughed aloud. "You..." She touched him as if she'd never known a man before. Had no idea how one might be constructed. Needed to know. *You shy, wild thing, don't ever stop touching me!*

CHAPTER SIX

PANIC WAS GIVING WAY to a rush of pure adrenaline.

It works! She surfed a cresting wave of triumph, his hands at her waist almost seeming in the dark to hold her aloft. *By God, it works!* Thirty-six hours at least since he'd inhaled her formula. Durand's response should be fading. Instead, he stood as if he'd never let her go. *Bonded. Still. Now if only I knew why and how!*

But she'd find the answer. Because tonight she could do anything. She fingered the rock-hard tendons where his forearms joined his upper arms. He laughed, a breathless growling laugh, and another wave of adrenaline rushed through her. Such glorious *power,* this. She'd never dreamed... He was hers for the touching—beautiful, wondrously hard.

Her hands had crept up his arms of their own volition. Now they followed the hot curves of his biceps. At her touch, he flexed them, and she laughed in delight as the muscles bunched. Such a *guy* thing to do. Absurd...absurdly thrilling. *"Hard* man!" she whispered mockingly and gripped them more firmly. Such power under her hands.

Hers because he had bonded to her, while she...? She was free.

"Hard all over," he growled, and pulled her against him.

Free—and snared fast in his arms. The power was all his, only lent her on his whim. The realization slammed home as he loomed over her. Lifted up on tiptoe, she arched herself instinctively into him, her head falling back for his kiss.

His mouth drove her down into darkness, a slow, swooning back dive. Her arms wrapped around his neck, dragging him down with her. Floating all around them, his scent of danger…of daring. He tore his mouth away to kiss her chin, the tip of her nose, her eyelids. Plunging his nose into the hair at her temple, he stood shaking, inhaling her essence in ragged breaths. *"D…"* he whispered fiercely.

No, oh no. Not D at all! Like a swimmer fighting the riptide, her mind surfaced, caught a breath and protested. No, this wasn't what she'd planned…wanted. This wasn't her at all, kissing a stranger in the dark. She'd come here to…to—

His hand found her breast, his lips her mouth, and she went under again, drowning. So this was what it was like, sex with an alpha male. *Anything you want…everything I want. Yes…*

She whimpered wordlessly when his hand left her breast. Her own hand had found its way inside his shirt. She threaded her fingers up through curly, rough hair. Over sloping hardness. His heart slammed beneath her cupping palm. Hers! Bonded to her.

Bonded to D. She clenched her hand into a fist, slipped it out of his shirt…

His hand slid down her thigh, his other around her back. He swung her easily off the floor—and kissed her when she opened her mouth to protest, long…deep…liquid…a dark, floating dream of a kiss.

He ended it before she would have. She found she'd twined her fingers through the thick, silky hair at the back of his head. That she gripped him as if this was all that saved her from drowning.

He brushed his mouth back and forth across her cheek, his own voice a drugged growl. "I'm not making love to you in a basement. Not the first time. Which way is out of here?" His back bumped a wall. "Left or right?"

"Left." Unless she was turned completely around. But she was. She hadn't come here to...

To have someone carry her. But he did. *Warm, enveloping arms. Her own arms wrapped around a wide, warm neck. Powerful shoulders. Utter safety.*

Terrible danger. Her breath snagged in her throat. She wriggled against his chest, but his arms only clasped her more tightly, increasing her sense of enclosure...of a trap...a walking trap... *Arms that could never be trusted. Arms that would surely fail her...* She was walking right into a trap!

"I want to watch your face the first time I come into you." His words rumbled against her side, and a fresh wave of panic broke over her.

He'd seen her face already. It hadn't impressed him. The thought of his own face, incredulous, when he saw whom he held...who it was he thought he wanted... "Put me down!"

"I'd rather carry you." He stopped, his shoulder touching the wall. "Here's a corner. What now, darlin'?"

She wasn't his darling, wouldn't be his darling at all when he saw her in the light. From the corner it was only thirty yards to her stairwell door. "Put me *down!*"

"All right." He set her gently to earth, then hooked an arm around her waist when she swayed. His fingertips found the side of her upturned face, then her eyebrow. They traced it delicately inward from her temple, soothing, caressing. "Shy, darlin'? I'm moving too fast?"

Way too fast. But her panic was skulking back into the shadows now that she stood on her feet. Her own two feet. The only safe way, for her.

The tip of his thumb found her mouth, followed the curves of it back and forth. "I'll settle for watching your face while you drink a cup of coffee with me, if that's all you want." His thumb pressed gently down on her bottom lip, seeking her dampness. *"Tonight,"* he added huskily, the word hanging between them, heavy with promise. *If not tonight, then soon. You know it. I know it.*

What he wouldn't settle for was letting her go without a look. Without seeing her safely home. Even half-mesmerized by his caress, she knew it. Because he was bonded. Still. She pictured two newly mated voles moving in tandem, the male walking a half step behind, his chin riding the female's shoulders. His bright eyes searching the world with passionate ferocity for any male who might dare to covet his lady.

No, Durand wouldn't take her if she wasn't willing. She knew that now. But neither would he let her go. His thumb intruded too far and she nipped him—hard.

"Witch." Laughing under his breath, he withdrew. "Which is it? My bed or a cup of coffee?"

Neither, she thought desperately. *This researcher chooses NA. Not applicable.* But try to tell *him* that in his present mood. Words wouldn't begin to do it. So. *Desperate times call for desperate measures.* She reached for his belt with both hands and heard him suck in his breath.

"Hey—"

"Here," she whispered. "Now." *And who has the power now, big guy?*

"No, babe, not like this." His hands closed over her own, on his buckle.

"*Like* this," she insisted, starting to smile—and slipped her fingers over his waistband. She tugged at it, drawing him closer, drawing a low groan out of him. *Make me want you, will you? I'll show you...*

"Little witch!" he protested on a laughing growl. "Cut it out."

Make me. She stretched a thumb to touch the bottom of his zipper, then stroked slowly upward. He felt enormous...hot...hard as a rock. She'd never touched a man like this. Teased one like this. *Blame it on D. This can't be me.*

He let out a shivering gasp and she grinned. Power, how sweet! *Who's trapped whom now?*

"Babe..." He made a clumsy attempt to stop her hands, but she brought her face to his chest and rubbed it luxuriously against him, smiling, while her fingers slipped through his and insisted. The buckle parted.

"Wait."

And lose the advantage? *She who hesitates is lost.* And she didn't mean to lose herself or this game. Not to any man. She slipped his waistband button through its buttonhole, then played the back of her knuckles down his zipper and up again. Taunting him. *Well, big guy? Should I change my mind?* "You'd rather have a cup of coffee?"

"I-I-I..." He growled a helpless, growling laugh. "You..."

She dragged the zipper down.

And wished suddenly, keenly, for a light. Her smile rounding to an unconscious *O*, she knelt. Touched him with just the tip of one questing finger, finding thick cotton stretched taut over rampant hardness, volcanic heat....

"Oh, *babe*...D...what you're doin'..." He plunged trembling hands into her hair, caressing, tugging....

What the hell am *I doing?* But it was too late to turn back now. *Press on regardless.* Her fingers curling over the elastic of his shorts, she leaned to press her face to his skin, just above that band. Closed her eyes and took a deep, shivering breath. Inhaled clean, hot male, the heady scent of musk and, most potent of all, what she could not smell, androsterone, the male pheromone, source of all her problems at the moment. *It's now or never, girl.*

She tipped back her head and stared up at him blindly. *Crash my experiment, will you? Turn me upside down with a kiss?* She shook her head to shake off his caressing hands, sucked in her breath. Then, with tender care, she pulled his shorts down around his knees, his trousers sliding down with them.

He whispered something dark and wordless, then "D...*sweet*...devil woman..."

Not me. Somebody else. She hadn't meant to touch him again, but suddenly the impulse was—irresistible. *Just a simple scientific inquiry,* she told herself as she reached....

As if she could see in the dark, she found him unerringly. Her hand closed around him. Heat. Vital springing hardness. Her fingertips could not meet her thumb. "Yikes!" She forgot to whisper it.

"Yikes?" He laughed. "What kind of—" Then, *"Hey!"* as she released him and stood.

Left hand to wall for returning, and you can't go wrong. Presuming she wasn't turned around 180 degrees and headed the wrong way. But how could anything else dare go wrong? She'd never meant for this evening to go like this, *end* like this.

Behind her, clothes rustled. *"D!* Where the hell are you—"

Nicola broke into a run. *Twenty yards...ten...*

Running footsteps behind her—Lord, he was quick! Her hand bouncing painfully along stone. *Doorway, doorway, where's the damn—* Her hand bumped the jamb. She hurled the door open, kicked out the block and yanked the door shut—as something large and furious hit the far side.

"*D,* dammit!" Fists hammering on steel. "*D?"* The doorknob rattled.

She hadn't meant it to end this way. Nicola flicked on the stairwell light.

"*D!"*

Just got out of hand, she told the vibrating door with regret. Then glanced down at her own hand. And grinned. *Game two to me, big guy! Crash my experiments at your peril.*

The door shook again and she winced. It *ought* to hold. But even if it did, in a minute Durand would recall the way he'd come into the tunnels. For all she knew, he'd left that door propped open. *Outta here*, she told herself, *with all alacrity*.

Somewhere on the far side of the campus, she'd stop and find a phone. Call Security. Tell them something very large and very noisy was raising holy hell in the steam tunnels below the science lab. "Be patient just a few minutes," she told the door. Then realized it had gone silent.

Omigod, he's on his way! Heart in her throat, she shot up the stairs.

HOLDING HAMSTERS was a bit like holding quicksilver. Just when you thought you'd grasped one, the lithe body slid through its own loose skin and slipped away. General Hannibal's head popped up through the gap between Nicola's thumb and forefinger. Dark eyes bulging, whiskers shivering, he shoved his way through—to drop into her left hand waiting below. "Gotcha," she said absently, then wished she hadn't.

She wandered over to her office window, the hamster peering anxiously over each side of her hand at the distant floor. "Don't even think about it," she told him. Told herself. *Ha.*

Gotcha. Durand's hands holding her, playing over her, driving her wild. Making her crazy. The things she'd done last night...*crazy.* Her cheeks burned and she pressed her forehead to the cool windowpane. *Wasn't me. Must have been D.* To dare to touch him like that...

She could blame it on D, that hotheaded irresponsible wench, or she could blame it on his cologne. Nicola turned back to her desk, where she'd piled copies of magazine articles. She'd spent the morning at the library, researching Durand's pheromonic cologne, Irresistible.

It had hit the fragrance market with great fanfare some eight months ago. Articles in *Cosmo, Glamour,* even *Playboy* had all breathlessly noted its advent, with each of the male reporters trying a sample, then recounting with gusto their adventures with women in singles' bars, airplanes, grocery stores.

Some of the writers had raved about their results; some had been doubtful. All had wondered. Was it all in the head? Or in the bottle? Madison Avenue hype or true scientific—and sexual/social—advance?

Good question. Nicola set the hamster down on her desk.

After the first onslaught of articles, they'd tapered off dramatically. The last one she'd been able to find was published in *Forbes* two months ago. After that the print media had observed a total blackout, apparently gone on to some other six-month wonder.

This last was a straight interview with Durand and his partner, the biochemist who claimed to have isolated the male pheromone, which was the basis of Irresistible. Its author had noted the staggering profits to be made in the fragrance industry. Then he'd recounted Durand's self-transformation from brief bright tennis star to entrepreneurial wunderkind, calling him a brilliant, self-made millionaire.

But like all the other writers, he'd skimped on his scientific facts. "Dammit, couldn't just one of them have asked Durand *which* male pheromone they're using?" she demanded of Hannibal, who had stopped to groom himself frantically on the edge of her desk. "Androsterone? Testosterone? Something else entirely?"

It wasn't as if there was only one sexual pheromone. Possibly there were a dozen or so, though nobody had discovered them yet. It wasn't till the mid 1980s that scientists had even admitted that human mating behavior, like animals, might be influenced by pheromones. But isolating those elusive attractants was another matter, like landing a manned rocket on Mars. Easy to imagine, not so easy to do. Had Durand and his partner done it?

Not that she cared either way. Aside from a truckload of embarrassment, she didn't give a fig about Irresistible's effect on herself. That didn't matter, scientifically speaking.

Not to her. What mattered was how Irresistible interacted with *her* formula to affect Durand.

"He was wearing his own cologne," she told the hamster, capturing him as he stepped down onto the handle of her top drawer, his fat rump pointing skyward. "He probably splashes it on his neck and jaw. So he's breathing in that pheromone already, right?"

She set the hamster back on the desk. "Then on top of that he inhales my stuff. And they interact. His stuff boosts the effects of mine, and we get..." *Dynamite.* Her body throbbed with a slow subsonic rhythm. As if he'd set off some explosion within her last night, its echo still rebounding from peak to internal peak. "That's...my...theory, anyway." The sensation subsided and she opened her eyes.

Like all premises, it would have to be tested. The problem was how. She supposed she could dash out and buy a bottle of Irresistible. Combine it with her own formula, then try to replicate Durand's response.

But even if she obtained the same supercharged bonding response, she'd be testing blind. Using an unknown substance to obtain her results. If she tried to write her dissertation based on that, she'd be laughed out of the field. She might as well claim that she'd caused men and voles to bond by sprinkling them with rose pollen or eye of newt.

"We need to know his active ingredient, General." She collected the hamster and let him cascade from hand to hand to hand, water seeking its own level. A first-rate chemist, given six months and the most advanced cracking equipment, *might* chemically isolate the pheromone from the perfume in which it was embedded.

But that task was far beyond her talents or time available. Irresistible could easily contain four hundred or more organic substances to make up the scent part of the liquid. The pheromonic portion of the recipe would be a tiny fraction of the whole, a chemical needle lurking in a fragrant haystack.

No, the only efficient, the only *rational* approach was to simply ask, "What pheromone did you use?"

"Right," she told the hamster. Mr. Ask-me-no-questions Durand would really tell her that! Not that she'd even get the chance to ask.

Because she wouldn't be seeing Durand's face around here after last night. Her own face warmed at the memory. Humiliating a man like that, even though that hadn't been her intention. Still, with his pride and his ego, bonded to her or not, he'd probably sooner throttle D than kiss her at this point. And if he found out that D was *she*... Nicola shivered.

"Goose waddling over my grave," she explained as the hamster froze and seemed to focus on her face. "That's all. And your playtime is officially ov—" She looked up as someone rapped on her door, then opened it while speaking to somebody out in the hall. The widening gap revealed a decisive profile, hooded eyes, dark hair—

Oh, no, not— A tidal wave of blood roared toward her face. Another second and she'd be glowing stoplight, tattletale red. Nicola yanked out her bottom desk drawer and dropped the hamster into its depths.

THE KID WASN'T going to like it. No matter that he was doing her a favor, she was going to hate this. All the more reason he should tell her himself. He'd always believed in doing his own dirty work.

And it had been dirty enough so far this morning. After his breakfast with Hadley, Reese wanted a shower. *I'll be doing her a favor, taking her away from that creep.* But try to tell her that. He rapped briskly on her door, said over his shoulder, "Give me ten minutes," then entered.

His first sight was of her bottom, clad in jeans, mooning him from around the corner of her desk. "Ms. Tightbuns," the guys in line had called her, he remembered with a grin, and strolled around for a better view.

She knelt, head and shoulders thrust deep into the lower

drawer of her desk, rummaging furiously. "Lose something?" he asked mildly.

"A hamster," she growled from the depths. "They're blasted escape artists." Without emerging, she dragged forth a stack of writing pads and dropped it on the floor beside her. A box of pencils followed, then a bag of sunflower seeds, a set of screwdrivers, a field guide to mushrooms, a hand-bearing compass.

He squatted alongside her, and picked up the instrument. "What's this for?"

"For fun," she muttered from her cave, and shoved something else aside. "*There* you are, you little— Hey, come back— *Ouch!*" Some part of her anatomy slammed against metal. "*Damn!*"

"Want some help?"

"*No,* thank you." She pulled out a baseball cap and a small framed photograph, which she placed glass-side down on the pile beside her.

Reese turned it over. Three children sitting on a porch step somewhere, sometime. On the left was the eldest, blond and solemn, maybe twelve. She stared gravely at the camera. The middle one, maybe eight and also blond, was scanning the sky with blank-faced detachment. She'd seen a bird at the moment the shot was taken? The other bookend was a child of roughly five wearing a baseball cap, a baseball glove that swallowed her right hand and half her tiny forearm, and a proudly defiant look. Her reddish-brown hair was cut boy-short. "This is you?" Or a brother, though there was something too pixieish even at that age—

"If you *don't* mind." Her hand groped over his, located the photo, set it back on the heap, glass-side down again.

Leaving him with the memory of delicate fingers playing over his hands in the dark. His breath coming faster. *Enough of this.* Time was flying. "Not at all." He quelled an impulse to slap her once on those trim buttocks. That would bring her up for air quick enough.

"Got—you," she finished primly from the back of the

drawer. Nicola Kent slithered out, her hands cupping golden fur. He caught a glimpse of a pink face, then she swung away and rose. Popped the hamster into one of the cages on her counter. Dropping gracefully to her heels, she reached below the shelf and came up again with a bottle of cleanser and paper towels.

He backed off hastily as the spray misted the air. Without a glance his way, she scrubbed down the counters. A stickler for cleanliness, was Ms. Kent. He supposed it went hand in hand with scientific precision. Sanitation is next to godliness?

All very well, but contrasted with a laughing wraith playing hide-and-seek in a grimy cellar? Kneeling before him in the dust? The scent of wild honey…or of ammonia? He knew which he'd choose every time. But then, one led to the other. "Nic."

With almost insolent deliberation, she put the spray bottle away, then turned. Her gold-green eyes collided with his, then shot away. She stalked over to her desk to flip a stack of articles facedown.

He'd noticed them already. "I see you've been checking me out." With amusement, he watched her face flush from shell pink to midstrawberry. An open book, was Ms. Nicola Kent, with a complexion like that. He didn't mind. It gave him an edge. Not that he didn't hold the whole pack of razors this morning.

Still, it was only polite to keep them in his pocket unless and until needed. "My offer from yesterday still stands." After last night he would have doubled it, but no need to tell her that. The deal had been fair as first stated. Besides, his expenses had trebled, thanks to Hadley.

And still worth every penny. He closed his hands over palms that still held the shape of her. *Later.*

But right now Ms. Kent was frowning her cool precise frown and speaking. "…you the first time, I'm not interested. As far as I'm concerned, that subject is closed." She plucked a paper from a stack on her desk and pulled it in front of her. "But about this evaluation form—"

He laughed aloud. "You don't quit!"

"Do you?"

"No." She had the eyes of a young gunslinger, looking up at him, level and cool. He had a sudden image of himself at fifteen, calmly facing his first world-class opponent across a net. Hell, no, he didn't quit. He'd played his heart out that day—and the guy had stomped him.

Welcome to the real world, kiddo. She was lucky it was he who'd deliver the stomping. He'd do it gently, just one of those learning experiences on the way to adulthood. Reese drew the paper from his pocket and set it before her. "Recognize this?"

CHAPTER SEVEN

FROM HIS NOTE of satisfaction, Nicola knew what it was. *Trouble.* Her eyes skimmed the page to her signature at the bottom. She'd signed this when? Where? She glanced up at him and frowned. "Where'd you get this?"

"It's a copy of course. The original is filed at the registrar's office. I believe you signed it two years ago?"

She remembered, and ice water sluiced down her spine. This paper was part of a packet she'd signed upon her admittance to the doctoral program in biochemistry.

"This is the contract you signed granting Rhode Island Institute of Technology a legal interest in any of your research that originates in its labs, Nic."

She knew what was coming—she just couldn't believe it. *You bastard!*

"As I read this, the university claims a piece of any work or product that you might develop while a student here if it can be commercially exploited."

She remembered hesitating, then shrugging and signing the document. Two years ago, the chances of her research leading to anything with commercial applications had seemed remote. Besides, she'd had no real choice. They'd have never financed her studies if she'd refused to sign.

"If you'll read the fourth paragraph, RIIT also reserves the right to negotiate all licenses should some company want to exploit your research. The university protects you, as well as itself, of course. You'll share in any patents that might result, and you'll get the larger share of all profits."

But whatever rights of hers they'd protected, they hadn't

left her the right to say no. *No, you can't use me and my work.* Her hand clenched, the paper crumpled to a wad. "You *bastard.* Who—" Her eyes flashed past Durand as her door opened. One look at Hadley's smirk and she knew. "Oh, you slimy, sleazy—" She hurled the contract at his head.

Hadley squeaked and ducked. Durand caught the missile midair, his eyes never leaving her face. "We're still working out the details, but the terms will be roughly what I outlined yesterday. You'll be a very rich woman, Nic, if your formula translates into a successful cologne." He tossed the paper into her wastebasket, then casually collected the stone paperweight from her desktop and pocketed it.

"And what does *he* get out of it? Thirty pieces of silver?"

"I'm endowing a chair in the biochem department."

A chair to accommodate Hadley's ample bottom. So that was how Durand had bought his allegiance! A chair was a plum position within any department, a professorial post with its own discretionary budget, its own generous salary and sometimes its own dedicated mission. She could imagine what Hadley's mission would be—to redirect her research in Durand's best interests! Her eyes teared up and she locked her jaw. *I won't cry in front of this bastard. I will not.*

"I still want you on staff, as well as your research."

Blinking furiously, she kept her eyes on his hands as he flattened them on her desktop and leaned closer. Both men knew she was on the edge of tears. *Damn* them. She gritted her teeth. "And if I refuse?"

"Then we use your data and we go on without you. Professor Hadley tells me he suggested this line of research to you originally."

"And you believe that?" She didn't hide her contempt. Durand's fingers tapped a restless tattoo. *You don't believe it,* she guessed. But he was too shrewd to say so at this honeymoon stage in the negotiations. *Some bedfellow you've chosen!* She felt her cheeks warm at the thought. Those long fingers, only last night they'd been touching *her*, tempting her to his bed, and now... *You bastard. I wish I'd never set eyes on you. Let you kiss me.* Thank *God* he didn't know!

"Take your time deciding," Durand said. "But meanwhile, I'd like a look at your test papers."

She jerked her chin Hadley's way. "Your pal has a copy."

Durand's fingers stilled, then drummed faster. "He has a copy of your experiment's *results*. But I want the rest of it. A copy of every interview. A list of all...the participants."

At the hitch in his last phrase, she understood at last. *Gotcha!* Her widening eyes rose from his fingers to his hard, unsmiling face. *You want D's name—that's what this is about! I wouldn't give it to you, so now you think you've bought it!* Her hands clenched to fists in her lap. *You think you've got me? Well, I've got you, Mr. Almighty Durand! You're bonded, buddy, tight as any prairie vole the morning after!*

But if she had him, she had him the way one grabs a tiger by the tail. Now what? "First, I'd like to talk to my..." Her mouth almost puckered on the word. "My adviser. Alone!" she added viciously.

"Right." He pushed off her desk and glanced at his watch. "I'll be back in an hour to take you to lunch. We'll talk."

"No, we won't," she said to his back. But if he'd heard her, he didn't stop to argue. *Oh, you arrogant—* The door closed.

"Nikki, Nikki, Nikki." Hadley shook his head, reproachful from a safe distance. "When someone drops a fatted calf in your lap, luv, you don't toss it out the window."

"And when you find a golden goose, I suppose you pluck it bald?"

He shrugged and tried a winsome smile. "Doesn't every-one?"

No doubt he believed that. "I don't suppose you told Durand that this particular golden goose isn't laying eggs reliably quite yet? That with a correct response rate of only fifty percent, my test was a failure? Did you tell the man that, oh, adviser?" She couldn't believe she was running down her own work. But now? Now she was desperate.

"Of course I did. But I understand our padrone took part in the test himself? And that his experience with your for-mula was, um, persuasive?"

His lips, persuading hers to respond. If she'd known what was coming, she'd have bitten him.

"For many people," Hadley continued owlishly when she didn't speak, "personal experience overwhelms sec-ondhand data. A jock turned businessman? He's just the type to operate on instinct rather than statistics."

If only he'd been twenty-fourth in line, rather than twenty-third! If Durand had received the placebo, none of this would have happened. Her life would still be rolling merrily on its way, not...not *derailed.* "Look, you don't have to do this to me. No good is going to come of this, not for anybody. I'm not even working with pheromones, did you explain that? I can't imagine there's a way that my findings can be applied to perfumery."

Hadley shrugged. "He's woefully ignorant, scientifically speaking. That's not where he's coming from. I understand his partner is the chemist. When we meet Baggett we'll talk technicalities."

"On the other hand," she forged on, "Durand *has* opened up a whole new window on my thesis. He's the one I was telling you about, whose bonding response spiked right off the scale. I think there's some sort of drug poten-tiation going on between the pheromone in his cologne and my formula. That's why his response was so..." Words failed her. So...

Overwhelming. She stood for an instant on tiptoe, pliant

and eager, her body arched to his, her heart slamming against his in the dark. "So intense," she finished lamely, grabbing at her scattered wits. "If I can learn the active ingredient in his cologne, combine it with my—"

But Hadley was shaking his head. "No, no, no and *no*, Nikki."

"I'd have the basis for a knockout dissertation! We'd be invited to read papers at every—"

Hadley snorted. "You don't think I've been there before, Nikkikins?"

He had. Thirty years ago Hadley had written a paper that had electrified their field. It was the author of that famous paper she'd sought out to be her mentor—some twenty years too late. There'd been no further breakthroughs since the one that had made his reputation. He'd been cruising on that legend ever since.

"Nic, when opportunity knocks, you open the door and you seize it by its scrawny throat! I learned that the hard way. Now I pass it on to you. Durand is a *gold* mine. You'll thank me for this someday."

"No, I won't."

He shrugged. "Or if you're a foolish little ingrate, then you won't. But meanwhile, I advise you to make nice with our moneyman. Sometimes it pays to simply lie back, spread your legs...and enjoy."

"Get *out!*" She yanked open her top drawer.

"But of course." Hadley blew her a kiss and pulled the door shut—as a box of paper clips hit it and exploded.

No decision she made right now could be remotely rational. *Just move, go, sort it out later!* She stacked the four cages into two groups of two. "We're outta here, guys."

No, wait. Couldn't forget her experiment. Hadley might have tossed it out the window, but she had not. Not yet. She threw extra response forms into her book bag, the subjects' interviews, the description of the experiment itself and its outcome. She paused. Durand had asked for a copy of everything. *Well, you can kiss my...*

He already had, or all but. She shivered with violent loathing. *Damn you! Damn me for letting you!*

She could defy him completely, ignore his request. But defying Hadley was one thing. Defying Durand might be something else entirely. *Just go. Run.* It wasn't long till he'd come walking back through her door, and if he did... She could see herself flying at his throat and the inevitable outcome of *that.* No, today the power was all his. She had to run and fight another day, when she could bring her brains to bear, not her sadly outmatched brawn. She had to *think.*

But meanwhile... *You want a copy of my experiment?* She grabbed a box off her bookshelf, dumped it out on her desktop. *So take a copy.*

All but for one vital page—the page that listed her original female subjects, along with their addresses and phone numbers. She ripped that sheet free of its staples, folded it and crammed it into her pocket. "There you go, then. Read *all* about it, big guy. You bought it. It's yours."

Her heart was pounding. She felt as if she could feel his approaching footsteps moving toward her down dark corridors, as fast as the beats of her heart. *Out of here. Get out. Away!* Tucking two cages under each arm, the book bag containing her experiment bouncing across her back, she staggered out of her office and left the door wide open behind her. It was Durand's office now. Let him shut the damn door.

WHEN SHE WAS ANGRY, when she was blue, or when she felt too sorry for herself, Nicola visited her sister Margot. Because wandering with her around the grounds of the home, sitting with her on the grass near the duck pond, Nicola usually regained her sense of proportion. Regained her purpose.

"Mom sends you a big hug." A verbal hug—Moo didn't like to be touched. Which was just as well, since their mother had moved three years ago, following her new hus-

band, an army major, to a U.S. military base on Guam.
Hadn't been back to the States since.

Moo.

"Dana?" Nicola flopped back on the grass and crossed
her arms behind her head. "Haven't heard from her since
April. I owe her a letter." Their older sister was out in
Oregon teaching high-school English.

Moooo-oo-oo.

"Dad? Well, you'd know more about him than me." His
check arrived like clockwork every month to pay for keeping Moo here at Pembroke House, just south of Boston.
Nic herself hadn't heard from him in years. She picked a
stem of grass and examined it against the sunlight. "It's
funny, something made me remember, the other night..."
Down in the steam tunnels. "Dad leaving. The day after
my sixth birthday, remember? He gave me a baseball
glove?"

And tried to teach her how to use it down at the park.
"D'you think if I'd caught his balls, hadn't been such a
klutz?" Hadn't thrown like a girl? Hadn't cried, finally,
with frustration, like a stupid... She swallowed around an
unexpected, foolish lump in her throat and managed a wry,
reckless smile.

Moooo.

"Nah, you're right, that's dumb. He'd have left, anyway." Their father had come from a family of five brothers.
Had wanted sons of his own. Instead, he'd gotten two
daughters, or maybe Moo counted for half a daughter? *And
then me, the third, who was supposed to be Nick. I was
supposed to save the day—and I blew it.* Being Nic, his
little tomboy, daddy's little trier, hadn't been enough in the
end.

*So he left. Walked away. Men do that, you know. Can't
trust 'em. No ties that bind. No remorse. Just gone before
you can blink.*

Leaving behind a child determined to show him he'd

been wrong to abandon her. She'd been a keeper, as good as any boy, *better* than any boy.

Mooooo-oo.

"He sent me a letter on my birthday—my fourteenth—did I ever tell you that?" An awkward, fumbling apology for his sudden departure—precisely eight years too late. And the suggestion that she might like to visit him and his new family sometime up in Alaska. Meet her two younger half brothers. *Ha!* She'd never answered that letter, and he'd sent no more.

But that letter... She'd redoubled her efforts in school after that. By then the boys were as tall as she, growing stronger and faster by the day. There was no beating them on the playing fields anymore. But in the lab she could hold her own. Could show them. Science was supposed to be a man's world, but with her brains, she could show them. Shine in the end. Hit 'em where it hurt, with her success, just as she'd been—

Moo-uuuuuhhhhhhhh. Moo scowled ferociously, shook the toy and turned it again. *Moo.* Her face relaxed.

Nicola turned to consider the small cylinder her sister held, the cylinder with a smiling black-and-white cow painted on its side. Upend it and it mooed—some sort of tiny bladder inside, she supposed. "That one's wearing out, isn't it?" Soon she'd have to bring Moo a new one. Arrange for her attendant to switch it while she slept.

The yearly maneuver was something they all dreaded. Moo knew every moan and squeak of her toy intimately. It was the only thing in the world she talked or listened to. If its voice changed even slightly overnight, she knew something was wrong. The first few days after a switch could be very bad.

Moo-oooooooooo.

"We'll wait till July," Nic decided, wimping out. "How's that?"

No answer. Moo's blond head was tipped back as she studied the treetops. She looked at trees, never at faces.

Nicola sat up. "Well, gotta go. I've got a tide to catch." She'd decided to take her boat out of Narragansett Bay, get away from it all for a few days. Think what she would do about Durand. How she could beat him. Or if she should just leave him in control of her research, just turn and walk.

Quitters never win, and winners never quit, their father used to say. And that was what her life was about, wasn't it? Winning.

Mooo.

And you, she told her sister silently. She stood and waved to an attendant, who watched discreetly from the back steps of the home.

IN A WEEK of indignities, somehow this was the crowning one. Nicola glared at the address painted above the door of the Thai restaurant. Three ninety-six Massachusetts Ave. She glanced down at the note she'd found waiting on her lesk, anchored by her own beach rock three days ago when he'd returned after five days of self-imposed, seething ex-le.

The note was written in Durand's slashing hand:

When you decide to stop sulking, you can report to work at company headquarters—Pherotics Inc., 396 Massachusetts Ave., fourth floor, Cambridge. If you want to move to Boston, I'll cover all expenses. If you prefer to commute from Providence, feel free. But I expect to see you daily, on time, in your lab here in Cambridge, Nic. Your clock starts running the second week of June. Any days you miss after that are your own vacation days.

R.D.

"Three ninety-six," she muttered, staring up at the number. But this was a two-story building, not a four-story or more. Perplexed, she stared up and down the street. It was a slightly seedy commercial strip, a jumble of textures—brick, stone and glass. A muddle of colors—shop signs in garish red, blue or peeling yellow. Buildings of varying heights and periods, the floors at street level a mix of ethnic restaurants, a laundromat, a copy and print shop, an auto-parts store. The floors above seemed to be home to personal-injury lawyers, dentists and chiropractors, intermixed with the occasional struggling biotech or software firm.

This was the unfashionable end of Cambridge, a street sandwiched between residential areas with grand old trees and grander homes fallen to student housing, perhaps half a mile from the Charles River. A low-rent location for young businesses headed up in the world or tired old ones on the way down.

Durand, where the hell are you?

Across the way and down a block, the buildings rose higher, a granite warehouse converted to modern use, flanked by something a century more recent in glass and steel. Nicola started walking. What was one more block in a journey that included a three-day, hundred-mile leg up the coast in her antique powerboat, followed by a row ashore in her dinghy, then a hike to a T-station, a five-mile journey by transit train and a trudge through half a mile of the back side of Cambridge on a hot and humid June morning?

She wiped a trickle of sweat off her sunburned nose. *Let's see...* She'd catch a bus back to Providence this afternoon, collect her trusty ten-year-old Toyota. A car would shorten the commute from her boat, which now lay on a rental mooring at a marina in East Boston, by a good half hour.

Always assuming that she found Durand's company headquarters. And assuming she could stomach working for the grabby bastard.

You've decided that already, she reminded herself. Though the terms and the purpose of her employment would be somewhat different from what Durand had envisioned. He thought he'd bought himself a useful little slave with nimble hands and a nimbler brain for his profitable exploitation.

Think again, wise guy. You've bought yourself a raider. Opened your gates to a Trojan horse.

Because Reese Durand wasn't the only one who could operate with a hidden agenda. She'd come to Cambridge to work for herself, not for him, although he could pay her salary while she did so, and serve him right. *Coming to get you, Durand!* Or at least to get his trade secret. *Crash my experiment? Derail my career? At your peril, big guy!*

"Don't even *think* about it, buddy!" The angry male voice could have been an echo of her own thoughts.

Across the way, in front of the warehouse conversion toward which she was headed, a small man stood astride an enormous motorcycle. It was wedged front-wheel first into a parking space between two cars. The rear of a battered pickup occupied the other half of that same space. As Nicola watched, the truck lurched another foot into the slot, its crumpled rear bumper threatening the shiny chrome of the big Harley.

"I was here first!" howled the biker, shaking his fist at the pickup.

"The hell you were!" The driver of the truck threw it into Park, swung open his door and stepped out, his chin thrust forward at a comical angle.

Testosterone. Male territoriality at its finest. One of these days women *would* rule the world, when all the men had finished one another off. Meanwhile, she'd be silly to cross the street and try to edge past the fray. Nicola turned, instead, into a small sandwich shop and walked up to its counter. "An orange juice," she decided, glancing at the menu on the wall. "And have you ever heard of a company called Pherotics around here?"

The young woman shook her head, three hoop earrings in each ear jingling.

"A man called Reese Durand?"

"Reese-baby?" The girl's solemn face lit up in a wide smile. "Hunk to die for? Sure, that building across the street."

Which proved to be number 369 when Nicola looked some ten minutes later. She strolled past the pickup truck, which apparently had won the confrontation. The Harley was parked three spaces farther down the block. All that yelling for nothing.

When she stepped out of the elevator on the fourth floor to face a sign that announced Pherotics, Inc. in bold gilded letters, Nicola heard more yelling.

CHAPTER EIGHT

FOLLOWING HER EARS, she walked down a wide hall with closed doors to either side.

"...had no *right!*" yelled the distant voice. "I leave town for two weeks—*two weeks*—and I come back and you've changed *every*thing?"

Another voice, pitched more deeply and calmly, answered the first. She couldn't catch the words. As she walked, her gaze flicked past another closed door on the street side. Its top half was frosted glass. The name on the glass registered, and she stopped short.

Peter Hadley, Ph.D. winked at her in freshly gilded, smugly ornate, four-inch letters. Biochemical Consultant was the fulsome title lettered below his name.

Jackass and Traitor, she amended, for once regretting that she wasn't the type to carry a lipstick in her book bag. Hadley wanted a fancy title? She'd give him one. *Pimp to His Own Students.*

"But this is a total *goose* chase! You're spending the last of our working capital on *what?* A half-complete, half-baked dissertation by a kid who hasn't even earned her doctorate? She's not even a *real* chemist. She's some sort of hybrid—half animal behavioralism, half biochem. A know-nothing in both fields, I bet you!"

Oh, yeah? Nicola bristled. *Says who?* She reached an intersection with, on her right, a door leading to what must be the coveted corner office overlooking the street. Tim Baggett, Ph.D. was the name gilded on the door glass, in—

eat your heart out, Hadley—five-inch letters. The title below it read Vice President.

The corridor turned left, running perpendicular to the street. More closed doors, then the last stood ajar with a red sign glowing above a stairwell exit just beyond. On this door black two-inch letters spelled out the name Durand, an announcement almost breathtakingly arrogant in its stark simplicity.

"...her stuff works," said the deeper voice as she neared that open door. "I've tried it, Tim, and *believe* me, it works."

But is it working still? That question had haunted her all the way up the coast. To learn its answer was a good part of the reason she stood here now.

"*My* stuff works!" the other man yelled. "If you'd give it a fair chance! You know damn well they say it takes ten million to launch a new scent! We've only spent seven so far!"

"*Only?*" The softness of that question ruffled the short hairs at the nape of Nicola's neck. Tim was pushing it.

"And the package stinks! You don't think that affects sales? And the name—Irresistible? If we'd called it Hitman, like I wanted, or Here, Babe—"

"Tim—" Durand didn't raise his voice, but something in his weary tone cut the other man short "—Irresistible's been out eight months. And we're getting lousy customer response. Not just lukewarm, but *lousy.*"

That wasn't the picture Durand had painted for her! She'd pictured a company with one successful fragrance now reaching for another. He'd said he wanted it all, the whole market. But he didn't have *any?*

"Something's gone wrong, Tim, if they're not reordering. And we can't throw good money after bad. We haven't got it. We've *got* to take this chance."

"I say we stick with the game plan!"

"And *I* say we don't." Soft words, with the weight of a tiger's paw behind them. "And since it's my money we're playing with, Tim, you can come along and play the new game or…you can bail out."

"Well, *screw*—" a short man flung himself out the door, then spun back to punctuate his exit line with a jabbing finger "—*you*—" registering Nicola's presence at his elbow, he jumped violently and whirled to face the new threat "—Durand," he finished absently, his finger now aimed at her startled face.

He was the same man she'd seen earlier on the oversize Harley. Looking quite a bit the worse for wear, with a fiery red face and one eye half-swollen shut. It would be black by tomorrow. A bent pair of glasses peeked from his shirt pocket.

"And who the hell are *you?*"

She felt her own temper rise at the question and the accusing finger.

"Nicola Kent." Durand loomed in the doorway. "Nic, meet my partner, Tim Baggett." He reached out to push Baggett's finger down.

It bounced right up again. "*Th-this* is—?"

"Yes. Now go put some ice on that eye and we'll talk tomorrow." Durand grabbed Nicola's wrist and hauled her past the sputtering chemist. Closing the door in Baggett's face, he tugged her several steps into the room, then let her go. "So—" he swung around to prop one lean hip on the edge of a large desk, crossed his arms and scowled at her "—what have *you* got to say for yourself?"

He was expecting an apology? From her? As if she were a twelve-year-old truant or a runaway slave? "Well, for starters, I'd say you're a bully, Durand. That guy doesn't come up to your chin."

His blue eyes narrowed, then suddenly he laughed. "*I* didn't punch him, Nic. He picked a fight with somebody over a parking space."

"Oh." She remarshaled her anger, but Durand pounced first.

"Where the hell have you *been?*"

As if she had to account for every minute, or any minute at all! "Around." She shrugged, a picture of an island anchorage at night sliding across her mind, standing on deck in the windy blackness, stars never ending, lovely, lonely...a good place to soothe the soul. A place she'd never tell *him* about.

"Around..." Durand purred, his brows drawing together.

"You're lucky I got here at all," she snapped, beating him to the attack. "You wrote down the wrong address, 396, instead of 369!"

With his tan it was hard to be sure, but Nicola thought he reddened across the cheekbones. "I did? Sorry. But you found us, anyway."

"Such as you are."

His brows tilted. "Meaning?"

"Meaning you hijacked me and my research, dragged me kicking and screaming into a company that's *failing?* Whose single product is a bust?" She could feel her blood pressure mount, charge by charge. "Your song all along has been that, sure, you're derailing my life, but, oh, don't worry, Nic, you'll make me rich to compensate. That's what you said, isn't it?" She'd stalked closer with each word, and now they stood almost toe-to-toe, though she had to look up.

He met her glare unflinchingly. "It is."

"But now?"

"Now I stand by it."

Oooh! As simple as that? He was so sure of himself, standing there, she wanted to flatten her hands on his chest and push him ass over teakettle! "How *can* you if you're running out of money?"

His lips twitched. "I've got a couple of million or so still stuffed in my mattress, Nic. Look, why don't you let me sweat the money end of things? That's *my* job. You do your part and we'll come out of this smelling like roses. And the first thing I want from you," he added with smooth determination, "is a list of the names and addresses of the

women in your test. That page seems to be...miss-
ing...from my copy.'' *No more games, Nic,* the glint in his
eyes said.

And so here they were again, at the crux of the matter.
High noon in Tombstone. She squared her shoulders.
''No.''

''*No?*''

How could he pack so much menace into a single soft
word? ''No.'' She shivered openly and stood her ground.
''The chief concern of my female volunteers, Mr. Durand,
was that my formula might work *too* well. That one or more
of the male subjects might form some sort of permanent...attachment and end up stalking them. So I promised
the women complete and absolute anonymity. Forever. And
I stand by that.''

''But—''

''And it looks as if their fears were well founded,'' she
pressed on. ''When I stopped by campus a few days ago,
I picked up a copy of the *RIITWORD.* Somebody's running
an ad offering a reward for the names of the women who
took part in my test.'' She cocked her head. ''Know anything about that?''

A faint bloom of color climbed his lean cheeks. He
scowled.

Got you! Still, she had enough sense to swing away as
her grin tried to spread. *You may have me, big guy, but I
have you, too!* She wandered over to a picture on one wall.
It was a Winslow Homer print of a schooner at anchor. Its
frame was slightly off level. She straightened it idly.
''You've bonded, haven't you?'' She smiled again at the
thought. *Power!* Not what she'd been seeking at all, but
sweet all the same.

''What the hell do you mean by that?'' he growled at
her back.

''You haven't read my test papers yet, beyond looking
for the missing page? Too busy writing...want ads?''

''All right, all right, you've got me. I placed that ad,

since you'd gone AWOL and I didn't know when or even if you'd..." He drummed his fingers against some surface. "I mean to meet D again, Nic. She was...something. And I have the usual tastes for a man. I like women."

"Been dating any others lately?" she asked, her voice achingly casual.

"That's none of your business."

"Well, actually it is. That's question three on my follow-up response sheet you never filled out. Did you ever wonder why I ask it?" She turned and felt his eyes meet hers, a current leaping the gap. Yellow sparks to blue flame. He shook his head.

"The formula you inhaled is based on my study of male prairie voles versus male mountain voles—the relative quantities of a certain hormone in their brains, how that hormone affects their relationships.

"For instance, with prairie voles, a virgin male and virgin female meet, and they...mate, the first time, for approximately forty hours just about nonstop." She found her own cheeks warming at the look on his face.

"A veritable marathon of volish bliss," he summarized gravely, his eyes dancing. "'He has the stamina of a prairie vole.' I'll have to remember to use that sometime."

"After which honeymoon," she continued, refusing to share his amusement, "the male is bonded to the female, Mr. Durand. *For life.* You'll always find them together, in the same burrow, within touching distance of each other. They cuddle and groom each other with great frequency. He'll attack any vole that dares to look at his mate or his offspring, defend them to the death. He's a monogamous family man."

Durand's amusement had faded. "What about mountain voles?"

"Mountain-vole males are much more like human males," she said, careful to keep her voice light and level, with no trace of bitterness. *Like every man I've ever met, anyway.* "They jump any female they find—for maybe forty minutes—then they go their merry way. They're cads. It's strictly 'wham bam, thank you ma'am,' then out the door and on to the next. They don't send flowers. They don't call the morning after. If they leave any offspring behind, well, that's *her* problem.''

''Bonded!'' Reese muttered blankly. His mind had stopped with the word, like a car ramming a prison wall, its wheels still spinning. ''I don't want a cologne that would cause men to *bond* to women.'' *I might as well try to sell men leashes and choke chains to fit their own necks!*

Why, bonding would mean an end to flings, to affairs, to…to excitement. To *romance,* dammit! To be trapped by the nose into loving only one woman? With no choice of *which* woman? ''If I had to think of a man's worst nightmare…'' He shook his head at the image of men fleeing in panicked droves from his cologne. *This is what I've spent the past week buying with almost the last of my…*

This is…what I inhaled? He stood blinking as it hit him.

''You're right,'' the kid said from across the room. She wasn't smirking, but he'd have sworn her voice was. ''You don't want a bonding agent. What you want is a sexual attractant.''

What he wanted was to sit down! ''What's the difference?'' He stayed on his feet, jammed his hands into his pockets, jingled his keys.

''A sexual attractant would attract *any* man to *any* woman or vice versa, depending which pheromone you used. The way truffles work on pigs.''

Voles were bad enough, but… ''Pigs?''

''Truffles contain a huge amount of androsterone, a male pheromone produced by both boars and men in their sweat and saliva.'' She paced the perimeter of his office as she talked, like a lecturer prowling the front of a classroom. Maybe she *had* given this lecture; she'd been Hadley's teaching assistant, he recalled. ''It's what makes truffle hunting possible.

''A female pig smells a truffle and she thinks she's smelling the world's sexiest boar—buried under a meadow. So she digs up the fungus, and the truffle hunter takes it away from her. So the poor sow goes looking for another mate, and she digs up another truffle, instead.''

"But she doesn't fall in love with any *particular* truffle," he muttered, beginning to get it, and sank down on the edge of his desk.

"Right. Because androsterone is an *attractant*, not a bonding pheromone. So, one of the issues I'm trying to determine in my experiment, and in particular with you, is—are you simply attracted to this D? Or have you bonded?''

The switch from abstract to personal was a bucket of ice water splashed full in the face. "*How the hell would I know if you won't tell me her—*" he tuned his roar down to a snarl "*—name*, dammit!"

He could hear D laughing somewhere out in the dark. Waking or dreaming, he'd been hearing her laughter all week. He needed to shake her within an inch of her sweet life for that trick she'd pulled. Needed to put his lips to hers and swallow that laugh, dive right after it into her honeyed mouth. And all that stood between him and his laughing witch was this maddening, rock-stubborn little bean-counting brat of a scientist, who stood now watching him with those odd, green-spotted gold eyes. Like a fox cub peering out at him from the bushes.

"It's very simple," she said now.

He bet all her life was simple—simple, logical and precise. *A leads to B leads to C.* Lists and calculations, measurements and experiments. Passion running along a narrow line ruled straight to the horizon and beyond. Emotion reduced to chemicals in a sterilized test tube. "*What* is?"

"To know if you've bonded. Have you been attracted to any other woman since you met, uh, sniffed D?''

He'd noticed no one since D, but that didn't prove a thing. Once upon a time he'd been famous for his ferocious concentration, and he worked that way still, like a lion locking onto a moving target. You don't blink till you've downed your antelope.

But once downed, there's always the next one. He was obsessed with D simply because he hadn't had her yet. That was all.

"Have you?" Nic insisted.

No, but— Knowledge is power. You don't give your power away. He wouldn't have answered that question if his own mother had asked it. And to tell this one? She was going to be hard enough to keep in line as it was. No *way* he'd hand her ammunition like that. Reese bared his teeth in a smile he didn't feel and shook his head. "Put your microscope back in your pocket, Nic. I'm not part of your experiment anymore. I gave you your money back, remember?"

She stuck out her pointed chin. "But—"

"No buts, Nic, and no more excuses. I'm the boss now. I pay your salary. And now…your boss is giving you a *direct order. Tell me D's name and where I can find her.*"

She crossed her arms and shook her head. "Sorry."

"Nic…" The one word promised fire and brimstone.

Her chin tipped higher. "So fire me."

You couldn't shake the employees, no matter how you wanted to, or swat them. Not in Massachusetts. Though a swat would have done Ms. Tightbuns a world of good— and him, as well. "You'd like that, wouldn't you?"

"Well, since we've already agreed that I can't help you…"

"We've agreed no such thing." And even if they had, he'd never have let her go. She was his one link to D. D, who refuted Nic's every statistic and reasonable argument simply by being.

Let the kid talk, he knew what he felt about D. And feeling was believing. There had to be some way to use Nic's stuff. Had to be some way to put this kind of dynamite, this sexual yearning into Irresistible, he was sure of it. "No. Tomorrow it's you, me, Hadley and Tim. We sit down and figure out a game plan, a way to keep the sizzle but throw out the bonding effect.''

If that even existed at all. Because he didn't really buy it. That part, he'd bet, was simply Ms. Nicola Kent trying to scare him. *Nice try, kid.* But he didn't buy it. He wasn't *bonded* to D. No way.

It was just that he'd die if he didn't get her, and soon.

CHAPTER NINE

ON HER WAY UP in the elevator the next morning, Nicola glanced at her watch. She was late for Durand's council of war, scheduled to start at nine on the dot.

Three minutes wasn't as late as she'd intended. She'd thought ten minutes' tardiness precisely right to express supreme indifference to his pleasure, while stopping short of outright defiance. But her timing had been thrown off when she'd found a parking space directly behind the building that housed Pherotics.

Stop by the lab, then, to kill a few more minutes? she wondered. Pherotics occupied the third and fourth floors of this converted warehouse. The labs and her own office were located on three, but looking up at the light over the door, she saw that the elevator had carried her past that retreat.

All right, all right, I'll settle for five minutes late and a surly disposition. He'll get the picture. Because the more she'd thought about it after she'd left him yesterday, the more outraged she'd grown. Durand had strong-armed her into a *failing* enterprise, with Hadley's collusion. She wasn't sure which of them she loathed the most! The only thing that made this situation bearable was her chance to turn the tables. To walk off with Pherotics's own pheromonic formula and a chance at an even better dissertation than her original. To walk away from Durand with the last laugh. *The game's not over yet, big guy!*

The elevator door rolled back, and Nicola turned right down the corridor, passing the open door of Pherotics's secretary-receptionist, Kay Grunwald. A glance into Kay's office showed her an empty desk. Perhaps the older woman was taking notes at the meeting?

But when Nicola pushed through the double doors that led to the conference room, situated at the core of the fourth floor, she found only one man awaiting her. Seated at the head of the long mahogany table, Reese Durand looked up over his cup of coffee with baleful blue eyes. "You're late, Nic."

"Am I?" She helped herself to a cup of coffee from an urn on the sideboard. Where were the blasted others?

"Sit down." Durand tipped his dark head to the side, indicating the seat to his left.

She settled, instead, for a seat three down the table from her boss. One place closer would have seemed friendly if not servile; one place farther would have been openly rude. Durand traded his pen for his coffee cup, and a twitch of his lips registered her fine distinction.

Not that the snub broke his heart, she realized, burying her nose in her mug. What did he care if she was angry, as long as he got what he needed?

"I meant to tell you yesterday," he said, setting his cup aside. "That's quite an improvement." When she raised her eyebrows in question, he added, "That perfume you're wearing. Nice change from counter cleaner."

"Is it?" She found her cheeks warming under his gaze and looked away. If he wasn't teasing, then he was being kind, because actually she reeked. Yesterday she'd bought a cheap rose scent at a drugstore on the way in to Pherotics, and she'd practically drenched herself with it. She'd repeated the dose this morning. The unsubtle fragrance should be as good a camouflage for her own personal scent as spray cleanser and was no doubt a good deal easier on her skin. But she felt like a tart wearing it, and if she felt like that, then what must Durand— Her cheeks burned hotter as it hit her. *He couldn't think I mean anything by wearing perfume around him, could he?*

She looked up with relief as someone entered the room,

then frowned when she saw who it was—Hadley, complete with ingratiating smile and a large box of doughnuts. "My, my. Our prodigal returns at last!" he caroled, seeing her. "Jelly doughnut, my dear? No? Reese?" He plunked the open box in the middle of the table, then, after an oddly wary glance at the younger man, chose a seat directly across from Nicola. "Sorry to be late. Traffic up ninety-three was bumper to bumper."

Durand glanced at his watch. "Perhaps that's what's delaying Tim. Let's get started, anyway, shall we."

It wasn't really a question, but Hadley beamed and nodded. Nicola studied Durand levelly over the rim of her cup.

"Purpose of this meeting is to discuss how we can incorporate Nic's formula into the existing formula for Irresistible. Since our cologne as currently composed is apparently ineffective—"

"But it isn't." Looking like a very short gunslinger who'd pushed through the saloon doors with a showdown on his mind, Tim Baggett glowered from the doorway. His magnificent black eye only enhanced his belligerence. He stalked over to the sideboard to pour himself a coffee.

"Good of you to join us, Tim," Durand said to his back. "But our latest focus-group findings don't bear you out. Ericson's survey of sixty men who tried Irresistible concluded that eighty-five percent of them would not purchase the cologne at its existing price."

"So we lower the price. I told you that from the start. We priced it too high. Once they've tried it and loved it, we can always—"

"Eighty percent of the same sample," Durand continued relentlessly, "stated they wouldn't purchase Irresistible even if we cut the price in half. Here's a quote from the sample— 'If my girlfriend gave me this stuff, I'd get a new girlfriend.'"

His freckled face turning a splotchy red, the vice president sat at the foot of the table. "Your sampling method's flawed. That's all this proves. Our original tests, before we decided to go to production—"

"Were extremely promising," Reese agreed. "I wouldn't have invested a nickel otherwise. But whether you buy the results of Ericson's survey or not, we can't get past this fact. *Nobody's reordering.*"

"That just means it's selling slower than projected, not that it's not selling! And sales momentum's a function of our ad campaign—whether we've put out enough ads and put 'em out in the right places."

"Tim, I'll be happy to go over the figures with you later on in my office." *In private,* was Durand's unspoken message. "The picture's come pretty clear in the time you've been away on vacation."

Tim half lifted out of his seat. "You're saying I shouldn't have gone on—"

"I'm saying I've made up my mind. Sales aren't impressive. Maybe that'll change as more figures come in over the next few months. Nobody hopes that more than I do. But in the meantime, we're not going to sit here with our thumbs—" Durand glanced sharply at Nicola, whose eyes skated away as she bit her lip to keep from smiling. "We're not going to sit here wringing our hands. We're taking action while we've still got room and cash to maneuver.

"Till we know otherwise, we're proceeding as if we have a problem. And that's why I've brought Nicola and Professor Hadley on board. Nic, let's start with you. What are your thoughts on how we can combine your formula with Irresistible?"

Her thoughts had been straying to alpha males, how one man could dominate a group without raising his voice, while another man couldn't achieve the same effect with yells and tantrums. She found herself stage center with a nasty jolt. "Uh...I *don't* think it's possible."

Tim Baggett uttered a crow of delight as Hadley blurted,

"What Nicola means is, uh, she thinks it would be difficult!"

"Nicola thinks it won't be *possible*," Nicola repeated, her eyes flashing. "Sexual attraction wasn't the point or the purpose of my experiment. I wasn't trying to—"

"Suppose we call it a by-product, then," Durand suggested. "You're not going to deny that your volunteers felt—" he paused, face reddening as he met her narrowed gaze "—sexual dynamite? I know what I felt, Nic. I don't give a damn what you hoped or thought you were testing for. One sniff and I..."

She wanted to smile. Wanted to laugh in his face with triumph. *And you bonded! To me.* She looked down at her hands, clasped demurely on the table. *Go on and say it, big guy. Are you tough enough to say it?*

"...and I knew we had a winner," he said, instead, with his infuriating ability to change directions. "If we can bottle your stuff, add it to Irresistible, then our cologne *will* be irresistible. Women will mob any man who wears it. Which means every man will buy it. Which means—"

"But it doesn't work that way," she cut in, then watched a muscle flutter in his cheek. That was another characteristic of alpha males, she supposed. They were more used to interrupting than being interrupted. "Even if I was investigating pheromones, which I'm not, one pheromone doesn't generally work in both directions like a telephone line.

"The female silk moth broadcasts a pheromone that says, 'Here I am. Come and get me, boys.' It travels *one* direction—female to male.

"Boars and men exude androsterone, which says, 'I'm the sexiest stud you're going to find, babe. Choose *me* if you want a good time.' That message passes male to female.

"Human females in dormitories or other close-contact situations put out a pheromone that says, 'Okay, girls, let's synchronize our monthly cycles.' A female-to-female message. Then honeybees—'' Beneath the table, something thumped her knee.

Across the way, Hadley had sunk in his chair till his eyes were barely level with the tabletop. Looking like a bullfrog glaring up from a swamp, he kicked her again. She shoved her chair back out of reach. ''A pheromone is simply a biochemical message, Mr. Durand. What the message says varies with the messenger. And a message meant for one sex doesn't necessarily reach the other at all.''

''Nicola, I'm afraid you're boring us.'' Hadley wriggled upright in his chair. ''I'm sure Reese and Tim know all about pheromones, since that's the present basis for Irresistible.''

''Tim is the technical half of our partnership,'' Durand said soberly.

''And if you'd left me in charge of that...''

Durand quelled his partner with a glance. ''And as such, he's our pheromone expert, whereas I handle the business end of the equation. But let's back up a step. Maybe Nic *should* start by explaining what she was trying to do in her experiment.''

''You still haven't read your copy of my test?'' The minute she asked the question, Nicola realized she'd stepped over some invisible line. Durand's dark head swung up and his eyes impaled her.

At the other end of the table Tim laughed nastily. ''No fear *there!* He's waiting for the movie to come out.''

Durand didn't move, didn't blink, yet suddenly the air...vibrated. Nicola couldn't hold his gaze, turned helplessly, instead, toward Hadley and saw that whatever it was, her adviser had caught the same danger signals. They reached for the box of doughnuts as one.

Their knuckles collided and Hadley burst into a nervous cackle. He swallowed it with a gulp. ''Please! Go ahead.''

She took her time choosing a doughnut she didn't want, took a bite, then risked a look at Durand.

"No, I haven't," he replied silkily as if no time had passed. "So suppose you *tell* us, Nic?"

"Umm." She swallowed hastily and nodded. "I've been studying a hormone that's present to varying degrees in the brains of men and in male prairie and male mountain voles. Oxytocin. I've been comparing the number of oxytocin receptors in the brains of each—"

"Back up another step. What's the difference between hormones and pheromones?"

"Not much," Hadley chimed in, unable to resist a spotlight no matter how harsh. "Very little, biochemically speaking. A pheromone serves as a messenger between two members of the same species. A hormone serves as a messenger within a single body.

"Take our Nicola. Midway through her monthly cycle her pituitary gland sends a surge of its luteinizing hormone to her ovaries. That's a message meaning, 'Release an egg.'"

Nicola glared across the table, but he continued undaunted. "It also serves as a message meaning, 'Go find some sperm for that egg.' For the next few days, whether she knows it or not, Nikki is on the prowl. She's a hundred times more sensitive to the male pheromone androsterone than she is for the rest of the month. And since normally a woman is already a hundred times more sensitive to that component of male sweat than any man ever is, she's now a *super*charged little detector. Her radar for men is switched on high, as…"

Nicola made a savage cutting motion across her neck, but Hadley sailed blithely on. "…is her sexual receptivity. For instance, were she married, ovulation is the time of month she'd most likely commit adultery."

So his instincts had been right, Reese told himself. Hadley did have the hots for his student, though she wasn't even half his age. Strange taste some men had. She seemed to Reese as prickly as a little hedgehog. Attractive, yes, but sexless, like a stone putti in a Renaissance frieze. But maybe that was what attracted the professor—that unaware, unawakened quality. *Child snatcher*. And meanwhile, if someone didn't intervene, a certain bright child was about to stuff the rest of her doughnut down the professor's unctuous throat.

"Testosterone is another well-known hormone," Nicola cut in coolly as Reese opened his mouth. "For instance, as it wanes in the aging male, the message it's sending is 'Slow down. Stop seeking extra mates you can't handle. Take up shuffleboard. Stay home with your own wife before you make a silly fool of yoursel—'"

"We get the picture." Durand swallowed a laugh as Hadley bristled. "Now what about oxytocin?"

"Oxytocin is a hormone that's generated in both sexes before and during intercourse—by stimulation of the lips, the skin, the breasts, the...genitals." Her eyes focused now on her clasped fingers, she turned a delicate shade of strawberry.

"When a large enough concentration builds up in the body, then orgasm occurs," Hadley added, recovering himself.

Reese kept his eyes on Nicola, who had deepened a shade. "But why should you care about that?" There were easier ways to reach satisfaction than by hormonal inhalant, surely. He found himself wondering for the first time, if the kid had ever experienced the traditional method.

"I don't!" she snapped. "Not in the least! That's beside the point. The point is that, in large enough doses, oxytocin promotes *emotional bonding*. That's why prairie voles bond, and why most men, and all mountain voles, do not. Because prairie voles have more oxytocin receptors in their brains than men or mountain voles. They receive a larger dose of oxytocin for a longer period of time—during that first honeymoon I told you about."

Reese nodded encouragingly, though where she was headed with all this, he hadn't a clue. "And so?"

"And so I've created a synthesized form of oxytocin. A

synthetic, volatized version of the hormone that can be inhaled—the way you received it during my test. It docks with the brain's oxytocin receptors, and once docked, here's the difference—*it's not reabsorbed by the brain as quickly as the real stuff.* So in effect it's *stronger* than organic oxytocin. And it lasts longer.''

Like the dose the ever-faithful prairie vole receives on his forty-hour honeymoon, Reese realized, the hair slowly rising on the back of his neck.

"You're working on a damned *fidelity* drug!" Tim exploded, popping to his feet. "*That's* what she's working on, Reese, dammit! That's what you spent the last of our money on—a drug to make men faithful to women? *Right*—that would really sell! They'll *lynch* us!"

Everyone was talking at once, Hadley with frantic eagerness, Tim in a sputtering rage, Nic with dogged determination, Reese calling for quiet. At last his voice prevailed, and he aimed a finger. "*Is* that what you're working on—a monogamy drug?"

"No, no, no, *no!*" Nicola shook her head till her braid whipped from ear to ear. "I don't give a damn about that! I'm working on a cure for autism."

"*Huh?*" Tim dropped slowly back to his seat. "You're *what?*"

"You know what autism is, don't you?" she appealed to Reese.

He knew. There'd been an autistic kid born to a family down the street from his own. The boy sat on his front steps all day long every day twirling a string, his favorite toy. You could try to talk to him, but he'd look right through you.

"Autism is the inability to connect," she continued fiercely, her eyes locked on his. "An autistic child can't bond emotionally to another human being. Not to her family, not even to her own mother. She's lost in a world of her own—frozen in a block of ice. So if I can learn what causes emotional bonding, how it works, how to make it happen..."

Reese got it now, and his stomach twisted as it hit him. He'd told himself he was doing Nic a favor, yanking her out of her academic playpen into the real world. But if she'd really been on the track of something useful, something that in the scheme of things was quite a bit more useful than any cologne could ever be... He'd have to think about this. He hated reconsidering actions. One of his rules in life was that you acted and moved on. You didn't look back. But this time...

And even if I do reconsider, it's too late, he realized, staring at her. The contract he'd signed with her university with Hadley's help... He'd meant to bind her tighter than tight. If he was investing this much in the kid's research, then he damn well meant to reap the benefits. But like most contracts, this one obligated both parties. If she was handcuffed to him, then he'd also handcuffed himself to—

"Thank you, Nikki," Hadley said, breaking Reese's train of thought. "You've summarized your goal beautifully. But in science, one must stay open to serendipity. Columbus was seeking India and its spices when he discovered the New World. He had to settle for Aztec gold, instead. In your case, you seem to have blundered upon a key to sexual attraction, and what we're trying to help you do here is see a way to exploit *that*, rather than..."

And Hadley had known what the kid was up to, Reese thought, letting him burble on. *Hadley knew, but he never once tried to explain it to me.* He sold her down the river for a chair at RIIT, an ego-puffing title as Pherotics's consultant and a yearly salary Reese had few illusions he'd ever earn. It was a payoff in all but name.

"But aren't we forgetting one thing?" Tim swaggered over to the coffee urn. Turning, he leaned against the sideboard, arms folded. "One teeny tiny detail?" His grin was close to a smirk as he glanced at his partner. "I stopped back by the office last night and read your copy, Reese.

And one thing stands out like a sore thumb. Whatever Nicola was trying to prove, she blew it. Her synthetic hormone had *no measurable effect* on half the participants in that test. I could do as well by flipping a coin. That test proves nothing!''

''I know it looks like that,'' Nic protested, ''but—''

''But nothing! You're a long way from finding the cure for autism, Nicola. You're a long way from anywhere.'' Tim turned his back on her to refill his cup. ''It pays to read the fine print before you buy,'' he added, that last remark apparently addressed to the wall.

It found its mark all the same. For a moment Reese cherished the image of himself dropping Tim headfirst into the coffee urn. But anger was a tool to be used, not a self-indulgence. Ignoring the gibe, he followed the information. Nic's test was a failure?

No. It worked. He should know.

But although Tim Baggett was a social idiot, he was no fool in the technical world. If Tim said the results of Nic's test spelled failure, then... Reese brought his gaze to bear on Hadley. *Then that's one more thing you didn't tell me, Professor Sleazeball. A teeny tiny rather crucial detail that didn't come up—once—in our negotiations.*

Hadley squirmed in his seat, opened his mouth like a goldfish, then closed it again with an ''aw shucks'' smile. ''Umm...''

Yeah, think fast, Professor. How are you going to gloss over this one? Leaving him dangling, Reese cast the net of his anger wider.

Tim? No, you couldn't blame Tim for defending the work of a lifetime. He was inflexible, but Reese had known that from the start of their partnership. It hadn't mattered until this need to change directions had arisen.

Nic? No, she was the one person at this table he could never blame. She'd fought his attentions every step of the way. Never lied once, he'd give her that. Like that compass he'd seen in her desk, Nic pointed true north. Even if the rest of the world was marching south.

No, the real target for Reese's anger had to be…himself. This was his fault. *Didn't do my homework. Should have slogged through every damn page and chart of Nic's experiment before I laid down a penny.* But he'd been so sure, every instinct howling, *This is the one!* As sure as gravity. As the tides. *Grab it now—grab her—before she gets away.* It had been that gut-level knowing that had moved him to close the deal.

Moved him still. *It doesn't work? The hell it doesn't!* Tim had to be lying. Or in his eagerness to find a flaw, he'd imagined…

But then, look at Hadley, the picture of guilt. *Would you buy a used car from this creep?*

Reese's investment so far would have bought a thousand cars. If they all were lemons—

"Tim is precisely right," Hadley blurted, breaking the silence. "Nikki's test is a failure."

"Now wait a minute—" Nic spun to face him.

"Her synthetic hormone did *not* elicit a reliable, predictable response from every test subject. You're absolutely correct, Tim. Sometimes it seemed to work—though only mildly, mind you. Sometimes it fell flat on its funny little face. But if your test was a failure, Nicola, it was a most *productive* failure." He gave her a courtly little bow, worse than any sneer.

She *would* throw that doughnut she held, Reese decided, and he didn't blame her. Still, rioting among the troops was the last thing he needed. He picked up his empty coffee cup and drifted toward the sideboard at her back. "And so?"

"Most evocative of all was the response of number twenty-three. Of yourself, Reese."

"*Haaadley…?*" growled Nicola on a rising note of disbelief.

"Your response was strongest of anyone's—by far."

Avoiding her eyes, Hadley spoke louder and faster. "Off the charts!"

"Oh?" Reese hadn't known that. He'd assumed his experience was typical. He moved closer to the table as the kid's right hand, holding her doughnut, gradually lifted.

"And I have a theory about that," Hadley plunged on. "I believe you were wearing your own cologne that day? Irresistible?"

"Oh! You…" Nic's hand arched back.

Catching her wrist, Reese plucked the doughnut from her fingers just as she launched it. "Go on," he said calmly to Hadley, then gave her the fish eye—*Cut it out, kid*—when she tipped her head backward, shocked to find him there. She tried to yank free and he tightened his grip on her slender bones. *Be still.*

She froze, then simply looked away from him, back at Hadley. Only her rocketing pulse gave her indifference the lie.

Holding her as casually as she ignored him, Reese took a bite of her doughnut—and grimaced. It smelled of her perfume, roses thick enough to strangle on. Odd scent for someone so boyish.

"I believe what we have here is a drug interaction," Hadley continued eagerly. "The pheromone in your cologne seems to be potentiating—boosting—the effects of Nikki's synthetic oxytocin. That being true, if we combine them, I'd say we have every reason to hope—every reason to believe—that we can create a successful pheromonic cologne. Irresistible *can* be made irresistible if my theory proves correct." He beamed at one and all, a magician who'd pulled a forty-pound jackrabbit from his hat.

Nicola tugged her hand again, but weakly. Interpreting that to mean she'd behave, Reese let her go. Her shoulders lifted in the faintest of defeated sighs, and he suppressed an impulse to pat her.

But if he couldn't offer comfort, he could understand.

Hadley had just ripped her off. Again. Youth and talent were no match for age and cunning, as the saying went.

On the other hand, she clearly hadn't meant to tell *him* about the drug interaction, Reese reminded himself. It wouldn't pay to let his natural inclinations blind him. No matter how sleazy, Hadley was his ally in this endeavor, Nic the honorable opponent.

"Good," he said, jerking himself back to the matter at hand. "Very good." His eyes swept the room. The troops were exhausted; time to give them a break. But it was important to end on a positive note. "So what's our first step toward that goal?"

Hadley steepled his chubby fingers. "We try to replicate your response. At the animal level first, then later with humans." He tapped his forefingers thoughtfully. "I helped Nikki design an experiment last year for her initial work with mountain voles…"

Reese automatically glanced down at Nic and saw her shoulders stiffen. *Who designed?* He could guess.

"I think a repeat of that test is in order," Hadley continued judiciously. "This time using a combination of your pheromone *plus* Nikki's hormone. If the results prove as promising, why, then…"

"Good, that sounds like a plan. You and Nic draw up a list of the supplies you'll need, also a projected time line to completion, and get back to me by three." Reese turned to his partner. "Tim, let's meet after lunch."

He set a fingertip on Nic's shoulder as she started to rise, and she jumped, then subsided. "Nic, a word. The rest of you?" His smile dismissed them. He waited till they took the hint and walked out.

Reese shoved his hands into his pockets and paced the room, his smile fading to a thoughtful frown. He had no time for baby-sitting, nor the inclination. But then it was he who'd yanked Nic out of her lab, where she'd been playing happily. So he owed her. But what? "Sorry" wasn't a word he used much. And it didn't quite apply here. Given the circumstances, he'd do it again. Still…

"My experiment *worked*," she said in a soft fierce voice. "Not all the way—something went wrong somewhere. Maybe in the procedure, or…" She paused. "But it worked." *I wasn't a failure,* her eyes said defiantly.

His gaze flicked to her full bottom lip. Child soft and trembling. "I believe you." And realized he did. If Nic said so, he believed. Or, at least, he believed that *she* believed.

But she'd seen his hesitation, and suddenly her face closed. Her chin tipped up. Her shoulders squared. Nicola Kent against the world.

The least he could do was buy the kid a pizza. Let her pour out her woes over lunch. His usual noon workout could wait. "Come on." He jerked his head toward the door. "I'm starved."

She trudged silently beside him down the corridor, head down, smelling of too many roses. Anchovy pizza, Reese decided, to drown her out.

"There was one thing I've been wondering," he said as they waited for the elevator. "About your experiment. I understand you're not working on a fidelity drug—" the door opened and he ushered her aboard "—but if that was a potential side effect… Didn't you worry, Nic, giving forty men a dose that you hoped would make them bond to one of your test women? What if it worked *too* well?"

She shrugged. "With mountain voles, the bonding effect degrades in thirteen to fourteen days."

He digested that. "But you'd never tried it before on human males?"

"Right."

"So it might have affected men differently? What if the effect *didn't* fade?"

Nic shrugged again. "That's why I won't identify the women."

"I'm talking about the men. What about them?"

"Oh—" another shrug "—I didn't think about that."

As bright as she was? "I find that hard to believe." The door slid open at the ground floor, but she simply stood there, looking up and through him, so he put out a hand to keep it open. "How could you be that—" okay, he'd say it "—irresponsible?"

She tipped her coppery head, considering. "Maybe I didn't care?"

"But…" She stepped out of the car and he had to follow, his fury rising. *He* was one of her guinea pigs, dammit! "You can't just—"

When he caught her shoulder, she spun on her heel, out of his grasp. "Why can't I, when men do it every day?"

"Huh? Do what?"

"Make women love them, bond to them, then just…just walk away. Out of their lives. Maybe it's time *they* learned how it—" She turned and banged out the front door, leaving him standing there in the lobby.

How it feels, Reese completed automatically, staring after her. His mouth curved in a slow rueful grin. *Well, well, Ms. Nicola Kent!* Not quite a virgin, after all.

CHAPTER TEN

LEAVING NICOLA to make their report to Durand, Hadley ducked out before three, with the excuse that he had an urgent appointment in Providence. Wanted to beat the fierce Boston rush hour, Nicola translated, and wished him an overturned tractor trailer blocking all southbound lanes of the expressway for eight hours or so.

Because Hadley's claiming credit for her theory of the interaction between Durand's pheromone and her own synthetic hormone was the final straw.

Never mind that he'd stolen her brainstorm. That had stung, but with Hadley, what else should she have expected? No, what she couldn't forgive was that, out of sheer piggish vanity, simply to brownnose Durand, Hadley had weakened her hand against her enemy. Hadley, in so many self-serving words, had told Durand that she needed *him*—that if she held the key to the puzzle, then Durand held the lock. Their substances worked better together than they did apart.

The only question that remained was, did the entrepreneur realize what power he'd been given? Blast Hadley, anyway!

Nicola rapped smartly on Durand's office door, which swung halfway open—revealing a vacant room. Terrific. She'd steeled herself for nothing. She was suddenly as irritated by the man's absence as she would have been by his presence. *Dump it and run,* she told herself grimly, stalking toward his desk. She smacked the sheaf of papers down, then whirled as a door on a side wall opened.

"Nic?" Durand leaned out, giving her a startling glimpse of tanned, naked shoulder and dark tousled hair, wet from a shower. "Be out in a sec." He disappeared again into what was apparently an executive washroom, leaving his image strobing in her mind's eye, her hands remembering the hard curves of his biceps. *Hard man.*

Hard all over.

Cut it out! she told herself fiercely. Arms crossed tightly across her breasts, she walked to his window. He'd chosen the office with a river view, the one she'd have taken, even if it was tucked away in the back. She turned, seeking other images to drive out Durand's. She noticed file cabinets, a bookshelf, which held a set of large dumbbells, phone directories, a pair of scuffed tennis shoes. A bicycle water bottle, a compact CD system with a rack of CDs, and what must be a toolbox—just about everything a man might conceivably need, except books.

And no tennis trophies, she noted, though apparently he'd won his share. Hadley, who fancied himself an aficionado, had been regaling her with Durand's feats this afternoon while they worked. He'd won Wimbledon twice, the professor had said proudly, as if somehow that stardust brushed off on his subordinates. *No trophies.* So Durand didn't dwell in the past. Needed no props to bolster his ego.

Her eyes moved on. Over walls covered only in sales charts and projections, an outsize calendar thick with notations, the designer's mock-up for Irresistible's package and bottle. No personal photos or artwork, except for the print of the schooner. So Durand didn't decorate. A private man, giving nothing of himself away.

Completing the survey, she scanned the ceiling. He had the same gridded panels that were used throughout their two floors, with the lights concealed above the pierced screens—a sleek high-tech look imposed by the previous tenants, a biotech firm gone on to grander quarters, Hadley had told her.

"Sorry to keep you," Durand said, walking into the

room. His hair was freshly combed and still damp. "Have a seat, Nic." He nodded at the chair that faced his desk.

Unwillingly she perched, ready to run. "It's pretty self-evident—" she started, nodding at her list, then stopped when he put up a hand.

"Good. But first there's something I've been meaning to say about your doctorate."

My late lamented doctorate? What do you care about that? She lifted her eyebrows and waited.

"Maybe Hadley explained. But in case he hasn't, part of our deal was that you'd be able to finish your degree while working for me. That when I wasn't using your time, you could work on your own research. At company expense."

"I..." It was unexpectedly generous. He wavered before her like an image in a suddenly tilted bowl of water, ruthless user a moment ago, and now? "D'you mean—"

"Of course your synthetic hormone can't be disclosed in your dissertation. From now on it's Pherotics's proprietary secret. But Hadley says he can help you come up with a different angle that doesn't include—"

"Right." She sat back in her chair. "Hadley'll help me cobble together some pathetic excuse for a dissertation, then, as my adviser, he'll charitably accept it. *That'll* help me a lot!"

Durand's dark brows drew together. "Look—"

"No, *you* look. A dissertation isn't just a hoop you jump through. That paper's tied to your tail for the rest of your life. A great one can make your career. It wins you invitations from prestigious labs to do postdoc research. A chance to work with the movers and shakers. To *become* a mover and shaker.

"A slipshod, mediocre one that fails to break new ground gets you nowhere. Oh, maybe I'd end up qualified to teach in some junior college in the boondocks if I was lucky, but *that's not what I'm aiming for*." She found she was on her feet, hands braced on his desk, leaning over him. She straightened and backed off. "So thanks, Durand, but no thanks. You're offering me nothing.'' Salve for his own conscience was all he'd proposed. *I'll take the whole cake, thank you, not the crumbs from your table.* She sat abruptly.

A muscle ticked in the side of his lean jaw. Alpha males weren't accustomed to having their gifts—no matter how condescending—thrown back in their teeth. ''From what I hear, you *have* nothing,'' he said at last. ''An experiment that was half a failure or only half a success?''

''*You* thought it was a success!''

''I did,'' he agreed in a silky growl. ''For *my* purposes. But for yours? You could be years away from a cure for autism, Tim tells me. Odds are very good you'll never find it.''

Oh, you'd love to believe that, wouldn't you? She started to speak, but he put up a hand.

''But in the meantime, Nic, in the *meantime,* I could make you rich.''

''I doubt it.'' And even so, was that all he cared about? Money?

''We'll see. One step at a time.'' *And now fun and games are over,* his expression said plainly. He'd made his offer, she'd refused, and so his conscience was clear. ''Tell me about the testing you'll be doing with mountain voles. What supplies do you need and when can I expect results?''

She nodded at the stack of papers. ''It's all there.''

''*Tell* me.''

She opened her mouth to protest, then—from something in his tone, or simply all the pieces falling together at last—it hit her. Her lips rounded to a startled *O. You don't like to read, do you?* Was *that* what Tim had been jeering at?

But you can *read,* she protested inwardly. He'd filled out her first response form after the test. And he could write—witness the note he'd written D. So...dyslexic, then? Reading was painful for him or very slow or... He'd reversed the numbers in the Pherotics address he'd left her, hadn't he?

But if Durand had trouble with letters or numbers, he had no trouble at all reading expressions, she realized as she refocused on the man. He knew precisely what she'd been thinking—and he was furious. All the more so because of her dawning pity.

She snatched up her papers and buried her nose in them. "Well, I'll…I'll need the voles for starters. I can order them from my usual supplier, or if you have a source you—"

"Do it." He stood and swung away toward his window. "What else?"

She told him, taking her time, making it dry and banal and as soothing as a grocery list, giving them both time to recover, thinking all the while, *but if he can't or won't read, then how did he come so far? Do what he's done?* The tennis she could understand—athletics would have been a natural outlet if he'd been thwarted in academics. But tennis had only been his launching point. The sheer teeth-gritted *determination* it must have taken—

She jumped as he flicked the back of the papers she was holding. "*When*, Nic?" he demanded, apparently not for the first time.

"Till we're sure of our results? Roughly two weeks."

"Two weeks! This is business, kid, not an academic free ride with somebody else picking up the tuition tab."

"Two weeks," she repeated. "Till the bonding response has faded to zero." *Or has not*, if her theory proved correct. If his pheromone was truly boosting the effects of her hormone.

"I told you I'm not interested in bonding!"

Ah, but I am! She shrugged. "We're trying to replicate my original experiment, Mr. Durand. Besides, if you don't want your cologne to cause men to bond to women—"

"God forbid."

"Then I'd better learn everything I can about the effect in order to learn how to suppress it, hadn't I?" Not that she meant to stick around Pherotics long enough to tackle that problem, even if it was solvable. All she wanted was the time and working space to verify her own theory—that and his pheromone, which he'd have to hand over if she was to complete this round of tests. *Two weeks and I'll have the last laugh, big guy. Kiss my fingers to you and I'm gone.*

She'd still have to find a new adviser, but with her new improved thesis, it should be easy to woo one. She might lose the fall semester, might even have to transfer to another university if Hadley cut up rough. But her gains should be worth it. *She who laughs last, laughs best.*

He growled a wordless assent. At least she supposed that was what it was. "That's everything you need, then?"

She shook her head. "I'm completing my original study on the side. It may have all kinds of useful applications." *For my future thesis, if not for you.* "And we're coming up on the two-week follow-up. I'll be contacting my other thirty-nine subjects, and so—" she whisked a response form out from under her list of supplies "—if I could ask *you* a few questions about how you're feeling today..."

He laughed—a sudden bark, as if she'd punched it out of him. "You just don't get it, do you?" He caught the arm of her chair and hauled it around so that she faced him, then caught the chair's other arm and leaned toward her, braced on the armrests. "Read...my...lips, Ms. Nicola Kent."

She looked at them, beautifully carved, wickedly knowing, then panicking, looked away. At his laughing eyes—oops, bad mistake!—then over his shoulder, fighting the urge to squinch her own eyes shut like a cornered child.

Because somebody had flipped the gravity switch. She could feel her body trying to rise, float upward to meet that smiling mouth. She clamped her fingers around the edges of her seat to hold herself down and blushed. *Damn* the man!

He laughed again softly, well aware of her discomfort. "This is the last time I'm telling you, rosebud. This guinea pig resigned, remember? What I feel is my business. *Mine.* Nobody else's."

"All right," she said to make him let go, get out of her face. "*Be* that way." Not that she'd stop trying. She needed his response more than all the others put together. But clearly the frontal approach was a loser. She'd just have to think of another way.

"I will, thanks." He glanced at his watch. "Are we done, then?"

He could reduce her to melted taffy, then glance at his watch, bored with the interview? Her blush this time was one of pure shame. *But in the dark,* she reminded herself, *who has the power then? It's just that he doesn't know who's really on top here.* Pity she couldn't remind him.

"No, I forgot. There's one other thing." *Say it casually—no hesitation, no greedy gleam in the eye.* "I'll need the formula for your pheromone and its molecular structure."

He'd started pacing again while she spoke, but the last words stopped him cold, facing away from her. "For your test on the voles," he said at last, his voice carefully neutral.

"Yes. The pure pheromone, without its fragrance." She clasped her hands together, then yanked them apart as he turned to look at her. "I'll be mixing it with my synthetic hormone fifty-fifty. And naturally I'll try other proportions—seventy-five to twenty-five..." *Stop babbling.*

"Of course." He turned his head, his eyes holding hers. "That's no problem."

Gotcha! She leaned down to scratch her ankle and grinned against her kneecap. *I've got you!* So he'd missed the implications of Hadley's announcement, after all.

"In fact, I can do better than that," Durand added as she straightened, her grin under control. "We've got a supply of it already made up. Just let me know how much you need."

"Umm..." That would never do. If he simply handed

her a beaker of the unknown liquid, she was back to working with eye of newt. She'd have to have it analyzed somewhere. "I'd really like the formula. It's nice to know what you're working with."

"Nice," he agreed blandly, "but hardly necessary, given the kind of basic testing you'll be doing."

You're suddenly a scientist? She glared at him, temper rising. But Durand was right, blast him. For his purposes all he needed to know was if some combination of their substances worked as a sexual attractant. Any lab flunkie could mix two unidentified liquids. "But—"

"Nic, I've told you. Secrecy's everything in the fragrance world. Industrial espionage is rampant. Spies are everywhere.

"Look, to show you how careful we are, I commissioned the creation of Irresistible's scent from an essential-oil house in New York. Once I'd approved the fragrance, they made it in bulk. Then we shipped the batch up here. Mixed it *here* with our pheromone. Tim supervised some contract lab workers so the New York people wouldn't get their hands on the pure pheromone.

"Then we shipped the mix back to New York to let the Nose make her final adjustments to the scent. Then we shipped it back here, bottled it, boxed it, shipped it and so on."

He came to lean against his desk, looming above her. "You understand? Tim and I know the formula. *Nobody else in the whole world knows it.* At Pherotics, we operate strictly need-to-know. And you—" his eyes held hers "—you may want, kid, but you *don't* need."

Reese imagined a bottle of strawberry soda, shaken with the cap on. Frothing just this side of explosion. Ms. Nicola Kent had no fondness for the word *no*. At least not for receiving it.

Nor did he, for that matter. He'd spent his whole life hammering *no*'s into *yes*es. Careful not to show his amusement, he admired the rapid batting of her lashes as her thoughts sought a way around his roadblock. *Get used to it, kid. I'll always be one jump ahead.*

"But—"

"No." Professor Sleaze's grandstand play this morning had alerted Reese to an advantage he hadn't realized was his. *Nic needed his pheromone as much as he needed her hormone.* She might hold one piece of the jigsaw, but seemingly, he held the other.

Pity that they each wanted to use both those pieces to complete two different puzzles. *Sorry, kid.* But when it came to winners versus losers, Reese knew which side he meant to be on. And a large part of winning in this game was to keep Ms. Bright Eyes in line. Keep her working with him, not against him. *All for your own good in the end, kid, though you'd sooner spit in my eye than believe it.*

And the best way to keep Nic in line, he suspected, was to hang on tight to the piece of puzzle she wanted. While he held that, she'd follow him anywhere.

Meanwhile, she had her temper in hand—just. *Time to poke up the flames,* he told himself. He'd learned that lesson on the streets years before he ever faced someone across a net. Make your opponents lose their tempers while you kept your cool, and you were halfway home.

And he meant to win home—today. He'd waited long enough. *Too long.* A shaft of sensation shot through him, and he clenched his stomach muscles. *Coming to get you, babe.*

"Well, if that's all..." she said stiffly.

He nodded with an easy smile and waited till she reached the door. "Oh, Nic? One thing more. I want D's phone number and name. Now."

Her hand closed on the doorknob. Without turning, she glanced over her shoulder with a gleam of foxy eyes, or maybe it was that russet hair catching a shaft of light from the window that gave the impression? "No," she said coolly, and walked out his door. Fox slipping into the bushes.

He swore and went after her. Tactical mistake, letting her reach the exit. *Don't walk out on me, my girl!*

The stairwell door was just squeaking shut as he hit the hall—she was quick as a fox. He slammed through the door and into the stairwell. She was turning the landing below. "Nic."

She froze, didn't look back, simply stood waiting. He could hear her shallow breathing as he came down the stairs. *Look at me, damn you!*

Third step from the bottom, his knee jabbed him. He'd strained it biking to the gym during his lunch break, and now it was payback time. Reese stopped for a second, blinking and breathing harshly. *Dammit!* And damn him. Who'd lost his temper? Lost control?

Like a lovesick horny kid. It came from wanting too much—a nasty, unfamiliar sensation. Wanting and having no way to satisfy your want. Someone else holding your strings. A serious loss of control. Dangerous. *Which ends now.* "Nic—"

"I told you—"

"You told me and I don't buy it." He'd planned his attack already, but now the words came with unplanned force. "There's something else going on here."

"What?" The look she gave him as she turned was warily wide-eyed, almost fearful. "What d'you m-mean?"

"I don't think you're protecting D. I think you're... jealous."

"I'm— That's ridiculous! Of— Why should I—" But the blood was surging to her face. "Don't be absurd!" She spun, clattered down the last flight of stairs and lunged for the door to the third floor.

As she opened it, Reese banged it shut again. He left his hand flattened against it, his elbow locked, his arm grazing hers. She shied, then whirled to face him, her back to the wall. "If you *don't* mind..."

"Yeah, I do." It had cost him, moving that fast. "I mind all of this, having a jealous little—" he couldn't think of a word "—twit. Schoolgirl. Standing between me and what I—"

"*Jealous!* You think I— Oh, you fatheaded, stupid—" She spun back to wrench at the doorknob.

He held it shut easily, then braced his other arm to her right, hemming her in.

She bounced off that arm, then tipped back her head with frustration, calling the heavens to witness. *"Ooooh!"*

Reese dropped his mouth to her ear, his cheek almost brushing her temple, his chest her shoulders. He lowered his voice persuasively. "If you're not jealous, Nic, then why not let two adults make up their own minds? We don't need *you* for a nanny." He took a breath and inhaled the whole rosebush, nearly gagged on it. "Just give me her number. She wants to meet me."

"No, she doesn't."

An elbow to his ribs would have felt the same. "How the hell would you know?" *Did* she know? It had never crossed his mind before that D and Nicola might be acquaintances, or even—his stomach lurched—friends. He'd assumed D must be a recruit, as he had been, someone drawn from the RIIT community. "*She* told you that? To keep us apart?"

"I..." Nic moved away from him, the only direction he'd left her. She rested her forehead against the door and let out a despairing sigh.

D didn't want to see him? Ever? Sucking at Reese was an emotion he couldn't name, but it felt like...loss. Being lost in the dark. Home was out there in the blackness somewhere, but receding. Unfindable.

This wasn't a feeling to dwell on. He shoved straight past it to cold fury. "I don't believe it." He would not. "You're jealous!"

"Of you and her? *Ha!*"

"Then prove you're not." Catching Nic's elbow, he pulled her around to face him. "Give me her number."

"*No!*" Tears of rage stood in her eyes. Her bottom lip trembled.

He didn't care—should have, but didn't. She had it coming, trying to keep them apart. "Then give her *my* number, Nic," he said, and the way he said it, she had to know. This was his final offer. Refuse that and he'd stand here all day, gagging on roses, till she gave up and gave in. *She's mine, and you won't stop me. Not you, you stubborn brat. Not anyone.*

She closed her eyes, shook her head, let out a long, slow breath—then shrugged. *On your head,* the gesture said, plain as day. "Sure." Her mouth quirked suddenly, as if laughter fought for a moment with tears. "All right. Whyever not?" She took the card he brought forth from his wallet and jammed it into her pocket.

And now that he'd won, Reese wanted to apologize. But wouldn't. Had no need, he told himself, and knew that he lied.

But guilt was swept away on a wave of rising anticipation. "You'll reach her tonight?" he demanded as he opened the door for her.

At the belated courtesy, Nic made a sound halfway between a laugh and a snarl and slipped through to freedom.

"Nic?" he called after her as she stalked away, knowing it made him look weaker, showing his eagerness, but unable to help himself.

"Maybe," she growled without turning.

"*Nic…*"

"All right, all *right*—if I can!" She reached her office door and shot through it. Banged it shut behind her.

Reese grimaced—then promptly forgot her.

Tonight. The word moved through him, bright with promise, warm as sun shining through a jar of wild honey. *She'll call me tonight.*

CHAPTER ELEVEN

HE'D WON every round.

Bare feet dangling above the water, Nicola sat on the stern of her little powerboat. She scowled at the glittering fairy towers of nighttime Boston, some five miles across the harbor. Her nose pointing to the gentle sea breeze, *Madame Curie* swung on her anchor line, and Nicola glared to the north of downtown, off toward Cambridge—and Pherotics. *Every round, damn and blast him.*

He'd kept her from getting her hands on his pheromone, and had done it so smoothly she still wasn't sure if he'd guessed how much she wanted it and why. Or was this simply Durand being Durand—cards clutched tight to his vest, one hand on his six-gun, trusting no one? Playing his own game by his wary lonesome? *Damn* him.

Then, adding insult to injury, he'd forced that promise from her. Manipulated her as easily and efficiently as she might deal with a balky hamster. His accusations of jealousy... Her hands clenched into fists. Had that ploy been simply ruthless, calculating manipulation?

Or was that how Durand really saw her—as a woman with *reason* to be jealous? A twit, he'd called her. A schoolgirl. Not particularly attractive—certainly not sexy. Without a man of her own? Why wouldn't she envy his mystery woman, his precious D, a woman who clearly had whatever it was Nicola Kent lacked?

Ha! What a joke.

A joke that had left her seething all afternoon. She'd stormed out of Pherotics on the dot of five, hit the gym in

Cambridge she'd joined only yesterday. A shower to scrub the stench of roses away, a sweat-slinging workout, a second shower, then home to *Madame Curie,* still nearly hopping out of her skin with a shamed and restless fury. *Damn* him.

Once aboard, she hadn't been able to sit still. And she'd soon tired of pacing the cockpit—twelve steps from stern to the bulkhead that supported the steering wheel and formed the rear end of the cabin, six steps thwartships, then back to the stern—a prisoner in an open-air cell. An hour before sundown, out of sheer desperation, she'd finally dropped the mooring pennant and gone on a putt-putt. At least she could charge up the batteries and explore a bit if she was good for nothing else.

Boston Harbor was miles wide and as ragged as an unraveling mitten. Dozens of little harbors nestled between fingers of land, which pointed out toward the harbor islands, then beyond these, the sea. With the last shreds of a crimson sunset, she'd found herself miles away from her rental mooring at the marina in East Boston. Rather than risk returning in the dark, she'd dropped anchor on the edge of a fleet of lobster boats. Off Quincy, according to her chart. She could even pinpoint the exact dock that jutted from the shore a hundred yards to the west. She was now debating whether to row the dinghy in and take a walk in the park that bordered the water or try to settle with a book in her cabin below.

Or call Durand. She wouldn't even have to go ashore to call him. With a portable phone, she could reach out and touch Durand any time she pleased. *I don't please, the rat.*

But she'd promised to give D his number, like an idiot.

"So call him, D," she said ironically, with no one but a late-homing seagull to hear. *Call the brute and tell him to bug off. You can tell him you're married, tell him you're gay, tell him you hate pushy men, tell him you're leaving for Antarctica—tell him whatever you please.*

Because D was an imaginary lady. Just a figment of his

blindfolded, overfevered imagination. She could be whatever she liked.

And if he pushes you too far? Well, then, you'll just go...poof! Up in smoke. Gonzo, Durand, and too bad about you. What a girl wants is a little respect.

What a girl wanted was a little revenge for the drubbing she'd taken this afternoon. She'd felt like a puppy, with him dangling his pheromone over her nose like a dog biscuit, just out of reach.

Teasing her? *No problem, Nic. I'll give you all the stuff you want—but oh, no—not the formula.* Had he been laughing at her all along?

But then, if he *had*... Nicola sat up straighter and stared off toward Boston. If he had, well, two could play that game! She could dangle what *he* wanted above his nose. Make him beg. *Who has the power now, big guy?*

Seven numbers, her heart pounding louder with each one she punched out. Nicola knelt on the short ladder that led below, staring out into the dark cockpit. *What'm I doing?*

"Hello," a familiar voice snapped. He'd picked up on the first ring.

She shivered, his voice as near as if they shared a pillow, then smiled. *Were you waiting right by the phone? For me?*

"Hello?" Durand repeated, his voice hardening with impatience.

She wasn't teasing so much as tongue-tied. *And now what?*

"D, is that you?"

So what if it is? She smiled off toward Boston.

"Are you shy, D, or slow, or just the kind of woman who likes pulling the wings off—"

She laughed aloud, remembering. *It's you!* He wasn't quite the same man in the dark, either. "Hello, Twenty-three." Spoken in a whisper. "Did you miss me?" *How much on a scale of one to ten?*

"Like the sound of leaves rustlin' in winter." He drew a breath, then, "And you? Did you miss..." The rest of his question faded to silence, or maybe the radio waves faltered between them?

Like the kiss of snowflakes on my face in July. "No," she whispered, instead, then laughed. *Take that from a twit!*

"Ah." He said no more, and they simply breathed together, measuring the silence. Wary. Waiting. Connected. "Where are you?" he said at last. "Providence?"

"Closer." Though there was no earthly reason to tell him that.

"Not close enough," he growled.

They considered that together, breathing. Nicola touched her eyebrow with a fingertip, drew it slowly down her cheek, her skin aching for a touch—not this one. *Why did I call?*

"Wherever you are, I can be there," he said at last. Huskily. Tentatively. An offering.

Himself. She closed her eyes and thought, *Why not?* There must be a dozen reasons why not, but somehow they weren't coming to mind. "No."

"What?" Durand raised his voice slightly.

"I said no." She raised hers, as well.

"Sorry, I can't— Must be the connection. These damned phones. Say that again?"

She could hear *him* clear as a bell. "I said no, Twenty-three."

"Repeat that?"

"Negative. No way. *Nyet!*" She'd raised her voice almost to normal. She hissed with exasperation, then whispered, "I can't."

"*Damn.* I'm sorry, I can't hear— Look, wouldn't it be better if we talked in person? Can you hear *me,* D?"

"I hear you fine. And I said *no.*"

"No? Well, if you can't hear me and I can't hear you, what should we do? Hang up?"

But they'd only just started! She shook her head emphatically.

"D? D, are you there?"

"I'm *here,* can't you—"

"D? D!" he called, as if she was running away from him. "Well, hell," he said to himself, and disconnected.

"Damn!" Nicola stared at her mute phone. *"Blast!"*

"WHAT THE HELL have I done?" Reese muttered, staring at his car phone. Traffic stormed past to his left; he'd been driving when she called, had pulled over, the better to talk. *And now I've hung up on her. Will she call back? Call me, D, darlin'. Devil woman.*

"Why the hell did I *do* that?" He thumped the steering wheel. He'd waited for days, hours, minutes that had dragged like years. She might never call again!

But deep down, he knew why. She had to learn, and she'd better learn from the start. The cardinal rule of Durand's Rules to Live By. *Nobody* pulled his strings. She'd been teasing him, playing hide-and-seek again. *I can call you, but you can't touch me.*

If he'd wanted her less, it wouldn't have mattered. He'd never minded games, even liked them, as long as he won in the end. But this time…something was different here. She had too much power already. "So much—and no more," he said aloud, grimly. *But call me, babe.*

"She'll call." He drummed a restless tattoo on the wheel. *She will. She has to.* Because whatever those strings were, they stretched both ways. No one had made her pick up that phone tonight. No one had made her meet him in the tunnel. There *was* something between them. Had been from the start.

Nicola Kent's magic bonding potion?

No, he told himself. No friggin' way. If he were *bonded,* helpless as a sucker vole, he'd never have been able to hang up on her. His free will was working just fine, thanks.

He wasn't bonded—just cross-eyed with lust. *Call me! Why the hell did I ever—* He jumped violently as the phone rang. *Yes!*

Reese eyed the phone as it rang again. Then again. He

should have let it ring one more time to throw her off balance, but he couldn't. "Hello?" *Babe?*

"Twenty-three?" That same sexy breathless whisper. "Can you hear me now?"

Hear you? I'm coming to get you, girl! He glanced at the traffic whizzing past his parked car and snapped, "Yeah, but I can't talk. Traffic's murder. Where can I meet you?" *Come on, girl, come on. You want us, too.*

"I..."

"*Get out of my* lane, *you*—" Reese slumped lower in his seat and laughed silently at himself. *Come* on, *girl.*

"*What?* Oh." She sighed, a soft sound of perplexity.

And his stomach muscles clenched. *I want you to do that again, in my ear. I want to make you do that.*

"There's a park in Quincy," she whispered quickly, as if someone might jerk the phone away any second, then told him where. "There's a dock..."

Yes! Hand cupped over the mouthpiece, he started the Porsche. Quincy. Half an hour, traffic willing. And factoring in the time to stop and buy a flashlight... "Be there in forty-five minutes," he said, and hung up before she could change her mind. The Porsche shot out into traffic and roared off to the south.

LAPSE IN PHONE RECEPTION? Or a trick? A few feet off the dock, Nicola dipped one oar to turn the dinghy in a lazy circle. Didn't matter, she told herself. Whatever Durand was up to, she'd taken precautions.

He wanted to talk? So they'd talk. She wanted to talk, too, she had to admit.

But no *way* was she letting him near her. Nicola dipped the opposite oar, halting her clockwise motion, to spin idly the other way.

In here near shore the water was black as pitch. There were no streetlights this side of the park. Nor stars and moon tonight; the sky was overcast. *Perfect darkness.*

And she was a mere shadow drifting on the dark. She

wore black jeans, a navy sweatshirt, the hood pulled up to hide her hair and most of her face.

Spinning the boat again, she glanced skyward. Big clouds were mounding in from the southeast. Rain, maybe, by morning? Waiting for Durand, she'd rigged the canvas awning over *Madame Curie*'s cockpit. That way, when she motored off at dawn, she'd have shelter, rain or no.

The dinghy revolved and she stared out toward her own boat amidst the others. *Madame Curie* was a patch of tar on black velvet. You wouldn't see her if you didn't know she was there. *Good, but now where the heck is he?* She'd give him five more minutes, then forget this. *This is crazy, anyway.*

Not so crazy, she defended herself. She still owed him, and what better way to pay him back? She could tease him from a safe distance. Show him what it felt like to be thwarted, powerless.

That's why you're doing this? an inner voice jeered.

Not the only reason. She also had data to collect. His two-week response sheet to fill out. And one question towered over all—was he still bonded? Or after two weeks, was his response fading?

He's driving halfway across Boston to meet me. I call that bonded.

Not necessarily, she argued. Durand hadn't had access to D for twelve days now. So how was he to know if his need had faded? *He wants his memory of me. But will he want me?* "That's the question."

"And what's the answer?" A shadow loomed at the end of the dock.

Reese laughed as she yelped and dropped an oar, then wished he hadn't spoken. Maybe she'd have come ashore? Or said something else? She'd spoken so low he hadn't gotten a real sense of her voice.

"Where the blue blazes did you come from?" A furious whisper while she reseated her oar. The rowboat glided to a position below him, where the shadows were deepest.

Handles it well, he noted. *No stranger to boats, then.* "Tennessee." He'd parked far back from shore, cutting his lights for the last hundred yards. In strange encounters he preferred to be the surpriser.

"I mean..." She shrugged, he thought, then her voice softened to humor. "Well, *you're* a long way from home."

Funny, he felt right at home here. Not home as he wanted to be, but...close, some sensation that eased his always tense shoulders and his mouth. "And where are you from?" Boston? The school year was over at RIIT, he reminded himself. So now she was home for the summer? *God help me, I'm chasing a college girl?* He needed his head examined.

"Around..."

Reese stirred impatiently. He'd always kept himself to himself, but this went past simple wariness. Why all the secrets? *Come closer, darlin', and I'll have them out of you, every last one.* "What d'you look like?" he asked on impulse.

"Umm..." She dipped an oar, swung around, looking back over her shoulder, a swan flirting. "Two eyes. The usual number of noses..."

He considered jumping into the dinghy, then discarded the notion. From a good eight feet up, he'd probably hole it. Not a class entrance for Romeo. "Got a mouth?"

"You know it."

So she *could* stand and deliver. "I do, but not half as well as I mean to."

"Ahh..." It was more breath than word.

Rattled you, did I? He laughed softly, then, "C'mere, D. You've got nothing to fear and you know it. I don't lose control."

"I..." It looked as if she shook her head. "I can't."

"Won't." *Then what the hell did you call me here for? Are you just a tease? Unzip me and run? I don't need this.*

He needed *her.* At the thought, his temper blazed. *The hell I do! Don't need anybody, least of all a—*

"Won't, then." She sighed. "This was dumb. Bad idea. G'night." The oars swept down like wings, and the dinghy glided away.

"Wait!" Need curled around him and wrenched tight, a rabbit snare around his guts.

The oars lifted rhythmically. Paler than her boat, they were all he could see now. *Wait,* he called, but his teeth clamped tight on the cry—he didn't beg for what he needed, he took it. *Damn you, wait!* And he remembered his flashlight. "D!"

The beam caught her looking off over her shoulder, showed him a slim figure clothed in black, a hood of dark cloth, a pale chin in profile. She jumped wildly as the light touched her, then her left oar sliced into the water and the boat pivoted—she turned her back on him. Sat there motionless a moment, then with great deliberation, dipped her oars forward. The dinghy crabbed out into darkness that sucked his light to nothing.

No way. If she left him now, she'd never call again, he knew it. *No way it ends like this!* He jammed the flashlight into his jeans, kicked off his shoes and dived.

Shit! The water was colder than cold. He shot to the surface with an incredulous laugh, shook the hair from his eyes and surged after her. *Coming to get you, babe! You teased the wrong man.*

A dozen strokes and he stopped while he checked his course. Ahead, a dark shape twirled. She was turning the dinghy. Giving in—coming back for him?

No, she'd turned to face him, the better to row. The boat shot away.

He swerved and went after it. All those years in pools since his knee went, now was the payoff. He settled into his stroke, cleaving black ice, his breath exploding with each turn of the head. *Coming, girl, coming...*

He was fast, thrusting through the water. The boat, gliding atop it, was faster. Didn't matter. His will hardened to stone. No different from a match. You simply said, *I will,* and that was that. Didn't matter what the other guy wanted. It came down to will—wanting the most, paying the price for your want. *Coming, girl.* He stopped to gasp and tread water. Where was she? There, off to the right. He shuddered violently—*cold*—sucked in a breath and pursued.

"Go back, you idiot!"

Had he heard that or dreamed it? His ears were full of water. Didn't matter. Reese stroked like a machine, stopping only to shudder and catch his breath, then on…and on…on… As long as it took…whatever it took…on…

"Get away from me. Go back!" The boat floated perhaps twenty feet away, oars poised.

"D-d-doesn't—end this way." He stopped, treading water and shivering. *Damn*, it was… The thought slipped out of reach.

"With you drowning—that's how it'll end. Go *back!*"

"I d-don't…do that." He stroked on, but he was tired. She had to take him in. That or he'd— *No.*

"Damn you! You stupid, stubborn…" But she waited, wings poised, a wild bird adrift in the black.

Easy. Don't scare… Reese lost the shape of the thought. *He* was scared. How far had he come? How far down was solid ground? He dangled in blackness as she stooped to meet him, angel on high. His hands clamped tight on the stern of her boat. "G-God, it's cold!"

"*Now* you notice that— No! Don't try to climb aboard. Can you hang on? It's not far."

Thank God. "Oh, sure. No problem." She'd spoken aloud, once or twice, but his thoughts were too muzzled to hold the sound of her voice. He knew only that it was low and angry. While he—he was starting to smile. *Won again. All it takes is—*

"Here." The dinghy bumped something hard. "I'll put over the swimming ladder."

The next few minutes were a shivering blur. She had to help him up the ladder, her hand hooked in the back of his belt, her swearing, him laughing, dopey—it felt like a champagne high. *Victory!* She landed him like a drunk seal, dropping him in the bottom of the cockpit, then vanished, swearing. He let out a satisfied breath. Home.

She returned, growling under her breath, her arms full of blanket, which she dumped to one side. She flattened a hand to his chest and he shivered against it. "Strip!" she whispered.

"Thought you'd never ask." He fumbled his shirt buttons. "Uhhmm…"

She hissed with impatience. "Oh, here!" She peeled him out of his shirt, then his jeans, standing to yank them down his legs. The flashlight fell out as she straightened.

He grabbed for it, but she beat him easily, then dodged back a step. "I suppose it's waterproof?"

"It'd better be." He held out his hand for it. *Mine.*

The beam shot out, lighting her feet. They were ridiculously small compared with his own. He reached for one, curled his fingers around a high, delicate instep. *Mine.* The light arced over his head, ending in a splash. "Hey!"

She dropped to her heels before him, their noses almost touching. "House rules, Durand. *No* lights."

"Yes, ma'am." So she could be fierce. He liked that.

She toweled him off with ruthless efficiency—and no apparent appreciation—then wrapped the blanket around him, muttering something about hypothermia and lunatics. He caught a strand of her hair. Not blond that would show in any light—but could have been any shade darker.

She whipped it from his fingers with a wordless snarl, stood and vanished through a companionway forward, her feet rattling down steps.

With a contented sigh, Reese leaned against a side of the cockpit, his teeth chattering. A boat. What the hell was she doing on a boat? Overhead stretched some sort of awning, making this space even darker than the night, a sheltered back porch, fresh with a sea breeze. *The lady has taste.*

"Here." She popped up from below, a mug in each hand. "Get this down quick."

Normally he didn't care for orders, but tonight, the winner, he could be magnanimous. He sipped hot chocolate with a slug of rum. "Good." His teeth clicked against the rim.

She knelt beside him, put a hand to his shivering stomach. "You're still cold."

"A little." *Take me below, babe. Put me in your bunk.*

She let out a vexed sound and settled instead beside him, their shoulders touching. "Drink up, then I'll make you another."

Clearly she hadn't seen the same movies he had. "There's an easier way." Reese shoved his arm and a wing of his blanket behind her. "Like this." He caught the two ends of the blanket in his fist, held it closed across their chests, a two-lover tepee.

"Ummm..." She hummed a soft sound of protest and worry.

Don't worry. Nothing will happen that you don't want. He leaned to press his lips to the softness below her ear. "Thanks for comin' back for me," he murmured against her skin. Tasting honey and chocolate and salt.

She'd stiffened at his first touch, but now, slowly, she relaxed, his lips upon her. "I had a choice?"

He smiled against her. "You always have a choice." *And you chose me, don't you forget it.* He rubbed the side of his mug, warm and smooth, along the line of her jaw, coaxing her face toward his. *You're cold as I am, babe, and it goes deeper. Thaw you out is what you need.* He offered her his cup, she hesitated, then drank. *Yes!* His whole body shivered and hardened.

He took a sip, his lips touching where hers had been, then set the drink aside. *I need honey, not chocolate. You, not a blanket.* He took her own mug and pulled it free of lax fingers. She looked up at him with a look that in the dark could have been dread, might have been hope. *Trust me, babe. We need this.*

CHAPTER TWELVE

IF YOU DON'T KNOW the way, I do. He laid a knuckle under her chin, tipped it higher. Then waited. *You're mine, do you know it?*

She sighed...leaned...slow as the stars wheeling overhead. They met in the middle. One kiss and he was lost...found...his feet on the road for home...his soul her center. There was warmth waiting for him.

She turned in his arms as he urged her, then slid a slim leg across his lap to kneel astride, never breaking their kiss. Hot...his...alyssum and burnt honey...*home*...her whimpering a greeting as he cupped her taut hips and pulled her closer.

He broke the kiss to gasp, "*You!*" then sought her breast, found it through the fuzziness of her sweatshirt—another first, his mouth on her there. The fabric an intolerable barrier. He nipped her and she cried aloud, arching against him. He unzipped the thing—*who's unzipping who now, babe?*—and sought her again, groaning with delight. *You, no other!*

He rolled backward on the planks, taking her with him, then simply held her, his arms locked around her, their hearts thundering, her face pressed to his throat. He stared up at the wind-shivered canvas above, trying to get a grip. *Easy, man, easy! We've got all night.*

He'd die if he wasn't inside her in the next minute. *What in God's name is happening to—*

She reached back, cupped her palm around the underside of his bent knee. Dragged her hand slowly, slowly, up the back of his thigh. He gasped, closed his teeth on her shoulder to keep from crying aloud—*witch, devil woman!*—then she found him. And he was lost...hers...even as he had her.

With no time to reckon the cost.

REESE AWOKE with a start when she sighed and started to ease off him. *No.* He spread a hand on her bottom to keep her in place. *Don't leave yet!* "Sorry. I don't usually drift off like..." The words were muffled against her shoulder. There was no usual here. No other woman he'd usualled with. *Only you.* Incredibly, he felt himself harden within her. *How do I get enough of you, girl?*

She'd felt him awake, too, squeezed a fluttering "Welcome back" that in turn squeezed a groan out of him. Tipping her hips, she slithered up his body, inching him deeper. *You...you're the...* He brought his hand up her rear, celebrating lush bottom, the deep curve of waist, the hard, hot back. He wanted to roll her over and drive deep, but not on these boards. "Shouldn't we go below?" She'd have a berth.

"No, here...*now*..." An imperious, urgent whisper, both of them laughing as they remembered where she'd said that last.

As you like, my lady. Later there'd be time for his likes, too. Images of their future couplings twined in his mind with the now. All long limbs and soft body, she enveloped him, protected him, needed his passion—pleading for it finally in a wordless, exultant chant that dropped an octave toward the last, then rose in a cry of...wonder? Triumph?

No, the triumph was all his, him shouting aloud as he planted his seed in her. *Mine!* From this moment on...and he'd never even seen her.

REESE DIDN'T AWAKE this time when she left him, but he dreamed her gone, him groping alone in the dark.... He was thirteen again...the third or fourth time he'd run away after his father's death. *Never goin' back. Nothing t'go back to.*

And nothing ahead except himself, Reese, standing alone. Feeling his way down a dark alley, he sought some kind of shelter, a Dumpster or box where he could sleep. Was raining—

"Reese?"

"Uhh!" He lurched upright at her touch, had yanked her nose to nose with him before he awoke. "Ohh..." He softened a bruising grip, turned it to a caress. "Sorry, I was..."

"S'okay. Come to bed, sleepyhead. It's damp out here." Her hand cupped the back of his neck, stroking, coaxing. "C'mon."

He pulled her hand aside, held it. He didn't need soothing like a cat or a child. "Why d'you always whisper?"

Her fingers stilled, then curled around his. "It's a night for whispering. Come below."

No answer, that, but he was too sleepy to argue. Too pleased to be taken to her bed. That was a kind of trusting in itself, he thought. The rest would follow.

Her hand drew him forward through a small cabin, not ten paces long, his free hand groping the slickness of varnished panels, the softness of a seat cushion, a pot on a stove. She guided him into a narrow hallway—"Watch your head." A door to either side—a toilet and locker, he reckoned. Then she scrambled up into a V-shaped berth built into the bow and he followed.

The feel of clean sheets, the scent of alyssum and honey—he was at the heart of the matter, her nest. The rain tapping on deck some four feet above. "I *like* this."

Lying apart from him, she laughed her low sexy laugh, with a touch of...what? Uncertainty? He reached for her and she rolled into his arms with a small satisfied sound. *You need an invitation after tonight, babe?*

Neither did she seem to know quite how to lie with a man—where legs and arms fit—outside of sex. He liked that, too. Hauling her to him, he fit her spoon-fashion to his chest, her head pillowed on his arm, her hips enough to make a man cry if he hadn't been so...happy? It wasn't a word he used much.

Rain pattered on wood. This beat a box in an alley, or any of the beds he'd had since, hands down. Reese kissed the nape of her neck and remembered. *You used my name. How...* Then realized. Nic must have given her his card.

Knowing his name, she was one up on him. Soon mended. He kissed her ear. "Babe, what's your name?"

"Mmmmpph." She wriggled against him, an invitation to ravishment if he'd had the means, slid one warm calf backward between his, drew a long contented breath—and slept.

Later for all that. Nose buried in her hair, he smiled. *D for devil woman...for darlin'. Dulce* was Spanish for sweet, *Dolores* meant sorrow. None of the above? All? His lids drooped. *Or danger,* a voice suggested at the back of his mind. Reese smiled—*no way!*—and slept.

THE BOAT NODDED its head to some swell—a passing ship's wake from across the harbor?—and Reese awoke. Still dark. It didn't feel as if he'd slept long, but he felt refreshed. She still lay curled in his arms. His hand crept up of its own accord to cup her breast. *Perfect fit.*

Her nipple rose against his palm. She moaned in her sleep and rocked back against him. *Yes.* He leaped to attention, his cock rising between smooth thighs.

No. Gritting his teeth, Reese pressed his forehead to her back, and willed himself to stillness. *Better not.* She was fine-boned and delicate. Fit him tight as a kid glove. As an angel's glove. And though he'd tried to be gentle, she was bound to be sore.

And she's inexperienced. Something—everything—told him that. If she'd awakened, invited him... But she slept on, kitten-limp in his arms. A gentleman would leave her in peace till morning.

As for Reese Durand? The only way *he* could manage such forbearance was to slide away from her. He eased off, hoping for a protest.

She murmured and rolled over, fast asleep. *So be that way, darlin'*. He slid out of the bunk and thought about the head. Opted instead for a fine stance on the stern, shivering in the breeze, sleepy and sleepily exultant. What a night! But the drizzle put the kibosh to his hard-on, which was probably just as well. Reese considered. *Behave yourself if we go back to bed?*

No promises from below. Oh, well, he could always explore. He commenced a braille investigation of the steering station. Domed compass and what must be engine dials, fixed on the dash above a steering wheel. His hands played over gear levers, engine controls. *You run all this, babe?* His instincts had been dead-on. She was special. A man's kind of woman.

Still hoping to be ordered back to bed—*at your service, ma'am!*—he drifted down four steps to the main cabin. His hands moved over shelves above the settee cushions. Crammed with books, more books than she'd need for a weekend jaunt, or he'd need in a lifetime.

In the tiny galley his hands brushed the metal intricacies of handles and burners—a stove. He bumped his head on something hanging—a hanging plant. Another plant sat at the back of the counter space—basil, by its smell. *You don't leave plants aboard, cooking herbs, if you're only using a boat weekends. Who'd water 'em between times? So she's living here?*

He'd heard of live-aboards but never met one before. The situation implied a spirit of austerity, making do with so little. And adventure. Along with a kind of competence not many women he'd met had attained or even wished to attain. And a willingness to undergo loneliness. Because this tiny world was isolate, a small planet hanging in liquid space. *Who are you, D? Where have you been, where are you headed?*

His hands returned to the stove. Burners...flames... Would their light carry forward? He wanted to see her. *I know you, yet I don't.* He was tired of mysteries. No lights, she'd said. House rules. *But why?*

And since when had he followed rules? Reese turned a handle. Heard the rush of gas, but no spark leaped to life. *Damn.* He turned it off again. Needed a match, he supposed. Matches, where would she keep them? Rummaging quietly, he found a drawer below the counter. Silverware. A second drawer held plastic bags, napkins, odds and ends, no matches.

She'd keep them here in the galley, it only made sense. Still he searched the shelves above the settees—with the same results. *Nothing.* She rubs sticks together?

Or...she hid them. It was a disturbing thought. *What are you hiding?*

"*Ahh!*" If someone had stabbed her to the heart, she'd have made such a sound.

"I'm here, babe!" He stubbed a toe against a bulkhead, getting to her. She sat bolt upright, panting. He wrapped his arms around her—held on when she jumped—then nuzzled her nape. "You okay, babe? Dreamin'?"

She nodded furiously and sucked in a shuddering breath. Her heart slammed against his forearms. "S'all right. S'okay. I'm here, babe."

She nodded. "Yeah." A rueful whisper. "You sure are."

Whatever that meant. He kissed her smooth shoulders. Burnt honey. Nuzzled her hair. Alyssum. Maybe loving would chase the nightmare away?

"Time to get up." She spun in his arms, slipped off the berth to slither past him, pattered aft through the cabin.

"Are you kidding?" It couldn't be past three, four at the latest. Reese followed her to the cockpit, where she was scrambling into her clothes. "What are you doing?"

"Going ashore. Get dressed."

"At this hour? Why?" She'd had an attack of the munchies? They were off to find an all-night diner?

"I…just feel like it."

Taking me ashore to dump me, he translated with sudden conviction. The alley of his dream flashed through his mind's eye, black, desolate; then the night turned red. She might as well have punched him in the gut. He stood very still, mastering the emotion. Considering options.

Make me, was the first thought that came to mind. It would take her plus the U.S. Marines to evict him if he dug in his heels. *Can't let it end that way. And maybe I'm wrong?* Swearing under his breath, he dressed in sodden clothes, then clambered down into the dinghy where she waited, a dark huddled shape, nothing but shadows beneath her sweatshirt hood.

But he could *see* the hood—just. No sign of dawn yet, but it was coming. Her oars flew like wings, a frightened bird. *What's your mystery, dammit?*

By the time they reached the shore, he had his temper in hand. Whatever her reasons, he'd no right to protest. If she wasn't having him for breakfast, she'd still shown him every other hospitality woman could show man. It would be churlish to demand more. *So take this point, babe, if it makes you happy. The game's not over, and you're playing the guy who never loses.*

The boat nudged the shore. She rose and leaped to the beach, stood there, a small resolute shadow as he stepped down beside her. *Doesn't end here, babe. No way,* he thought, looking down at her. The question hovered on his lips: *You'll call me?*

He'd have sooner drowned himself than ask it.

Besides, he knew the answer, even if she didn't. *You will.* Call him conceited, but he knew when he pleased—he'd pleased her big-time. Better yet, he'd surprised her. She hadn't come to him expecting such pleasure. He didn't know how he knew that, but he knew. *So you'll call me for more. Soon, I hope to God.*

If not, he knew now where to find her.

Her toe scuffed the rocks. "Well…"

Well, hell. He caught her by the waist—such slenderness. His thumbs pressed a little harder than they should have—so soft. How could he let her go? He felt a sudden sharp relief when her head tipped back. *Yeah, don't deny it. You feel this, too.*

He broke the kiss before she would have; a man had his pride. Still, the words escaped. "Sure you want me to go?" He cursed himself for asking.

She looked away, down, the hood shadowing her face. Small, mysterious...lonely? She nodded.

"Then see you round, babe." *I guarantee it.*

He had to walk to the head of the dock, then down its length for his shoes. By the time he reached the end, she'd faded into the night.

Unwilling to go, Reese sat, feet dangling over water. The rain had ended. Come morning, maybe she'd come ashore? If she rowed right by him, he wasn't going to close his eyes. Meanwhile, his lids drifted shut, the better to remember. He slumped backward, propped on his elbows, then gradually sank flat. "Whoof!" Slowly a smile spread across his face. *What a...*

When he awoke, a wisp of cloud gleamed overhead, flamingo bright. Reese sat up. Silhouetted against a lemon sky was her boat, with a slim, hooded shape leaning over the bow.

What was she...? He scrambled to his feet. She was raising an anchor!

You don't live here, on a mooring? The sound of an engine reached him faintly across the water. With long, graceful strides she walked aft along the cabin side, jumped down into the cockpit. The little boat hovered, eased gradually forward, gathered weigh, puttered off toward the rising sun.

Watching her go, Reese didn't know whether to laugh or shake his fist. *Fooled me again, girl!* She was good—really good.

But he was better. *So call me, babe.*

And if she didn't?

Reese shrugged and headed for his car. If she didn't, so be it. He'd have to take the thumbscrews to poor Nic again.

Luckily he didn't mind a challenge.

CHAPTER THIRTEEN

STUPID, STUPID, *STUPID*! How *could* she have been so stupid, making love with Reese Durand last night?

Couldn't have been me. Must have been D. Making love with the enemy.

Love with a rock-stubborn, set-on-having-his-way alpha male! Eyes on the sunrise, Nicola lifted one hand from *Madame Curie*'s wheel to touch her lips. Found them puffy and bruised. She smiled.

Then scowled when she caught herself smiling. *Stupid!*

For a woman who prided herself on *not* being stupid—who'd nothing much but her brains, after all, to justify her existence—it was a nasty blow to wake up and realize she'd spent one whole night not thinking but feeling. *How could I have let him do…* all the things he'd done?

I had a choice? she asked herself.

You always have a choice, a mocking male voice reminded her—and sent a shiver right down to her toes.

Once safely moored back at the yacht club, she needed a plan for this discombobulated, dazzled day. Nicola's first impulse was to stay away from Pherotics. Because if Reese laid eyes on her today, surely he'd know? She felt as if she were stamped with his imprint—her mouth bruised and wearing its odd come-and-go smile, her skin glowing, her body shuddering with random aftershocks. One look and surely he'd know?

I could visit Moo. It had been, what, two weeks since her last visit?

But if she played hooky from Pherotics today, then

mightn't Reese put two and two together? Because whatever he was—*arrogant, exasperating, terminally bull-headed*—Reese wasn't dumb. So better to go in and act perfectly natural.

Natural—ha! Naturally loved within an inch of her life. She stretched, looked up at the sky—and grinned. How could she ache all over and feel so…*smug* about it?

Run down by an alpha male and lived to tell the tale, that's all. Survivor's giddiness. No more than that.

SHE SPENT the morning tracking down the men from her original study for their two-week evaluations. She had a dozen or so still to reach, and it was good mindless work for someone whose attention was addled. By noon she had only seven subjects left, and still no sign of Durand. "Question three—have you dated anyone since we last spoke? Yes? How many dates, if you don't mind my asking?"

Sixteen didn't mind—he'd had too many dates to count over the past two weeks. Well…maybe a dozen or so. Um, *precisely?* Um, three—with three different women.

And your sense of bonding, six on a scale of ten the first day, is now approaching zero. Still she forged on through her form, finally asking, "Do you miss woman A?" The woman to whom he'd originally bonded in her experiment.

"S'funny…" Puzzled young voice. "I remember telling you I missed A—a lot—two weeks ago. But now…I d'know, who says absence makes the heart grow fonder? World's full of women."

No male mountain vole could have put it better. Emotionally he was free. The effects of her hormone had degraded to zero.

The next five were also fancy-free, which left only two to go—Durand and Forty. Forty was the one other man of her original group, besides Durand, who'd been trouble from the start.

He was the one who hadn't bothered filling in his ID

number on his response sheet the day of the test, and that bit of carelessness had proved typical of his style.

She'd yet to catch up with him since the experiment, though she'd left countless pleading messages on his campus answering machine. *Jerk.* So much for his agreement to submit to her follow-ups. Still, she needed his data.

His summer home was listed as Newton, a rich suburb west of Boston. She hadn't thought to ask for his parents' names on the questionnaire, but a search of the phone book gave her two likely candidates. Nicola dialed one—

The sound of a distant heavy door closing—the stairwell door? Tim and Hadley preferred the elevator. Brisk footsteps coming down the corridor. Reese? Nicola swiveled her chair, turning her back to her office door. *Oh, God, I'm not ready yet!*

"Nic?"

Him. Without turning, she raised her free arm, rotated her palm to face him and gave an impudent four-finger flapflap. *Hiya. Can't you see I'm busy?* The back of her neck belied the casual act. It felt as if it had been dipped in boiling water. "Um, question five," she mumbled to the still-ringing phone. "On a scale of one to ten—"

"Oh, sorry. I'll catch you later," Reese said behind her.

You've done that already. One of those odd, shuddering spasms started in the soles of her feet. She scrunched her toes as it shivered up her thighs. His footsteps moved away. She let out her breath and felt her mood descend a notch with each ring of the phone. *He didn't know me.*

Somehow she'd thought he would.

JUST AS WELL Nic had been busy, Reese told himself, walking away. He hadn't known quite why he'd gone to her, what he'd meant to say.

She's as close as I can get to D right now. That was it. She was his only link, besides the phone. And he'd grown tired of jumping every time it rang, only to find the voice of one of his salesmen at the other end, instead of a sexy, laughing whisper.

He gritted his teeth as he headed upstairs. Not having her phone number, having no way to reach her if he chose. When he chose. *Someone else pulling my strings.*

But only as long as I choose to let her, he reminded himself. Because as long as he had Nic, he could lay his hands on D in the end. *Besides, even if I had her phone number right now, I wouldn't call her.* It was too early, not twelve hours since they'd parted. Didn't pay to let a woman think you needed her.

Didn't pay to need a woman. He never had before. Didn't intend to start now. It wasn't need that drove him to D, some kind of bonding, as Nic would put it. It was plain old-fashioned desire.

FOOL. WHAT HAD SHE hoped for, expected? For Reese to point a finger at her and cry, "Aha! It's you"?

That was the last thing she wanted. Because the next thing after that would be her watching his face as the realization hit home—shock fading to disappointment. Lift the velvet mask of darkness and you find, not the sexy, mysterious stranger of your imagination, but—*surprise, sucker!*—plain old Nicola Kent. Schoolgirl. Twit. The same woman who's been leaving you cold and uninterested for two weeks now.

Then watching his disappointment shade to—what? Anger? That she'd played him for a fool?

Or amusement? Serious, unsmiling Nicola Kent could make such noises in his arms? Proud Nic could beg for a touch like any other woman?

Or pity. Maybe that was what he'd feel. *Poor* Nic, who had to resort to trickery to lure a man to her bed?

Nic broke her pencil in half and threw the ends up in the air—then ducked as they clattered down again. *Just shut up and stop thinking about it! What'd you expect, after all?*

It was time to remember who she was. Nicola Kent, not

D. Coolly rational scientist, objective researcher, single-mindedly driven author of a dissertation—if she could ever put it back together—that would show them all. Win her a place in the sun. A future full of achievement and honors.

That was worth remembering. Worth fighting for. Unlike last night, which was merely a dream. A fantasy. A crazy interlude, now ended forever. Back to the real world—and her goals that would make that world real.

IT WAS A FUNNY FEELING, nothing he'd ever felt before. It felt like hunger, but it wasn't that. The ham-and-swiss he'd eaten at his desk didn't put even a dent in this...hollow feeling.

Tired, Reese told himself, and he should be after last night. But this wasn't tiredness. It felt edgier than that, kept him prowling around his office, cursing the phone, the point around which he revolved. Like a dog leashed to a tree.

He felt as if he'd lost something somewhere—something essential like his car keys. Or as if he'd forgotten something, a name or a word, and it danced on the tip of his tongue.

This feeling couldn't be what Nic meant when she talked about— *Naaah*. This was simply irritation. Knowing that what he needed was just downstairs, locked in Nic's desk or her brain, seven numbers that would change everything. Turn him from a man waiting into a man acting. Not that he'd use them even if he had them. Not yet. But if simply *having* D's phone number would ease this gnawing feeling... Reese cast a last scowl at his phone and headed for the stairs.

TWENTY T-MAZES. Nic looked from her order list to the boxes delivered that morning and counted twenty. *Check!* She opened another type of box, found two dozen sterile beakers. There were five of these boxes and she'd ordered one hundred and twenty beakers, so...*check!*

She looked up as the lab door opened, expecting Tim or even Hadley. Then she froze. *Reese.* She jerked around and put her hands blindly on a box. *Do something!* She tore off its brown wrapping tape and lifted the lid.

He reached past her to pull something from the package. "What's this?"

"A harness. Each of the female mountain voles will wear one." There should be forty. She counted a dozen out onto the countertop slowly, wishing him gone. Why was he standing there?

"You harness them? Why?"

"So they'll stay put. One female will be tethered in the left room of each maze and a second female in the right. You drop in a male, without a harness, free to go where he pleases." Wasn't it always that way? "You check back later, and if he's staying by one female, grooming and cuddling only her..."

"Then he's bonded?"

"He's bonded." She opened a third box, counted more harnesses. *What do you want?*

"Seen Tim?" he asked, and drummed his fingers against something.

"Not today."

"Hadley?"

"Nope." Work was something Hadley left to students and other fools.

"So when do you start?"

"Tomorrow, assuming the voles come this afternoon. I'll give them the night to settle." When he said no more, she added, desperate to fill the void, "Today I finished contacting all the men from my study." *Except Forty and you.*

"Um, how's that going?"

"'Bout how I predicted."

Come on, come on, give! I need to know. Reese fought an urge to reach out and tweak her braid. "And how's that?"

She shrugged slender shoulders and opened another box. "They're all dating again, or trying to date."

"Which means?"

"Which means I'm wondering...did D contact you? And did you go out?"

"Mind your own biz," he growled. "But if they're dating other women, that means?"

She counted out another stack of tiny harnesses. "Means their bonding response has degraded to zero. Which is why I'd like to know about you. You're the only one who got the mixture—your cologne plus my hormone. The combination we'll be testing tomorrow."

Say a guy was bonded, what would it feel like? Sharp as Nic was, he dared not ask. *Would it feel as if I were missing...something?*

No. Can't be. Trapped by the nose like a dimwit ratty vole? No way!

But there was no way now he could ask Nic for D's phone number. Not at this moment, anyhow. She'd say he was bonded.

AN HOUR PAST SUNSET, standing on the dock where he'd last seen her. Half-a-dozen lobster boats moored out there, but nothing like her powerboat. *Where are you?* She hadn't called all day.

She will. The night was young yet.

Or maybe...maybe it hadn't been as good for her as he'd thought?

Naaah. Her incredulous laughter each time at the end, those tiny nonstop kisses she'd showered over his face, his throat, his shoulders afterward, almost as if she'd been *thanking* him... How could he mistake that? A woman fake that? *No.*

So, then...what? *Where the hell are you, babe?*

To hell with it. He turned away, then turned back to glare one last time across the harbor, squinting for some approaching speck, black on silver water. Saw nothing but a tanker, sliding out to sea. Gulls winging home for the night.

As he should be doing. He was tired. But picturing home, he didn't see a house in West Concord anymore. Home was... Where the hell *was* she?

Night's young yet, he reminded himself. She had his number. She'd call.

Or he'd go crazy.

CHAPTER FOURTEEN

NICOLA LAY on a lab table, gazing up at the tiny gaps in the gridded ceiling while Tim Baggett bustled around the lab. *What have I got myself into?*

After a toss-and-turn night on sheets that still held the faintest hint of Reese's cologne, she'd awakened early—to find herself hugging the pillow he'd used. *Fool! Sentimental idiot!* She'd marched off to Pherotics, grimly determined to resume her quest. Find the formula for his pheromone and get out fast, while her objectivity was still intact. That was the only rational response to this…this aberration. Digression. Glitch in her plans.

And Tim Baggett was the key to getting her hands on a sample of the Pherotics pheromone, she'd decided. Tim had discovered the substance, after all. So maybe if she appealed to his vanity? A scientist craved an audience as much as any artist or actor, and preferably a learned one. Who better than she, another biochemist?

That had been her approach this morning when she arrived at the lab—that, plus two coffees and a bag of doughnuts.

But flattering Tim had proved a thankless task. He'd merely grunted at her first humble questions, though he'd grudgingly accepted a honey-dipped cruller.

Any other woman would have switched right there to the usual feminine weapons—smiles, batting lashes, the easy, semisuggestive banter that had never come easily to Nicola. She'd spent her teen years competing with boys, not enticing them.

So she'd tried subtle goading. How could Tim think his pheromone worked as a sexual attractant? Reese's marketing surveys seemed to show it as a failure. And no one was buying Irresistible—not twice, anyway.

With that, she'd found his button. Tim had almost tripped over himself in his eagerness to prove he was right, and Reese was wrong. His pheromone worked—Irresistible worked—if only Reese would give it a decent chance, damn him.

Got him! she'd exulted privately. If she couldn't beat Reese one way, she could beat him another.

But instead of producing his formula's molecular structure for her inspection, Tim determined to give her more dramatic proof—using her as the guinea pig. Half intrigued, half apprehensive, she now lay waiting for him to finish his preparations.

"You know what the vomeronasal organ is, of course? The VNO?" He asked, booting up the computer that sat on a counter alongside the table.

She studied him for a moment. Even from this angle, Tim looked short—he was only a couple of inches taller than she was, though he must have outweighed her by a good forty pounds, most of that muscle. Lifted weights, she suspected. Bodybuilding as compensation for his lack of height? Or his Coke-bottle glasses?

Whatever his reason, his pumped-up width only made him look squat. Tim wasn't ugly, exactly, but somehow his effect was...unappealing. Maybe because he always seemed to be looking for offense—and too often finding it?

Or maybe that was just his manner toward her. She was the interloper, after all, brought in to show him his business.

"You haven't heard of it," he concluded on a note of happy condescension.

I have, but you're going to tell me, anyway. And she supposed she'd better let him. "It's in the nose, isn't it?"

"Yes. It's your sixth sense—for sensing pheromones. Discovered first in 1703 by a Dutch military surgeon who was doing dissections after the battles. The VNO is located beneath the septum in your nose, quite invisible except for a pit the size of a pinhead to either side. Nothing anyone will ever see unless they stick a microscope half an inch up your nose."

"So if they discovered it back in the eighteenth century, why do we never hear about it?"

Tim examined a rather ominous-looking device of stainless steel—it looked like a twenty-first-century water pistol—then plugged it into the wires leading to the computer. He pulled a trigger and air hissed. "A highly respected anatomist in the 1930s was the next to go looking for the VNO, as per the surgeon's description. Didn't find it—the pits are easy to miss. She declared the surgeon wrong. Humans *didn't* have such an organ, though most mammals did, for reasons they couldn't imagine back then. So everybody forgot about VNOs till research on pheromones boomed in the 1980s."

At which point they looked again, Nicola summarized to herself, more carefully, and lo and behold, humans had one—bigger than that of a horse. *All the better to sense you with, my dear!*

"People think that because the VNO is located within the nose, it's used to detect smells. But it isn't."

"Pheromones have no odor," Nicola agreed. She was tired of playing dumb. Nerves from the VNO ran directly to the most primitive part of the brain, the part of the brain that dealt with emotions. Let a vaporized pheromone enter those tiny pits to either side of her septum and her mind would receive whatever message that pheromone carried. *Fall in love. Run for your life. Fight me.*

Tim brandished his device. "Now this gizmo will deliver a puff of any chemical I choose to your VNO. Then it'll suck it back up again before it reaches your olfactory nerves, higher up your nose. So you won't *smell* what I'm giving you, you'll…" He shrugged.

Precisely. Because no one had known that the organ existed, the English language had never evolved a verb to describe how your VNO dealt with a stimulus. Your eyes saw. Your nose smelled. Your ears heard and your tongue tasted. But your VNO? All you could say was that it *received* an impression and then you knew what you felt— love, hate, fear, whatever the message that particular pheromone carried.

"So first we attach these electrodes to your temples."

Her body tensed as he bent over her, his eyes eerily remote behind their thick lenses. She grimaced at the coolness of the conductive paste, then the grip of the tiny suction cups, and suppressed a shudder. *Night before last, I let a man come as close to me as a man can come.* But now, letting *this* man near her? Letting him lay hands on her even in this completely impersonal way? It felt oddly...wrong. As if she was being...disloyal. Giving away something that was no longer hers to give. She clenched her teeth. *Don't be ridiculous!* She owed Reese nothing, certainly no sort of... Her mind shied away from the word, then pronounced it anyway. *Fidelity.*

Nonsense. This was a simple scientific inquiry. Nothing more or less.

Just as the night before last was? an inner voice jeered.

"Okay." Tim straightened. "If you watch the monitor, Nic, it'll show you whenever something stimulates your hypothalamus."

The part of her brain that recognized and processed a pheromonic message. "So you'll give me a puff of the pheromone you're using in Irresistible?"

"Yup. But I'll also give you a puff of a few other harmless things. You tell *me* when I give you my pheromone. Now. Roll over so you can watch the screen. Come on, relax."

Ick. He taped the probe in place, then backed off, beaming.

All I wanted was to get my hands on your formula, dam-

mit! But if submitting to this pleased Tim, turned him from hostile competitor to cordial colleague...

"Ready?" Tim poured clear liquid from an unmarked beaker into a cup at the butt end of her gun. "Watch the screen."

Her toes curling inside her shoes, Nicola stared at the line pulsing along the bottom of the monitor—her hypothalamus in a state of rest. *Get it over with.* She jumped at a sensation of coolness, a blast of air.

But the line on the screen stayed flat. "My VNO and my hypothalamus are not impressed."

"Right. That was saline. Means nothing to your brain. No message sent, no message received."

"What the *hell* are you two—" Reese's voice came from the direction of the door.

Wonderful! Nicola felt a blush rise from her toes. She'd have sooner Reese caught her with her hair in pin curls, than to be caught like this. The only blessing was that with her back to the door, he couldn't catch the full glory of her position. Yet. She closed her eyes. *Bug off, Durand. Can't you see I'm busy? Stealing your secret, if I can.*

HE'D SPENT MORE of last night staring at his ceiling than sleeping, waiting for the friggin' phone to ring. And by this morning Reese was fighting mad. Was this how a hooked trout felt, the barb sunk deep in its flesh and pulling?

Driving to work, he'd had to muster every last ounce of his willpower to stop himself from detouring by the dock at Quincy to see if her boat might be there. And winning that fight hadn't cheered him in the least. He'd never had to fight before. Never had the least trouble keeping his women in perspective—pleasant diversions to be treated with all due gallantry, then promptly forgotten. So what was wrong with him now? Wanting was one thing, but *needing*...

I don't *need.*

He needed to shake Ms. Nicola Kent within an inch of

her earnest, single-minded, irresponsible life for doing this to him. This was her fault.

He needed D's phone number, and that Nic would give him. This morning, first thing. Then maybe he could rest. It was this...this helplessness that had him going. The realization that if Nic chose—or if D chose—it could end right here. Might have ended already.

And he'd have no recourse. No way to put his hands on her, to change her mind, win her back if for some reason she'd decided to—

But she won't. She felt it, too.

Yeah? Then where the hell is she?

Nic would tell him. No more nonsense, no more stalling. This was her fault—let her fix it. He shoved through the lab door, saw Tim bending over her outstretched form and felt his temper blast off like a moon launch. "What the *hell* are you two doing?"

Three strides and he faced Tim across her body. He wanted to clap one hand on her cocked hip and plant the other square in Tim's face, then give a good shove. *Get away from her, damn you!*

"I'm showing Nic how my pheromone affects women," Tim said, glaring back at him.

"So I see." Reese glanced down at Nic's lobster pink profile. She was steadfastly ignoring him, her eyes fixed on the computer screen—Queen Victoria in her bath, refusing to acknowledge the plumber who'd bumbled in to fix the pipes. One good smack on her tight little buns and he'd have her undivided attention. He jammed his hands into his pockets.

"Got any problem with that?" Tim's muscles were flexed, his chin stuck out farther than was wise.

There was no reason, really, why he should. Tim had shown him this experiment when they were first discussing their partnership back in friendlier times. This demonstration was what had sold him, more than all Tim's facts and figures.

He drew another breath, felt his temper drop a notch from rage toward manageable anger, groped for a rational explanation for all this resentment. A way to vent it. "I thought you were starting your experiment this morning," he growled, leaning over the table. *Notice me, dammit!*

"Just as soon as we finish this," Nic said coolly, her eyes locked on the screen. "Give me the next one, Tim."

Tim squeezed the trigger and her body jerked. Reese's eyes flicked to the screen. Flat line.

"Saline again?" she guessed.

"There you are!" A woman's voice, laughing, musical, just the hint of an exotic accent. Reese turned to find Demi Cousteau posed in the lab doorway, one arm extended along the doorjamb, head tipped, glossy black hair brushing one shoulder of her cropped jacket, amber-skinned face vivid with amusement. Breaking the pose, she danced toward him on her high, high heels and leaned to kiss his cheek. A fragrance of flowers, like the first breath of spring. "Reese. So *good* to see you again."

"Demi." He hadn't thought of her in weeks. "What are you doing here?" She belonged to New York, as rooted there in his mind as the Brooklyn bridge. Demi Cousteau, a handful at the best of times. Just what he needed right now. Still, he found himself smiling as he turned to Tim. Men always smiled around Demi.

"Tim, this is our Nose, Demi Cousteau." Also their creditor. Reese had bartered for her usually sky-high services, trading them for a ten-percent royalty for five years on their net profits on Irresistible.

At the time he'd cut the deal, it had seemed more than generous. But now, almost a year later, with Irresistible still in the red? He glanced at her sharply. *Is that why you're here?* Any man who thought Demi Cousteau was just a frivolous knockout was setting himself up for another sort of knockout entirely.

Demi's delicately hooked nose swerved unerringly toward the table and its beet red occupant. Her nostrils quivered, her jet brows shot up, she took a step back. "And this is?" she asked on a pitying note.

Reese hurriedly introduced them, then said, "Demi's a Nose—a perfumier. The best in the country."

Demi's huge brown eyes flashed, then she laughed. "In the *world,* thank you!"

Well, one of the five best in the world, according to Reese's research. But she was the youngest of those in the first rank, and the most daring. "Demi created the fragrance for Irresistible," he added for Nic's sake. "She's head of an essential-oil house in New York." A fledgling firm that fit the budget of his own start-up company, cutting corners wherever it could.

"I see," Nicola said tightly. "How interesting. Tim, can I have the next puff, please?"

Demi prowled around the table to face Nicola. "What are you *doing* to the poor girl? Torturing her?"

Tim stopped to give an explanation, which made up in length and enthusiasm for what it lacked in clarity. Men tended to talk as long as Demi deigned to listen.

Nicola tapped one foot against the table, then cleared her throat.

Reese bit back a smile and took Demi's arm. "Let's leave them to it."

"Oh, *no,* I want to watch." She swept her lashes at Tim. "Give her a puff, Tim. Please?"

Nic jumped, then let out a snarl while the line on the screen pulsed flat and true. "You plan to give me the *real* stuff in this lifetime?"

"You were expecting it that time." Tim smirked at Demi. "Everybody thinks the third time's the charm." He fiddled with his beakers. "Maybe *you'd* like to try this, Demi? See what puts the punch in your cologne?"

"All my scents have...punch, Tim, though I'd use another word." She made a comic face. "But, thank you, no. I'm not as brave as Nicola. I fear to look like a..." She paused, blinked as her own words registered and shrugged.

"And of course, since I live and die by my nose, I pamper it. Foreign utensils. Brrrr…"

"Ready, Nic?" Tim squeezed the trigger, Nic's body jerked, and the line on the monitor spiked straight up, hit the top of the screen—and zagged down again.

"*Oh!*" Demi caught hold of Reese's arm. "That was it?"

"That was it," Nicola said in a low humming voice.

Reese frowned. *Now where*— Demi tugged at his arm. "That was it, your pheromone?"

"*My* pheromone," Tim snapped. "Took me eight years, working days in a commercial lab, stealing lab time at nights, to isolate that sucker."

"Do it again," Nic said in that same far-off voice.

"Sure." Tim poured, pressed his trigger.

Bam. The line spiked. "Impressive," Nic purred, her eyes fixed on the screen.

Demi edged up against the table. "How does it feel when he gives you that? Does it feel…sexy?"

"Nooo…not exactly." Nicola removed the probe and suction cups and sat up. She felt as if someone had been brushing her hair—her skin tingling and velvety, a little warmer than normal. But that might simply be Reese's eyes upon her? "It happened so fast. It's not like the prolonged dose you'd get if your date was wearing it in his cologne. And I was looking at a computer screen, not a man, when I took the jolt. I'm not going to fall for a computer, no matter what my hypothalamus signals."

"But it works?" Demi insisted.

Nicola shrugged. "Got my attention, I'll give it that."

Demi flattened a hand on either side of Nic's feet and leaned forward. "But if it works, Nicola, why isn't it *working?* The word's out on the street—Irresistible's a *dog! No* one likes it. Why? The scent is superb—the best I ever made for men. So that can't be it. But then *why?*"

Reese caught her arm. "Demi, come to lunch."

"Not yet, Reese." She shook him off. "If the pheromone

does work, then why aren't the women mobbing the men, the way Reese promised?''

Nicola glanced at Reese. He gave her a fierce look over Demi's shoulder, the muscles in his jaw bunching. But if he wanted her to alter the truth for his sake, he could think again. "Because people aren't animals, Demi. That's why nobody's had much luck with a pheromonic perfume so far. It's not so simple.''

Demi's dark eyes gazed unblinking. "How do you mean?''

"Animals—especially the lower ones—operate on instinct. If you rub a female hamster's pheromone on a stuffed toy, a male hamster will mount it. He's working on instinct *alone.*''

"But people have instincts.''

"They do—and they also have memory. Learning. Logic.'' She drew her legs up, crossed them, set her hands on her knees. "Look. Suppose you meet a man who's been *dipped* in Tim's pheromone and your instincts are shrieking, *Grab him!*''

Demi's lips curled upward. "I throw him over my shoulder and run?''

Nicola shrugged. "Could be. But what if he happens to be married and your mother taught you to never date married men? And your sense of logic tells you that if he cheats on his wife, he'll cheat on you, too? And he's blond, and you remember that every blond man you ever dated was a creep. You see? Humans bring another layer of complexity—layers and layers—to the table.

"Sometimes those layers contradict the instincts. Sometimes they reinforce them. That's why humans are unpredictable. They just don't *have* knee-jerk responses.'' *Or if they do, no one's found them yet. Am I getting close?*

"I see,'' Demi murmured. She frowned, flashing her big eyes at Reese, a look that said, *Trouble for you, my friend!*

"But if all things are equal?'' Tim spoke up. "If all things are equal, Demi, if the guy's presentable and he's wearing Irresistible, then *shazam!* You saw Nicola's reaction—off the chart. One sniff and he's got her."

Demi widened her eyes. "*You're* wearing Irresistible, Tim." She swung to look at Reese over her shoulder—held the look so long that Nicola clamped her teeth till they ached. "As are you, Reese. So...have *you* two been...getting much lately?"

Tim's face turned a dull, mottled red. Reese laughed aloud. "Wreaking havoc wherever she goes!" He caught Demi's arm and towed her away. "I'm glad you dropped in. I have a plan to fix Irresistible. Come to lunch and I'll tell..."

Demi cast a comic look of apology and farewell over her shoulder, then followed him out the lab door.

That was a kindness to Tim, saving him from answering, Nicola thought, and she liked Reese for it. Hated him for liking Demi as much as he clearly did, though who could blame him? She drew a jagged breath, stole a glance at Tim, then turned away.

So that was how jealousy looked, was it? Like loss? Like frustration stewed with misery and anger? *Was this why you chose to work with pheromones, Tim? So the other guy wouldn't always get the girl? To make life fair again?*

But if Tim looked like that, then she... Nicola was grateful she held no mirror.

CHAPTER FIFTEEN

"So..." DEMI BROUGHT her steepled fingers, long and golden, to her mouth, drawing his eyes there. "You really think Ms. Rosepatch can fix Irresistible?"

That was just what he'd been saying all through lunch. Still, she cocked one dark brow, waiting. As if his answer was the most important message she would ever receive. As if he was the most important man she'd ever know. One of Demi's many charms was making a man feel like that. Reese smiled inwardly.

"I do. Don't underestimate her, Demi. She looks like a kid, but she's sharp as a razor."

Demi bounced her forefingers reflectively against her lips, indenting their lushness. "And you really think she can separate the—how did you say it—bonding effect from the sexual attraction? Throw out the bonding but keep the come-hither?"

She had to. If she didn't his creditors would pick his bones, this lovely bird leading the flock. He'd stopped by his office before taking Demi to lunch. There'd been a fax waiting for him, cancellation of an order from one of his biggest customers, a nationwide chain.

"Reese?" Demi reached across the table to touch his hand.

He jumped, felt an odd twinge of...discomfort at the contact, moved his hand to his wineglass. "Yes. I think she can do it."

But *would* she do it? A tricky problem, that, how to keep Nic motivated and nose-to-his-grindstone even while he yearned to hang her by her heels till she talked. At least Demi had brought his mind back to business. And wouldn't she be mortified if he told her that?

Demi narrowed her eyes at him, then smiled against her fingertips. "You know...if she can't separate the effects...,"

His stomach knotted. "But she will."

"If she *can't*, Reese, you could simply...change your aim. Don't sell Irresistible to men so they can score women. Change the perfume's name. Let me redesign the fragrance, make it more floral, and we market it to *women*. I'm sure there are millions of my sex who'd spend their last dime if they could buy a perfume that would attract a man, then keep him faithful." *The poor things,* was her unspoken comment. Demi Cousteau needed no such assistance.

And Reese Durand needed no such advice. "Maybe," he said, meaning, *Maybe when pigs fly.* Sell a perfume that put a ring in every man's nose? *Like Tim said, they'd lynch us!* The waiter glanced his way and Reese nodded. Didn't women get what men were about? *Freedom is all we have.* A man wasn't a man without his freedom. Not for long.

His own father, loving too long and too well...loving the wrong woman, a spoiled, insatiable daddy's girl...

If love hadn't chained him? If he'd walked away, instead of struggling to give her everything she demanded—a house in the suburbs, instead of one rented deck of a three-decker on the tough side of town? Clothes, car and trinkets to fit the dream house? If he hadn't taken that second job driving a cab, the late-night shift? Shot in the back of the head for eighteen lousy bucks in fares—it had been a slow night, his last night.

And if that was all he'd brought home that night, she'd have bitched, instead of getting down on her knees and thanking God for a man who tried to give her everything she asked for. Maybe if he hadn't died, she'd have broken him, anyway, in the end, with all her demands.

Or maybe he'd have wised up and walked one day. Taken me with him.

Instead, he'd had to turn and walk without his dad—*for* his dad—as soon as he was able. Looking for freedom enough for both of them. *Take a big bite out of the wide, wide world.*

And money was the way to take that bite. Money bought your freedom, and hard cash kept it. If you had enough money, no one could touch you, chain you down, *grind* you down with soul-killing drudgery. Reese started as the waiter cleared his throat, then extended the credit slip for him to sign. Across the table Demi studied him, wide-eyed.

Wise enough to sense his mood, she stayed silent till he'd parked the Porsche in front of Pherotics. "So you're sure Irresistible will make it as a men's cologne?" she asked again when he'd cut the ignition. "I really need my money, Reese."

Choosing his words, he came around to her door. Demi waited for the courtesy, whereas Nic would have beaten him to it. "That's why you came?" He took her hand to help her out.

Nylon-clad legs, pressed elegantly together from knee to ankle, swiveled out to the pavement. Demi stood up under his chin, within kissing range. She was very kissable, he remembered remotely—as if their one weekend together in New York had happened to a friend of his. That he'd heard about it secondhand.

Demi tipped up her face, gave him a slow, wicked smile. "It's not the only reason."

Movement beyond her caught his eye—Nic, sailing out the front door of his building. She turned sharply left and strode off down the street. Off to lunch, he supposed. Had she seen them and chosen not to speak? Or was she oblivious—off in her own head somewhere, mixing chemicals, devising theories? Junior Einstein hard at work.

Demi tugged on his tie. "Ahem."

Expecting a kiss. But he wasn't in a mood to fulfill expectations. *I told you back in New York we should stick to business, remember?* He rubbed a finger along her chin instead. Surprise flickered in her lovely eyes. "A bit of your lunch—spinach," he lied gravely, and dusted his hands.

"Wher*ever* did you find this tie?" She let him go, wheeled in one graceful movement and stalked into the building, dark head held high.

So MUCH FOR BONDING! Funny how it hurt so. She'd had theories that failed to hold true before. A scientist could— should—only expect that. The better you were, the more hypotheses you put forth—the more came crashing down when the facts failed to support them. But you couldn't let a failure hurt you.

All her attention was behind her, her senses craning backward although Nicola refused to look back. They'd be kissing about now, damn them. *Damn him.* So much for bonding—he was a mountain vole at heart. *Wham, bam, thank you, ma'am.* The idea of lunch suddenly turned her stomach. Her stride lengthened almost to a run. She'd walk to the river, instead.

An hour of fierce exertion cheered her somewhat. Maybe she'd jumped to conclusions too soon. You needed facts to disprove a theory, as well as to prove it. She'd turned her back, rather than gather those facts.

But maybe, just maybe, Reese had been the kissee, rather than the kisser. Demi was clearly a woman who'd kiss any man she pleased, whenever she pleased. Not that he'd been exactly fighting her off. Still... *Test your hypothesis, dope.*

But how? She was passing the copy shop. *Ah!* As inspiration hit, she spun on her heel and marched back to the shop, then up to the man at its counter. "You send faxes, don't you? If I give you one, could you send it, not now, but—" she glanced at the clock on the wall "—say, at one-thirty? Precisely?"

SHE KILLED the half hour tethering two female mountain
voles in their respective rooms of each T-maze, food and
water within easy reach. Forty virgins in waiting. "Soon,
girls." And soon for her, too, she realized, glancing at her
watch. Time to get up there.

At precisely one-twenty-five she rapped on his half-open
door. It swung inward to reveal Reese at his desk, one hand
massaging his temples, a scowl on his face as he looked
up from the paper he held. "I'm ready to start downstairs,
Reese. All I need is your pheromone—one liter at its stan-
dard concentration." Headache? she wondered, looking at
him. Or grouchy because Demi had abandoned him? The
best Nose in the world was nowhere in sight.

"About time." Reese's eyes flicked to the print of the
schooner on the wall. "Send Tim up and I'll give it to
him."

Her temper, uncertain all morning, slid upward. *You
don't trust me as far as you can throw me!* "Tim's gone
to lunch."

"When he comes back, then."

Oooh! She could see herself grabbing him by his tie, as
Demi had done. She'd swing astride him, there on his chair,
yank him nose to nose— She blinked, her heart hammering.
And then? Anger and passion weren't precise opposites, she
realized for the first time in her life.

"Yes?" Reese said dryly, but she could see the smile
lurking at the corners of his mouth.

You think I'm funny, do you? We'll see who laughs last!

"Nicola!" The door to Reese's washroom swung open,
and Demi stepped forth. Her welcoming smile faltered as
their eyes met. She sat regally on the edge of Reese's desk,
one hand braced behind her, almost between Reese's own.

She needed more proof than this? There was a washroom
down the hall, but Demi had used his. Had borrowed his
toothbrush, for all she knew.

"I'm interrupting something?" Demi crossed her legs
casually.

"No!" Nicola and Reese snapped together.

"I was just going," Nicola added. One-thirty on the dot, but who needed more proof? She spun and stalked out the door. So much for bonding!

"What was *that* about?" Demi murmured as the door closed with exquisite care, louder than any slam.

"Chess," Reese said absently, staring past her. *And check, you little fox, you!* She just kept trying. You had to admire such persistence.

At his back, the fax machine hummed, then started printing. He turned to look. More bad news? He'd had enough for one day. And he didn't like Demi watching while he struggled to read it. Still he reached, tore it free—and froze.

"I met a man on the plane this morning," Demi said behind him. "He told me about a new restaurant down on the waterfront. It sounded heavenly. I thought maybe we…" She paused when he didn't respond.

Four words, printed large and clear enough that even he had no trouble reading them. A simple question—aimed straight at his heart. He felt as if he'd been punched there, the breath stuttering in his lungs.

Do you miss me?

Like a hawk who's lost his nest! Damn her, was she taunting him? Or missing him, too, like a nest missing the sound of wings?

"He offered to take me there this evening, and I thought I'd take him up on it."

"Good," Reese muttered, his eyes locked on the page. Was there any way to trace a fax? *Devil woman, why is this so hard when it should be so easy? You and me, we belong—*

As the door slammed, he jumped and looked around. Demi was gone. He frowned—what was that about?—

shrugged, looked back at the page.

Printed by *her* hand. They'd twined fingers the last time as they came. Had held hands till they'd drifted off to sleep. *This is bonded, missing her like this? Not wanting Demi? Wanting only her?*

A black wave that felt like fear but had to be rage rose slowly within him. Was this why his father hadn't walked when he should have?

Bonded. No choice in the matter. To D, simply because that's the woman he'd been with when he sniffed the dose? A chain around his throat! He crumpled the paper and threw it at his basket. Snarled when it missed. *Damn* her! And most of all, damn Ms. Nicola Kent, mad chemist and meddler in men's lives. Bonded. Wouldn't she laugh if she knew!

He looked up savagely as a jaunty knock sounded. The door pushed open and Peter Hadley beamed at him. "Who *was* that exquisite woman I passed in the hall? Twelve on a scale of ten!"

"I'm busy, Hadley." Looking for a hacksaw. Chains could be cut.

"Oh…well, this will only take a few minutes. I have a proposition to make, Reese. Something that should benefit us both."

Like your last deal? To keep his hands off Hadley's lapels—or maybe his throat—Reese put his desk between them. "Two minutes. Talk."

"ONE LITER." Tim held up a bottle filled with clear liquid for her inspection. Pherotics's pheromone, at last.

"Thanks." Nicola nodded at her workbench. "Put it there, please."

"Sorry, but I have to do the mixing myself." Tim didn't look sorry at all.

On Reese's orders, Nicola realized bitterly, though Tim would never admit that. Reese was determined to keep the pure substance out of her hands. "Fine. I'll need one liter of fifty-percent solution and one of twenty-five percent your stuff to seventy-five mine." Not that this whole exercise mattered anymore if Reese was no longer bonded.

Still matters, she argued with herself. He'd stayed steadfastly bonded for fourteen days, with none of the gradual tapering off of desire her other subjects had shown. She'd hoped for a permanent effect, but even a ten-percent gain in the bonding period was a significant advance. *So press on regardless. Get what you came for, then run.*

But how, with Reese countering her every move?

While Tim measured and stirred, she went down the line of mazes, lifting each clear plastic lid to tuck a ball of cotton under each maiden vole's harness at the withers. "So where do you keep that stuff if it's not stored down here? Or does Reese mix it up to order in his bathroom sink?"

"Huh!" Tim snorted at the idea of Reese mixing anything. "I distilled this batch months ago. We keep it in the company safe."

And the company safe would be under Reese's thumb, since alpha males liked control. She made the leap—the off-kilter picture that first time she'd entered his office. "The one on Reese's wall? Behind the sailboat?"

"That one." Tim sniggered and shook his head.

"What's so funny?" She tucked another ball of cotton under another harness. The vole twitched her ears, then went back to her sunflower seeds.

"He can't remember the combination to his own safe. He's hopelessly dyslexic, y'know. I'd lay my Harley to your roller skates he's never read a book cover to cover in his life. But for some reason numbers give him even more trouble than letters. He jumbles 'em every time."

You think that's funny? Looks to me like he's gone twice as far as you have, little man, with half as much. "So how does he get into his safe? Call you?"

"When I'm around, yeah. He makes some excuse and

calls me." Tim laughed again. "But I caught him the other day with a card he'd made out. A picture of the dial, with the combination numbers marked in. He holds that up next to the real dial, makes sure everything looks just the same, scowls like his head's in a vise, holds his breath, then—*hey, presto*—he cracks the safe."

Good for him. And where did Reese keep this card? In his desk? Her heart quickened. Find that and she was home free. With a pure example of the pheromone, she could find someone with the equipment to analyze it.

Or better yet, did Reese keep a copy of the pheromone's *formula* in his safe? As its inventor, Tim would know it by heart. But even if he couldn't read it, Reese would want a copy. As backup should something ever happen to his partner. *Ten minutes to scribble that down and I could be out of here. Blow you a kiss and goodbye.* The thought didn't cheer her as it once would have done.

"Done," said Tim behind her.

"Great. And thanks, Tim."

"Not so fast. I'm not supposed to... Uh, I don't like to take my eyes off this stuff. It's top secret. Industrial spies are—"

"Everywhere," Nicola agreed grimly, though she hadn't seen one yet, and suppressed a sigh. So Reese had instructed Tim to make sure she didn't get her hands on a drop, mixed or pure. No doubt he'd take the leftovers with him when he went.

Okay, so there's more than one way to skin a cat. "Fine. Then you can help me. If you look at the tag in front of each maze, you'll see which female gets the combined dose and which gets the placebo." She lifted the first tag. "See? Vole one-A gets the real stuff. So if you'll use this dropper and squirt exactly one cc on her ball of cotton, I'll handle the saline for vole one-B..."

"And then?" Tim asked, following her down the line of mazes.

"Then the gentlemen come calling."

REESE SWERVED his bike around an in-line skater and nipped back into his own lane, just missing two oncoming joggers. The jogging path along the Charles River was crowded this morning. He glanced at his watch. Time to head back to Pherotics.

He'd spent another half-waking night last night trying to drive her from his dreams. Three nights now since he'd held her. If D hadn't called by now, she wouldn't be calling. The fax was just a tease. *She* was a tease. *Forget her. Right. Tell the trout to forget its hook.*

Up with the sun, he'd driven in to work—might as well slog through some paperwork before the others arrived. But after an hour of that he'd given up and gone for a spin on the bike he kept in a first-floor utility closet.

A good move. The exercise had cleared his head at last. He knew now what he had to do. How to set himself free. *Fight fire with fire.* Demi Cousteau—now there was fire enough to cauterize any wound....

She'd told him yesterday she'd be in Boston for a few weeks. One of her many admirers had loaned her his condo on the waterfront while he was out of the country. No doubt she'd drop by the office at some point today. Or if she didn't he'd track her down, invite her out tonight.

And then? Reese felt no quickening of his pulse, nothing but grim resolve, unswerving purpose—and a twinge of guilt. He shoved it from his mind. Demi had come hunting *him*, after all. And like him, she knew how to play while guarding her heart. A passionate little fling would suit them both. Hurt no one. Set him free. *Goodbye, D.*

So fill the void with something else. Business. *Hadley.* He snorted, remembering, as he cut away from the bike path and off through a back street. Hadley's proposition. The professor had figured out how tight working capital was growing at Pherotics. *Talked to Tim?* Hadley had offered to give back his yearly consulting fee—one of the sweeteners with which Reese had purchased the professor's cooperation in bagging Nic.

In return for which, Hadley would take company stock—twenty percent of Pherotics, he'd suggested.

Reese turned another panting breath into a snort. *Right!* It was bad enough being partnered with Tim. But add Professor Sleaze to the mix? *When they play ice hockey in hell!* He'd sooner pay Hadley his yearly blood money till the company rolled tits-up, *not* that it was going to.

And he'd told the professor so—not as tactfully as he might have, given his mood yesterday. Hadley had stormed off, somewhat bruised in his dignity. *Not the only place I'd like to bruise him.* He was a nuisance, but not an amusing if maddening one like Nic. More like a wad of gum you'd stepped in.

The only encouraging thing about the whole transaction was that Hadley had wanted Pherotics stock. *So he thinks Nic has a chance of pulling this off. He sees the potential, even if Nic can't or won't.*

That was a good thought—the thought he'd hold through this day. *Get your mind back on business. Forget about D. Right.*

IT WAS HARDER than she'd foreseen, searching his office. There was no reason to feel guilt, Nicola kept reminding herself as she pulled out each drawer in his desk and examined its contents. Reese was the one who'd started their feud—bribing Hadley, hijacking her research, offering her the Hobson's choice of inventing a new dissertation from scratch or working for him in Boston. He'd stolen her work to help himself; now she'd help herself to his. *And serve you right, Mr. Mountain Vole Heart.*

Well, she'd help herself if she could find the combination to his safe.

Not in his desk, or even taped to the undersides of the drawers, she discovered the hard way. Nicola stole a glance at her watch. Seven-fifteen. She'd better scram soon. She could imagine Reese's face if he caught her here. With a grimace she looked around the room. In the bookcases? She started on the top shelf, left to right.

Three minutes of searching turned up zip. *Where else?* Taped to the back of one of the sales charts or design sketches tacked to the wall?

No.

Taped to the bottom of the wastebasket? She lifted it— no—set it down, stepped back to survey the room. *Three minutes left, not a second more.* She could *feel* him approaching, her heart thumping louder and louder, her nerves stretching like rubber bands. *Has to be here. Where else could it be?*

His washroom? The back of her neck crawled as she stepped through that door. At least in the outer office she might hear him coming in time. She left the door open and dashed for the sink. Above it, a medicine cabinet. Filled with aspirin, ointment, Band-Aids, deodorant—first-aid kit for a jock. Two bottles of Irresistible cologne.

Nicola frowned. *Have you been getting much lately?* All night she'd wondered, lying there in her berth, hugging his pillow. Was he lying with Demi? Getting much more than she could ever give him? Schoolgirl. Twit. No one he'd ever noticed by daylight. *Shuddup! Got to get out of here. Find the stuff and run.*

The card wasn't in the shower, of course. Her fingers flew over the stainless-steel apparatus bolted to the wall beside it, one of those on-demand propane water heaters. Nowhere she could see to hide a card.

Scratch the bathroom and scratch the search. Get out of here before he busts you! Bolting for the door, Nicola noticed the clothes hanging behind it.

A spare set of business togs? She patted one trouser pocket, felt something. Drew forth a folded paper, its surface crinkled as if it had been wadded, then smoothed flat again. She unfolded it and read.

Do you miss me?

Do I? All last night, sitting up in my berth to peek through the porthole, stare at the moon—it's so beautiful, nearly full now. Wondering where you were. If you were seeing it, too.

Somewhere a door squeaked, and Nicola sucked in her breath. The door to the stairwell, which always squeaked! *And the only one besides her who used it...* She pushed the bathroom door back to the position she'd found it, slid between it and the wall as Reese walked into his office.

Oh God, oh God, oh God— Don't let him come in here! She'd stand here all day on tiptoe if she had to, to avoid the oncoming humiliation.

Something thumped to the carpet in his office. Sounded like tennis shoes being tossed aside.

Holding the note over her head, she folded it as best she could, then slipped it into his pants pocket and drew a shallow sigh of relief. Marginally better. As her hand withdrew, it brushed something hard in another pocket. She traced the shape through the fabric—squarish, hard but resilient. *A wallet.* Her heart stopped.

This wasn't a spare change of clothes. *These were his clothes for today.* He'd been out exercising. Which meant, any second now—

Move or die! Move or die! Survival instincts kicking into high gear, she slithered sideways along the wall on tiptoe, snatched a paper cup from the dispenser above the sink. Fill it? No, he'd hear. *Fake it.* Jamming one shaking hand into her pocket, she strolled casually out the door, bringing the cup to her lips as she stepped into view...

And found herself staring at a magnificently masculine torso. Reese, pulling his T-shirt over his head.

She stood, drop-mouthed, eyes snagged on ridges of sweat-sleekened muscle—shapes she'd memorized in the dark.

What am I doing? Now's my chance! She spun on tiptoe, took three giant strides toward safety—

"Nic?"

"Ummm..." Nailed by a word, she sank flat-footed. Glanced over her shoulder. Reese stood scowling, his T-shirt wadded in one hand.

"Needed a drink of water." She held up her cup. "Thanks!" She shot into the hall, hitting herself in the forehead with the paper cup as she went. *Brilliant, Nicola, just brilliant! Excuse of the century!*

Behind her he called from the door. "Did you want something?"

"No-no. Not really. I was just passing by." *Oooh, that's brilliant, too!* She stiff-armed the stairwell door and clattered down the stairs. *Damn, damn, damn. Damn!*—one curse for each step.

Reese found himself smiling for the first time that day. Weird kid. *What was that about?* She'd never seen a half-naked man before?

Or—his eyes scanned the room—*looking for the formula, were you, you fox?* His eyes flicked to the schooner print.

It hung perfectly level. He always tipped the right side half an inch higher. *Ah.* So she'd found the safe. Not that it'd do her much good. Unless...

He headed for the bathroom, fished his wallet from his trousers. Checked the card inside. *Good.* She'd missed it. So, no harm done.

This time. But from now on, that card would live in his pocket. Frowning thoughtfully, he wandered to the water heater and switched it on. He turned as the phone rang. Early for business. Unless it was one of the London accounts?

Or Demi proposing a lunchtime rendezvous? He sighed at the thought, tossed his sweaty T-shirt into the sink and headed out the door, closing it behind him. The phone rang for the third time. "Okay, o—"

A cannon boomed in the bathroom—or maybe God stamped.

Time slowed as it always did in a crisis. Reese had all the time in the ending world to spin and watch something silver punch its head through the door. As he dropped and rolled to one side, the door folded leisurely outward—then blew apart.

CHAPTER SIXTEEN

SPLINTERS AND SHRAPNEL riddled the shelves and the far wall. The glass on the schooner print shattered. Metal ricocheted around the room. Arms wrapped around his head, deafened by the concussion, Reese lay catching his breath while time sped up to normal. The propane heater...a gas leak...but how?

And who cared? He was alive. And bleeding. He sat up slowly, examined his upper arm as it started to hurt. A four-inch splinter of wood from the door sticking into it. He gritted his teeth and pulled it out.

He looked up to find his secretary, Kay, standing in the doorway, her hands clapped to her mouth. If she was making a sound, he couldn't hear it. "See if anything's burning in there," he said, since his legs were shaking too much for him to stand. She looked at him wildly and he wondered if he'd yelled the words. Or maybe whispered them. He had no way of judging, with his ears ringing this way. Damn, if his ears...

Someone shoved Kay aside—Nic. Her face went green-white when she saw him. She landed beside him on her knees, touched his arm, then his forehead with one fingertip.

Cool. He closed his eyes and leaned against her touch for a second, felt immensely better. Nic could cope. "Nic, check the bathroom. See if there's a fire."

She nodded and went, stood in the shattered doorway, staring. Her arms crept up till she hugged herself and shuddered. She turned, met his eyes, shook her head.

"Oh, my God, *Reese!*" Demi Cousteau swooped down upon him—where had she come from? Blocking his view of Nic, she ran her hands across his chest, cupped his face. "Oh, Reese! You're all *right?*"

He could hear her. He let out a long breath of relief. For a minute there, he'd feared—

She kissed him square on the mouth. He returned the kiss automatically, then set her aside. "I'm fine, Demi. Just a gas leak. Calm down."

"But you could have been killed!"

"Yeah." He shoved himself to his feet, clenching his teeth at the pain and Demi's unwelcome assistance. He stood swaying, then propped himself against his desk to assess the damage.

Bathroom totaled, office a mess, a trip to emergency for him. He'd need stitches to close this bleeder. Then home, he realized, since his office clothes lay in shreds around the room. So much for *this* morning. "Shit."

HE COULD HAVE BEEN KILLED. Seeing again that pipe from the water heater rammed halfway through the shattered door, Nicola swallowed hard against her nausea. If Reese hadn't stepped out of the bathroom when he had… *Don't think about it.* She couldn't stop. *Reese…*

She'd wanted desperately to hold him. Simply to hug him close and feel his heart beating steadily against her. Instead, she'd had to watch Demi kiss him, fuss over him, whisk him off to emergency while she and Tim stayed to clean up the mess. *I could hate her if I put my mind to it.*

Not fair. She couldn't blame Demi for being charming and beautiful. And Demi had seen him first. Not that that would have made a bit of difference. First claim or last, Demi was a winner, while she…she was simply Nicola.

Hotshot scientist, she reminded herself.

Second-rate woman? jeered an inner voice.

Am I? She wondered. That had never been an issue before. Until now there had never been a man who had made her remember her femininity, much less like it.

She didn't like it now. If this was what it was to be a woman, longing for a man, she hated it.

She needed to get out of here. Find satisfaction in her own way, the way she always had.

Sure. All you need is his formula. The combination to his safe. It was in his wallet, she was convinced. *Should have guessed that from the start.* She didn't carry much in her own wallet for fear of muggers or pickpockets. But Reese, Mr. Alpha Male himself, would have no such qualms.

She looked up as the lab door opened and Demi strolled in. "How is he?" Nicola asked before she could stop herself.

"Patched and surly. God help the plumber who installed that heater when Reese gets his hands on him." Demi wandered over to stare down at the mazes, each with their trio of voles.

"*Where* is he?"

"He insisted on driving himself home for a change of clothes. Wouldn't let me—" She stopped. "These are adorable! Gerbils?"

"Mountain voles."

Demi walked the line of T-mazes, her eyes downcast. "It's always two cuddling, one lonesome. Why is that?"

Because life's a bitch and then you— Nic shrugged. "In each case, the male had to choose."

"Really? Couldn't he run back and forth? Most *guys* I know…"

They shared a rueful grin. "If he was a normal mountain vole, that's just what he'd do," Nicola agreed. "Run himself blissfully ragged. But in this case—" she read the tag fastened to the seventh maze in line "—when number seven checked out female seven-B, he sniffed that bit of cotton on her back and inhaled a dose of the Pherotics pheromone mixed fifty-fifty with my synthetic hormone. He hasn't left her side since. He's acting like a monogamous prairie vole. Bonded.''

"So it *works*..." Demi hung over the maze as if she gazed at a display of crown jewels, not two furry rodents crouched shoulder to shoulder.

"Yes." It had worked every time, at both concentrations. Twenty males had chosen their predicted partner. Unlike her human trial, where only half the men had chosen correctly. "For a while."

"How long?"

Nicola shrugged again. "With men, the longest bonding effect lasted...fourteen days." *Till you came along.* "This is my first trial of this combined dose in voles. I've no idea."

Mountain vole seven stopped nibbling. Facing his partner, he drew small, dextrous hands through her fur, ruffling it backward. The two animals touched noses. "How will she feel," Demi murmured, "when he falls out of love with her?"

How would it feel to spend the rest of a wintry lifetime listening for the sound of leaves? "I wouldn't know, Demi."

Or in the end, maybe she would.

BY THE END of the day, Nicola still hadn't seen Reese. He was upstairs, Tim informed her, but not in a pretty mood. She could imagine. No doubt he was occupied, putting his office back to rights.

At five she gave up waiting and headed upstairs. A progress report on the voles was her excuse. In reality, she simply needed to see him. The memory of his impaled door still haunted her. If she wanted to sleep tonight, she had to replace that horror with his unharmed face, scowling or otherwise.

But Reese was gone. "You just missed him." Kay pulled her purse from a desk drawer. "He left ten minutes ago."

With Demi Cousteau? Without her? Nicola could think

of no way to ask. "Was he feeling all right?" That was safe.

Kay smirked. "Mr. Bombproof? He had me make dinner reservations at the Harborside Hyatt—for two. What d'*you* think?"

Ignoring her wink, Nicola shrugged and turned away. *I think it's a very short way from a table overlooking the harbor to the honeymoon suite upstairs.* He'd be in for an expensive evening. But then, Demi looked as if she expected the very best.

A BEAUTIFUL WOMAN by his side, her arm bumping confidingly against his own. Stretched out below them, beyond the veranda railing, Boston Harbor, the setting sun turning it to a cauldron of copper and quicksilver. He'd lived when he might have died. Any sane man would be celebrating life to the fullest tonight. *And if I had D...*

Reese stamped on that thought, turned to Demi and quirked an eyebrow.

"Beautiful," she murmured, staring out at the view, seemingly unconscious of his inspection. "Absolutely beautiful!"

As was she, he told himself. But nothing stirred within. You could look at the Taj Mahal and still be...homesick. He ground his heel on the word. *What's wrong with me?*

Nothing that a laughing whisper wouldn't cure.

Demi nudged him, and he smelled the fragrance in her hair. Something rich and alluring, reminding him of Casbahs and palm trees, dark eyes and drifting veils.

He needed something simpler, fresher...the scent of honey and hay, tiny flowers called alyssum. You buried your face in them on a summer's day, and the world was...right. *This isn't working.*

He clenched his teeth. *Give it time.* It had to work. He wanted his freedom back. No chains to bind him.

Demi's hand smoothed along the brass railing, then casually, as if by accident, touched his. *This isn't working.*

He eased out a sigh, slowly against the sea breeze, so she wouldn't hear.

And what if I *don't work?* His stomach lurched with the thought, a new one for him. *Not possible,* he told himself immediately. No way in hell not. *Nic, if you've done that to me, I'll...*

Demi turned her gaze on him. Held the look, her eyes wide. *Well?* she was asking. Challenging.

Sure he could perform—with Demi how could a man not? But was that the point—to give a performance? Fake what he felt? He'd never done that before. Always before he'd been sincere, if only sincerely in lust. But now, what he was feeling...

He didn't know *what* he felt—yearning, fear, anger, dismay? He'd never felt *confused* before. Had always known his path, however steep and rough. But now he stood in the dark, waiting for a whisper to guide him...*where?*

Damn you, D! He broke free of Demi's gaze, turned to the sea again. *Damn you, are you out there somewhere? Floating free on your little boat, wind in your hair, laughing at me? Devil woman, I won't stand for this!*

"Reese?" Demi rubbed her nose back and forth against his shoulder.

The best nose in the whole wide world, he reminded himself, dredging up a smile from somewhere. *But not for me.* This wasn't the way to win his freedom.

So find another way. He turned to meet her puzzled, lovely eyes. "I think I'm fading, Dem. It's been a helluva day. Would you mind if we cut it short?"

RESTLESS AS SHE WAS, she couldn't go to her boat, pace the planks where they'd loved in the dark. She needed to *move* tonight, and pacing wouldn't do it. Neither would chugging aimlessly around the harbor at six knots, trying to keep her eyes off the Hyatt.

No, she needed speed if she hoped to outrun her thoughts. Nicola went to her car and drove.

She headed west, leaving the coast to Reese and Demi. Reached Worcester before dark then turned north, found her way by dusk to the lofty flanks of Mount Wachusett. From there she could see the loom of Boston's lights. *Reese.* Lost somewhere amidst all that glitter. *What did you expect? One sniff of your magic potion, and he and you...* It was too laughable for words. *Get real, girl!*

Get back to the real world. Where she had a boat waiting for her, books to read by lamplight...an intriguing biochemical problem yet to solve...the ambition to show them all. That should be enough for any sensible woman.

But who, given the choice, would be sensible?

And who said you had a choice? She sighed and turned her car for home. Avoiding highways, she cut across country, taking the winding backroads past hills, forest, fields, sleepy New England towns. It was familiar territory. She'd spent her teen years west of Boston, her mother commuting by train into the city to her job at an ad agency. Working hard to support two daughters at home. Nicola's father had sent checks for Moo, but that was all he could or would do. Nicola's mother had shouldered the rest. By herself, standing on her own two feet.

As I'll do. Ten miles from the edge of Boston, the road led her past a turnoff she'd known as a kid. Nicola smiled. A granite quarry lay down that rutted trail. Other girls had gone there with their beaux to neck and skinny-dip. Nicola had spent one whole summer observing salamanders there, studying their mating habits. *If I'd studied boys, instead, like the other girls...?*

The moon peeked over a hill, full and pumpkin gold. *Are you seeing it, too, Reese?* Or was he much too busy, with eyes only for Demi?

Her route took her through Stow, then the western edge of Concord. Reese lived somewhere hereabouts. Hadley had mentioned it a few days before. Not that he'd be home tonight. On impulse, she swung into a gas station.

When she pulled back onto the road minutes later, Nicola

turned south instead of east. One glance in a phone book, a question to the attendant and she knew the way. *This is stupid, stupid, stupid. Pathetic!* Driving past his house like a moony teenager. Like a lovelorn vole, scouting her beloved's burrow.

Just curious, that's all. What kind of house does an alpha male choose? This detour was a simple scientific inquiry, that was all.

The road swooped around a bend, bringing a low hill into view, meadow to the top. With something modern and low-slung on its crest, open to the stars. She laughed in spite of herself. *I knew it—top of the hill! Master of all he—* She saw the Porsche parked out in front, and her foot lifted off the gas.

So he brought her home. Somehow she'd thought he wouldn't. Maybe had blocked out that possibility, with its implications of intimacy, a long-standing affair.

So now you know. Satisfied? Feeling better? She stamped savagely on the gas and drove on.

She pressed on as far as a strip mall a few miles down the road, but at the sight of a phone booth along the end wall... *You can't be that stupid!* She swerved in and parked. Got out of the car. *What are you going to do, dope, if he answers? Ask him if Demi's there? Listen for her moaning in the background?*

Nicola punched out the number she'd memorized days before. *I just want to hear his voice—okay?*

Reese answered on the first ring. "Hello!"

Ohhh... it's you. Eyes glazing with tears, she smiled up at the moon. *Hello!* And now what? Just to hear his voice was enough. She hadn't thought beyond that.

"D, that's you, isn't it?"

Yes, it's me. But if she spoke right now, her voice would be choked with silly tears. *You're alone, aren't you?* Funny how she could tell—something in his voice.

"Are you shy, D, or just slow? Or more and more I'm wondering, are you the kind of woman who likes to—"

"Hello!" she whispered, laughing. *Oh, hello, you!*

They breathed together for an endless moment, then, "Where the *hell* have you been?" His voice was rough, almost angry.

As far as the moon. Near enough to touch you. "Around."

"I want my arms around *you*. Want you...around me."

A rush of heat swept up her thighs. *I want that, too!*

"D? What do *you* want?"

I want you. But how could she have him? She turned her face to the moon. So bright tonight. One look at her face by this light and the spell would be broken. No princess, only Nic.

"Devil woman?"

She laughed aloud. *You think* I'm *a devil, the way you've made me feel, you with your Demi? But was I wrong? Are you still bonded? To me?* "Did you miss me?" *How much, on a scale of one to ten?*

"Not for a minute."

"Oh..." Her smile wavered.

"I missed you—like the sun misses the moon. And you, did you..."

Did I do anything but *miss you? The moon doesn't shine without the sun.* "Want to come out and play?" she whispered.

His breath hissed. "Tell me where!"

Her eyes lit on the drugstore at the far end of the strip mall. Ten minutes to shop, ten miles back down the road... "Meet me in an hour. Go north on route ten..."

THE MOON WAS BRIGHT enough to read by. *This time you can't help it, girl. I'll see you.* She had to know that.

So this was surrender. *And about time!* His blood surged with the thought, fast as the speeding car. He hadn't waited her mandated hour. From now on, he wasn't waiting. He was calling the shots. *Tonight's my turn to be on top.* In every way. His foot settled on the gas, and the car snarled around a bend.

When he reached her described turnoff from a two-lane country road, his mood changed to match his speed. The Porsche swung onto a dirt track, branches above and to the sides brushing the paint. Reese gritted his teeth and bumped along in first gear, headlights bouncing over tree trunks, thickets. The moon hardly pierced these woods. Didn't matter. This time he'd brought matches. He'd light a torch of deadwood if he had to, to see her face.

His torch was burning already. His stomach filled with moths to swarm around the flames. *So I see her. But what if she's...ugly?*

An ugly thought. He wasn't the world's prettiest face himself. Still, it mattered. In his mind's eye, she was...magic—silk, fire, fragrance, softness in his arms, an odd stirring around the heart. *But if her looks don't match that—and how could they?—how do I feel then?*

Right now he felt frightened, then furious as a branch clattered down the Porsche's side. *Devil woman, why d'you make it so hard? We could be loving each other in my king-size bed. Or on my living-room floor if you have to rough it. But this? I should have brought a machete!* As another branch scraped the car, he groaned, then laughed aloud—and gave up on the Porsche's paint job. *No pain, no gain.* The car burst into a small clearing, and the moon broke free of the trees, turned it to whitened sand, an arena for moon dancing.

With no car waiting. Reese cut the engine, and silence swooped down upon him. He stepped from the car to meet it. His shadow leaped to crouch at his feet. He checked his watch without numbers; its hands were clearly visible. Twenty minutes to go. Twenty years, it felt like. He prowled the clearing.

The resiny scent of pines. Hardwood leaves overhead, filtering the moonlight along the edges of the space. Cricket song. Lots of car tracks. This would be a parking place for lovers. Local knowledge, hidden as it was. *So you've used it before, babe.* He was instantly jealous. Wanted to reach into her past and grab his rival—most likely some spot-faced teenager—by the collar and run him right out of her life, past and present.

And future? *Forget the future. This is about now. Tonight.*

Reese stopped when he found the path. The moon was bright enough to show him three branches on the ground, laid out to form an arrow aimed down that track.

The tip of the arrow pointed to a letter, "D," traced in the sand. Below the shaft of the marker, she'd scratched a number. "23."

Me to you, he translated. *Flying straight to the heart of you!* He started down the trail, headed for home.

CHAPTER SEVENTEEN

A HUNDRED YARDS IN, the path brought him to an outcrop of boulders, white in the moonlight. He stepped up on a rock—and his breath snagged in his throat. He teetered above a well of blackness—this was cliff's edge. An old quarry, its rim overhung by tall trees. If he'd taken one step farther? *Might have warned me, girl!*

Something broke the dark waters below—an arm carving a graceful arc. Some pattern of leaf shadows flowed over her face—he couldn't see her clearly.

Soon mended. The path followed the lip of the quarry, descending to the bit of beach that edged its low side. Heart hammering, Reese started down. *Coming to get you, girl.*

Out on the bright sand, a small square of darkness, was a pile of folded clothes—hers. Unbuttoning his shirt, he scanned the water. The pool was maybe sixty feet in diameter, moonstruck in the middle, shadowed around the margins. Something rolled like an otter below the cliffs. He dropped his shirt, stripped off his pants, stepped free of his shorts.

No way to use matches out there. Didn't matter. Moonlight would reveal every freckle. "D!" The water was cool, not frigid, his blood fired enough to overcome the chill. She swirled to face him, then waited, treading water, long hair tenting her shoulders, face hooded in shadow.

Reese launched himself smoothly toward her, his hands burning for the touch of her, his eyes hungry. *To see you at last.* How could he have doubted? Just the lift of her head on that graceful neck—this was beauty, waiting for him. She was beautiful.

And elusive as ever. She laughed her low, liquid sound and dived, pointed toes arrowing into the black. Ripples spreading in silvered circles.

He stopped, treading water, heart thumping. *Coming to meet me? Or gone again?*

For a nasty second he imagined her gone forever, swallowed by the depths. His breath stuttered, then caught again. *No way. Doesn't end like that tonight! Ends with me having her. Knowing her. No more of this maddening come and go.*

Guessing her direction, he swam to meet her. She surfaced only feet away, drew a laughing breath as she tossed back her hair—then yelped as his arms encircled her and they sank.

Lips sought and found lips. They molded their bodies together—fire within, ice without—as they drifted down, down into colder water. She wriggled and he let her go. They broke the surface together, gasping.

He reached for her but she shot away, headed for the cliffs, feet churning water to silver. He laughed and pursued, caught her in a dozen strokes, snared a slender ankle. She twisted around with a wordless cry, half fear, half pleasure, as his feet found bottom.

He stood chest high in the water and scooped her up, all long limbs and slippery warmth. "Gotcha!"

"Oh, you think?" She wrapped her arms around his neck and hid her face against his throat, laughing against him.

"Babe, I know." And she was shy, he realized all over again. Was that why she always ran? Shy, hiding her face from him like this, yet also—he shuddered as she nipped his ear—yet also wanton, bless the gods. Carrying her, he waded shoreward. She'd led him to a tiny island, he saw now, a long fallen boulder tucked below the cliffs.

Standing on soft sand, he set her down, her face still hidden against him. "Come out from under there." Far

above, the trees leaned over, their leaves shattering moonlight to a million shards of ebony and jagged silver. Still,
it was enough to see. He caught her chin. "Look at me."

Slowly...reluctantly, her face came up—then lifted defiantly. The light touched it—and he gasped.

Swirls of dark stripes where a face should have been. He
held a tiger woman! Or was it only the leaf shadows? No,
too dark. *God help me, I've fallen for the tattooed lady!*
"What the *hell?*" He touched a spot on her nose. It
smeared, and he laughed aloud. Some kind of makeup? The
wench was wearing camouflage—nothing but. "You—"

Her teeth caught the light as she laughed up at him.
"Like it?"

Like it that she'd fooled him again? He wanted to shake
her till she cried for mercy. He caught her waist, lifted her
high and whirled her around and around and around, growling with exasperation as she giggled. *"No!"*

Yes, lady, oh, yes! Frustrated as he was, he had to admit
the weirdness was a turn-on. Making love with a moon
tiger? Reese brought his face to her painted breasts, and
beyond the scent of water, smelled honey. *He was home.*
He brought her down slowly, sliding her seal-slick length
down his body till her toes touched the sand. Then he
kissed her, hot, deep, slow, bending her backward over his
arm. Crazy or sane, spotted or striped, she was...the One.

HIS SANITY RETURNED slowly, sometime much later.
"Sorry, I..." She lifted her head lazily to meet him, her
kiss sipping the words from his mouth. He'd blacked out
entirely there at the end, as if she'd called his soul out of
him to dance in the moonlight. *And if I never came back?*
He shuddered at the thought.

Her hands smoothed down to his buttocks to hold him
in place, and he shuddered again with pleasure. Pressed
himself deeper. *Witch! Darlin'...*

Dark lady. He could barely see her face; his own head
blocked the fall of shifty light. *I swore I'd be on top this*

time, and here I am. He thumbed her cheek, smearing another stripe.

She murmured and turned her face to his cupping hand. Kissed his palm and fell asleep in the act, her lips relaxing to a smile. *Or am I on top?* he wondered, staring down at her. Can a man hold power over what he doesn't know? He wouldn't know her under those stripes if he passed her on the street tomorrow, not unless he put his nose to her skin.

And he couldn't go sniffing every woman in Boston.

You aren't giving me anything, babe. Lying limp in his arms, pinned to the sand, she hadn't surrendered at all. She still held her essence apart. *Is this all a game to you? You have me on your chain—bonded—while you stay whole and free? Come and go as you please? Is that your plan?*

Well, think again, babe. He kissed her cheek, her ear. She sighed like a child in her sleep. *By devil or angel, I won't be owned. Bound by my nose to any woman? Not me, babe.*

But he was. He wasn't any freer now than he'd been a day ago, aching for her. For just a heartbeat, when she'd cried aloud and arched up against him, her nails striping his back, for that one moment he'd owned her. But not now. She could be anywhere, with any man, smiling in her sleep.

You could be married for all I know. I could be your man on the side. Something to visit at your whim. Nothing more.

No way. Think again, babe. Chains were made to be broken. How to snap this one?

Such a fragile chain, you'd think. Her profile was delicate, he could make out that much. And oddly familiar. But every bit of her touched familiar, and had from the start. He lifted a strand of her hair, held it out to a ray of moonlight. Lighter than black, he was fairly sure. Darker than blond. Brown, he guessed, like maybe a million women in Boston.

Her body was also fragile—swan neck, wide but slender shoulders, boyish hips, endless legs. Young Lauren Bacall in Key Largo, mischief in her eyes, dancing across the floor to meet Bogie? *If you want me, all you have to do is…whistle.*

One whistle from her and he had come running. Panting. Bonded. *Like a dog on a chain.*

Break the damned chain, but how? Trying to forget her sure hadn't worked. Demi had been no solution.

She sighed, shifted, and his attention snapped back to her. *Too heavy for her.* He rolled to his side carefully, taking her with him. She didn't awaken. Simply pressed her forehead to his chest and snuggled deeper into his arms. He smiled and stroked her, but the feeling that rushed through him was *terrifying.* So small and fragile, his to hold and protect. If another man had dared look at her right now, he'd have killed him.

Was this how they got to you? Nic had told him once that bonded voles would fight to the death to defend their mates. *Blast you, Nic, wherever you are! I've held more women than I can count. Why this one?*

No reason but Nic's friggin' chemistry…bonded.

Break the chain, but how, if Demi couldn't do it?

She sighed again, pressed closer; her breasts burned his chest. He let out a harsh breath as he stiffened.

The only way out is through. He brushed his lips along her velvety temple. That was the solution, had to be. If he couldn't forget her, then he shouldn't try.

He should have her. Have her till he was sated. Have her to oblivion. Have her till he couldn't bear the thought of her. He'd cured himself of tequila in one night-long binge at fourteen, hadn't touched a drop since. The taste of it still made him sick. *How long till I'm cured of you, babe?*

Five times? Fifty? A day, a week, a month? He had no way of knowing, but he knew the magic number was out there waiting to be reached.

So, sooner begun, sooner done. He lowered her till she

lay back in the sand. So fragile. Maybe he should let her sleep awhile longer? He hardened his heart. Drew one lingering fingertip from her navel up her silky middle, spiraled it slowly, slowly up her breast to dance on the tip, king of the hill.

She sighed in her sleep, arched her back in a breathtaking stretch, her body following his touch, then opened her eyes. Smiled up at him, a drowsy moon-tiger smile.

Now, Reese decided, his own smile fading to intentness. And no cure could be sweeter. His fingers traced their way southward, southward till she purred. *Coming to get you, babe.*

Get you out of my life.

WHEN SHE AWOKE AGAIN, Nicola faced upward, her head pillowed on the hard swell of Reese's arm. For a long while she simply lay, her body rocking deep within, the way the waves ruled you long after you'd left the ocean. She arched her neck, caught her breath and smiled in sudden, vivid triumph, remembering. *Yes!* She'd given, as well as taken last night, hadn't she?

She shifted her head cautiously to see him. Did he look as different as she felt?

Reese's face was turned her way, his lashes lying thick and still on his cheeks. All his daytime hardness had been washed away by their loving. He might have been fifteen but for the bristles.

Bristles... She could see him, *really* see him. Her heart lurched. That light beyond the trees, she'd thought it was the moon going down. But that was east. The sun was coming, driving all enchantment before it. *Omigod!* She bolted upright. Reese growled a protest and caught her arm. *Oh, God, now what?* Her disguise might do for moonlight, but by the hard, cruel light of day? *I'll look like a clown!*

She *was* a clown to think she could get away with this. What had she been thinking? Had she thought at all? Or only wanted, and then thrown rational thought out the window?

Fine for the night, but now? She lifted his hand free, set it on his chest, stooped to kiss his fingers. *Good night, sweet love.* She walked into the cold water without a backward glance and swam. The trees stood knife-edged against a rosy sky.

Shivering, she waded ashore, then looked behind. Reese was a dark shape stretched on the sand. She was safe. Hurriedly she dressed. Looked again. *If only I could stay, sleep with you. Kiss you awake in the sunshine.* But she couldn't. Nicola turned, seeking the start of the trail that led to her hidden car. Her eyes alighted on his pile of clothes.

His wallet—was it there in his pocket? The combination card within? Moving on yesterday's impulse, she knelt and lifted his shirt. Found his wallet by touch. Paused, her hand resting on it. *I have you in my power.* She could memorize the numbers on his card, beat him to work, snitch the formula from his safe. Reese need never know, not until she'd published her dissertation. This was truly power. Steal this and she'd won.

She couldn't do it. Not like this, not this morning, not after last night.

"D!"

Her head shot up. Out on their island, Reese sat, staring.

She set his shirt down, smoothed it carefully. Rising, she kissed her fingers, lifted her hand to set the kiss free, let it fly to him.

He stood, but he didn't call again. Didn't ask her to stay. Reese didn't beg any more than she did.

If I could stay, I would. Can't you see that in my eyes?

He moved toward the water, not running, but like a lion walking after a herd of antelope, intention plain in every line of his body. Then he began to swim. She turned and fled.

By the time Reese reached shore, she'd faded into the woods. Nymph at dawn. He cursed savagely. Stalked, dripping, to his clothes. *And what did you want with these, my darlin'?* For a moment, hope leaped. She'd tucked a message between their folds? *Your phone number would do.*

No such luck. She'd left him nothing. *Maybe you meant to steal kit and caboodle, leave me stranded, buck naked?* God knew, she had a sense of humor, but he'd have sworn there was nothing obvious or crude about it. So what, then? One more mystery among too damn many.

GIVEN HIS DRUTHERS, he'd have gone straight home to a bath and bed. Reese stopped by his house, showered and headed in to Pherotics. He'd let himself think when he got there. Right now if he thought about D, he'd break something.

Trudging up the back stairs, he stopped at floor three to consider. Nic had started her trial with the voles yesterday. He ought to check on that, and... Reese frowned, trying to think. There was something else. Something he needed to say to her...*or maybe ask?* He couldn't bring it to mind, tired as he was. *Later,* he decided. First a cup of coffee and a moment's peace at his desk. A moment simply to remember the night....

Three cups of coffee later he still sat staring into space, caffeinated to the red line, his thoughts anywhere but here. *If I could have her till I didn't care anymore...*

Last night hadn't done it. Hadn't been half-enough. Hadn't scratched the surface of his desire for her. His body had faded first.

But given the time—and the stamina—to reach satiation point? *Say, forty hours nonstop, like a blasted prairie vole?* If he could have her till he didn't care anymore, then...*then maybe it would be safe to have her?* As long as he was the one in control? The one who could walk away?

What the hell's the point of that?

He wasn't sure what the point was anymore, beyond needing her. *Need to sleep. Think about this later. Get to work, Durand.* Nic, he needed to see Nic. *About...?* He hit the wall again. Later for that, too.

A cheerful knock-knock, and Demi skimmed into the room, bright as a summer garden in her flowered sundress, bringing with her a subtle drift of fragrance. Reese pictured the tropics, a lei wrapped around his neck—twelve times. He sighed and fetched a smile. "Demi."

"Good Lord, Reese!" She dropped her purse and a straw hat trimmed with orchids on his desk. Came around its corner to perch on his blotter. She put her palm to his forehead. "You look terrible!"

"Thanks." He caught her wrist and removed her hand.

"Did you sleep at all last night? Are you in pain or did you just have nonstop, horrible nightmares?" She glanced toward the shattered washroom.

"I was a bit restless," he admitted. But not reliving any explosions, at least not the kind fueled by propane.

"Poor baby. But serves you right. You should have let me distract you last night rather than gone home and brooded about it."

"You're distracting me now."

She mistook the complaint for a compliment and gave him a brilliant smile. "Good."

"So what can I do for you?" He didn't need Demi on his plate this morning on top of everything else.

"Well..." Kicking long legs meditatively, she studied him from under her lashes. "I have a...proposition to make. I meant to make it last night, but somehow we never..." She shrugged. "But I'm not sure this is the time and the place, either."

Spit it out, beautiful. He drew a breath, schooling himself in patience. "Let's have it, Dem."

"All right." She turned to pull a bottle from her purse. "This is my latest scent." Removing the cap, she dabbed the perfume on the crook of her elbow, then leaned forward to present it.

Reese sniffed dutifully, smiled in spite of his mood and

closed his eyes. An image of firelight formed in his mind. Orange blossoms, embers and autumn. Golden, foxy eyes, so close to his own they swallowed him up. "It's—" he opened his eyes "—wonderful." An inadequate word, that. The scent resounded in his mind, images linking one to another, all in a hot palette. "Golden?"

"Ah…" She beamed at him. "I call it Firefly. You have an excellent nose. But I knew that already."

"Pity you can't give this one to Nic. Trade it for that rose stuff she wears." Which had never seemed to suit her somehow, any more than her original counter cleaner.

Demi's smile faded. "Anyone who could wear that junk willingly doesn't deserve this. I can hardly stay in the same room with her."

Who asked you to? "It's a wonderful scent, Dem. And so?"

"So all my scents are wonderful…" She frowned. "You aren't making this easy."

He leaned back in his chair, turned his hands palm up. *What d'you want from me, woman?*

"But there are lots of wonderful scents on the market… I've been thinking, thinking a lot, since I…met you a year ago. And also waiting." She tipped her head, gave him an enigmatic smile, a big-eyed expectant look.

"Waiting for what?" he asked with the last of his patience.

"For *you*, idiot! To come to your senses." She slid off the desk and settled in his lap. Her arm hooked around his neck. "I keep thinking, he'll be back. Give him time. He's a busy man. But that one night we had together… You're not an idiot…" She frowned comically. "I think?"

"Dem." He couldn't lean backward any farther. Couldn't dump her on the floor. He supposed he'd asked for this. Deserved it. But today of all days? "Demi—"

"I know you said we shouldn't mix business with pleasure, but that's where you're wrong, Reese. We could make it *all* pleasure. I can't think of anything more pleasant than making zillions of dollars—''

"Huh?" She'd thrown him again. He thought they were talking sex.

"And that's *just* what we'd do. Your pheromones mixed with my scents? We'd take the world! But not with just one cologne for men. We should be marketing a whole *line* of men's fragrances, each using your same pheromone. We should have one line for men and a second line for women. Maybe six scents in each line."

"Demi…" He didn't need any more partners—and he damn sure didn't need a partner who conducted business perched on his lap.

She leaned closer, her lush lips only inches from his own. "It's a merger made in heaven. Pleasant by daytime…and by night, Reese? You and me? You call this merely… *pleasant?*"

He managed to say, "No, thank you," just as she closed the gap. Their lips grazed as he turned his head aside. Her lips pressed to his cheek, he looked blankly past her— straight into a pair of burning eyes.

Nic, standing in his doorway. "You…" He lost the rest of that thought. Simply stared. She looked different, some-how—changed her hair maybe?—as well as blazing mad. *I have to talk to you!* About…?

Demi turned her head to see. "If you *don't* mind, Ni-cola?"

"Not at all." She was gone, fox fading back into cover.

Reese stood, not easy with Demi draped from his neck. He dropped her on the desk and started away. "Excuse me."

"*Reese!*" She caught his sleeve. "Where are you— What—"

He gritted his teeth. *Okay, okay. First things first.* "Dem…" He peeled her fingers gently from his shirt. "You're a gorgeous woman." Whose lower lip was quiv-ering. He winced. Looked helplessly down at his desk. *Hell.*

He lifted her bottle of scent and held it out to her. "You're a true genius when it comes to scents. This one is magnificent."

She took it from him. "But?"

He drew a breath. "But I don't want you for a partner. I'm happiest traveling alone." *Am I?* Was that true anymore?

Her eyes narrowed. "Then last year, what d'you call that?"

Oh, boy. "A pleasant evening between two adults?" he hazarded, retreating to his chair.

"So you *used* me!" She snatched up her purse, collected her hat.

"Huh?" If anybody had used anybody and used him hard—

"You seduced me to knock my fee down."

"*I* seduced— Lady, you came on like a Mack truck!"

"*I didn't!*"

"Inviting me to your apartment to smell your best scents—"

"I didn't have my own office yet!"

"Fine, but you had to showcase your perfumes in nothing but a silk caftan? With the very best one poured down your cleavage?"

"Well, if you weren't interested, you never should have—"

"You've got *that* right. But if I hadn't, I'd have hurt your feelings."

"My *feelings?* You think I was *that* desperate, Reese Durand, that I needed a conceited lout like *you* to— *Pah!* You think I can't have any man I want—whenever I want?"

Any man in the whole world but me. The realization launched his temper into orbit. No more Demis? No more flings? *I'm going to hunt Nic down and*— No, strangling was a felony in Massachusetts. He drew a ragged breath.

"Well, why don't you, then? Go have some other lout."
Any other lout. "Give me a break."

"Give you a—*fine!* Here!" She didn't wind up, didn't
hesitate, she simply threw.

And he ducked—right into it. Trust Demi to throw like
a girl. Aimed at his head, her bottle hooked into his coffee
cup. Smashed a scant inch from his descending nose. Wet
heat splashed his face, his wide-open eyes, turned to liquid
flame. His lids slammed shut in reflex and he gasped—
inhaled alcohol, a scorching fragrance called Firefly.
"Ahhh!" He clawed at his eyes, then stopped himself.
Glass fragments, maybe, as well as alcohol, to hurt like
this? *Don't rub. Can't.* Damn the crazy bitch! He stood
blindly, shuddering with pain, tears streaming from his
eyes. *Get to the bathroom.* The sink still worked.

Something moved near the doorway—light footsteps. He
clenched his fists. He was helpless, blind like this. Open to
anyone.

"Reese!" Hands closed on his shoulders.

Nic. He sucked in a breath of relief—inhaled more of
Demi's hell brew and coughed.

"Sit." She pressed him back into his chair.

"My eyes—"

"Yes, I'm getting water. Sit still." She was back in a
moment. "Tip your head back." Her palm cupped his jaw.
"Keep your eyes closed." Warm water trickled over his
forehead. Bathed his eyes. "Good." Her thumb swept his
cheek. "Don't open while I get more."

At least he could breathe now. He nodded blindly. She
was back in seconds. Her hand cradled the nape of his neck;
it felt like a caress. "This time open your eyes."

Reese cracked them an eighth of an inch, fought to keep
them open while she poured. He yelped as the water hit.
"Damn that hurts!"

"I imagine you earned it." She pattered off to the bathroom.

She was mad at him, too? Was half the human race

crazy? Still, he was lucky that it was Nic come to his rescue and not Tim or Hadley. Lucky that Demi hadn't stayed to finish him off, helpless as he was.

Confining herself to clipped directions, Nic washed his eyes again and again till he could open them. While she went for more water, Reese wrenched his shirt open, not bothering with the buttons. He'd never wear this one again. He struggled out of it, threw it aside. "You'll have to go buy me another," he said when she returned.

"I'll do that after I take you to a doctor."

"No doctors. I've had enough quacks. If you'll just give me one more rinse." Much as the treatment stung, he liked her hands on him, which was odd, since Demi's touch left him— He inhaled at the wrong moment, sputtered under the flood. Putting up a hand to fend her off, he bumped her cup. It clattered to the floor. "Sorry."

Nic growled something wordless—her mood wasn't much better than his own, he realized—and came round his chair to find it. She knelt and reached under his desk.

Her braid fell to one side, baring a graceful neck, one delicate ear as she turned her head. *A streak of mahogany red along her nape at the hairline.*

Reese sat motionless, the world revolving beneath his feet. *Nothing made sense.*

Nothing made sense, but...but *he knew that color.* Had spent half an hour this morning scrubbing smudges of it from his hands, his face, his chest. Some sort of rouge. *I missed a spot, touched Nic and it rubbed off on her?*

He might have touched her hands this morning. No way had he touched the nape of her neck.

Can't be. Cannot possibly be. His inner compass reeled. He'd been marching south all the time he'd have sworn he was headed north?

She stood with the cup in her hands and turned. "What's the matter?"

"They still hurt." All of him hurt. It hurt to breathe. There was no D? Anyplace in the world, reachable or not?

Only this stubborn, willful, foxy child, nothing at all like he'd imagined?

"Small wonder. If you have a chip of glass—"

"So rinse me again!" He drew a breath, tempered his snarl. "Please." He didn't need it. Just needed her gone. He had to think—couldn't think, He'd been punched in the gut. Felt sick to his stomach. D didn't exist? *How can you love someone who doesn't exist?* He closed his eyes, tipped his head back.

A small hand, nimble and strong—he recognized it now—cupped his jaw. "Open your eyes, Reese."

And high time he did. Had he been willfully blind? How could he have not known her? Recognized her here, under his thumb the whole time? He yelped as the water splashed and burned. "*Dammit!* Stop!" He jerked out from under her hands. *Damn you, girl!*

"Fine. I think you'll do now." She headed for the door. Long legs, lithe tomboy's walk. The devil's own pride. How could he not have known?

Did I want not to know? The mark came running to embrace the con man, they always said. But was he such a fool? "Go buy me a shirt, Nic. Neck seventeen, longest sleeves you can find. Want money?"

"My treat."

She thought she could buy him off that easily? She'd murdered D, and she thought a shirt would clear the debt?

Not by a long shot, babe! Reese slumped back in his soaking chair and closed his eyes. Drew a breath that felt black in his lungs. His *heart* felt black…lost in the dark. God, he was tired. With no place now to lay his head. No place to call home. *I imagined it all.*

CHAPTER EIGHTEEN

IN THE LEFT WING of maze seventeen, male seventeen and female seventeen-A lay curled in one ball of snoozing bliss. Nicola made a check on her chart. Still bonded seven days after their honeymoon. Which gave her seventeen faithful pairs out of seventeen so far. The effects of the Pherotics pheromone, combined with her own hormone, were still holding.

For mountain voles, yes, but for humans? One human in particular? *Reese.* His name evoked the usual response, a wave of warmth shivering up from her toes, a backwash of longing. She hadn't seen Reese since Demi's tantrum the morning after their night at the quarry.

The day after that, he'd flown off to Chicago to meet with his Midwest marketing director. More orders of Irresistible had been canceled, and with their commissions in jeopardy, his sales team was near mutiny. After he'd stamped out that fire, according to Hadley, Reese had flown on to Seattle to consult with his ad agency, something about slowing down Irresistible's campaign till Pherotics had revised its product.

As per my suggestions? Nicola bit her lip. So far she hadn't any. Fixing Irresistible wasn't why she'd come to Pherotics. This test had been Hadley's idea, and she'd only gone along for her own purposes. To try to get her hands on Reese's pheromone.

But now that she cared about Reese and swiping his secret wasn't possible?

I'll have to think. If there was some way to help him,

some way to make Irresistible live up to its original promise, then perhaps a trade might be possible. Her suggestions
in return for his pheromone formula?

But how to fix Irresistible—assuming it was fixable?

Start by reviewing all of Tim's data? Not the formula
itself, since they wouldn't let her see that, but what they
did with the formula? Either it had worked as a sexual
attractant originally and something had gone awry in its
application to a cologne, or it had never worked at all. *I
could start out by determining which, then take it from
there?*

Meanwhile, this test of the voles addressed her own con-
cerns more than Reese's. *Has he bonded?*

Maze eighteen. Nicola consulted her list. Female B had
worn the combined dose in this cage, female A was the
control. In the B room of the maze, the harnessed female
and her unfettered mate crouched shoulder to shoulder. The
correct pair was still bonded.

But is Reese? Thinking of him, she swung toward the
lab door—and started violently. "Yikes, you scared me!"

"Guilty conscience?" Reese pushed off the doorjamb
and sauntered toward her, lazy and dangerous and oh, so
very male.

"No more than usual." She looked down at her chart,
then retreated to the next maze. Stood there, staring down,
registering nothing but his advance.

"How's it going?"

I miss you night and day. And you—do you... She
shrugged. "About as predicted. Everybody's still bonded
tight." *But are you?*

"And how long is your little experiment going to run,
Nic?"

Little experiment. His anger pushed at her, a palpable
wave, shoving her down the line of cages. She marked
nineteen as bonded, then moved on to twenty, flinching
inwardly as he crowded her. *Why are you mad at me?* Or
was he just in a mood? Had the news out West been that

bad? "I don't know. We're trying to repeat your experience on the rodent scale, remember? How can I guess how long they'll stay bonded when I don't know about you."

"I told you to leave me *out* of your experiments, remember that?"

Her temper flared to match his. "Yes, I do, but d'you recall who crashed my experiment in the first place?" *And if you got more than you bargained for, big guy, whose fault is that?*

They both wheeled at the sound of clicking heels, a woman's low, furious voice. "I have *never* in my life been so—" Demi Cousteau stalked into the lab, towing a bloody-nosed Hadley by his shirtsleeve "—so *humiliated!*" she declared, making a beeline for Reese. "I understand you have ice in here?"

"In the fridge." Glad of the interruption, Nicola ran to get it.

"What happened?" Reese asked the professor, who wore a shy, fatuous smile beneath his battered beak.

"This hero," Demi announced to the room at large, "fought with the UPS man for the honor of opening the downstairs door for me."

"What else could I do? He was insolent. The creep leered at you." Hadley accepted a clothful of ice cubes from Nicola.

Demi jabbed him in the chest with a ruby-tipped fingernail, evoking a sillier grin. "He was simply being *pleasant,* Peter!"

"Well, he hit me first."

"*After* you shoved him. And he was seventy if he was a day."

"No more than sixty! And a bruiser."

"Oh, sixty, well, that makes everything just *fine,* Sir Galahad." Demi caught Reese's arm. "Would you call me a cab, Reese? I've had all the gallantry I can take for one day."

So much for getting to the root of Reese's evil mood.

Blast Demi and her theatrics, anyway. Reese didn't spare her another glance as he escorted his Nose from the lab. Nicola turned to glare at her adviser.

He held out his bag of cubes. "I believe these would work much better if they were crushed, Nikki. D'you think you could—"

"No, I don't. And I don't need the smell of blood upsetting my voles, Hadley, so if you'll just..." She sniffed again. Blood and... "Irresistible?"

He gave her an embarrassed smirk as he retreated toward the door. "Why not? Everybody else wears it around here."

Three out of three guys do, you mean. Closing her eyes, Nicola felt the room shift subtly around her. There was a pattern here somewhere. Reality distorted, turned rubbery as she tugged at its pieces, struggling to rearrange them, then it snapped back to the status quo. She sighed and opened her eyes. *Imagined it maybe?*

As she'd imagined Reese's caring for her? That Reese and she might be bonded, hand to hand and heart to heart forever and ever? She shook her head. *Whole lot of dreaming going on around here.* Reese and Tim dreaming of fortunes. Hadley imagining he could have Demi. And she, *God,* she hated being a fool. That was all this pain was. Consulting her chart, Nicola moved down the row to maze twenty. Still bonded.

WHO WAS SHE? Slouched low in his car, Reese watched her approach in his rearview mirror, a brisk, slim shape in the twilight. *I thought I knew you.* Stubborn, sexless as a recording angel, a single-minded, brainy kid, all passion channeled ruthlessly into the will to know. Love reduced to nothing but chemicals in a test tube. All surfaces wiped squeaky clean with ammonia. Science, not poetry. *I had you neatly summed up. Didn't know you at all.* Only those foxy eyes to give him a clue, and arrogant fool that he was, he'd ignored them.

Golden eyes... He'd pictured D's eyes as violet, midnight eyes for his nighttime lover. Reese's fingers gripped the steering wheel till they ached. *Damn you, Nic.* All this week out West he'd fought to hold on to the image in his head, D as he'd imagined her. Midnight eyes, clouds of glossy brown hair, laughing whispers in the dark.

But that image was supplanted now. Gone forever. He imagined D now, lying beneath him, her face dark and delicate in his cupping hands, lashes trembling on her cheeks. But when those lashes slowly lifted—*Surprise, sucker!*—it was Nic who gazed up at him. Fox under cover, wild golden eyes peering out from the leaves, laughing.

Damn you. Have you been laughing at me all along?

Or even harder to stomach, simply studying him like a bug under a microscope? Not warmth waiting for him at the end of the chase, but cool, clinical detachment. Numbers checked off on a questionnaire.

Behind him, Nic had reached her old Toyota. *Who are you, lady?*

He meant to find out. Meant to find out everything. *Where do you go? Who do you see?* As her car eased out from its parking space, Reese leaned below dash level. Lights swept the ceiling of his car and passed on. He sat up, gave her to the end of the block, then started the Porsche. *And what do you want of me?*

"HE'S GETTING on my nerves, Moo. Seems like every time I turn around this past week..." Reese was watching her. Pausing in her office doorway. Scowling at her through the window of the deli across the street when she went out to lunch.

Mooo.

And not only was Reese everywhere, he was mad. At her. "Because he's desperate for results, I suppose." Once he'd learned that she assessed the voles twice daily, at nine and four, he'd taken to hovering, glowering at every mark on her tally sheets over her shoulder. Not that there was much to see. The mountain voles had passed the eighth day of their test, bonded. The ninth, bonded. The eleventh, still merrily bonded. "So now we're coming up to the crucial date, Moo."

Her sister stood and trundled off through the park, her toy sounding like a tiny cow heading home to be milked. Nicola sighed and strolled after her.

They were coming up on the thirteenth day. On that day the first time she'd conducted this experiment, her male mountain voles had abruptly rediscovered the delights of polygamy. Devoted family men had turned back to heartless cads.

So this was the telling point. If Reese's pheromone was truly boosting the effects of her hormone, she'd know it soon. They'd stay bonded after the thirteenth day.

"For how much longer?" Reese had demanded again yesterday.

Tell me if you're still bonded and maybe I could guess, she'd wanted to say, but hadn't dared. Not with him in this mood. She'd simply shrugged. Sixteen days? Eighteen months? Maybe forever?

And if they stay bonded forever, then that means... "It would be safe to love him." She whispered the absurdity aloud. *If he could never leave me, then wouldn't it be safe to—*

Mooooooo.

STANDING AT THE END of the marina dock, Reese could just make out her boat, moored some fifty yards out. *So, girl...* One by one he was learning her secrets. *I know where you sleep now at night. Where you buy your coffee and doughnuts in the mornings.* The health club she went to, after work to wash off that damned cheap perfume.

He was learning her secrets, but her mind? *What would you do, Nic, if I stripped off my clothes and swam out to you? Would you laugh and take me in? Or fend me off with a boat hook?*

He'd half a mind to find out. See how she'd like a surprise. Because, looking back, he realized, every time they'd met, every time they'd loved, she'd been the one in control. The one who chose the place, the time, yes or no. The only one who knew the players.

Well, no more of that. Now it was *his* turn to hold the power. While he knew, and she didn't know he knew, he was the one on top. The one who could watch in secret, who could secretly laugh.

The light in her portholes flickered, then faded to black. Bedtime. His fingers curled as he remembered her berth, her body nestled against his in the rocking darkness.

No. He wrenched himself away, then headed up the dock. Not tonight. He wasn't ready to give up his advantage yet. Not till he knew what she wanted.

And what *he* wanted. Revenge? The last laugh? Or simply…her.

THE FOURTEENTH DAY, and every vole remained bonded. From now on, they moved into unknown territory. Only Reese had gone before, and what he was feeling, he wasn't saying.

Still, they'd made it this far, and Nicola felt like celebrating. She'd considered asking Demi out to supper, changed her mind. Tim, her fellow scientist, would have been the logical choice. But he went around these days with a brooding, wounded air that put her off. Nicola knew who she wanted across her table, but she couldn't ask Reese. He'd see no cause for jubilation in monogamous voles. Anything but.

So she'd celebrate alone. Treat herself to a bowl of chili and a beer in the bar of her health club and take along some paperwork. One of the surveys that Reese had commissioned months ago, this one was on women's reactions to Irresistible. Pleasantly tired after an aerobic workout and a hot shower, Nic sat, oblivious to the meat-market atmosphere of the bar around her, spooning chili into her mouth and reading.

Each woman had been exposed to three men, of whom two wore no cologne and one wore Irresistible. After meeting each man, the women rated him. Nicola thumbed slowly through the papers. *No wonder Reese thinks he's in trouble.*

The women didn't like the Irresistible guys at all. "Too pushy," "Too aggressive," "Thinks he's God's gift to women," "Came on too strong," were some of their comments. Nicola frowned. "Wouldn't want to meet that one in a dark alley!" She paused, spoon frozen midair.

Ahhh. The sounds of the crowd around her blurred, drifted away. Nicola stared into space. Could it be...?

"THE BLONDE with the hooters? An eight," said the guy down the bar from Reese. He and his pal were rating every woman in the place. Eyes fixed on Nic, Reese shifted irritably away from the morons. What was she thinking about right now? Or whom? She looked a thousand miles away.

"The little redhead with the spoon?"

Reese suppressed a strong urge to turn around and punch the guy. *Don't even touch her with your eyes, creep.*

"A seven? Not much on top, but her legs make up for a lot. Wrong attitude, though. I tried to buy her a brew last week. Uppity."

"So give her a point for those pins, subtract two for snottiness, and that makes her a six. Now, the babe coming in the door?"

Six? Reese was too incredulous to even resent it. *If you think she's a six, fool, then you're too dumb to wipe my hands on. She's a six thousand.*

Four weeks ago, he wouldn't have spared Nic a glance—hadn't.

But now? Now he just wanted to put his nose to the nape of her neck, close his eyes and smell her. Her hair was still wet from her shower. She wouldn't smell like a truckload

of blown roses right now, she'd smell like...*sweet alyssum*.
Like honey and hay...and home. Reese carefully put down
his mug and stood. *Nic. Ms. Nicola Kent.*

SHE SAW THE PATTERN before she focused her eyes. A figure standing alone at the bar, the people around him giving
him a wide berth, an oddity in this jam-packed room. The
man started toward her and the crowd between them parted.
Not suddenly, but with a steady, mindless drift, like bits of
steel repelled by the wrong end of a slow-moving magnet.
A swath opened before him, and her eyes rose to his face.
Reese. *Of course.*

The pieces rearranged themselves, a kaleidoscope, bits
of bright color rotating to make a lovely new pattern. Reese
parting the crowds like Moses the Red Sea. Hadley with
his bloody nose, Tim with his black eye. Three men sitting
as far apart from each other as they could at a conference
table. *Pushy. Not in a dark alley.* Her own terror even, the
first time he'd kissed her. She put down her spoon and
laughed aloud.

"What's so funny?" Reese pulled out the chair opposite
and sat.

"I just had a thought." She'd have to test her premise
before she spoke, but already she was sure. *I have a present
for you.* She felt as giddy as a sky diver floating down, toes
pointed, from the perfect jump. She could have grabbed
Reese's hands and swung him around.

"Yes?" his voice sounded odd, husky and strained.

Touch down. Her feet came back to earth with a jolt.
Reese, here in her club. "What are you doing here?"

"I..." He glanced down at her papers, looked up again,
his gaze like a blue slapshot. "I want you to contact D.
Tell her to meet me. Tonight."

Ten seconds ago she'd been happy. She should be happy
now. Twenty faithful mountain voles showed that he should
be bonded. His desire to see D was almost conclusive
proof, as was his irritation at her resistance. His eyes nar-

rowed dangerously as the silence stretched out between them. *But if you're bonded, it's not to me. You don't even see me, do you? I'm just your link to D.* Her hands clenched under the table. "D's out of town."

"What?" He came halfway out of his seat.

"You heard me." She stood, shoved her pile of surveys into a stack. *If I can't have you, why should I give you D? How could I if I would?* The situation was ludicrous. Impossible!

He caught her wrist. "Then tell her to get her ass *back* to town. Now."

"This guy bothering you, babe?" A mountain of a man loomed between them, one of the free-weight crowd. He probably bench-pressed Reese's weight and her own combined.

Reese let her go and stood. "Get out of my business." He looked almost happy, as if he'd just found what he needed.

"Reese, please..." Nicola looked around desperately. Three more men were bearing down upon their table, others turning to stare. Not one of them would take Reese's part if her theory was correct. "Reese—"

"Meet me at my car, Nic." He stood easily on the balls of his feet, his eyes skating from the bodybuilder to the converging trio.

If he couldn't or wouldn't run, then she should. Every instinct cried out for her to stand by her man, but she was the excuse for the coming mayhem, if not its reason. Remove herself from the equation, and maybe— Grabbing her papers, Nicola plunged off through the crowd.

She stopped when she reached the bar's entry, looked back and sucked in a gasp of relief. Reese was backing warily toward the exit while her would-be protectors stood bristling. He looked like Daniel backing out of the lions' den. *Thank God.*

But with Reese safe, it was time to look to her own

escape. Meet him at his car, he'd said? Meet him tonight as D?

She couldn't. This whole situation was absurd. *I want you. You want D.* She was headed for the worst kind of heartache, only making it worse each time she met him. *I've got to think.* Nicola turned and took to her heels, bound for the sanctuary of her boat. The one place Reese would never find her.

ONCE HE'D HAVE SWORN that Nic pointed true north. Maddening, yes, pigheaded and difficult, you bet, but when she spoke, he'd believed.

D's out of town. "You little liar," Reese said bitterly, leaning on the sill of his office window. Across the Charles, the brick town houses of Beacon Hill blushed rose with the setting sun. *Liar.* He'd wanted to shake her within an inch of her life last night. *How you could look me coolly in the eye and say that...*

He was probably lucky that her muscle-head pal had intervened before he lost it and threw the truth in her face. *You're D, babe, and I know it. I know the sounds you make when you come, the smell of your skin, the weight of you in my arms. I know you, girl—and I've known you.*

But what he didn't know was why she was doing this. Playing with him as if it were a life-and-death game.

When he'd left the health club last night, he'd set out to run her to earth. Corner her on her boat and drag the truth from her, then see where that left them.

With him in that temper, it was probably lucky he hadn't caught up with Nic. The Porsche had lost a front wheel just as he swung out onto Storrow Drive.

His near accident hadn't just given him time to cool down, it had sobered him. Brought him back to his realization in the bar, when everything had suddenly seemed simple. He didn't know that he wanted Nic, but last night he'd realized he wanted a chance to find out what he felt for her. If their magic had survived somehow. And holding her should give him some kind of answer.

And then she'd pulled that on him!

Little liar! But where did that leave him? He couldn't confront her without saying how he knew that she lied. And that would tip his hand. Give away his last advantage.

She had so many already, knowing what she wanted, what the point of her game was. He, without a clue, was trapped between outrage and desire. No, he wasn't ready to surrender his only edge yet.

Reese turned to the phone on his desk as again one of its buttons lit up. Someone was using one of Pherotics's two lines—had been every few minutes for the past few hours.

Not Kay. His secretary had gone home at five. He'd heard the elevator collect her, then sink again. Nor could it be Hadley. Professor Sleaze hadn't bothered to show his face in the office today, and neither had Demi. Tim had dropped by to say a curt good-night, more than an hour ago.

So the busy caller could only be Nicola. *Who are you trying to reach, Nic? A lover?*

If she had one somewhere, Reese hadn't found him yet. *If you want to call someone, Nic, why don't you call me?* The button blinked out. He reached for the phone, then swore as it lit up again.

A NIGHT OF THINKING, thinking, thinking and pounding her pillow hadn't solved anything. Some messes you couldn't think your way out of, no matter how hard you tried. Nicola was learning that the hard way.

But if wits wouldn't serve, where did that leave her? She had no faith in her heart to find the way out—it had made a fine muddle of things so far. Led her on this fool's errand from the start. All the time she'd told herself she'd been seeking a cure for autism, a brilliant dissertation, she'd been seeking something else entirely.

Deep down in her foolish heart of hearts, she'd dared to hope that Reese's bonding might last forever. Because if Reese could never leave her, it should be safe to love him.

So now, when it seemed her crazy wish might come true? When with each day of the test that passed, each day that her voles stayed blissfully bonded, she should have felt safer and safer? Happier and happier?

She didn't feel that way—anything but. *How can it be safe to love you when you love D?* Reese didn't even seem to like her these days. She was just the roadblock he'd have to smash through to reach D. The situation was ludicrous. *If it didn't hurt so, I'd be laughing.* Nicola picked up the phone again.

But if her personal life was a shambles, there was always her work. With the voles in their fifteenth day still bonded, she had the makings of a dissertation that would set her field agog.

Which meant that, flawed as it was, her first human trial was more important than ever. The results of that experiment were the baseline against which she'd compare all future trials.

She'd spent the whole afternoon contacting her original subjects. This was the fourth week since the study, and she needed their final responses to conclude the experiment. She'd reached every one except Twenty-three, Reese—*a lost cause, that*—and Forty, who still wouldn't return her calls. She'd left half-a-dozen messages on his answering machine this past week, to no avail.

But she was hot on the little fink's trail. For the past half hour his line had been busy. Somebody was finally home. Nic punched his number again, and this time a woman answered.

"Hello," she said brightly. "This is Nicola Kent from RIIT. May I speak to Jed Feinstein, please?"

"Oh, it's *you!* You certainly may not. Jed's not here, but my son asked me to give you a message, young lady. He said to tell you that he never took your stupid test and that he's sick of your badgering him. Now *don't* call us again.''

"But—" Nicola winced as the phone slammed down. "But I have a photo of Jed right here, you silly hen!" And a five-page questionnaire he'd filled out the day before the test. And the response form he'd filled out the day of the test, then forgotten to number. *And I need his data, dammit!* Nicola hit the redial button. "Look, Mrs. Feinstein," she said as the phone was picked up.

Click!

"Blast, are you nuts, lady, or am I? He *did* take my test. He was Forty." Nicola reached for the redial button, then paused. Better not, not till they both cooled down. She hung up, then jumped as the phone rang under her hand. Jed's overprotective mama having a change of heart? Nicola snatched up the phone. "Yes?"

There was a moment's pause, then an amused masculine drawl. "And the question *is,* can I buy you a drink?"

Reese. She sucked in her breath. "Um…I'm working late."

"So am I. Why don't we call it a day and go out for a brew, Nic?"

"Ah…" He hadn't given her a really cordial word or a smile all week. To be with him alone, not as D, but as herself… Her nerves skittered and twirled, tap-dancing a tiny rhythm that felt something like happiness. *He's asking me, not D?* Though on second thought, this was probably Reese's way of softening her up before he asked her to contact D again. "Um…"

"Good," he said, interpreting that to suit himself. "Let me wrap up a few things. I'll be down in five." He broke the connection.

Alpha male. Nicola made a face that ended in a smile, then drew a deep breath and headed down the hall to the washroom. She just had time to rinse her face, reapply some rose perfume, maybe even a dab of lip gloss.

Standing before the mirror, Nicola cocked her head.

Somebody was using the elevator. She could hear it humming through the adjoining wall. Reese? He never used it to reach her floor. More likely someone from the accounting firm on floors one and two.

ORDERING THE PAPERS on his desk, Reese paused at the sound. Nic, coming up to meet him? But she always took the stairs. The contract cleaning service that the firm below used, he decided.

He spent a few minutes in his restored washroom, splashing his face, combing his hair. *Nic.* It was a summer night out there, balmy, a night made for walking and talking. *Or finer things.* Perhaps a walk by the river after their drink? If they both relaxed, took their time, maybe the knot would pull free tonight? Why did it have to be so hard, a man wanting a woman? If she'd only trust him enough to step out from behind her mask.

Locking his office, he pushed open the stairwell door, grimaced at the hinges' creak. He'd oil them for sure tomor—

All the lights were off in the stairwell. Reese paused. What bozo had switched them off? Letting the door swing shut behind him, he moved blindly toward the switch located at the top of the stairs.

At his second step he frowned. *What the*— What was that, crunching under his foot? As his hand found the switch, he realized. *Light bulb glass!* The switch flipped up, but the darkness remained. He spun around, ducking, and threw up a hand as the blow smashed out of the black.

CHAPTER NINETEEN

LOCKING HER OFFICE DOOR, Nicola turned toward the stairwell and frowned. That noise—it had to be Reese coming down, but would his footsteps carry past the metal door and firewall? "Reese?"

When she tried to enter the stairwell, something blocked her way. "Reese!" Nicola put her shoulder to the door and shoved. The weight slid grudgingly, gradually. "Reese, are you...?"

She thrust her head through the widening gap into darkness, then a beam of light hit her face. Squinting in its glare, she looked down. Reese lay motionless, eyes closed. "Reese!" She wriggled through the gap, glanced up at the light. Her hammering heart stopped cold.

Someone stood on the landing, aiming a flashlight bang in her face. "Who—" she threw up a hand to shield her eyes "—who's there?"

Silence. Whoever it was should be rushing down the stairs to help, not standing there watching. Hiding behind that light. "Who the hell is..."

The light bobbled on her face, then steadied. Beyond the blood pounding in her ears, Nicola heard a scraping footstep. The light wavered again. He—she?—was retreating up the well of darkness in horrible silence, blinding her with the light as he withdrew.

Reese groaned and moved.

Light, she wanted light—her own light to drive out monsters! Groping for the switch at the base of the stairs, Nicola found it and flipped it—again and again. She let out a word-

less whimper, spun toward the watcher above. "*Damn* you!
Get away from us!"

The door above squeaked, closed again with a deafening
echo. Darkness clamped down. He was gone. Nicola's
knees gave out and she crawled. "Reese, what did he *do*
to you?"

Fingers sweeping, she found his out-flung arm. "Reese,
please, *please* say something!" His hair was silk beneath
her fingers, wet— "Oh, God!"

She had to have light. Yanking off her shoe, she leaned
over his body, wrenched open the door, jammed it in the
gap. A blade of light from the hallway sliced into the blackness. She knelt over him, cradling his head. "Oh, Reese…"
She kissed his eyes, his warm, unmoving mouth, then
jumped violently as somewhere up on the fourth floor
something crashed.

Methodical, crunching blows echoed down the stairwell.
Whoever the intruder was, he hadn't gone far—could return
whenever he pleased. To do whatever he pleased.

Call the cops. Call the rescue squad. She couldn't leave
Reese to do either, not with that watcher so near. "Reese,
wake up, love, wake up!" He muttered and stirred. She
sobbed with relief—then yelped as he caught her wrists in
an iron grip.

Pinned nose to nose with him, she didn't struggle.
"Reese, it's me." Was he even conscious? "Reese?" He
was crushing her bones. "It's Nic. Can you sit up? We've
got to get out of here."

The sounds upstairs had ended. Somehow silence was
worse. "If you'll sit up, I can open the door." She gasped
with relief as he growled something and released her.
"Come on, let's get you into the light." Hauling and coaxing, somehow she helped him around the door's edge and
into the third-floor corridor.

But he wasn't safe yet, not near the door. Dazed as he
was, he'd be easy game. She couldn't lift him, but with her
urging, Reese crawled the few feet to her office. Only when

they were inside and she'd wedged a chair under the doorknob did Nicola phone for help.

TIME FOR MORE ASPIRIN. Filling a glass at the sink in his
private washroom, Reese inspected himself in the mirror.
Not a pretty sight. Three days after his mugging, the bruise
striping his cheekbone was a Technicolor wonder. Not that
he was complaining. If the weapon—blackjack? crowbar?—had hit him an inch higher, he'd be sporting a permanent eye patch. He swallowed the pills, grimacing as he
tipped his head back. The rest of the damage, acquired at
various points in his tumble downstairs, was hidden by his
hair or his shirt.

Just as well. He was ready to forget the incident, as were
the police. Just a simple office break-in. Some loser looking
for money or drugs or both. Nothing unusual in Cambridge
except for his blundering into the proceedings and nearly
having his check canceled.

Returning to his office, Reese frowned at the schooner
print, a replacement for the one his washroom explosion
had shattered. He'd like to forget, but there were still a few
questions that bothered him.

How had the thief found his safe so fast? Nic had estimated the creep had ten minutes of working time, max,
before the police arrived. *He jimmied my office door, then
went straight to the safe.* Did his damnedest to pry it open
with a crowbar and hammer. The dial had been battered,
the edges of the door scraped and dented. But the safe had
held fast. No experienced burglar would have expected otherwise.

So he was an amateur, a newly hooked junkie still learning his trade. *But if he was an amateur, how did he find
my safe so fast? Why didn't he go for my desk, the easy
target?* Why did he stick around at all when he knew Nic
must be calling the cops downstairs?

Nic. Reese sat and propped his aching head against the
backrest, gazed up at the tiny gaps in the gridded ceiling.

That was the one thing to be thankful for in all this. If the creep had started on three, instead of four—and that was strange, too—he'd bypassed the first three floors of the building to start at the top. Well, he could thank his lucky stars that he did. If he'd dared to touch Nic… *You'd be a walking dead man, creep. I wouldn't rest till I found you.*

As for himself, he could forget, if not forgive. There was just one more question that haunted him. The minutes between the first blow and his return to consciousness in Nic's office were a blank. So Nic's hands on his face in the dark, her lips soft and frantic on his—was that an actual scrap of memory? Or just the byproduct of a nasty whack on the head, a wistful dream?

EVERYONE SEEMED to be hovering nowadays when she assessed the voles. Tim had dogged her steps through yesterday's four-o'clock session. Halfway through this morning's rounds, Demi had wandered in, was now poking aimlessly along the workbenches on the far side of the lab, safely beyond range of Nic's rose perfume. "So what's your score?" she called as Nic turned away from maze number twenty.

"Every last one is still bonded." After eighteen days. She wished there was someone besides Demi to share her triumph. One particular someone.

"Do you know what this means?" Demi demanded.

That if nothing changed, she'd found just what Tim had feared a month ago. A fidelity drug. Maybe Reese would want D forever.

As he imagines her. But would his wanting transfer to me? Nicola couldn't see it. Could see no way to find out without risking everything—his wrath, his contempt, the chance to be near him in even the humblest lab-flunky guise.

"It means we're sitting on a gold mine!" Demi pirouetted on her heels. "I keep trying to *tell* Reese we should be making a perfume for women, not for men. Just think what women would pay for a fragrance that would make a man stay!''

This was the first Nicola had heard of this. ''What does Reese think?''

''Pah—I could shake him! He just laughs at me and says it would never sell. Because no man would ever, ever forgive a woman who trapped him that way.''

So, there it was, the answer to all her agonizing in a nutshell. Let Reese discover she was D and it was over. Before it had even begun. Nicola felt sick to her stomach.

''And I've tried to persuade Tim, but he believes this is a wild—'' Demi had the grace to blush.

''Goose chase,'' Nicola finished gravely for her. ''Yes, I know.''

''It's not that he doesn't admire you, Nicola. It's just that he has faith in his own work. Tim thinks we should go back to the original formula and stick it out. That it will sell in the end if we promote it enough.''

It would never sell. Nicola had begun experimenting yesterday on male voles, scenting one with Irresistible, then dropping him in a cage with other males.

Put two voles together and the unscented male fled. Put two unscented males with one scented, and both turned tail and ran. Put *three* unscented males in a cage with one wearing cologne, and given the courage of those odds, they'd attack. Mr. Irresistible would have been killed if she hadn't been there to scoop him out, squeaking his outraged defiance.

''But Peter agrees with me,'' Demi continued.

Hadley believed in her work? Nicola had assumed he was simply milking this windfall for all it was worth, taking Reese's money till Reese realized he'd been had. Or was the professor only siding with Demi in hopes of fringe benefits? As if Demi would consider Hadley while Reese was in the world.

''Now if *you'd* talk to Reese, Nicola, I think maybe he'd listen to you.'' Demi cocked her head coaxingly.

Nicola burst out laughing. "Not a chance, Demi. I'm not on Reese's A-list, in case you haven't noticed." Nor his B-list. His invitation the night of the burglary had been his last. *Thinks I'm bad luck maybe, after that?* He had an odd way of watching her these days. As if she'd grown a second head. "No, if you can't persuade Reese, he's not persuadable."

"I suppose not." Demi fingered the pearl in her earlobe. "But...what about you? Are you under contract to Pherotics?"

"Meaning?"

Demi lowered her voice and spoke faster. "Meaning *you* see what we have here, even if Reese is blind. Could you walk if you wanted? Bring your formula with you? I have a lab in New York, my own essential-oil firm. Together we could—"

"No, we couldn't. I am under contract, Demi, and even if I wasn't—" she wouldn't betray Reese "—it wouldn't do any good. It's not my original hormone that's making these voles stay bonded. It's my stuff *mixed* with Reese's—Tim's—pheromone. And their formula is Pherotics's proprietary secret. The recipe's upstairs locked in Reese's safe." Quite unreachable, as the burglar had found out. Nicola blinked as a thought stirred, then turned as Kay Grunwald leaned in the door.

"Nic, didn't you hear your phone?" When Nicola shook her head, she added, "You have an urgent message. I left it on your desk."

THE PHONE RANG again, but Reese didn't look up. It was Kay's job to field callers. He'd enough to do teasing meaning out of the rows of writhing figures on the spreadsheet before him.

Not that the bottom line wasn't brutally clear. If Nic didn't pull a rabbit out of a hat soon, he'd have to fold Pherotics. Reese grimaced. *Try to convince Tim of that.* Tim would want to keep throwing money—Reese's money—at the problem till they slid all the way down the greasy chute to bankruptcy.

The phone was still ringing. Kay must have strayed from her desk. Reese picked up instead. "Pherotics."

"Hi, this is Joe Dominguez, returning Nicola Kent's call."

Dominguez, Dominguez. A picture formed in his mind. The big, good-looking kid who'd helped Nic with her experiment back at RIIT. Reese's brows drew together. A man who had a prior claim on her, was a part of her life before he'd known her—someone admitted to Nic's charmed inner circle? While he—he was left to prowl the perimeter like a cold and hungry wolf?

"Nic's not available." *Not to you anymore.* "Want to leave a message?"

Hanging up a minute later, Reese stared down at the words he'd penned on a pink phone-message form. The tone of the message was professional rather than romantic. So maybe Dominguez wasn't a threat? Or he was just good at concealing it?

Of course there were forty subjects. I counted them coming in the door, then counted their post-test evaluation forms before I gave 'em to you—forty. What's the deal? Off to Baja for specimens. Call me early next week? Joe.

Reese picked up the slip and stood. He'd felt too battered these past few days to do more than wonder about Nic. But now he felt his heart lift as he moved in her direction. He'd deliver this himself. Watch her face while she read it. Every clue took him closer to mystery's end. *And then?*

But Nic wasn't in the lab, nor her office. Gone to lunch? Reese schooled himself to patience. He'd catch her later. His eyes lit on another pink form, crumpled on her desk.

Smoothing it out, he recognized Kay's baby-round hand.

"Your sister's toy broke last night," it read. "Can you bring another? Alex Brady." The message was followed by a phone number and two extension digits.

Sister. He hadn't even known Nic *had* a sister. He knew nothing about her, needed to know all. He was way over the line, Reese thought as he lifted her phone and punched out that number. *And I give a damn?* She'd invaded his life first.

"Pembroke House," sang a woman's voice.

"Yes," he said, thinking as he spoke. "Could you tell me where you're located, please?"

NIC'S SISTER. Cancel his first assumption, which had formed while he drove up a tree-lined drive that ended in a parking lot before a sprawling brick mansion. Pembroke House wasn't a private school for the wealthy, not with those steel-mesh-covered windows on the third floor, a pair of hands laced forlornly through the grill at one room. So Nic's sister wasn't a student, still young enough to play with toys.

Pembroke House wasn't a school. Some other sort of institution. Moving with casual purpose around a side of the building—he'd bypassed the sign directing him to check in at the reception desk—Reese swept his gaze across vast lawns dotted with groups of people.

Not a hospital or a nursing home, he decided, passing a gaggle of shrieking and giggling adults in headlong pursuit of a soccer ball. The man with the whistle who shouted advice and encouragement was clearly a therapist. And the players were patients. A young woman sat down abruptly in the midst of their playing field and wept. The coach knelt beside her, speaking in hearty tones.

Mental home of some sort. So this was what lay beyond that wall Nic had thrown up between them—a secret that grieved her so much she couldn't admit to even having a secret? A secret she bore in silence, head high, slim shoulders squared, without a whimper? The devil's own pride—

admirable, exasperating. *You don't need to be that strong.
I'm strong enough for both of us.*

His gaze snagged on a distant shade of autumn fox—
Nic, sitting on the bank of a pond. Using a clump of lilac
bushes for cover, Reese drew nearer. Not that he had a need
for stealth. Nic's whole world had narrowed to the woman
who sat beneath a nearby tree, her face tipped up to the
leaves, rocking, rocking, rocking.

Reese knew that rocking. Years ago the kid who'd lived
down the street from him had rocked like that. Autistic. Nic
extended an object she held in her hand toward her sister,
then turned it.

Moooooo.

The blond woman, Nic's sister, paused, then rocked
harder and faster, not acknowledging the toy's sound, not
acknowledging Nic in any way.

Autism's the inability to connect. To bond. "I'm working
on a cure for autism," Nic had announced that day in the
conference room. Yes, but Reese had never dreamed her
quest was personal. Was more than just the subject of a
high-flying dissertation. *You never told me.*

But no surprise there. Nic never begged, never asked for
quarter any more than he did. Because asking laid you bare,
left you open to refusal. Having to ask proved you weren't
self-sufficient, weren't safely armored against the uncaring
world.

*And if you had? If you'd come to me, Nic? Trusted me
enough to simply tell me why I should let you go, let you
get on with your work?*

But what had he ever done to earn such trust? He'd come
into her life as a raider. Intent on saving himself, and devil
take the hindmost. He couldn't even say for certain that
he'd have let her go if she'd begged, not with him thinking
she was his only link to D. He laughed silently, bitterly. *I
used you, Nic. D'you hate my guts?*

Nic turned the toy again.

Moooooo.

Locked in her own airtight world, her sister rocked on. Nic rose, set the toy within her reach, then backed away. New toy, Reese remembered. The blonde snatched it up, held it a moment—then inverted it.

Moooooo-ooooo.

She shrieked—an eerily inhuman sound—and hurled the toy across the lawn. Nic's shoulders slumped. After a moment she went for the toy, returned and sat down again. Held it out and turned it.

Moooooo.

Pained and oblivious, the blonde rocked on. But Reese put his money on Nic, his stubborn lover; he wasn't even sure she knew *how* to quit. She'd turn that new toy a hundred times, ten thousand, till familiarity made it sound right and her sister accepted it.

Meanwhile, he'd as soon she didn't catch him spying. She had enough to forgive him already. Hands jammed in his pockets, head bent in thought, Reese turned and walked.

Moooo-oo-ooo.

NIC BARELY MADE IT back in time for her four-o'clock rounds. Her wrist was sore from turning the blasted cow toy, but finally something had clicked. She'd left her sister rapt, intent on exploring every nuance of the new toy's voice, like a violinist let loose on a Stradivarius.

Stowing her book bag in her desk, she hurried back to the lab. All the males were still bonded. If anything, they showed an increase in tenderness, as if they'd realized their mates were carrying. Nicola had long suspected there was a pheromone to announce the happy event. *Now if everybody will just stay happy, then maybe I could—* She wouldn't think about it.

Returning to her office, she stopped short in the doorway. Demi stood behind her desk, in the act of closing a drawer. "Need something?"

"Oh, Nic!" Demi blushed scarlet, no easy trick with her

honeyed skin. "I didn't know you were back. I was looking
for—" she wrinkled her nose "—for a tampon. You
wouldn't have any, would you?"

"Back of the top right drawer." The drawer Demi had
just closed. She'd missed them, or… Nic handed her one,
then watched her hurry off toward the restroom. Or that
wasn't what she'd been looking for. Interesting. Her interest
faded as her eyes fell on a note tucked under the edge of
her phone.

Nic, see me ASAP. R.

HE THOUGHT BEST when he moved. Reese had been pacing
his office ever since his return. *Nic, how to make amends?*

He could set her free, find some way to break the contract that bound them both. Let her go back to her life
before he'd barged into it.

The thought of Nic in Providence, him ninety miles north
in Boston, with the only admitted relationship they shared
at an end—not acceptable. *I need you here, Nic, under my
thumb.* Under him, period. Whatever had changed, that
hadn't. That was growing clearer day by day.

But before they could go forward from this point—sort
themselves and this weird relationship out, see where it
led—he needed Nic's forgiveness. *I need a clean slate.* No
wonder she'd been dancing away from him.

Reese reached his window and swung around, grimacing
as his knee complained. How do you win forgiveness? Beg
for it? But if Nic was no beggar, neither was he. He'd
always preferred to *buy* whatever forgiveness he needed,
by cash or by deed. *How do I buy yours, Nic? What can I
give you for it?*

He'd ripped control of her own research from her hands,
so he could start with that. Give that back to her.

Plus damages. But money wouldn't make it right; money
had never rung Nic's chimes. So what, then? Reese turned,

his eyes skimming across the schooner print, then skating back. That was it. Nic wanted Pherotics's formula for the pheromone to use for her own ends. She'd been trying to get her hands on it from the very start.

Something wriggled at the back of his mind, something...not good. Reese stopped, frowned...shook his head as he lost it, paced on.

She wants it, she's got it. Proprietary secrets be damned. He'd figure some way to protect Pherotics and still see that Nic had the use of it. So, good, that took care of what she wanted.

And what I want? He paced, thinking. More than touching her, having her, he wanted...honesty. *Meet me face-to-face in the sunlight. Then let's see what we've got.* That was what he wanted. Had to have. But she had to come to him freely. Ripping her mask off wouldn't do it, he saw now. *You've got to trust me that far, Nic. I need that trust.*

Let her only trust, and then he'd be set free. Free to meet her, to show her... He had no words for what he could show her, only the image of his arms around her. The feeling of coming home.

A brisk rap on the door spun him around—too fast. Pain sliced up his thigh. He halted, silently swearing.

"Are you all right?" Nic's eyes moved from his face to his knee.

"Yes." He hated it, people noticing. He tightened his jaw. "Sit." She was here too soon, before he'd ordered his thoughts or the words to present them. "I have a proposition for you." He stopped, snagged on a sexual connotation he hadn't intended, but that beguiled him all the same.

She sat primly waiting, golden eyes veiled—fox well under cover. Secretly mocking him? *Devil woman, why is this so hard?* He wanted to rip her damned mask off, put his nose to her skin.

He'd sworn he wouldn't do that. Couldn't, if she was ever to trust him.

But what was wrong with nudging Nic toward trust if

that's what it took? *So you're shy, love, or you're slow, but I'm tired of waiting.* "I want to trade."

"Trade what?" Her hands sought each other.

"I want to give you the formula for the pheromone, Nic. I believe you've been wanting it?"

She tugged at her fingers. "In exchange for?"

I'm opening the door, babe. Take off your damned mask and step through. "In return for D's name and phone number." *Just tell me it's you, Nic, and the rest will be easy, I promise.*

"Ahhh…" Her mouth kicked up in a wry little smile. She swung away from him to gaze out his window.

Leaving him free to stare at the nape of her neck. *Say the word, darlin', and I'll set my lips there.*

Nic swung back and he frowned. Some trick of the light made her eyes glitter. She blinked rapidly, looked at her clasped hands. "If it's a trade you want, Reese, then I've got a better deal for you."

He didn't want to stand here haggling like a couple of rug merchants. Maybe trade had been the wrong word to use?

She tipped up her chin, once again reminding him of Billy the Kid at thirteen. The cool, deadly eyes of an innocent, taking aim for a heart shot. "You give me the formula for Pherotics's pheromone and let me go back to my own work, my own world…and I'll tell you what's wrong with Irresistible. How you can fix it."

His mind stuck fast on the first half of the deal. She'd take his formula and go, giving nothing of herself in return? Would simply back out of his life, fox withdrawing into the bushes? Leaving him…where?

Nowhere, with nothing left that I want. Not home, but lost…empty…wanting. *But what good is wanting when the one I want doesn't…* Bile rose in his throat. His hands fisted—

—as the rest of her proposition registered. "You know what's wrong with Irresistible?" All these weeks he'd been sweating bullets, Nic had known? She'd made him want her, need her, and all the while— "And you want to use *that* in trade?"

Her eyes widened at his words, or at the rage with which he'd spoken. "Yes. I've come up with a theory…"

Damn you and your theories, Nic! Damn your cold, clinical, unloving heart! "Well, here's a news flash, kiddo. *You've got nothing to trade.* Anything you thought on the job, while taking my paycheck, is mine already. So give. Come on." He turned his palm upward and flicked his fingers, the gesture to come closer and fight. "Let's have it."

Her eyes narrowed to slits. "What? You think it's fair to trade when *you* set the terms, but when *I*—"

"That's right, hotshot, you got it in one." Two strides put him looming above her. "*No* deal. You can't trade what you don't own. That's not the way it works in the real world. So. Tell me."

"Reese…" She cocked her chin and met his eyes. "You can whistle for it." Calm words, delivered in a voice that shook. "You can pucker up and *blow* for it, big guy, till hell freezes over!" She lunged to her feet, her heaving chest nearly touching his own.

He could have put out his hands and had her. Could have yanked her up against him and shown her with one kiss that he didn't need to deal at all, that he knew who the hell she was. That he held all the marbles. *All but the one I want!* But furious as he was, he didn't dare touch her. He backed off and she shot away. "Nic—"

"Forget it!" His door slammed so hard behind her the walls shook.

Devil woman! Sucking breath after shaking breath, he stalked to the window, almost punched it, then leaned his forehead against the cool glass, instead. And now what?

MIDNIGHT, AND HE HADN'T been able to sleep. He'd driven nearly to her marina before he'd mastered himself. Now he drove aimlessly along the coast road, chasing a crescent

moon that gleamed through scudding clouds like a derisive
grin. He'd botched it. Should have handled her some other
way. But what way? He couldn't think straight for wanting
her, but if she didn't want him back...*to hell with her.*

The Porsche swerved from its lane as his car phone rang.
Let it ring, he told himself even as he grabbed it. "Yes!"

Silence to make his teeth ache. *It's you, Nic. I know it.
Devil woman?*

A soft, shaky laugh. His heart surged at the sound of it.
"Twenty-three?"

Her lips at his ear. He eased the car off the road and
turned to look south over his shoulder, across some fifteen
miles of ocean. So near, but a man couldn't swim it. Anger
and hope swirled sickeningly in his stomach. *You're calling
to apologize, Nic?* Or even better, to confess? "So you're
back in town," he said evenly.

"Ahhh..."

He bared his teeth. *Forgot your own lie, did you?*

"Yes—" a shaky laugh "—I guess I am."

So. Reese slumped against his door. The dance goes on.
*No way, my moon tiger. I'm through dancing. At least to
your tune.*

"I was wondering..."

"Yeah, that makes two of us." The pause lengthened,
and he beat his clenched fist against the wheel. *Come on,
spit it out. What's your game tonight?*

"I wondered..." She paused again, uncertain, or was she
teasing him, drawing it out like this? "I wondered if you'd
like to get together?" she whispered in a rush. "Come out
to my boat? The moon is...nice, tonight."

This was her way of apologizing for their fight? *You'll
give me your body, Nic, for amends? Your body, but not
your trust?* But without one, what good was the other? He
could find that anywhere. "Who's asking?" Even to his
own ears, his voice sounded as cold as chipped ice.

Silence, echoing between them. Stricken silence? Guilty?
Or mocking? "Devil woman?"

"*I* am. I just thought…"

"Well, you thought wrong. If you want to meet me, then let's have a *date*, D. Like real people. I'm sick of this slinking around. It was kind of fun in a kinky way at first, but now… Why don't I pick you up? We'll go grab a cup of coffee, talk…"

"I…" A sigh, soft, perplexed. It tugged at him. He hardened his heart. "I…c-can't. Not tonight."

"Tomorrow then."

"Ummm…"

"Tomorrow…or never, D." *I don't dance another step.*

"But—"

"You know where I work, don't you?" His grin was mirthless.

"Y-yes, but—"

"Meet me there, in the first-floor lobby, seven-thirty tomorrow night. We'll go out to eat like real lovers do, babe. Maybe go dancing…" *And I'll lead every step.* His arms ached for her, small and fragile and tough as a diamond, warm against his heart, their bodies turning slowly to a love song. It should be so easy. *All I need is your trust.*

"Reese, I don't know. I…"

He smiled with triumph. She'd used his name, not his number. It was a first, shy step. He had only to stand firm and she'd cave in. "You've got to make up your mind, darlin'. Come to me. You won't—" His jaw locked on the last word, too close to begging. *You won't regret it. I swear you won't.* "Seven-thirty and don't be late."

Slowly he put the phone down. *God, what have I done? If she doesn't come, won't meet me…then what do I do?*

The crescent moon grinned—a moon tiger smiling—and slid away behind the clouds.

CHAPTER TWENTY

SHE COULDN'T DO IT. Couldn't meet him. Moving like a sleepwalker, Nicola completed her nine-o'clock tally of the voles. In place of bonded rodents, she saw herself, that evening, waiting in the lobby downstairs. Saw Reese stepping from the elevator, his face alight with eagerness and triumph. Saw his face change the moment she turned and he realized.

God, I can't do it! His incredulous outrage she could bear. His disappointment would kill her. *Surprise, sucker! It was only me all along!* Uninspiring schoolgirl-twit, Nicola Kent. *It wasn't magic we shared. It was fraud, trickery. Abracadabra—princess turns into frog before your very eyes! How d'you like that trick?*

Yeah, he'd love it. She couldn't possibly do this.

But if she didn't? Making a last check on her chart—all voles were still bonded—she drifted blindly toward her office. If she didn't, then they were still finished. Because having delivered an ultimatum, Reese would stand by it. If she didn't go to him tonight, he'd never meet D again. Either way, it was over.

So given that it was over, wouldn't it be best to end with the magic intact, rather than smash what they'd had? Shouldn't she simply fade? Let Reese keep his fantasy lover, his memories of a crazy moonlit interlude of love and laughter. While she—she'd have his tenderness to treasure for the rest of her life. Why spoil irreplaceable dreams with clownish reality?

Yes, that was the best way, the rational way, the *only*

way to respond to his ultimatum. But that being so, why had she, for the first time all summer, worn a dress to work?

HE'D WON. As always, risking had proved smarter than playing safe. Too exhilarated to sit, Reese prowled his office. He'd stood firm, and as he'd hoped—prayed—she'd caved in. Circling blocks in search of a parking space, he'd spotted her down the street, headed to Pherotics. *Ms. Nicola Kent in a red dress, my, oh, my! We definitely go dancing tonight.*

AT FOUR NICOLA MOVED again down the line of T-mazes. Reaching the twentieth maze, she made a last check on her form. Bonded, every one.

Five o'clock. Nicola sat huddled at her desk. Every vole was still faithful. And Reese had received the same dose. He should still be bonded—clearly he was, the way he insisted on seeing D.

D. That's me. The man's bonded to me.

Six-thirty. Nicola paced around and around her desk. *So he's bonded to D. But is he wed to the woman he imagines—or to my pheromones? The scent of my skin? Who says he can't make the transfer from wanting D to wanting me?*

If Reese were a vole, the odds would be good for a smooth transition, a transfer of bonding. Beauty lay in the vomeronasal organ of a vole, not his eyes. If his brain received the same message, he felt the same emotion. Bonding. *Love.*

But humans were infinitely more complex. They didn't operate by instinct alone. Memory and logic came into play. As did pride. When Reese found she'd played him for a fool, surely he'd hate her.

I couldn't bear that.

So you're going to give him up without a fight? That's why you wore a dress and heels? Ten minutes left to decide. She wandered down to the bathroom, stared at herself in the mirror. Nobody special, with a braid gone all to wisps.

Automatically she rebraided her hair, her eyes peering beyond the glass. If he stayed bonded, then it should be safe to love him.

Nothing felt safe. Nothing felt sure. But was she such a coward that she wouldn't risk without a guarantee? Ripping a handful of paper towels from the dispenser, she wet them and began to wipe her face, her neck, her arms. Every place she'd dabbed the hateful rose perfume.

Seven-thirty. Locking her office door, she heard the hum of the elevator descending. Reese heading down to the lobby. She swung toward the back stairs, escape. *I cannot face him.* Pivoted slowly back again. *I must.* If she didn't take this chance, she'd regret it till her dying day. Drawing a final, steeling breath, Nicola let it go—and found the decision was made. Had been made hours ago. Perhaps since the day they met.

Sooo... A flurry of emotion, all red and gold and trimmed with sleigh bells, shivered through her. *Yes?*

Yes. Go for it. As she moved toward the elevator, her chin slowly lifted. *Ready or not, Reese, here I come!*

But skimming by the lab, she stopped. Had she shut off the lights? She ducked her head in the door to see. Hadn't. Hadn't been thinking straight all day. She danced toward the switch. *Reese, wait for me.*

He'd be boiling, blazing, raving mad at her, and who could blame him? But then? After the bomb had gone off, the mushroom cloud cleared? After he'd had time to get used to the idea. What then?

If he'll just give us a chance! If he'll only kiss me once, smell my skin, then maybe, maybe, maybe, oh, please...

And if he wouldn't kiss her? Her smile wavered—she forced it back to a curve. *Then damned if I don't grab him by his tie and kiss him!* If she was going down, at least she'd go down in flames.

Hand on the switch, she swept a radiant glance over her voles and flicked off the light. Stood frozen. Flicked it on again. Something was wrong, some pattern she'd noted below consciousness. What?

"No..." she whispered, walking closer to the mazes, shaking her head as she saw. "Oh, *no.* No way. Oh, you *rats!*"

SEVEN-FORTY. Reese paced the lobby. So her watch was slow. Or she was combing her hair. Nothing to worry about. *I've waited this long. I can wait a little longer.* Nic was worth it.

He smiled, thinking. She was bound to be embarrassed, then furious when she learned he'd known all along—well, almost all along. Served her right. *He who laughs last, laughs best, lover. When you play the guy who always wins, you're bound to lose a few.* But he'd make the loss up to her. His pulse quickened as he thought of all the ways he'd make it up to her.

Seven-forty-five. Reese scowled and shoved the fear from his mind. Nic was the last one upstairs. A call had come in while she was leaving, that must be it. And now she was trying to politely disengage, worrying that he might not wait for her. *Don't worry, Nic. An army couldn't budge me.*

Seven-fifty. He let out his breath between his teeth. Okay, so he should have expected this. His shy lover was stuck upstairs like a cat up a tree, unable to face him or to flee. *So what do I do—go up and get you? Dammit, I need you to come to me. Trust me, Nic. Is that so much to ask?*

Eight o'clock. His heart felt like a lump of lead. *Devil woman, why do you make this so hard?* She'd turned the dilemma back on him. He could go to her and, doing so, lose the high ground. What good was an ultimatum when he broke its terms himself?

Or he could turn and walk. Forget about her from tonight on. *Either way, I lose.*

Five minutes after eight. Face carved in stone, Reese stalked from the elevator. *Coming to get you, Nic, damn and blast you!* The day's sweet anticipation had turned to ashes in his mouth.

But his dance-away lover had deprived him of even the satisfaction of an end-it-all fight. The lights in her office, the lab and the washroom were out. She'd slipped down the back stairs and into the night. *Damn you for a coward, Nic! That's it. That's the end.* Reese stamped down the stairwell, banged out through the rear exit and headed for his car. *It's over.*

Outside, the night matched his mood. Fog had stolen upriver from the sea to wrap its clammy shrouds around the town. Dew-beaded cars, parked bumper to headlights along both sides of the narrow road, gleamed evilly whenever a car crept past. Reese walked midstreet, hands jammed in his pockets, his face misted and grim. A night like this they could have built a fire in his fireplace, sipped brandy. Close his eyes and he could see her bare body lit by the flames. *Damn you, Nic, what we could have had. You're a coward, hiding behind your mask.*

His shadow lengthened before him, grotesque, lonely, as a car purred up behind. Reese backed up against a fender to let it pass.

But if she's a coward, then what am I? The thought slid in sideways, a knife angled to take him between the ribs. He bared his teeth and shook his head, but it was in past his guard already. What was so brave about watching her from ambush while he prodded her to make the first move? Wasn't he keeping his guard up while he insisted she drop hers? He'd wanted her to trust. But was that fair when he gave her no guarantee that he'd welcome her unmasking, take her as she really was?

If I'm so brave, then why don't I take the first risk—drop my weapons and step out from cover? If I said, "Here I am, Nic, will you have me?" would she still turn and run?

At his back, slow-creeping headlights turned the cars

ahead to jeweled and gilded chariots. His shadow leaped
out before him, light-footed and eager, reaching ahead of
him into the night. *What if I swam out to you tonight, Nic?
Would you take me in?*

Behind him, a foot stamped on a gas pedal. Tires
shrieked on wet pavement, an engine roared like a charging
beast.

FOUR OUT OF TWENTY mountain voles had rediscovered the
lusty delights of polygamy. Two others had quit their pregnant mates to hunch sullenly in the central compartments
of their mazes, a Don Juan gleam in their beady eyes as
they looked back and forth from the old to the new. This
was precisely the pattern of bonding decay she'd seen in
her original mountain-vole trials. By morning, the rest of
the little brutes would be jumping anything in fur that remotely resembled a female.

Her twenty pregnant females would raise their pups without the comfort and support of a loving mate, just as her
own mother had raised Nic and her sisters when their father
strayed to greener pastures.

Damn, damn and *blast* all males! What good was it to
love them if they just threw your love away? What use was
it to offer her heart to Reese when, any day now, his bonding must surely decay? Why risk humiliation and rejection
at his hands if she hadn't a hope of a lasting prize?

She supposed she was lucky that the voles had warned
her in time. Arms clasped around her churning middle, Nicola trudged through the dreary night. It was over. Good
as over. She just wanted to be home on her boat. She'd
crawl into her berth and maybe never come out again.

She paused and looked around, her eyes scanning the
line of parked cars for her own. *Where am I?* This was the
block on which she'd parked, surely. She walked back a
car or two, peered farther...shook her head in bewilderment
and turned again. Next block, then. She passed four more

cars and stopped. *I parked under this tree this morning. I know I did.*

Some other car was parked there now. *I've been towed?* Tonight of all nights, she needed that like a hole in the heart! She walked another block to be absolutely sure, then turned back once more. But why should she be towed when it was legal to park all day? Theft, then? What moron would steal that clunker?

A block down, tires squealed, a car lunged into motion. Black against its oncoming lights, a figure raced headlong down the street. Nicola stopped short. *My God, didn't the driver see him?* Her breath snagged in her throat as she realized the driver couldn't possibly miss him. *Didn't mean to!*

And then, like a knife thrust to the gut, it hit her—the runner was Reese. *No!* She started moving, a nightmare wading through knee-deep water. There was no way to reach him in time. *Dear God!*

With the car snarling at his heels, Reese launched himself into the air—or had he been struck? From a block away she heard the impact of body against metal, then the screech of tires as, too late, the car braked to a halt. *Not Reese!* A branch hanging low over the sidewalk swiped at her face. She ducked it, tripped, nearly went sprawling as a heel snapped. *Oh, no, oh, please, oh, no, not Reese!* She stopped, tearing desperately at the straps on her shoes, threw them aside.

Ahead in the gutter lay a dark, bundled shape—his body, thrown over the hood of a parked car. Silhouetted by the headlights of the killer car, a figure loomed above it, then stooped. But not to help Reese, something told her—to harm. *"No-o-o-ooo!"* Shrieking like a banshee, Nicola flew down the sidewalk.

The figure leaped to his feet—raced back to his car, his scrambling shape a black spider against his own lights and the lights of another car coming up from behind.

"Reese!" Nicola flung herself down beside him. Out in

the street his attacker roared away. The car behind followed placidly, its driver unaware of their presence beyond the parked cars.

ONE FOOT MORE to the right and he'd have dived cleanly over the hood to safety. Instead, his shoulder clipped the corner post, skewing his trajectory, and his head smashed into glass. Like a stamped and broken toy, Reese slithered headfirst to the gutter, cracked his head again, surrendered with a long grateful sigh to darkness.

Hands groped his back and he shuddered. The hands patted his hips, found his wallet—this was no friend! Snarling, Reese tried to rise, but a hand between the shoulder blades shoved him flat. The darkness reeled. With the last of his strength he reached backward, chopped at the tugging hands. In the distance, something was wailing, like a train flying toward him down the tracks. Trains, he'd always loved trains, their seductive rocking carrying him off into the velvet night....

This time when the hands returned, Reese was ready. He snatched one and held on, in spite of a yelp of pain. "Want my wallet?" Using the resistance of his captive as leverage, he rolled over. "I'll shove it down your friggin' throat!"

"No, thank you." Nicola flattened her other hand to his chest, smoothed it slowly across him, rib by rib. "Do you hurt anywhere?"

Was there anywhere he didn't? "Where did you come from?" *I thought you'd left me.* He let her go, closed his eyes, let her run her hands up his neck, across his face, his ringing skull. Cool, sure, familiar hands. He shivered and kept his eyes shut, the better to feel her feeling him. *Don't stop.* He started to smile, then remembered again. She'd left him. *And why'd you go for my wallet?*

Her hand cradled the nape of his neck. "Can you sit, Reese? I...don't think it's good for us to stay here."

Nic helped as he tried, and Reese found himself sitting, their lips only inches apart. He considered closing the gap, but he felt sick to his stomach, and something ugly was tugging at the tattered edges of his mind. He'd turned to look before he'd started running—a mistake that had nearly cost him his life. But he'd gained something from it. The left front parking light of the oncoming car had been broken. He laughed to himself. *Makes a habit of chasing pedestrians?* And catching them.

Nic cupped a palm to his cheek. "Where's your car, Reese?"

An hour ago he'd have given everything for such a touch. But now? There was something nasty here—something nastier than Nic's walking out on him. That broken light. He'd seen it before. Where? *Where's my car?* "Up ahead, beyond that truck."

"Give me your keys."

He handed them over—waited, swaying dizzily, while she went for the Porsche and backed it up.

Leaving the engine running, she came for him—stooped from the darkness, angel on high. *Or devil woman?* Where had he seen that smashed parking light before?

"Can you get up?"

With Nic lifting, he could. Reese wobbled, his arm around her shoulders. He dropped his face to her neck, closed his eyes and simply stood, inhaling her. But she didn't smell quite right, a whiff of roses overlying burnt honey. Home, but something wrong about it.

"Come on," she said softly, and tugged him toward his car.

He balked when she brought him to the passenger side. "I can drive."

"Right." She opened the door and looked up at him, her chin angled for a fight.

He'd have won it, but he was too tired to bother. Reese struggled into the bucket seat, closed his eyes. Squinched them in pain when she ground the gears shifting into first. After that she seemed to get the hang of it. "What about your car?" he asked as they turned a corner.

"Somebody stole it," she said lightly. "But since we're off to the police station to report your hit-and-runner, we'll do a two-for-one deal."

No cops. He'd grown up in a world where you handled your own messes. He wouldn't have called them last week—that had been Nic's doing, too. The rest of her message hit home. "Somebody swiped that heap?" Again his mind itched. *Too many bad things happening too fast.*

"Speak of the devil!" Nic braked so fast the Porsche quivered and died. She shook her head, amazed. "What's it doing *here?*"

"Waiting for you, I'd say." But she'd already scrambled out of the car, and with a groan, he followed.

"I parked it one street over from here! I swear I did!"

An easy mistake to make, but he didn't say so. Instead, moving with a kind of dreadful, sick surmise, he walked to her, leaned on its hood. *Warm.* Moving casually to the front, he glanced back at the left lens, and though he'd half expected it, his mind stopped, its circuits blown. Blankly he walked to the driver's side of the Porsche. Got in and locked his door.

"Reese!" Nic leaned in the other side. "You're *not* driving yourself!"

"Wanna bet?" He didn't look at her. "Got your keys, kid?"

"I do, but—"

"So you drive your car, Nic, and I'll drive mine." He leaned past her to catch the door handle. She let out an exasperated growl, then moved aside. He slammed it, hit the lock. Laid rubber on the road as he tore away—but there was no outdriving this.

Stubborn to the end, she followed him all the way home, honked farewell as he headed up his long driveway, then she drove away. Reese hardly noticed. Strobing on his brain was the image of a broken parking light, left front. Nic's car.

IN DAYTIME the Beretta would live under his desk, taped to the bottom of his middle drawer, within easy reach. Reese smoothed the duct tape, then nodded, satisfied. After hours, he'd keep it closer.

He bolted upright as someone shoved his door wide. "Where have you *been?*" Nic charged straight at him, braced her hands on his desk and leaned over them, eyes blazing. "I've been calling you for two days *straight*, Reese! Didn't you get my messages? I said it was urgent!"

He'd gotten them, all right. Had collected them remotely off his answering machine. But since he didn't know yet what he wanted to say to her, hadn't a clue yet what he thought... "Sorry, I've been busy." *Thinking about you, missing you.* She was maybe trying to kill him and he'd missed her. Was this what love did to you—made you crazy, all the better to finish you off?

*"Busy—*oooh! I even drove over to your house this morning expecting to find you dead on your couch of a skull fracture or...or..."

"You must have just missed me." By two days actually. He hadn't slept at his house since the close encounter with her car. He'd stopped by there to pick up his gun and a few essentials, then he'd checked himself into a hotel not a mile from Pherotics under a false name. Once he'd ensured that nobody could walk up on him while he slept or booby-trap his Porsche, he'd crashed for twenty-four hours straight, then had awakened to think.

The wheels had been turning ever since. *Somebody's been trying to kill me for weeks. You, Nic?* His gaze wandered over her too-bright eyes, drifted down. "I thought I told you, kid, never to stick your chin out." Off balance as she was, a tug on her braid would tip her neatly into kissing range. His pulse leaped with the thought. Dangerous thought, he reminded himself. Distracting him when he should be focused. Disarming him when he should be wary. Who was the one off balance here?

"Thanks for the lecture, but you might look to yourself."

She backed off and sat, humming with tension, white-knuckled hands gripping his desk edge.

"Meaning?" *Talk to me, babe.* Every word, true or false, was a clue. Leading to what? *What do you want, Nic? If only I knew...*

She wet her lips and drew a breath. "Meaning, I've finally realized...there's a pattern here. You'll probably think I'm crazy, Reese, but, *please,* just listen." She held up a hand and counted off her points digit by digit. "First, your bathroom explodes."

He shrugged. "Propane leak in the water heater." Though the plumber had insisted his original installation was unimpeachable—as any plumber, guilty or innocent, would have done. *Still, I should have listened.* And should have thought twice. The heater had exploded only minutes after Nic strolled out of his bathroom that morning.

Nic jabbed a second digit. "Second, somebody mugs you."

Wrong, lover, that was the third attempt. Second was his wheel, its lug nuts loosened—a potentially lethal accident just waiting to happen. But only his would-be assassin would know about that one. *When were the nuts loosened, that's what I'd like to know. While my car was parked on the street outside here?* Or maybe at Nic's health club, when she'd fled that near brawl?

She waved her hand before his face. "You do remember a mugging?"

He shrugged again. "Sooner or later everybody in Boston gets mugged."

"But this guy wasn't your garden-variety mugger, Reese. You didn't see him—*I did.*" Nic leaned closer, dropped her voice. "There was something about him that was...horrible. He was so controlled, backing out of there. And his silence. The air was just thick with...with *hatred,* is what it felt like..."

His face stayed poker still, while the hairs at the nape of his neck stirred. Was that what this weirdness was all about? Not business, not money, but *somebody hating me? And you were all that stood between that and me, Nic?* His stomach heaved. He'd have been no help to her if that bludgeoning horror had advanced, rather than retreated.

Or maybe she'd been perfectly safe—because she was the hater. It would have been so easy to lie in wait for him in the dark. Then after she'd clubbed him, she'd tried to break into his safe. That was why the attempt had looked like amateur hour—it was exactly that, a grad student taking on a task that would have daunted the most optimistic burglar. Plus, she'd had only a few minutes to try before he'd started to revive. Then she'd called the cops, returned to the stairwell, brought him round.

And kissed me? Or was that part just his lust-inspired dream?

Or she clobbered me and kissed me, which means she's one very sick cookie, and this really isn't about business, at least not just. Something darker, something twisted. *But hatred, Nic? Could you really hate me?*

He found himself fixed on her lips. Nic pinkened, rubbed them and slogged stubbornly on. "Then third, somebody tries to run you down. You don't think that was malicious? Intentional?"

"Sure I do, but I don't think it was personal. That was a drunk, or some kids out on a joyride. I was just the available target."

"Reese, whoever it was *got out of his car,* bent over you. I don't know *what* he was trying to do, but he meant you no good. I'm sure of that."

And I wish to God I was sure that, whoever the hell it was, it wasn't you tugging on my wallet. He'd been muddled, dazed, might have been unconscious for only seconds—or for minutes. Time enough for Nic to park her car and run back, try for his wallet?

Because if there was a pattern here, that had to be it. This final attempt had tipped his secret stalker's hand. *Somebody wants my wallet.* Not for money—no one would go to such lengths for the cash in his wallet. But his wallet contained the combination to his safe. All these attempts were, directly or indirectly, aimed at his safe and its contents.

Except for the wheel sabotage.

But how did he know his secret stalker hadn't been following? If he'd had an incapacitating accident, he or she could have stopped, rendered assistance. *And lifted my wallet?*

Then there was the explosion in his bathroom. But that, too, could be viewed as an attempt to create chaos. With the entire staff semihysterical and swarming his office while he lay dead or dying, that should have been the perfect opportunity to steal his wallet—except that it had been blown clear across the room and under his desk. He hadn't found it himself till late that afternoon.

And there was one final, bitter piece to the puzzle—his glimpse of Nic at the quarry, her hands on his clothes. She'd stopped when he shouted, but was that what she'd been looking for, his wallet?

Or am I going mad? To look at her, those wide foxy eyes fixed anxiously on his face, you'd swear she was innocent.

She'd been playing two women for weeks—his whimsical lover by night, his honorable opponent by day. An actress who could pull that off—why couldn't she handle a third role? *A moon tiger.* Stalking his steps—ruthless, relentless. He shuddered and realized Nic was talking.

"...*sure* someone wants you dead. But what d'you think?"

"I...think you're brilliant." *Whatever else you are.* She'd covered her ass with the car in case he'd recognized it by suggesting it might have been stolen for the job, then parked again afterward. If he ever accused her, that would be her alibi. And now, by anticipating his suspicions and voicing them first, she'd set herself up as his ally. *And if you want to stab somebody, be his friend first. Offer to watch his back.*

Of course if she *was* his friend, she'd act the same. Reese rubbed his aching temple and wondered if he should have stayed away another day.

"Thank you. So what d'we do now? Go to the police?"

He laughed in spite of himself at her earnest naïveté—then stopped midlaugh. Wouldn't his intentions be just what she'd need to know if she was his stalker? "We've got nothing to go on but your theories, Nic. Cops like hard evidence." *And it all points to you, babe.*

Which was another reason to steer clear of the law. He couldn't imagine turning her over to the police, not if he found her bathed in blood to her elbows. *For better or worse, you're mine, Nic.* And one way or another, he'd deal with her.

Leaning across his desk, she brushed his left eyebrow with a fingertip. "What d'you call that? Face paint?"

"Cops aren't impressed by bruises." Her touch echoed down his veins. He wanted to lean toward it, call it back again. *If you aren't my secret stalker, Nic, then we've crossed some sort of divide.* Even a week ago she wouldn't have ventured to touch him by day.

She stuck out her chin again. "So then…what? You wait here like a sitting duck for the next attempt? D'you even believe me, Reese?"

He gave her a brisk, dismissive smile. "Well, it's certainly an interesting theory. I'll take it under advisement." He glanced at his watch.

"You'll—" She bounced to her feet. "You *don't* believe me."

"I said I'll take it under—"

"Fine, *be* that way—till you're dead! See how smart you feel then!"

Reese winced as the door slammed; his head needed that. Still, if his head hurt, his heart felt a tentative…hope? He did his unsuccessful best to quash it. Reached under his

desk to touch cold, sobering steel. Hope clouded perceptions. He couldn't afford it. *Wait. Watch.* Before he could
act, he needed facts as cold and hard as this gun.

CHAPTER TWENTY-ONE

How COULD YOU protect someone who didn't believe he was in danger? Nicola prowled her office, brows knit, mind spinning like an insomniac hamster on an exercise wheel.

Answer: *with great difficulty.*

"Not good enough!" she muttered aloud.

Answer: *catch whoever's after him.*

"Better." Nic had been working on that since the morning after Reese's hit-and-run. One after the other, she'd casually chatted up Tim, Kay, Demi and Hadley, finding out who'd been where and doing what while a car tried to smash the life out of her lover.

Because if you approached the problem logically, the odds were good that she knew the face of that faceless watcher in the stairwell. Murder between strangers was rare. Her best suspects were the people Reese was closest to, the people he rubbed up against, or maybe rubbed wrong. The people who knew his daily routines—where to find him, how to get to him.

But why?

Find the why, and she'd find his enemy.

And that took precedence over all now. That one moment, when she'd knelt by his body and prayed for a heartbeat, had been a moment of blazing revelation. Between one breath and the next, everything that didn't matter had been burned away—her pride, her fear, her desires and ambition. Leaving behind only one fact, as stark as a running figure, black against blinding light. Reese must live.

She could live without his love—plainly would have to, since his bonding had ended, or must soon surely end. But she could *not* live without knowing that Reese Durand was out there someplace, breathing the same air as she, moving through the same world—arrogant, maddening, immeasurably dear. That much she would settle for. But she would not settle for less. So, how to keep him safe?

Behind her someone cleared his throat. She squeaked and spun around. "Where are your voles?" Reese hooked a thumb toward the lab.

It took a moment to catch her breath, then she said evenly. "Back in their cages in the holding room. The females are whelping this week, and I wanted them to settle in before—"

"But what about your experiment? It's over?"

She nodded and retreated behind her desk. "While you were out. Their bonding decayed to zero. The last little cad left his mate yesterday. They're normal mountain vole-creeps again, footloose and fancy-free."

"So this means…" He shook his head, stunned, wordless.

It means you're free, or soon will be, just as you wanted. "Yes," she said, then unable to resist, she added, "Have you wanted to see D lately?"

"Mind your own damned business!" She opened her mouth, and he added savagely, "Yes, I know, you consider that your business. So tell me, hotshot, what does this do for you?"

"For me?" She'd expected him to be happy, relieved, not mad at her.

"How does this affect your own research? Is this a blow for science, or just what you'd predicted all along?"

"I had no idea what to expect. You were the only subject I could base my predictions on, and you weren't talking."

"Like your other guinea pigs."

"So I thought you might be more articulate than the average rodent—silly me." She reined in her temper with an effort. "For me, it's not the best. I'd hoped that bonding would prove permanent."

His restless prowling ceased for an instant. "You wanted that?"

"A permanent cure for autism? Yes, I did." She shrugged, but resuming his pacing, he'd missed it. "But even though I didn't get that—" *or what I really wanted* "—your pheromone extended the bonding effects of my hormone by almost fifty percent. If I haven't found a cure for autism, maybe I've found a treatment. Why not a pill a patient could take every two weeks or so?"

"So you still need the formula to Pherotics's pheromone," he muttered.

"Now more than ever." She drew a cautious breath. "And I still have something to trade for it—a way to make Irresistible work."

"You know what I told you. You can't trade what isn't yours."

"But—" She was interrupted by the phone. Lifting the receiver, she listened, then said, "Yes, he's here." She hit the mute button. "Kay says you have a call on line one. Want to take it?"

"In my office." He headed for her door, then stopped. "Nic, about the Pherotics pheromone?" He waited till hope dawned on her face. "You can whistle for it."

Reese paused on the fourth-floor landing, dizzy. Leaning against the cold concrete wall, he closed his eyes. So Nic still wanted the Pherotics formula. *Now more than ever.*

I should give it to her. If she was innocent, then he owed it to her. And if she was guilty? *If you're a moon tiger, willing to kill me for the formula locked in my safe?*

He should still give it to her. Maybe she'd take it and go. Leave him unmauled.

Give it to her, and either way, guilty or innocent, she'd go. And he'd have no way of ever learning which she had been.

Not acceptable. He wanted to know. *Meant* to know, whatever the cost. Because he was stuck in limbo till he knew, unable to move closer to her or to turn and walk. Limbo? *Purgatory!* He pushed through the fire door and snarled at its squeak. *Okay, okay, I'll buy some friggin' oil to...* A grim smile crossed his face as he realized. Oh, no, he wouldn't. He could hear that squeak from his office when he left the door open. It was a built-in early alarm, guarding the approach from this end of the hall. He meant to know—but he wasn't dying to know.

Reaching his own office, he jabbed the button on his phone, heard the voice at the other end, said, "Hang on a minute," then went back to close his door. It was the private investigator he'd hired yesterday.

"So," the man droned on, minutes later. "Your Demi Cousteau will take a while longer. She's never had a driver's license—not under that name. And her financial setup, I'm still diggin' into that."

Reese doodled an intricate heart around Nic's name, the first on his man's list. Nic had three traffic tickets for speeding—that was her record for twenty-six years. No sort of violence whatsoever that his man could find. His smile faded. *That he could find.* Nic was as bright as they came. If she applied her brains to crime, would she leave any tracks?

A water heater malfunctioning, a wheel coming loose, a mugger who miscalculated his swing, a hit-and-run accident. Had any one of those nailed him, the cops would have made a cursory investigation, then shrugged it off. Bad luck happened all the time.

"Now your Peter Hadley, he's a master criminal."

"Oh?" His hopes soared.

"One hundred and twelve parking tickets outstanding. And his first wife snitched on him to the IRS for cheating on his tax returns."

Reese snorted. "And Baggett?"

"Baggett's clean. No traffic tickets and a credit rating I'd give my left nut for."

No surprise there. Reese had checked Tim out thoroughly before they'd entered into their partnership.

"Kay Grunwald?" He'd told his man to leave unlikeliest for last.

"Haven't got to her yet. I'll call you with more tomorrow."

He'd hoped for an easy answer, a smoking gun—gripped in anyone's hand but Nic's. But of course, Reese thought, hanging up, things were never that easy. So...what next? His eyes lit on the schooner print.

The door to Tim's corner office was closed. Reese rapped on the glass, heard an inquiring grunt and entered.

Size-eight feet propped on his desk, Reese's partner lounged back in his chair, a half-finished paper airplane suspended between his hands.

"Got a minute?" Reese leaned against the doorjamb. He found that Tim irritated him so much nowadays, he didn't like to go nearer.

"Sure." Tim looked down at his creation and creased the trailing edge of each wing. He made wonderful origami gliders. His three best flew from fishing line threaded through the gaps in the gridded ceiling. "What's up?"

He should circle in on this question, find some way to broach it tactfully. He was too edgy to bother. "You know I keep a card with the combination numbers to the safe drawn in on it." No use trying to weasel around that, no matter how it embarrassed him. Tim had walked in on him once, caught him using it. "I need to know, have you ever told anyone about that card?"

"Hmm..." Tim folded the tail fin up. "I s'pose it's possible."

Meaning he had. Reese reached a decision he'd been moving toward for months. The partnership was over. He'd buy Baggett out if it took his last nickel. "Who?" *You pitiful little bastard.*

Tim didn't look up, but the tips of his ears reddened. "Demi, one day when we went out for a drink." He ran a thumb along the underside of a wing, creating an airfoil curve. "Oh, and I b'lieve Hadley was there."

Disgust and gratitude made an all-but-indigestible stew. Reese had stamped opponents before, but he'd never felt the need to sneer at anyone. Still, if those two were all Tim

had told, then… "No one else, Tim? This is important."
This is my life, you creep, so get it straight.

"Oh…and I guess I told Nic, one day in the lab."

He could have cheerfully stamped him now. So she
knew. "That's all, *partner?*" *Or do you tell that one on
me for drinks at the bars?*

Tim still wouldn't meet his eyes. "That's all." He put
down the plane and stared at it. "Guess I shouldn't have."

Reese didn't trust himself to agree. He turned to go.
Demi, Hadley, Nic. One of those three, then.

"Oh, Reese?"

He stopped, but didn't look back.

"I've been meaning to rearrange the furniture in here.
Would you have a minute to give me a hand?"

"I wouldn't."

DEMI CALLED HIM at four with an invitation to squire her
to a gallery opening. Their exchanges this past week had
been icily formal, each of them holding out for an apology
that wouldn't be coming. So this was a new development—
Demi meant to forgive him for not falling for her, if not
forget? That suited Reese, but he had other fish to fry this
night. "'Fraid I'll be working late all this week, Dem. I
got a postponement on taxes last quarter. Now it's coming
due."

That's one, he thought, hanging up. After that he called
each of the others—even Hadley was in, for once in his
life—and repeated his announcement, along with a request
that if they had any receipts or expenses, to turn them in
before leaving. Then he phoned for a pizza. Even a stalking
horse had to eat.

Nic arrived as the deliveryman was leaving, her stormy
face in perfect contrast to the pizza man's well-tipped grin.
"I can't believe you're doing this! You *can't* do it. Not
here."

"Why not?" Reese cocked an ear for the sound of the
elevator descending. Good. That was all of them gone, then.

All but his prime suspect. He refocused on her and smiled in spite of himself.

"Why *not?*" She stalked over to him, stood teetering, one step from shoving him in the chest, apparently. "Every attempt that's been made on you has been made here, Reese. You'd be crazy to work late!"

He'd be crazy not to. *I want this over, kid. I want you in my life or way the hell out of it, and till I know...* He shrugged. "There's only two sure things in life, Nic, death and taxes."

"It's not the IRS man I'm worried about!"

"Fine. You go home, *I'll* worry." Reese sat down at his desk. "Scoot."

"Ha!" She grabbed his visitor's chair and dragged it toward the hall.

"What the hell, Nic?" He shot to his feet.

"I'll be sitting out here, then, till you wise up and leave."

"The hell you will!" He caught an armrest, ending the chair's progress. How was he going to catch whoever it was with Nic standing guard out there, scaring him off? And if she was the tiger, he didn't need her lurking just out of sight, choosing the best moment to spring.

"Reese, in case you haven't noticed, this guy doesn't like witnesses. He's backed off every time I came round."

This was love? Never being sure if you wanted to kiss her or shake her silly—or both? He drew a breath. "Trust me, Nic. There is *no* bogeyman. Now go home and let me eat my pizza and do my taxes."

"No." She turned toward the hall. "I'll be out here if you need—" She squeaked as he caught her arm and spun her around.

Hauling both chair and her to the side of his desk—that left him a clear shot at the door—he let her go. "Sit. Have a slice of pizza." He aimed a finger at her as she started to speak. "Not another *word.*"

She closed her mouth, sat glowering while he finished his first slice, then took one herself when he held the box out again—ate it, her eyes blazing above the tomato sauce. Reese drew a long breath, smelling roses and pepperoni and a half-imagined whiff of honey. *I must be crazy.* Here he sat with a woman who maybe wanted to kill him, and he felt...happy?

Two slices of pizza later, Nic's compliance was over. She prowled his office, shooting dark glances at him, then ducking her head out the door to check the hall. "Want to know what I think?" She ignored his warning growl. "It's not Kay. She hasn't a thing to gain by your death."

"Agreed." He supposed he should hear her out. Smoke-screen or honest opinion, either might give him a clue.

"Same goes for Hadley. If you died, Tim would cut off his consulting fees the next day. Now Demi—" she flicked him a wary glance "—Demi might have a motive. She thinks there'd be a market for a woman's perfume that made men bond to women. Even though we've shown the bonding isn't permanent, I suppose a woman could always reapply the scent—keep dosing her guy to keep him faithful. But you're standing in Demi's way of using my findings for that."

"Tim doesn't like her idea any better," Reese pointed out dryly.

"Ah, but Demi could handle Tim if you were out of her way."

Could she? Tim had an almost religious faith in his own discovery. On the other hand, the way he mooned after Demi... Reese shrugged.

"But it's hard to picture Demi getting down and dirty," Nic continued. "She'd be much likelier to try an all-out seduction to get her way."

Which she had, but a gentleman could hardly say so. So once that had failed, Demi played hardball? She seemed desperate for money. But then, his investigator had said Demi had no driver's license. On the other hand, that was hardly a requirement for doing a hit-and-run murder.

"Then there's Tim." Nic popped her head out the door,

glanced both ways and turned back. "Tim gets Pherotics if you die?"

Once the key-man insurance paid out. "Yes."

Nic turned her hands palms up. "There's my choice. With you gone, Tim could fire me and Hadley, then go back to your original game plan, starring his pheromone. Tim thinks he stands to make millions—though he's wrong. Tim doesn't like you—doesn't like any of us, I'd say, except Demi. And she'd continue as his limited partner if you were gone. I vote for Tim."

Except that Tim had no need to steal the combination to the company safe. He'd opened it for Reese on half-a-dozen occasions, and after the second time, he'd had the numbers down cold. Besides which, Tim had no need to swipe Pherotics's formula—its structure was stamped on his brain. But Nic didn't know about that hand tugging at his wallet. Or did she?

"So what do you think?" she demanded.

"I told you, I don't believe in bogeymen."

She hissed her impatience. "Then, hypothetically speaking, if you did?"

"You don't quit." For better or worse, she didn't know the word. "Hypothetically speaking?" If she was innocent, then he needed her out of his way. Haring off after the wrong suspect might keep her safe. "Tim's a good bet."

She beamed at him as if he were a dull pupil spelling the word right at last. "On the other hand," he added evilly, "it could be you."

Her smile faded. "You think I'd kill you?"

Babe, you are *killing me.* "Hard to say," he said, keeping his tone light. "We fight like cat and dog." Her eyes glittered—tears or resentment? He'd have given his right arm to know which. "On the other hand, here you are, trying to save my miserable neck—from a bogeyman."

Her chin tipped defiantly. "Ohhh, I'd do the same for any…mutt."

He could walk across the room, lay his hands on her and make her eat those brave words. Whatever was wrong be-

tween them, it sure wasn't chemistry. Eyes locked with
hers, Reese shoved back his chair.

"What do you think *I'd* stand to gain?" she asked
quickly.

He got a grip, cocked his head. That question could be
injured innocence or delicate, deliberate probing. He'd have
given his life to know which—might, if he read her wrong.
Angel or devil woman? Trust my heart or my head?
"Well," he drawled, "Tim would send you and Hadley
back to RIIT so fast your head would spin. You've always
wanted that."

He edged a step closer to the cliff. "But now you want
the Pherotics pheromone to mix with your stuff. Would you
go without it?"

"You think I'd kill for that?" Nic crossed to his desk,
stood staring down at him, golden eyes shadowed.

*If it meant a cure for your sister? Fame and glory for
you? Revenge on a man who wronged you? I don't know,
lover. I wish I did.*

"I offered to trade, for Pete's sake!" she added when he
didn't speak. "Your formula for saving Pherotics."

"But I won't trade." *Not if it means I never know who
you are.*

"Then I don't need to kill you—you're committing financial suicide! Irresistible will never sell as it's formu-
lated."

"Why is that?" *Tell me. I need to know.* Once upon a
time, saving his company was all he'd cared about. He still
cared, but now it came second.

She shook her head. Her gaze traveled to the stacks of
receipts he'd shoved to one side. She flicked a pile. "How
fast are you going down?"

"We've gone down twice. Once more and we're
breathing water." *And I can't ask for your help. But, oh,
babe, if you put out a hand...*

She drew a long breath, then sighed. "Have you any of
Demi's pure fragrance left—before you mixed in the pheromone? I'd need that."

Triumph blazed in his eyes. She saw it, scowled and spun away, resumed pacing, her shoulders hunched.

He tried his best to keep the jubilation from his voice. Surrender, this was partial surrender—a scrap of the white flag if not her whole banner. "We don't have any here. But Demi may, at her lab."

"And I'd need your pheromone, of course. I need to mix the two myself, do some more tests. Then I'll know for sure."

His inner victory dance faltered. Meanwhile, she'd have another chance to lay hands on his formula. Was this really surrender, then—or a stall? One last attempt to get what she wanted? *You're the girl who never quits.*

"Well?" The word was a challenge, delivered in D's smoky whisper.

He who risks most wins most—or falls a long, long way. "All right, then. Let's do it."

BUT DEMI HAD NONE of the Irresistible fragrance in stock, Reese learned the next day. Her lab chemist would have to make a new batch—when he returned from his vacation in two weeks.

Not good enough, not while he sat here in limbo and his company slid down the tubes. For an exorbitant fee and the price of a round-trip fare—first class—Reese persuaded Demi to fly to New York and mix the scent herself. Three days to deliver it, she estimated.

Meanwhile, he kept his nightly vigil, using himself as bait. And night after uneventful night, Nic kept it with him, in spite of his exasperated protests.

By the afternoon of the fourth day, Reese was starting to wonder. Maybe the bogeyman *was* simply that, a myth to scare children after dark.

Or was Nic queering his hunt, keeping all evil at bay by her presence?

Or Nic was the huntress herself, a tiger purring on his hearth, waiting for him to turn his back, bare his nape, and then...

Whatever she was, she was doing him no good, sharing his waiting game. He needed a free hand, and he wanted it tonight. But how to get it? At the last minute on the fourth day, he found a way.

NIC GLANCED at her watch—nearly six-thirty—then rapped on Reese's half-open door and entered. "Are you working late tonight?"

"I am." Reese's gaze was a mix of annoyance and boredom when he looked up from his desk. "And you are not. I'm not getting any work done with you breathing down my neck."

"So work at home where you're safe."

"I'm safe here. There's no bogeyman, Nic, and what's more, I've finally realized you don't believe in him, either." Rising, Reese approached, lazy, sexy, his mouth curving with wry amusement. "Game's up, kiddo. I've figured it out at last. The bogeyman's just an excuse. You're stuck on me. That's why you've been hanging around."

"Stuck on *you?* You're stuck on yourself, Durand, if you believe that!"

He patted her cheek. "It's very cute, and I'm flattered, kid, but if I wanted a woman right now, somebody like D, then I'd—"

They stepped apart at the sound of heels clacking in the hall. The door flew open and Demi Cousteau stalked between them, Tim Baggett tagging meekly at her heels. "Put it there, Tim."

Tim placed a box on Reese's desk, then stood blinking behind his thick lenses, his eyes all for Demi.

She gestured grandly at the package. "There it is, Reese, two liters of Irresistible scent—and for that you owe me the finest dinner money can buy. We sat on the runway for two whole *hours* getting here—there are thunderstorms in New York. And when finally I made it to Boston, my cab hit the mother of all traffic jams in the tunnel. It has been an utterly *miserable* day. I'm frazzled, I'm famished, I want cosseting. Pay up!"

"Nothing I'd like better." Thumbs hooked in his pockets, Reese rocked back on his heels, amused. "But I'm afraid you'll have to take a rain check. I'm finishing my taxes tonight." As she pouted, he added, "So why don't you let Tim take you out—someplace wonderful—at company expense?"

Tim's mouth opened wordlessly. He looked like a frog fielding an unexpected fly. He blurted, "Uh, sure. Yeah! I'd be delighted to. Demi?"

Demi's eyes flashed at Reese; her pout deepened, then vanished suddenly in a rueful smile. She shrugged gracefully and turned to Tim. "Then I'm yours, Sir Galahad. Take me away."

"And take Nicola, too," Reese added. "She's been working overtime all week. Pherotics owes her something better than take-out pizza."

Tim's disappointment and Demi's annoyance would have been disincentive enough. But it was Reese's trying to get rid of her that hurt, that and his previous words. *If I wanted a woman...somebody like D...* Nicola shook her head. "No, thanks. I don't think I—"

"She's going," Reese said to Tim.

"Whoever's going, let's *go*," Demi decreed. "Give me two seconds to freshen up, and then..." She vanished into Reese's washroom.

"Tell Demi I'm grabbing my keys." Tim darted out the door.

"Reese, I'm not—" Nicola stopped as he caught her shoulder and dropped his mouth to her ear.

"You really think I'm in danger, Nic?"

His lips brushing her ear, she nodded and fought off a shiver.

"Then here's your chance for some real detective work. They're your two best suspects. Stick with 'em tonight and maybe you'll learn something."

"But—"

"C'mon, Nic. How can I be in danger when you're riding herd on your bogeyman? Or am I right? You never believed in him?'' He chucked her under the chin as if she were ten and he her uncle. ''You know, kid, I think you're sweet. And I'm *really* flattered. It's just that—''

''That you have a terminally fat head if that's what you think!'' she hissed, spinning away. Schoolgirl, twit—that was what he thought. *Thank you, Nic, but no thanks. If I needed a real woman...*

''Well,'' Demi demanded, emerging from the washroom, ''are you coming, Nic? With the two of us, Tim will think he's died and gone to heaven.''

''I guess I am.'' Reese had one thing right if all else wrong. If she kept Tim and Demi in sight all night, then nothing could harm him. Still, as she followed Demi from his office, she turned back for one last word. ''Promise you'll lock this door, and I'll go. Otherwise, deal's off.''

He scowled, then shrugged. ''All right, all right. I'll lock it.''

Reese stood in the corridor, watching her join Demi, then turn the corner toward the elevator. Stood listening to it descend. *Alone at last.*

Or was he? He walked all the way to the elevator, then back along the corridor, opening doors, checking each room. Nobody. Pherotics lay in dusky silence. *Get my taxes done, at least.*

Returning soft-footed to his office, Reese remembered his promise. He flipped the dead bolt to lock the door— *There, Nic*—then flipped it back to open. Settling at his desk, he reached for the gun. He had a feeling company was coming.

Let it be anyone in the wide world but Nic.

CHAPTER TWENTY-TWO

TIM'S PICKUP was the four-wheel equivalent of his Harley. A muscle truck, Nic thought with amusement as he unlocked it. Giant tires, roll bar—a chromed and shining declaration of the chemist's virility.

Tim pushed up his glasses. "Dem, can I ask a favor? I sprained my neck yesterday doin' a bench press. Should've used a spotter. I know you're tired, but would you mind driving?"

She shook her head instantly. "Poor Timothy. Nothing I'd love more than to drive this brute. But I don't have a license."

"You don't drive?"

Demi dimpled. "I once dated a Grand Prix racer whose idea of foreplay was...well, let's just say I drive superbly, but I'm a New Yorker. Why worry about checking your oil when you can catch a cab?"

Nic stepped forward. "I'll drive, Tim." Playing chauffeur would serve as a distraction from her anger at Reese, she reflected as they left Cambridge by the Mass Avenue bridge. And her growing suspicion. Had some note rung false in his you've-got-a-crush-on-me routine? Had Reese been *trying* to insult her, drive her away? *Just what are you up to, Reese Durand?*

Whatever, it was too late to turn back now. And his reasoning still seemed sound. While she shepherded her suspects, he should be safe. Meanwhile, Demi's bad transportation karma continued. They hit a traffic jam east of Fenway. "Big Red Sox game toni—" Tim paused, his mouth rounded in a perfect *O*. He slapped his forehead.

"Jeez, what a dimwit!" He groped in a pants pocket, then stopped himself and shrugged. "Oh, well, what the hell."

"What is it, Tim?"

He chuckled unhappily while Nicola gained a car's length, then stopped again. The streets were jammed as far as you could see. "I completely spaced it. I was going to the game tonight. Was going to meet a couple of friends. We had great seats."

Demi patted his knee. "Poor baby! Nic and I will make it up to you."

"I don't doubt that." Tim frowned out the window. "It's just that..."

That Tim had promised to meet his two friends ten minutes previously at a nearby sports bar—and that Tim was the one who'd purchased the trio's tickets. Had paid dearly for them, Nic deduced. "Look, we can drive by there. Find them," she suggested.

Except that the bar lay down a gridlocked side street— one way, the wrong direction. By the time they turned around and inched back to it... "They'll have given up and gone home," Tim predicted, "cursing my name. Look, if you'd pull over, I could run it faster than you can drive."

But there was no legal place to pull over. There rarely was in Boston. Tim muttered. Nic rolled her eyes. *I should have stayed with Reese.*

"Oh, crap! And while I'm forgetting things—" Tim dug a pink message slip from his shirt pocket "—I've been carrying this around for you all day, Nic. Took it at lunch-time, then I got busy and..." His mumble trailed off as she took it and read.

If you still want to talk to me, tonight's the only pos-sible night. Come to my house in Newton, 33 Sherlock Way, before nine.

Jed Feinstein.

"He called me back? I don't believe it!"

"He said something about it's gotta be tonight—he's off on a vacation or something tomorrow, if I got it straight."

Blast! She needed his data, longed for it in direct proportion to the trouble it was taking her to collect it.

"Look, I've got an idea." Tim braced an elbow on the dash and turned to beam at them. "Let's *all* go to the game. We'll dump my truck first parking lot we come across and see if we can find my friends. If we do, then I'm sure I can scalp a coupl'a extra tickets. If we don't, then I've got three already and we're set." He gave Demi a pleading look. "How 'bout a foot-long chili dog with extra cheese and sauerkraut, Demi, and a couple of beers? Is there a finer meal in the world than that? What d'you say?"

Demi bared her teeth. "Tim…I loathe sauerkraut. *And* baseball."

"And I've got to get to Newton," Nic added. They'd been headed in that direction from the start, to some French restaurant in Brookline that Tim had recommended.

The solution was obvious. A few minutes later the two women sat in the motionless truck, watching Tim jog off through the stadium-bound crowd that mobbed the sidewalks. He'd find his friends or he wouldn't. Would see the game either way, then catch the train home after that. Demi had elected to drive out to Newton with Nic, and then they would eat. The Nose sighed and drooped lower in her seat—a lily wilting.

Nic gnawed on her lip. *I was supposed to watch them both.* And the one she'd lost was the one she suspected most—though she found it near impossible to believe that Tim had anything but baseball on the brain at the moment. But was the elegant if disheartened Demi a more likely candidate? *Maybe Reese is right. The bogeyman exists only in my head.*

Or maybe it was Hadley. She smiled at the preposterous image. Her adviser was ninety miles down the road in Providence. If Hadley did any sneaking around tonight, no doubt he'd be sneaking out on his wife.

"So—" Demi sat up straighter "—we have to do this?

That wasn't just an excuse to ditch Tim? We can't go collapse in a wine bar?''

"I've been trying to catch this guy for weeks, Demi." Bracing herself for a tantrum, Nicola edged over one lane, angling for a turn up ahead.

Demi sighed resignedly. "Look, if I come along quietly, no whining, will you tell me what's wrong with Irresistible? Reese said you may have figured it out, and I really need to know."

"Ummm…" Nic made the turn. Heading away from the stadium, the traffic was lighter. Should she tell? But then, why keep it a secret? She was giving it to Reese for free. "Okay, but remember, this is only a theory." Beyond the sports fans' range, she turned west again. "Whatever pheromone Tim isolated, let's assume it was a male one. Something akin to androsterone, which you find in men's sweat and saliva."

"Saliva?" Demi screwed up her nose. *"Gaaack!"*

Nicola laughed. "Why d'you think people love to French-kiss—all those pheromones sloshing around?" A lane opened up ahead and she accelerated. "So assume Tim found a male pheromone, and let's say it worked—really did function as a sexual attractant in his early tests. You saw what it did to my vomeronasal organ in the lab." Demi nodded gravely. "So if it's a male message intended for women, it's saying something like, ''Here I am, babe. There's nobody studlier. Surrender."

Demi giggled. "Subtle!"

"Mother Nature gives a fig about subtle, as long as her message is clear—and effective." Nicola found the entrance to the turnpike she'd been seeking. A sense of urgency brought her foot down hard on the gas. Somewhere she could feel time running out, sand through a glass.

"Now, if it's a message aimed at women, then women should be more sensitive to it than men. For instance, women are *one hundred times* more aware of androsterone than men are." They passed an exit, not the right one. She pushed the truck up to seventy miles an hour. "Which means a man can 'broadcast' on the androsterone 'wave-length' and only women 'hear' him. The message goes right over the other guys' heads and into the women's ears—into their VNOs, actually."

"But what's this got to do with Irresistible?" Demi demanded.

"Well, Tim's a chemist, not an animal behaviorist. Suppose he made a very common mistake when he mixed your scent with his pheromone. Suppose Tim thought that if *some* of something was good, then *more* of the same thing would be better. What if he mixed it too strong—put too much of his pheromone into each bottle of cologne?"

Their exit flashed into view, and Nicola shifted down. "Is there a map in the glove compartment?" While she paid the turnpike fee, Demi dragged out a map of Boston. "If he did make it too strong," she resumed, "then, in effect, he's turned up the volume on his message too loud. Now it isn't going over the men's heads—*they're getting it.*"

"So?" Demi refolded the map to show the outlying towns.

"So when a guy wears Irresistible, he's coming on too strong. Imagine if Arnold Schwarzenegger walked into a cocktail party, tore off all his clothes and yelled, "Give me all the women!" What would the men at the party do?" Nicola turned right toward Main Street.

Demi grinned. "That's easy. They'd either leap out the nearest window or they'd pick up their chairs and brain him."

"*Exactly.*" Nicola pulled the truck over and reached for the map.

"Hadley had that ridiculous fight with the UPS man..." Demi murmured. "Over me!" She clapped her hands delightedly as she realized.

"And Tim got a black eye the first day I met him." Nicola found her route, started driving again. "And watch Reese, Tim and Hadley in any crowded room. They stay as far from each other as they can get. They're getting on each other's nerves *at the instinctive level*. On a conscious level, they just think they can't stand each other.'' She frowned, a pattern forming slowly at the back of her mind. A face moving toward her through the dark, coming nearer, clearer.

"Then men aren't buying the cologne twice because they get beaten up?"

Nicola nodded, checking the names of streets as they passed each block. "They wouldn't necessarily make that connection, but yes, that's partly why. They wear Irresistible, and it's friction, friction, friction wherever they go. They're uneasy. Their men friends snarl at them, snub them. They don't have a good time when they wear Irresistible."

She found the cross street she needed and turned. "What's more, a man wearing Irresistible is sensing *his own* pheromones, since the dose is so high. That makes him feel extra sexy. On the prowl."

"That's situation normal."

"No, because he not only wants it—*he feels certain he'll get it*. He thinks he's Mr. Irresistible. Then if he doesn't score, imagine what that feels like. Say you dressed for a party—a gorgeous dress, best perfume, your hair looks perfect. You figure this is *your* night."

"Situation normal." Demi's laugh was wryly self-mocking.

"Not for most women, it isn't. But imagine how you'd feel if you went to your party looking the best you'd ever looked in your life—and nobody asked you to dance. There you are in your gorgeous dress, looking perfect, feeling irresistible—and you bomb out. How d'you feel then?"

"*Major* disappointment. I'd never wear that dress again."

"Or buy that cologne."

Demi leaned forward urgently. "But I don't *get* it. If the pheromone is extra-strong, why don't the men wearing it get laid extra-often?"

"Because all a pheromone can do is make a woman *no-*

tice a man. That much is instinct. But after that she bases her decision on other things—her experience, education, logic.''

The truck rounded a bend and the sign for Sherlock Way swung into view at last. Nicola turned left, looking for numbers on the large well-tended houses set far back on manicured lawns. ''So imagine you're at our party one more time. Someone taps your shoulder, and suddenly you get an impression—the world's sexiest man is standing behind you. You turn around and there he is—five feet tall with halitosis and a bad attitude toward women, wearing Irresistible. D'you take him home to bed?''

''I don't *think* so.''

''Right. Because your brain contradicts your instincts. But since he's wearing a supercharged male pheromone— Irresistible—your VNO keeps on receiving his same message—'I'm a stud! I'm a stud!' Therefore your impression will be that the guy's coming on too strong. That he's conceited, pushy—because his cologne is *pushing that impression at you.*

''If he's small and unappealing, you'll see him as a pushy, egotistical little nerd, an embarrassing nuisance. If he's *large* and unappealing, he may even scare you. You'll see him as a pushy, sexually-threatening nuisance. A potential rapist.''

''Either way, Irresistible doesn't help him score,'' Demi murmured.

''Right. He'll get a lot more attention than he usually does—*then a lot more rejections.* And he paid one hundred dollars an ounce for those extra rejections.'' Nicola parked in front of number thirty-three, a large colonial.

''I see...'' Demi sat thinking. ''But say I turn around and it's Reese, or someone as sexy as Reese, wearing Irresistible?''

''Then your instincts, your experience, your logic all line up like three cherries on a slot machine—the guy hits the jackpot. But then most likely he would have won you, anyway. Irresistible maybe gives him an edge—what would have happened anyway happens a little faster, a little harder. Seems a bit more magical than normal. He gets your full attention, then he runs with it.'' *Runs off with your heart, like a football tucked under one arm.* She sighed and looked toward the house.

"Then if we remix Irresistible, that fixes the problem?"

"I think it will. If we lower the volume on the message, then we eliminate the male-friction factor. We also eliminate the letdown factor—the wearer doesn't feel so certain he's bound to score. Then if he doesn't, he's not as disgruntled.

"He'll simply notice that whenever he wears Irresistible, he gets more female attention. When he meets a woman he could have won, anyway, he'll win her faster. And when he meets a woman where romance was teetering in the balance, she'll be more likely to give him a chance."

"That should sell." Demi steepled her fingers and brought them to her mouth. "Yeeees...that should work. It won't be the million-dollar overnight sensation that Reese promised me. But as men find that it gives them an edge, word will spread. This could be one of those slow-building classic scents, the kind a man starts wearing at twenty— and wears till he's ninety." She clapped her hands with sudden glee. "Yes! It'll work!"

"Always assuming my theory's correct." Nicola opened her door. "Meanwhile, I still have a dissertation to finish. Wait for me here?"

REESE SAT AT HIS DESK rolling a pencil idly back and forth across its surface. *Come on, damn you, come on.* Instinct or wishful thinking, something told him tonight was the night. That even now the bogeyman was creeping closer through the dark. *Nic, Demi or Hadley?* Every choice was unthinkable, yet somebody was trying to kill him.

Nic. He found himself smiling as he pictured his fiercely earnest bodyguard of the past few days. His smile faded as he remembered the hurt in her eyes when he'd made that crack about a real woman like D. *You're the woman for*

me, Nic. Enough woman to keep him guessing and en-
chanted the rest of his life. Vulnerable child. Fey, moonstruck lover. Driven scientist. A staunch friend to watch his
back.

His bonding to her should be ending any time now if she
read her voles right, she'd said.

Reese couldn't imagine it ending. Ever. No longer could
remember what it had felt like before loving her.

*But if it's you trying to kill me, Nic? If this night ends
with me catching you in my nets like a crazed tiger, will
that end the bonding? Or would I be crazy enough to love
you still?*

He wouldn't have to make that choice. His every instinct
cried out that she wasn't his stalker.

But the needle on his compass had been reeling ever
since he'd met her. Did he know where true north lay anymore—or was he blindly following his cock? *Come on,
damn you, come on, whoever you are. I'm sick of waiting—
is that part of your crazy game? You lie low till impatience
makes me slip?*

The short hairs on his back lifted as the elevator's motor
kicked in, its distant hum like a growling reply. Tiger rising.

Thumbing the Beretta's safety catch, Reese headed for
the elevator. *Coming to get you, my friend! Get you out of
my life.*

WHEN NICOLA RETURNED to the truck, she was scowling.
"Weird!" she muttered as she started its engine.

"What's weird?" Demi held out a bag of airline peanuts.

Nic shook her head in refusal. "That guy back there,
Jed, was supposed to have taken part in my first experiment. But he didn't. He went through the first-day interview. Then he stood in line all the next day to take my
test—he should have been the last one tested, number
forty."

She turned off Sherlock Way and accelerated. Something
was nagging at the back of her mind, something bad...

something urgent. "But there was some sort of mix-up. When Forty finally reached the lab door after waiting hours and hours, Joe, my assistant, turned him away. Told him we already had all the subjects we needed—in other words, forty. So Jed stamped off in a rage for having wasted his whole day and he's been pouting ever since. Refusing to return my phone calls."

"Understandable." Demi offered the peanuts again. Nic nodded this time, and Demi poured the rest of the bag into her open palm.

"Sure. But what I *don't* understand is, how did I get forty evaluation forms on the day of the test? Who filled out that fortieth form, the one with no number, if Jed Feinstein didn't?" She'd have to think. Absently she tossed the peanuts in her mouth, scowled, stopped the truck at a red light.

"More nuts? I'm starving." Demi dug into the large shoulder bag that sat on the seat between them.

Glancing down, Nicola found herself staring at a small, gleaming gun, slipped in the side pocket of Demi's purse. "Good Lord. That's real?"

"What every well-dressed woman should wear in the city." Demi laughed and pulled it out for her inspection. "I dated a police detective for a while. He gave me this and insisted I learn how to use it." The lady's derringer was decorative as a piece of jewelry with its swirling inlays of leaves and flowers, gold upon silver.

"Pretty." But something more important than deadly toys was tugging at her attention. What? Nicola started as someone behind them honked. She put the truck into gear. "That wasn't the only weird thing. Tim didn't take that message today. He took it yesterday."

It was only luck that she'd found Jed at home. He'd been scheduled to leave on a cross-country road trip, leaving town early this morning. But his friend's car had broken down, so the trip had been put off a day.

Demi shrugged. "I suppose Tim forgot when he took the message. He was certainly rattled enough this evening."

"Or he forgot to give it to me yesterday, then was embarrassed to find he'd muffed the delivery—so he told a white lie." *Or he lied for another reason.* Nicola's stomach swooped, like the first dip on a roller coaster.

Demi gestured ahead. "I don't remember passing this shopping center."

Neither did Nicola. She pulled the pickup into the parking lot. "Could I see that map again?" She looked back over her shoulder, searching fruitlessly for a street name at the intersection they'd just crossed.

Demi yelped as something heavy clunked to the floor. Nic whirled back around. "What was that?"

"A foot breaker if it had been an inch to the right!" Demi sat up with a thick metal rod in one hand. "I guess this was tucked inside one of Tim's maps. I pulled it out by mistake." She set it on the seat between them. "A railroad spike?"

Lifting it, Nic turned it in the light cast by the mall's yellow sodium lamps. "No. It's a cold chisel." For cleaving metal. Its cutting end was jagged and silvery where it had encountered something even harder than itself recently. *Like a safe...*

Dark and ugly, the pattern formed, its pieces sliding into place like dry leaves slithering across a floor. Tim wanting someone else to drive—so it would be easier for him to beg off the excursion at a moment's notice. Tim holding her message till he could make use of it—to draw her away from Reese's side. Tim wearing a cologne that made him hate and envy Reese. *Tim at a Red Sox game, only twenty minutes from Pherotics by train.* "We've got to get back!" But dear God, where was back from here?

THE ELEVATOR HUMMED.

Gripping the automatic with both hands, Reese stood with his back to the corridor wall. To his right lay the corner where the hallway turned to parallel the front of the building. His bogeyman would step off the elevator, move down that front stretch, then turn left here to approach

Reese's office at the back. A nerve ticked in his cheek. *This is too easy. He's gotta know I hear him coming.*

But then, the bogeyman couldn't be sure that Reese had put two and two together—realized those accidents weren't accidental. Reese had admitted his convictions to no one. *Not even to Nic.* Therefore, his stalker couldn't know: was he sneaking up on unsuspecting prey? Or had hunter become the hunted?

The elevator stopped one floor below, at three, and Reese cursed heartily. Not so easy, after all. *So you step off below and then what?*

He jumped as the elevator hummed again—and rose. *Damn you!* Whoever he—she?—was, he was good. If he'd stepped off on three, then he'd be sneaking up the stairs, attacking from behind.

Or he was coming now—would burst out of the elevator any second. Reese slowed his breathing even more. *Fire door squeaks, I turn left. Footsteps to the right, I aim right.* Piece of cake. *Easy, boy.*

He stiffened as, around the corner, the elevator doors rolled open. Ears straining, heart pounding, he waited. No sound of footsteps—the guy was that light on his feet? Or he wasn't there at all?

The elevator doors rolled shut, the noise a perfect cover for a soft rush down the corridor. Reese leveled the gun and waited. *Damm you, make a sound!*

Nothing...for thirty seconds or so. And he who hesitates... Reese sank to a crouch. Rulé to Live By number five—or was it six? Never be where your enemy expects you to be. At dwarf height, gun ready, he lunged around the corner. "Freeze!"

The empty corridor mocked him. He clenched his teeth and rose. *Oh, you're good, my friend. You're very good.*

If he wasn't here, then the bogeyman must be down on third.

Or he was still down on first—had pushed the buttons for three and four, then stepped off the elevator. *A war of nerves to soften me up?*

Or he *was* here on four. While Reese had dithered around the corner, he'd slipped into a front office—Kay's, Hadley's or Tim's.

The other choices could wait. This was the first thing to determine. Nearest to the elevator, Kay's office was his best bet. Shoulders aching with tension, Reese drew a breath and moved.

"NIC, *DON'T!*"

Nicola stamped on the gas. Swinging out around the bus, the pickup stormed past its moving flank, headlights racing to meet it, horns blaring, then swerved back into its own lane and sped on. Demi cursed fervently.

"Sorry," Nicola muttered, not sorry at all. She'd missed the entrance to the turnpike. They were returning to Boston by a parkway, not making good time. Speed of light wouldn't have been fast enough.

"I can't believe Tim would want to kill Reese. *We're* the ones who'll be killed if you don't...slo-o-ow *down!*"

They shot under a red light, tires shrieking on either side as cars braked frantically, then honked outrage behind them. "Sorry." She'd tried to explain to Demi, but she couldn't as she had to drive and marshal her facts clearly at the same time. No doubt Demi thought she'd gone mad.

"Tim invited us to a *ball* game, Nic. He'd never have done that if—"

"If he thought we'd accept the offer. He's an improviser, Demi, and he does it brilliantly. If we'd accepted, he'd have shown us a great time and put Reese off to another night." Except that Reese had said he was finishing his taxes tonight. Tonight was too good an opportunity to miss.

"But it makes no sense! Why would Tim want to break into Reese's safe? He *opens* the safe for Reese sometimes, he told me— *Oh!*"

This light they had to stop for, or ram the car stopping ahead into the intersection. Nic beat her palms on the steering wheel with frustration. "My point *exactly*. Tim made

a point of telling you that! Don't you see? That's his alibi.
He didn't want to break into the safe—he wanted to make
it look *as if someone was trying to.* Me, you, a common
thief, an industrial spy—I don't think he cared who was
blamed. Oh, come *on!*'' The light changed. She roared up
on the car ahead, loomed over its bumper and honked till
its driver lost his nerve and swung aside.

"Look, why don't we call Reese if you're so worried?
Warn him."

"That's a great idea." But she wasn't wasting one minute to stop and look for a phone. "Tell me if you see
one…"

Three blocks farther on, they found a booth. Nic stopped
in the curbside lane and scribbled down the number of
Reese's private line while Demi scrounged for change in
her purse. "Just tell him I said it's Tim and that Tim is
coming for him—might be there already. Tell him not to
be a macho fool."

"I'm also telling him I think you're stark raving mad!"
Demi slammed the door.

Fine, as long as she warned him. Nicola clasped her
shaking hands together and looked down, willing herself to
calmness. *Cannot panic. Must not panic.* Pherotics was still
five miles away, at least.

And then? When she got there, she'd do whatever she
had to do. Protect him somehow. But with what? Her eyes
focused on the gleam of metal in Demi's open purse. *With
this.*

She slipped the killing toy into her pocket, then jumped
violently as Demi opened her door. "I can't get through.
His line's busy."

"Oh, *damn!* Here!" She snatched the paper from Demi's
fingers, jotted down Pherotics's main number. "Either of
these numbers will reach him. Just keep trying till you get
him, then give him my message. Please?"

"Oh, no. You're *not* leaving me here!"

"I've got to, Dem." Nic shoved Demi's purse into her

hands. "Just catch a cab—or look, there's a T-stop across the street. Phone him, then take the train. Demi, *please*."

"Tim isn't trying to kill anyone, Nic!"

"If I'm right and you're wrong, then Reese is *dead*. You want to take that chance?"

Demi closed her mouth with a snap. Eyes blazing, she slammed the door. Nic missed the next light, stopped and turned to look back. The Nose was phoning. *Bless you!* The light turned to green and she shot away.

CHAPTER TWENTY-THREE

HE'D CHECKED every room leading off the front hall. Found no one, which meant his secret friend still lurked somewhere below.

So their waiting game continued. Under cover of darkness, Reese waited in Tim's corner office. From here he had a clear view of the lighted corridor, a straight shot at the stairwell door. His ears were tuned for its faintest squeak. That would be the way he'd come. *She* would come?

Reese glanced up, stretching his stiff neck. Overhead, Tim's gliders hung motionless, pale vultures in the gloom. Waiting for a dream to die?

Whoever this is, is smart. Too damned smart. With nerves of steel, playing the game like this. Reese couldn't see Hadley lying coolly in wait, letting each moment stretch till it shredded. Couldn't see Demi, her mind moving out through the night to meet his, two wills circling silently in the dark, a deadly dance.

Whoever you are, I know you. Don't know you at all. But you're here, close. I can feel you thinking at me.

Nic. She was the one with the brains and the nerve. The one he'd danced with in the dark. Whose mind he knew intimately—and not at all. *Is it you, darlin'?*

Who else *could* it be?

Maybe there's nobody at all. Maybe I'm goin' crazy.

Or maybe *she* was crazy? He'd crossed her, bullied her, used her enough to enrage any sane woman. But Nic had a sister in an asylum, and who was to say it didn't run in the family? Those cool gunfighter's eyes. Her implacable determination. Push that over the edge and what did you get? A stalking moon tiger, as innocent as she was deadly?

No, it's not Nic. I'd stake my life on it.

That was just what he was doing.

Riiinng!

He rose to his feet at the first ring of the phone, heart lurching, breath snagged, then returning with a rush. The sound came again, from his office. His private line.

No question who that was. His thoughts had called her to him. *Let me pick up the phone, love. Hear your laughing voice with the sounds of a restaurant behind you. I hear that and I'm free—we're home and free.*

The phone rang a third time as Reese neared his office. He kept the gun up, covering the fire exit till he'd ducked through his door and thrown the bolt.

Riiiinng!

He reached for the phone—and saw. One of its buttons was lit already. A second one lit when he picked up. *Whoever's calling is calling from somewhere in the building.* Using the other Pherotics line. Calling from the third floor, since he'd swear the fourth was clean.

The only phone on three was in Nic's office. He dropped onto the edge of his desk and closed his eyes, feeling ill. The rage would come later. "Nic," he said into the receiver.

Silence…but someone was there, breathing with him. "Devil woman?" He wasn't frightened anymore, only tired.

Silence—implacable, awful, shredding the present and his future.

"Are you shy, girl, or just slow? Or maybe you're the kind of woman who likes to pull…" This was where she always laughed. But no one was laughing tonight, not aloud. The silence mocked him. "Who likes to pull the wings off flies." It wasn't a question anymore. *It's over.* Whatever he'd dreamed, here was the reality.

He waited for fifty heartbeats, twice that again, listening to her listen to him, then, "Nic, we've got to talk. This is stupid. Whatever you need, whatever you want, I'll give it to you. You don't have to kill me, kid. We can end this tonight.'' It was over already. There was nothing here worth fighting for.

Silence.

His nerves prickled, his hair slowly rising as he realized. What if she *wasn't* there? What if she'd set the phone down, was even now gliding up the stairs while he sat here mesmerized? She could be waiting outside his door by now, ready to spring.

I'd have heard the stairwell door squeak.

With his own door shut? He wasn't sure.

You fool! Just because you declare the game over doesn't mean she's done with you. Rage came trickling in to drive out sorrow. *You think you can trick me that easily, Nic? Use my caring against me? Damn you, girl!*

If he had nothing left, he still had his pride. Reese grabbed his gun and padded to the door. Turning the lights out, he dropped to his heels, opened the door. *So we'll do this your way.*

Outside, the corridor was empty. Silent as a tomb.

She was here already? Or still in the stairwell? No telling. And a man could waste a lifetime guessing and second-guessing himself. Action was the only sure answer. Reese paused by the stairwell door, gun lifted. *Does it end like this, Nic?*

He turned the knob, shoved the door. Heard...*nothing.* Two more heartbeats and it hit him—*no squeak.* The door rotated silently inward on oiled hinges. *Dear God, and I've been depending on this!* When? When the *hell* did she oil it?

He shut the door again and stood, his heartbeat rocking him. *Oh, you're good! You're so damned good.*

Too good? He wheeled to face the dark rectangle, the doorway to Tim's office. *You're here now, aren't you? Slipped by me while I listened to the phone.* Using his caring against him.

So here I am, babe. You want me? Take a big bite. Eyes

level, he walked toward Tim's office. It was where he'd have waited. *Got the guts to do me face-to-face, darlin'?*

He flinched as the phone rang in his office. Games, playful as a rendezvous in a steam tunnel, a skinny-dip in a quarry. But games for keeps this time. The ringing sawed at his nerves. It would cover any sounds she made when she moved to meet him.

He stopped in his partner's doorway. Scanning the gloom, Reese picked out the desk, the chair behind it. Tim's office rearrangement had changed everything. File cabinets that once stood along the wall now made an L-shape with his desk. Down the hall, the ringing stopped.

Where are you, babe? Behind the desk? Or ducked down in back of the files? He stepped to one side—neither. Behind the door? No. He felt more rage than relief. *What are you waiting for? Let's finish this!* His eyes swept from floor to gridded ceiling, fixed on three paper gliders, twirling slowly, silently...*in a breezeless room.*

Three heartbeats, four, and he realized—joy and terror dawning in a burst of light. He spun on his heel, dodged back into the corridor. Blind, he'd been stupidly *criminally* blind, and now maybe he'd pay for his blindness, just when life was—

Not without a fight he wouldn't. He walked briskly down the hall to the elevator, found the light switch across from it and flicked it, throwing the corridor into blackness. The entire floor was dark now.

He took three or four silent strides away from the switch, then looked up, breathing easier, considering. And now what?

Around the corner, the stairwell door banged open. "Reese?" His name was called in a sobbing half whisper. D's voice. *"Reese, for the love of God!"*

Don't turn on a light! he started to yell, but it was too late. Light from his office slashed into the hallway as he turned the corner. *Soooo...* He took a deep breath. And raised his gun.

"REESE!" NICOLA WHISPERED again, afraid to raise her voice. He must still be here, the door to his office had been standing wide open. "Where are you?" *Say I'm not too late!*

And where was Tim? He'd had more than enough time to…to… Her mind couldn't phrase the words, though it supplied the image. Reese lying behind his desk. A pool of blood. Half-blinded by tears, she went to see, let out a little moan of relief. He wasn't there.

"Reese?" She padded to his washroom and turned on the light. Swept the small room with desperate longing. Oh, let him be hiding here, safe, whole, hers… He wasn't.

She swung back into the office and gulped. Reese loomed large in the door to the hallway. *"Reese!"* She started for him, then stumbled to a halt as she saw the look on his face—and the gun. Aimed at her chest.

"So it was you all along." His voice was soft as a caress. Deadly.

"Me?" She still hadn't caught her breath from the flight up the stairs. Terror had narrowed all her thoughts to one— saving him. Now her mind fumbled the absurdity. He *couldn't* mean—

"It was you trying to kill me." He jerked the bore of his gun floorward. "Drop it, Nic."

Her eyes followed his to Demi's gun, held down at her side. "This?"

"Drop it, I said!"

The derringer clattered to the floor. "That's just Demi's. I brought it because—"

"You brought it to shoot me. The same way you tried to run me down last week. You thought I wouldn't recognize your car? You must think I'm pretty stupid."

"I'm starting to." She gulped a breath. "Or crazy, anyway. That wasn't *my* car that—"

"Yeah, babe, it was. You've got a smashed parking light, left side. So did the car that nearly nailed me." He advanced, gun outstretched.

Backing away from its lethal bore, she edged toward his desk. "If...if...even if it *was* my car, I wasn't driving it."

"Right. You left your keys in your desk and somebody must have swiped them. Copied them. Is *that* your line?"

He punctuated the question with a lunge that sent her scuttling backward, her hands raised to fend him off. "It *is*! At least that's all I can think... Tim must have..." Or maybe Demi? She shook her head, confused.

"Not Tim. *You*, babe." Gun unwavering, Reese leaned against the doorway to the washroom. "You've been trying to break into my safe for weeks, to steal Tim's formula. When you found out I kept the combination in my wallet, you started in after that. If you had to kill me to get it, you were willing—the explosion, the wheel on my car loosened, hit-and-run?"

"I *wasn't* willing! Reese, *listen* to me! I wanted the formula—I *told* you that. But I'm the one who's been saying all along you were in danger! Look, I figured it out tonight—it's Tim!"

"Don't make me laugh, Nic. It's you." His eyes never leaving her face, he reached in and casually flicked off the washroom light.

"It *is* Tim! You both wear Irresistible."

"What's Irresistible got to do with it?" Reese twitched the gun toward his desk, a mute command that she obeyed automatically.

"It contains too much male pheromone. It's making you compete with each other more than you normally would. It's put you on a collision course. Pherotics is the territory in dispute. And I suppose Demi aggravates the dynamics, a desirable woman up for grabs?"

"Demi?" He laughed aloud and jerked the gun at his desk. "Nice try, kid, but I'm not buying. You've been playing me for a fool from the start."

She shook her head. "I *haven't*!"

"Meeting me in the dark, pretending to be two different women?"

Her mouth dropped, the air whooshing from her lungs

as if he'd punched her in the gut. Her lips soundlessly tried to form word after word she'd yet to find. "Y-you *knew* I was..." She couldn't say it.

"D?" Slow and wicked, his smile spread. "I've known it from the start, darlin'. Devil woman..." He reached out to brush her cheek with his knuckles.

She slapped his hand aside. "You've *known?*" She could feel her cheeks blazing, her temper swinging to the red line and beyond. "So what've you been doing? Laughing at me? Sneering behind my back?"

Reese shook his head slowly. "Having the time of my life, darlin'."

At her expense, he meant! Laughing at her all the while, using her, while she... Her eyes swam with tears and she swiped at them furiously. His hand landed on her shoulder, warm, heavy, pressing her downward. She squared her shoulders. "*Damn* you!"

"Damn me for a lovesick fool," he agreed. "There I was, bonded tighter than one of your ratty voles, and you, babe? All the time you were trying to kill me." His hand urged her downward.

She locked her knees and resisted. "I wasn't!" she whispered, throat aching with unshed tears. "I *wasn't* playing you for a fool. I was...falling in love with you."

"Then why—" he stroked the barrel of the gun up her arm, a cold, oddly gentle caress "—why all the sneakin' and hidin', Nic? Why couldn't you own up? Drop the mask? Come to me?"

"Because..." Her eyes filled and overflowed. Her whisper was barely audible. "Because I just didn't see how you could l-love me back, if you found out I was D."

"Little idiot." His voice was tender, almost laughing, as he raised the gun to her face.

Her eyes widened. *"Don't!"*

His hand on her shoulder tightened, pinning her in place. The gun tipped higher, then lunged up and past her as he straightened his arm with a snap—and fired. Darkness fell with a clap of thunder, counterpointed by her yelp and the tinkle of falling glass. He'd shot out the ceiling light?

Her ears rang. Her knees buckled as Reese dragged her down. "*Under* my desk, Nic! *Now*. Get under!"

Another shot smashed the dark. She yelped again and crawled for cover, flinching each time a shot rang out. They came methodically, brutally, at two-second intervals— three...four...five—then a longer gap of pregnant silence. Then Reese's voice, its weary determination scarier than anger, coming from somewhere across the room. "Tim, I'll keep on punching holes in the ceiling till I get you."

Silence. Then another shot shaking the blackness, and another.

"*Don't!*" Nic cried, but a man's voice drowned her out, the same protest, ragged, tearful—Tim's voice, breaking like a boy's. "*Stop! Quit!*"

"Then drop your damn gun and come down, Tim. It's over."

Nicola started violently as something smashed onto the desktop. She drew a sobbing breath. "Reese?"

"It's over, love. But stay safe under there a minute longer."

In the distance the elevator hummed. "Who's that, Nic?" Reese asked from somewhere nearby.

"That'll be Demi, I bet."

It was. And the Nose had brought along the cavalry— two young Cambridge policemen, bemused, bewildered and entirely bewitched by Demi Cousteau, whatever wild tale she'd been spinning them. Their indulgent grins turned to something sterner when a grimy, tear-streaked Tim Baggett dragged one of the shattered ceiling grids aside, then dropped down onto Reese's desk.

HOURS LATER, after their statements had been taken, they were free to go. Reese, Demi and Nicola stood outside the Cambridge police station, waiting for the detective who'd offered to drive Demi back to her condo. She'd get her long-promised meal, Reese suspected, at some late-night greasy spoon, rather than a French restaurant.

Nic swayed on her feet and his arm tightened around her, snuggling her closer against him. They'd yet to find the chance to talk alone, and he'd be damned if they'd do it in public. But whenever they glanced at each other, she had a shy, wild hope in her face that set his heart to singing. *Soon, my darlin'.* Couldn't be soon enough.

"But how did you guess he was up there?" Demi was asking, a too-bright, too-brittle smile on her face as she studied their coupled stance.

"Things added up." Almost too late. "Tim had moved his furniture so he could step from desktop to file cabinet to reach the ceiling tiles." Enabling him to move one aside, then scramble up onto the beams hidden above the dropped ceiling. Giving him an invisible highway leading to Reese's office. It must have seemed the perfect ambush perch for a man who didn't dare face his enemy—above his quarry's head, affording a clear kill shot down through the decorative ceiling grids.

Thinking of the smug, twisted malice it took to ask a man to collude unwittingly in his own murder, Reese shuddered. *Asking me to help move his furniture!* Nicola's arm stole around his waist and he looked down, found her eyes, warm and golden, waiting for him. For a moment time stopped; the world spun away, leaving only the two of them. *You, babe. Just you and me, together.*

Demi cleared her throat and he looked up again. "When he'd climbed up and dropped the grid back in place, Tim didn't replace it perfectly—there was a gap between that screen and the next." Maybe a quarter inch. If he, Reese, hadn't looked up at the gliders, he'd never have noticed. "And he'd kicked one of his airplanes, climbing up. It was still moving when I checked his office. After that—" Reese shrugged "—it added up."

After I'd added it up all wrong. He had much to make up for if Nic would give him the chance.

The Nose glanced back at the station. "You won't press charges against Tim, will you? He's really rather pathetic."

"Probably not." Though Tim would be lucky if the cops didn't press charges on their own account. "But a night in a cell will do him a world of good." Tomorrow Reese would lay down his terms. He wouldn't press charges—as long as he never had to look at Tim's weasel face again. He'd be a silent partner from now on, with no say in Pherotics. He was welcome to his share of the profits, but he'd collect them by mail. If Nic was right and Irresistible could indeed be profitable, Reese figured Tim would settle for that and be grateful. Tim's lawyer would make him see the light if a night in jail didn't.

"Oh, *here* he is!" Demi cried, breaking into his reverie. Her detective came striding down the steps, jaunty and eager. "Well, you two—" her mouth quirked in a rueful smile "—take care of yourselves."

"At last!" Reese murmured, watching her walk away arm in arm with her new knight. "And *now*..." He swung to face Nic, his hands dropping to her slim shoulders. "Nic...I'm sorry."

Her eyes were luminous. She leaned inward against his grasp. "For what?"

He laughed softly and slid his arms around her, gathering her so close she had to tip back her head to see his face. "Where do I begin? For that act at the end there, for starters. Once you switched on the lights and Tim could see us, it was all I could think to do. Till I could make it dark again, I had to keep him too entertained to shoot. I imagine there's nothing he'd have enjoyed more than fooling me into killing you." Picturing it, he hugged her so tightly she gasped. "But I'm sorry I scared you like that. Forgive me?"

Her smile was slow, wide and generous. She started to speak, then simply nodded, the streetlights turning her eyes to stars.

Just that simple? Was that what it was to come home? Everything effortless and easy between them? Forgiveness for the asking? He desperately needed to kiss her but held off with an effort. "Okay..." His voice sounded strange to his own ears, husky and not at all sure of itself. "Then there's just one more thing—a question." He smoothed one hand up her neck, tipped a thumb under her jaw, felt her pulse hammering against his palm, a beating butterfly. "Did you mean it?"

"Mean what?" But her eyes gave her away, all shyness and expectation with just a hint of lurking mischief.

Make me work for it, will you? Fair enough. "That you'd fallen in love with me? That you love me, Nic?"

"I..." She drew a shaking breath.

"No games anymore, babe," he warned. "From now on we play it straight." *We play for keeps.*

Her smile came again, her chin tipped defiantly. "Yes, I meant it." She gasped again as his arms tightened around her ribs. *And you?*

She didn't ask the question, but he read it in her eyes. He dropped his mouth to hers and answered with a kiss. When they could talk at last, he said simply, "Then let's go."

NEAR DAWN, her little boat nodding to the southwest breeze that blew in off the ocean, they lay in her berth, the flame of a brass kerosene lamp turning their skin to gold. Nic had opened the hatch overhead. It framed a square of stars beyond Reese, diamonds on midnight blue, blocked out when he dipped his head.

Time stopped as their lips met. The stars wheeling across the night stopped. She inhaled, breathing in his scent, arching her back, her breasts rising against his chest. They cried out together, a wordless exaltation.

The stars resumed their slow dance. She laughed breathlessly, eyes closed, body shuddering with one aftershock after another. "Yikes!"

His lips found her eyelids—brushed one, then the other, lingered on her temple. "Yikes?" Laughter rumbled in his chest, then, *"Hey!"* He braced on his elbows to frame her face with his hands. "Tears, darlin'?"

"'Cause I'm so..." She turned her face, buried her lips in his palm. So happy. *And so scared.* To find this, then perhaps to lose it? She couldn't believe that such joy could come and stay. But, oh, while it lasted... She kissed his wrist.

"Me, too." His words were rough with emotion. Holding her to him, Reese rolled to his side so they lay face-to-face. He stroked her for a long while in tender silence, their hearts speaking one to the other in drowsy lovers' code. "'Bout thirty-seven hours to go," he said at last, and smiled.

"Till?"

"Till I equal a prairie vole's honeymoon record. They're the monogamous ones, right?"

"The ones that mate for life." She nodded, her eyes misting again.

"But I guess we've been bonded for weeks already," he mused. "Since that first time in the lab when I put my nose right *here*—" He brushed his nose along her temple, up into her hair, breathing her in, "—and I knew I was...home. Just took me a while to own up to it."

"That's what I'm—" She stopped. It was crazy to question such joy.

"What you're afraid of," Reese finished for her, his smile fading, "is that my bonding will end, since your little mountain-vole creeps went back to their tomcat ways." He curled his hand around the nape of her neck. "Ain't gonna happen, love. Trust me on this. Maybe that's how we started, D and Twenty-three, two guinea pigs in the dark. But, Nic, I've seen the light now. I'm a man, not a mouse."

How she prayed that he was right! She found a brave, sassy smile, raised it between them. "So I'd noticed!" She drew a knuckle from his navel slowly, slowly down.

"Had you now?"

"Hard to miss."

"Oh, yeah?" He caught her waist and rolled, lifting her,

giggling, above him for his leisurely, arrogant inspection, then lowering her to lie along his heated length.

"Yeah." Who could resist such joy, be it for an hour or a lifetime? She reached for him, murmured with wicked, mocking admiration, *"Yikes!"*

"Devil woman!" The sea breeze had faded with the dawn. The boat rocked on.

BEYOND THE HATCH, the sky blushed tender pink. The feathers of a gull winging past were tipped gold by the rising sun. Nic lay with her head pillowed on his arm, lips at his ear, talking in a drowsy half whisper, D's smoky voice. Reese watched the sky brighten slowly to blue. *So this is happiness.* He'd been a long time learning.

Bonded—the strings that tied him, linked his heart to hers. Pulled both directions. He'd lost his freedom—and found it again, here in her arms. He smiled. Nic feared this could ever end? He'd just have to show her then, hour by hour, year by year.

"Can't figure it out." She was recounting the previous night's adventures, the drive out to Newton. Number forty, who claimed to have been excluded from her test. "I'm sure it's got something to do with the way my results came out skewed, remember? The first twenty plus you bonded, or didn't bond, precisely as I predicted. But for the rest, my results went totally haywire."

"I remember." He liked this about her, too, that she was fierce about her work, as well as about him—passionate through and through, his lady. "So you learned one thing, anyway. You had forty-one men, not forty."

"Huh? How d'you figure that?"

"You ended up with forty evaluation forms filled out, and then Dominguez told your kid Feinstein to bug off, that you had all the subjects you needed already. So Feinstein must have stood forty-*first* in line." A memory stirred. Reese's brows drew together. "It's something to do with that redheaded kid. Got to be."

"What kid?" Nic propped up on an elbow to stare at him.

"The one you sent back into line when his interview papers were misplaced." Reese described the kid who'd stepped out the door in the outer hallway.

"Nobody's papers were misplaced!" Sitting all the way up, Nic spread both hands on his chest. Leaned over him, her eyes fierce as a moon tiger's. "And what door are you talking about?"

He described it. "A back way into the lab, I assumed."

"No, that's a broom closet!" She shook her head, starting to smile. The smile turned to a laugh. "A kid was hiding in that closet? All night, I suppose, and then he cut into line ahead of you?"

Reese grinned. "*Enterprising* son of a gun! The rumor was out you were testing an aphrodisiac, a love potion. Every last man on campus would have played guinea pig if you'd let him. Give that kid an E for effort."

"E?" She laughed, tears streaming down her cheeks. "I could kiss him!"

"Uh-uh." He sat up and growled, "Any kissing from now on, direct it my way."

She smacked him full on the lips. "You see what this means?"

That he wanted her again already. Forty hours was starting to look like a real possibility. He'd bow to no vole.

"Do you *see*?" she demanded.

"He cut in before Twenty-one," Reese recalled obediently. "So that means everyone behind him was bumped back one place, all along the line to Feinstein, who became the forty-first. One subject more than you needed."

"More than that, it means Twenty-one became Twenty-two, Twenty-two was really Twenty-three, and *you*..." Her eyes were glowing. She drew a lingering fingertip from his brow to the corner of his mouth. "It means you, sir, weren't the twenty-third man at all. You came through the green door twenty-fourth in line!"

"So?" Kissing her finger, he still didn't get it.

"So it means Joe checked you off on his list as Twenty-four, and he put you in Twenty-four's room."

"But I met you, anyway. That's all that counts."

"After you'd sniffed the dose Joe gave me for *Twenty-four,* you met me!" Sliding a leg over his thighs to kneel astride, she draped her arms across his shoulders and arched up against him, smiling with a shining confidence he'd never seen before. Reese didn't know where it had suddenly come from, but he loved it. She was meeting him for the first time as his equal, with no hesitation, no apology. His woman.

"Yeah?" he murmured, brushing her lips with his, his hands sliding down to cup her hips. "And so?"

"So you got the placebo, big guy! Nothing but saline solution."

He saw the joke at last. "Just salt and water? No hormones, no pheromones?"

"At least, not the kind mixed from bottles."

"Then when I sniffed you?" When he smelled honey and hay and home, as he smelled it now. The tiny flowers called sweet alyssum that bloomed where the world was right.

"That, my love, was nothin' but plain, old-fashioned chemistry."

His grin widened to match her own. No more doubts. No more fears. Nothing left but the joy. *The tie that binds.* "I can live with that."

"And so can I."

Outside, the breeze reawakened. *Madame Curie* swung her nose to meet it, bowed to the rising sun. And rocked on.

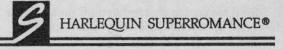

HE SAID

♥

SHE SAID

Explore the mystery of male/female communication in this extraordinary new book from two of your favorite Harlequin authors.

Jasmine Cresswell and Margaret St. George bring you the exciting story of two romantic adversaries—each from their own point of view!

DEV'S STORY. CATHY'S STORY.
As he sees it. As she sees it.
Both sides of the story!

The heat is definitely on, and these two can't stay out of the kitchen!

Don't miss HE SAID, SHE SAID.
Available in July wherever Harlequin books are sold.

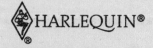

♦ HARLEQUIN®

And the Winner Is... You!

…when you pick up these great titles
from our new promotion at your
favorite retail outlet this June!

Diana Palmer
The Case of the Mesmerizing Boss

Betty Neels
The Convenient Wife

Annette Broadrick
Irresistible

Emma Darcy
A Wedding to Remember

Rachel Lee
Lost Warriors

Marie Ferrarella
Father Goose

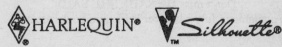

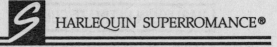

HARLEQUIN SUPERROMANCE®

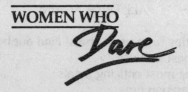

WOMEN WHO *Dare*

NOBODY DOES IT BETTER
(#741, May 1997)
by Jan Freed

It took brains, independence and nerves of steel for
Hope Manning to get where she is today, CEO of her own
company. And *nobody does it better.*

Jared Austin teaches others to find the peace he himself
discovered on a wilderness survival course. And *nobody
does it better.*

Blackmailed into "chilling out," Hope reluctantly joins
one of Jared's west Texas wilderness expeditions. And it's
war between the sexes from the start! Then a sniper
appears, gunning for Hope. To survive, she and Jared
have to put aside their differences and work as a team....

And nobody *does it better!*

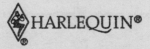